MW00914849

Communist
Number One

Life and Times of Joel Barr
Escape to Russia
Leading USSR Scientist

VOLUME TWO

A True Life Novel

Brian B. Kelly

Brick Hill Roads, Ltd.

Communist Number One, Vol. II

FIRST EDITION

© *2021 by Brian B. Kelly*

All rights reserved under the International and Pan-American Copyright Conventions. No part of this work may be reproduced, stored in a retrieval system, or transmitted in any form or by any means, electronic or otherwise, without the prior written permission of the copyright holder.

ISBN:

Communist Number One *is a work of fiction. All persons, organizations, and events herein are products of the author's imagination or are used fictitiously.*

Further info on Brian B. Kelly's novels at bbkwriter.com:

Tropic of Paradise, a Tahitian Love Story
Brick Tower Press February, 2011

SmartAss, an Awakening
Brick Tower Press January, 2012

The Irish Smuggler
Brick Tower Press October, 2013

Just Call Me Whitey
Brick Tower Press October, 2016

Our American, A Romance of Moscow
Brick Hill Roads, April, 2017

Mother Russia
Brick Hill Roads, Ltd December, 2017

Tiare Tahiti at Harvard
Brick Hill Roads, January, 2019

Tropic of Paradise, Second Edition
Brick Tower Press May, 2019

Two's Company… A Comedy of Sex, Love, Crime & Treachery
Brick Hill Roads, August, 2020

Communist Number One, Life and Times of Joel Barr…Vol I
Brick Hill Roads, February, 2021

Communist Number One, Life and Times of Joel Barr…Vol II
Brick Hill Roads, August, 2021

"…If only there were evil people somewhere insidiously committing evil deeds, and it were necessary only to separate them from the rest of us and destroy them. But the line dividing good and evil cuts through the heart of every human being. And who is willing to destroy a piece of his own heart?

"During the life of any heart this line keeps changing place; sometimes it is enough space for good to flourish. One and the same human being is, at various ages, under various circumstances, a totally different human being. At times he is close to being a devil, at times to sainthood. But his name doesn't change, and to that name we ascribe the whole lot, good and evil."

—Aleksandr I. Solzhenitsyn, *The Gulag Archipelago*

For all my grandchildren including Sophia, Zeya, Anya, Cyrus, Nyah, Lillymoon and Eva

INTRODUCTION

I have friends and acquaintances who say they won't read my books because they don't read fiction. There's certainly nothing wrong with that. I do consider the novel to be mankind's highest form of art, the greatest source of human truth. I don't claim to have exemplified that in my own work, but I have based this novel on any and all facts of Joel Barr's life I could find. That is to say I've tried to include all the interesting facts I could find and thread the story together from there. I've even done my best to invigorate less sensational facts of the story. This is a fact based story and that is why, like others before me, I call it A True Life Novel. In an appendix at the end of *Communist Number One, Volume III* I'm tempted to identify the chunks that are not factual, but are made from thin air and my imagination. So, yes, there are some non-facts, but Volume II is crammed with real solid facts. My aim is to tell Joel's real story in the best way I can.

I started this project in 1991, an agreement with Joel that I would write a true to life novel about his life. That agreement is now thirty years old. It took years before I realized that the hard part of this story was going to be finding out what happened with Joel and the Soviet Navy. It was a sort of myth: *Joel and his partner, Al Sarant did some work for the Soviet Navy.* That was about all there was, either from talking to Joel or from books written by other people about Joel. It took a while longer, a year or so, for me to realize that this *'work for the Soviet Navy'* must have occupied something like 5-8 years. I knew nothing about this giant hole in my knowledge of Joel's life.

When Joel had an hour long nationwide ABC network broadcast: *Nightline: American Patriot / Soviet Spy?* with Ted Koppel on June 15,1992, Ted crucified him as a traitor and spy which Joel weakly denied. Koppel went on to describe all the harm Joel had done in designing Soviet anti-aircraft weapons which shot down 'American boys' in Vietnam. Ted brought up all the available dirt his professional research team could find. But there was no mention of the Soviet Navy or their lethal submarines. So I didn't know anything and, as far as I can find out, nobody else did either. Then, long after I read Eric Firdman's book, *Maverick For Life Without Parole,* a few times, which is a colorful account of Firdman's life including his time with Joe Berg and Phil Staros, the new KGB generated identities of Joel Barr and Al Sarant, I got in touch with Eric and we hit it off and we had long conversations, not only about his working with Joel, but of course I asked him what else he could tell me about the submarine work for the Soviet Navy that wasn't in his book and what was Joel's role in that?

Eric said the guy you need to talk to is Mark Galperin, and good luck with that. But then Mark Galperin's book came out, *Prizhok Kita,* (Whale Jump), but only in Russian and it wasn't easy to get a copy either. But eventually I did get a copy and began tediously translating it using my very sketchy knowledge of Russian and a machine translation program. When a highly trained literary friend of mine read some of this semi-translated concoction, she asked, "What are you going to do with this complete gibberish?" Well the answer was to keep reading, re-reading and trying to figure it out. But, at the very beginning of the book, Mark Galperin, mentions that he has so many fond stories of Joe Berg alias Joel Barr and what a shame it was that there was not enough room to tell these stories in his book, which is mostly about Galperin's work on the Soviet computer guidance system for Soviet submarines. Perhaps needless to say, I found this statement terribly disappointing and I soon decided I must get in touch with Mark Galperin and somehow get him to tell me those stories.

Well, it took a while, but I did eventually reach Galperin who was kind enough to arrange for me to get the DVD version of his book which did have pictures and articles, but I never did find or get to hear the intimate personal stories that Galperin had alluded to. Even so, both the badly translated print version and the DVD version of *Whale Jump* proved very useful and were really all I had to go on for Joel's life during his work for the Soviet Navy. He worked developing what is called a Combat Information and Control System named the Uzel for their diesel electric combat submarines from 1965 until sometime in the early 1970s. I have used *Whale Jump* like a bible, its facts, descriptions and even characterizations of the people and situations surrounding Joel in Latvia. Often, knowing Joel as I do, I was able to read between the lines and further interpret what I had gleaned from Mark Galperin's important work. I can only hope someday *Prizhok Kita* will be professionally translated into English because I predict that Joel Barr's unique life is going to be of interest for many years to come.

Brian Kelly, Brooklyn, Augurst, 2021

Principal Characters Volume II

Joel Barr, aka **Joe Berg,** American engineer and ex-spy
Alfred Sarant, aka **Philip Staros,** Joel's partner in the USSR
Vivian Glassman, Joel's girlfriend and fiancée in New York
Julius Rosenberg, Joel's close friend and collaborator
Ethel Rosenberg, Julius's wife and co-defendant in trial
Anatoly Yatskov, KGB handler, first contact for Joel in Europe also a co-defendant in the Rosenberg trial.
Harry Gold, an American Soviet spy and messenger, convicted
David Greenglass, Ethel's brother, convicted with Ethel
Morton Sobell, Joel's friend, co-conspirator with Julius in spy trial
Bill Perl, another friend, classmate and collaborator of Joel's
Aleksandr Feklisov, Joel's stateside KGB handler
Viktor Taroikin, KGB handler of Joe from the earliest days in Prague and of both Joel and Al Sarant in Prague and the USSR
Vera Bergova Joseph Berg's Czechoslovakian Catholic wife
Peter Dementyev, Soviet Minister, instrumental in bringing Joe and Phil to Leningrad
Aksel Berg, major Soviet engineer and radar specialist, good friend to Joe and Phil, knows they were the spies who supplied all the radar info
Elvira Valueva, Joe's blonde Siberian girlfriend
Henry Eric Firdman, leading LKB engineer and protégé to Barr and Sarant.
Mark Galperin, second protégé, chief designer of the Uzel project
Sergei Gorshkov, Admiral of the Fleet of the Soviet Union and major military leader in the USSR
Nikita Khrushchev, Premier of the Soviet Union, General Secretary of the CPUSSR
Aleksandr Shokin, Minister of electronic industries, GKET
Dmitry Ustinov, top military engineer, USSR Defense minister
Sergei Korolev, secret chief designer of the Soviet space program
Andrei Tupolev, famous Soviet aircraft designer, anti-Stalinist
Eric Golovanov, Captain of Soviet Project 641 submarine B-103
Leonid Brezhnev, General Secretary of the CPUSSR
Grigory Romanov, Leningrad Communist Party boss, Politburo member

ONE

"You know something, Phil? I suddenly want to live to be very old. Very. I want to be around to see what happens. The world is stirring in very strange ways. Maybe this is the century for it. Maybe that's why it's so troubled... Maybe it won't be the American century after all, or the Russian century or the atomic century. Wouldn't it be wonderful if it turned out to be everybody's century, when people all over the world -- free people-- found a way to live together? I'd like to be around to see some of that, even the beginning. I may stick around for quite a while."

---**Mrs. Green,** *Gentlemen's Agreement,* **by Laura Hobson**

THE NEXT TIME THE FRIENDS FROM THE CCNY engineering class of 1938 met after the confrontation on July 5 1946 between Julius Rosenberg and Max Elitcher was in late August. The upbeat mood of most at the July party at 65 Morton Street, apartment 6I was missing at the Blue Mill restaurant in Greenwich Village. Once again they were defying the strict cautions of the Soviet KGB not to meet each other, and especially not to be seen together in public places. During the intervening seven or eight weeks, their sense of pride and celebration had ebb darker and more pessimistic. Max was not there, but Joel was, along with Julius, Bill Perl, Vivian Glassman, Bill Danziger, Morton Sobell, his wife Helen and one or two others. They were all conscious that the USSR was being cast as the adversary of the USA. They'd all felt the rapidly deteriorating spirt of alliance that had buoyed their war work.. The new mood made them feel that they hadn't really won after all. Never one to bare an awkward or uncomfortable silence, Mort spoke into the undertone of gloom:

"It's the same people who wanted Hitler to crush the Soviet Union that are now warning against—and are so hostile about Communism and the Soviet Union."

"The Axis had no monopoly on fascism," Joel said.

"Sure," Vivian said, her voice neither stern nor gloomy, "there are plenty of US fascists and plenty who are only too ready to follow them."

"The US is aimed at world domination and Truman is not as wise or broad as Roosevelt,' Julius said.

"You give them both too much credit,' Perl said.

"You still miss the Kingfish (Huey Long) do you Bill," Joel asked kindly, joking.

"Anyway," Mort said, "it doesn't look like the US is going to become a peace loving, democracy-promoting, socialist tolerating nation of compassionate winners and wise voters, at least not to me!"

"No it doesn't," Helen said. I'm sure we all agree on that, don't we? That Hitler is gone but fascism is still here? That Truman is not the man to stop it?"

"You're not wrong," Perl nodded his large head, his forelocks shaking above his eyes."

"It's not inconceivable," Joel said, "that in ten or fifteen years, we'll have a dictator ship right here. That'd be the shits."

"Let's not get carried away," Vivian said.

"It's not going to take ten or fifteen years," Julius said.

"I see no reason to stop what we've been doing," Perl said.

"No, nor do I," Sobell added, feeling he'd been properly convincing and glad Danziger was there, even though he had not passed anything to the KGB.

No, Joel thought, *there is no reason not to keep helping our friends from the land of Socialism. A balance of power may be the only way to stop the US from crushing Communism.* "I need to get a job before I can do 'what we've been doing'," Joel said.

"You won't have any trouble," Julius said.

"Don't be too sure," Mort said, thinking, *the hut (FBI) is slow and not too bright, but there are a lot of them.*

"Joel will finish soon at Columbia," Julie gently admonished Mort. "With an advanced degree. He'll get a good job."

Mort sniffed but said noting.

IN EARLY SEPTEMBER 1946, JOEL BARR received a masters degree in electrical engineering from Columbia University. His dissertation, Solving Transcendental Equations by Means of Lissajou Figures, was well-received and widely circulated. He appreciated the Soviet help in achieving this degree but he wanted to earn his own money again. He wanted to work, to engage the real challenges of new inventions. He applied for a job at Sperry Gyroscope, concealing his status as a security risk by saying he had never been fired or reprimanded. He did an impressive interview and was soon working on radar guided missiles, ICBMs.

Alfred Sarant, though, was ready to pursue bourgeois goals. He got Louise pregnant, quit his job at Bell Labs, took a job helping to build the Cornell University cyclotron and moved with pregnant Louise to Ithaca. He was losing touch with the old crowd.

On September 15, again violating KGB spy handler Aleksandr Feklisov's prohibitions, Julius Rosenberg went to see Joel. Aleks and his family were sailing that day on the *Stari Bolshevik* (the Old Bolshevik) from New York for Leningrad.

"We said good-bye two days ago," Julie said to Joel in a melancholy mood. "We may never see him again. He urged me to stay clear of all my friends and be ready to leave home and family on a day's notice. ...But I couldn't leave family behind."

"I was said out of devoted comradeship," Joel countered.

"Of course, but it's easier for him to go off to Moscow or Leningrad than it would be for us."

"So you think he's left us holding the bag?"

"No, I think nothing much will happen. The Elizabeth Bentley business will blow over. Things will settle down. After all, the war is over. Who'd want to start another one?"

"Don't be too sure," Joel used Benjamin's old line, "that there won't be plenty who will not only want to..."

"Alright," Julie said, "don't be offended if I don't make contact with you then."

"Of course, it's better to be careful." *This is all crazy,* Joel thought. *But Aleks is right, I can't see my friends; we're dangerous to each other.*

In Ithaca, Al Sarant and Louise befriended another couple, physicist Bruce Dayton and his wife, Carol, with whom Al and Louise at first shared a house. Soon the two couples would build houses next door to each other.

With Sarant gone from 65 Morton Street, when Bill Perl came from Cleveland to pursue a PhD in Physics at Columbia University, with a classified top secret thesis on 'transonic flows past thin airfoils,' he moved into 65 Morton Street, apartment 6I, with Joel.

On October 15, recently convicted Nazi war criminal, Hermann Göring, poisoned himself hours before his execution. Three days later, an FBI agent filed a note that Alfred Sarant was definitely a Communist and lived at 65 Morton Street in Greenwich Village. Ten days later, Joel started work at Sperry Gyroscope on a top secret long-range radar project and began providing microfilmed documents to KGB spy handler Boris Pronin, aka 'Archie'.

On November 27, Indian Prime Minister Jawaharlal Nehru appealed to the United States and the Soviet Union to 'save humanity from the ultimate disaster,' by banning nuclear testing and beginning nuclear disarmament. We know how far that got.

On Christmas eve, while American crime bosses met in Havana, Anatoly Yatskov met with Harry Gold to tell him that he must leave the US. When Gold told Yatskov that he had lost his job, but had been hired by Abraham Brothman, Yatskov lost his temper and shouted: "Are you some kind of jerk? You're destroying ten years of hard work! Anyone who reads newspapers knows Elizabeth Bentley has exposed Brothman as a Soviet spy! That story was everywhere last July." Yatskov threw money to pay for their drinks on the bar top and stormed out without looking again at Gold.

Moscow center, at the KGB's Lubyanka headquarters, it

was quickly decided to manage their key atomic spy, Klaus Fuchs, in Great Britain, sending experienced handler Aleksandr Feklisov to London. Yatskov was ordered to Paris to handle other agents and on December 27, three days after his angry meeting with Gold, Yatskov sailed in haste from New York for France.

1947. THE YEAR OF LAURA HOBSON'S RUNAWAY bestseller, *Gentlemen's Agreement*, and the motion picture starring Gregory Peck as Phil Green, exposing anti-Semitism in America. This year, 1947, was when Mikhail Kalashnikov joined previous designs with new ideas for a self-loading rifle, the **A**utomatic **K**alashnikov of 19**47**, the year Julius Rosenberg's machine shop business failed, and his partnership with David Greenglass eroded under the friction of that failure, while both were pressed by the needs of hungry young families.

On January 31, Soviet Communists took power in Poland. Six days later they installed former Soviet military intelligence (GRU) agent Boleslaw Bierut as President of Poland. On February 10, in Paris, peace treaties were signed with Italy, Hungary, Romania, Bulgaria and Finland. On February 17, the *Voice of America* began broadcasting US propaganda into the Soviet Union. On March 1, thirty-five-year-old Wernher von Braun married his 18-year-old first cousin, Maria Luise von Quistorp. On March 12, President Truman declared that the US would support Greece and Turkey economically and militarily to prevent their falling under Soviet control. He called upon the US to 'support free peoples who are resisting attempted subjugation by armed minorities or by outside pressures.' This *Truman Doctrine* outlined US foreign policy for the Cold War: financial, political, military and covert support for totalitarian governments in Third World countries, under the pretext of 'democracy and freedom', but using dictatorships to contain the spread of Communism and any other anti-colonial, anti-capitalist ideologies. 'Support' would include direct military invasions to remove duly elected socialist governments or those formed through popular revolutions.

In March, a federal grand jury was empaneled in New York to hear Elizabeth Bentley name over eighty of her colleagues in the Jacob Golos spy rings. "Here we go," Mort

Sobell commented when Joel, Mort and Bill Perl got together to see *Ivan the Terrible*. "An anti-Communist frenzy is coming," he accurately predicted.

The three friends enjoyed the show, feeling almost carefree at moments though Bill was put off by the 'lavish costumes and wasteful pageantry'.

"But the message is clear," Mort insisted: "Unity and power, Mother Russia above all."

"For a ruthless despot, Ivan was quite a prince," Joel joked.

By April, the federal grand jury investigating Elizabeth Bentley's confessions had called over 100 witnesses who refuted her claims or refused to testify. The government was getting nowhere.

"You see," Julius told Ethel, "it's all going to blow over."

She looked up from where she sat eight months pregnant. "I hope so," she said, "otherwise…"

On April 3, the loyalty program prompted HUAC to compile a list for the Attorney General of 'subversive organizations'. People from all walks of life wondered, *Am I on the Subversives List?*

On May 16, Robert Rosenberg was born to Julius and Ethel. Once again, quarantine measures of tradecraft were abandoned for the bris and Joel had a chance to talk with Julie:

"I don't entirely share your faith that the witch hunt will die out."

"Unless one of us talks," Julius said, "they've got nothing."

On June 5, Secretary of State George Marshall outlined his plan for US aid to Europe: Pay cash to keep Hitler's prediction from coming true, that Bolshevism would engulf Europe.

In June, the security detail of Joel's employer, Sperry-Gyroscope, asked the FBI to check-up on Barr. His file showed that the FBI had informed the US Army in 1942 that he was a member of the CPUSA. The FBI then requested his army records, and went looking at bank records and Western Electric employee reports, finding no sign of illegal income and only ample praise for Joel's professional performance. In fact, he had never received any money beyond minor reimbursements for his substantial aid to the Soviet Union.

In early July, Joel went to meet 'Archie', his KGB handler. Like Feklisov before him, Boris Pronin was a Soviet Consular employee operating under diplomatic cover. The stocky, balding man, at thirty-four, had spent two hours cleaning his trail before reaching the side entrance of the Lexington Avenue restaurant just as Joel came in through the front door. They arrived at the same table fifteen seconds apart, each carrying a tray with a sandwich, coffee and a folded copy of *The New York Times*. Archie's copy held a brown envelope containing blank pages of hotel stationery; Joel's copy concealed a brown envelope containing twenty rolls of film: the latest electronic designs for Sperry's guided missile control. The two newspapers lay together as the two men ate.

"I would tell you to be more careful," Archie smiled openly, "but I assume you are still sleeping with only one woman and only telling *her* what you are doing. I can only hope you swear her to silence. Then, there are your friends who already know our business because you are telling them also, eh?"

Despite this sharp professional perspective, Joel sensed a sort of collaborative leniency from Archie, as if Joel presented such a unique case that Archie found himself at a loss as to how to handle the forest of dangerous loose ends that Joel and his friends presented. Was there a trace of hope that their friendly collaboration would have some chance of orderly survival?

Pronin knew that whatever kind of mess it was, it was probably too late to clean it up. He also knew that sooner or later it would hit the wall, as untidy messes often do. Some of these people would need his help to avoid serious trouble if they weren't to betray him instead. They all presented dangers.

"Well," Joel offered a momentary engaging smile before lifting his sandwich to cover his mouth, "it may not be as bad as it sounds. We're an intimate group. We don't talk to strangers, and Al is out of it, gone from the scene. Besides, I don't tell even Julius everything."

"That's one of your best ideas. The two of you should never see each other."

"Speaking of ideas, I've brought you some quite advanced stuff, on controlling rocket travel and distant targeting. Very-long-range rocket propelled warheads are steps away."

"Yes, like it or not," Pronin agreed. "Meter," Pronin used Joel's KGB code name, "the stakes are getting higher and our activities are ever more dangerous. Your work is valuable to us, but you must be prepared to leave the country at a moment's notice. There have been serious security breaches and a rapidly changing climate of hostility, as you must know..."

"Some things I'm working on, the development of more compact circuitry, are going to be very influential. You'll see."

"We paid for your master's degree from Columbia, we can—"

"—Yes of course you did, but—"

"—No, look, we can send you to college in Europe as well, with a similar sort of small allowance for living expenses."

Mildly surprised, Joel regarded Archie directly again for a moment before lifting his ham-on-rye and taking a bite, chewing, eyes straight ahead, "I think I'd want to study music not engineering. There are some great teachers in Paris, for example. I just might want to become a composer myself. What would you say if I got out of engineering altogether?"

"Fine. That would be much better for all of us than you staying here. Study the hieroglyphics of the ancient Egyptians if you like." Archie looked at Joel, unblinking. "It's an interesting field. Not everyone can make sense of those curious symbols."

"Hmmm," Joel rolled his jaw and nodded slightly, enjoying Archie's sense of humor without smiling.

"If you go," Pronin muttered, "I've been authorized to say yes to whatever you decide to do over there."

"Well, I have to admit you've supplied food for thought. There are some good engineering schools over there as well."

Pronin nodded but said nothing, not wanting to disturb Joel's contemplation of a quick departure, or possible disaster to come, if he stayed. Pronin chewed his turkey club slowly, relishing the bacon. After a while he said, "Hitler is gone and Truman has made us the enemy."

"As a bourgeois capitalist, he fears your success and

survival."

They set the next meeting for September 8 at another restaurant. When it was time for Pronin to depart, as he took Joel's newspaper from the table, Joel flashed a panicked expression, as though he had done nothing until then to which he could be held accountable. As Pronin receded, Joel relaxed; his expression became cheerful, pleasant and benign. He retrieved Pronin's newspaper slowly, tucking it carefully under his arm as he left the restaurant. By the time he reached the subway entrance, he felt safe and secure, as much as he had at almost any other time in his life. He dropped newspaper and envelope into a trash bin.

In mid-July, the FBI began checking on the references Barr had provided Sperry-Gyroscope. Two were okay and the third was a Julius Rosenberg, who was not contacted. The FBI did not connect the Julius Rosenberg reference with the Julius Rosenberg on the Communist party membership rolls the FBI had burglarized from the CPUSA's New York offices.

On July 11, a ship, the *Exodus*, left France for Palestine with 4500 Jewish death camp survivors. A week later, following wide media coverage and special consideration by the UN Committee on Palestine, the *Exodus* was captured by British troops and refused entry at the port of Haifa. *Like the St. Louis, a refugee ship that shows capitalist, imperialist hypocrisy,* Joel thought.

On July 22, Harry Gold and Abraham Brothman were hauled before a grand jury and questioned. They confirmed each other's lies and remained free as there was no evidence against them. Though the KGB's New York station was very nervous, Feklisov's meetings with Fuchs in London continued regularly. Following their own need to believe it, the KGB counted on Fuchs holding up well if questioned.

On July 26 1947, President Truman signed the National Security Act, creating the Central Intelligence Agency, the Department of Defense, the Joint Chiefs of Staff and the National Security Council.

On July 29, the giant computer, ENIAC, after being powered down on November 9 1946 for a refurbishment, was turned on with a memory upgrade. It was to remain in continuous operation until October 2 1955. Joel read classified reports on the work done by ENIAC and knew its rapidly growing capacity could guide long-range missiles, run complex machinery and compute the answers to questions that would take human beings so long the answers wouldn't matter when they were reached. Joel thought he knew what the future looked like.

On August 3, the USSR invited Western military observers to the Tushino air show in Moscow where they were shocked to see exact copies of the US Air Force B-29 roaring by overhead. The Soviets didn't blink. They called the big four engine bombers the TU-4. US military men couldn't help thinking that, carrying atomic bombs, with US markings, those planes could fly right into North America.

After India and Pakistan had been freed of British rule and riots had broken out in France when the bread ration was reduced and just before Communists seized power in Hungary, the US Army received its first hints of the Rosenberg spy ring from deciphered KGB telegrams. This initial work had scrambled pieces of Joel's, Julius's, and Al Sarant's identities.

Feklisov would have six covert meetings with Klaus Fuchs from September 1947 to April 1949, one every three to four months in various London neighborhoods. To deliver the answers to Soviet questions needed to develop thermonuclear weapons in the USSR, Fuchs drove from the atomic research center in Harwell over little-traveled roads where it was easy to detect a tail. At a rail station mid-way he took the London train. Fuchs, when asked by Feklisov how he would reach London and what precautions he would take, answered in detail, as if he were a child wanting to show how good he was, emphasizing that he jumped onto the London train only at the last moment.

On September 3, in New York, the Army Signal Corp's file on Joel Barr arrived at the FBI office showing that the ASC had fired Barr from the Fort Monmouth laboratories following the FBI warning that Barr was a member of the CPUSA. On September 14, the FBI received a letter from a Barr neighbor saying the whole Barr family were Communists and their entire neighborhood was Communist, with everyone busy going to Communist rallies and handing out Communist pamphlets. The

Bureau had still not put together the information obtained from its illegal raid of the Communist Party offices that Joel Barr was a member of Communist cell 16b along with Julius Rosenberg, who he had given as a character reference.

On October 5 1947, the FBI notified Sperry Gyroscope security of Barr's FBI file and his status as a potential security risk. Joel was in his cubicle when he was summoned to his supervisor's office, a senior engineer who admired Joel's work ethic and ability to short-cut his way to rapid development of novel ideas. With sincere regret, the man informed Joel, "Unfortunately, your position here is over. I'm being forced to let you go immediately."

Joel blanched and a look of panic passed so quickly across his face that it was almost unnoticeable. "Why? What's the matter with my work?"

"It's not your work. You are deemed a security risk…"

"…So, it's politics, we have to say then?"

"I'm forced to insist that you not even return to your desk."

"Well, I have personal things. Let me get my jacket there."

"I'll have someone fetch it. Anything else?"

"There's a couple of photos…"

"Fine."

"Can't this be discussed? I'm sure it's a misunderstanding."

"No. The decision was made over my head and it's final."

"I have to think it's a sign of the times, that a contributing member of a scientific team is fired over his political views."

"Joel, I'm sorry. You've done great work here. If you'll follow these security fellows to the lobby, I'll have someone bring you your personal items."

Joel left thinking of Vivian Glassman, the love of his life, how to tell her, how to sound and remain optimistic. He knew what his KGB handler would say: *time to leave the country,* and he wondered, *How is Vivie going to take that?*

TWO

"[we are] going to continue to fight communism. Now I am going to tell you how we are not going to fight communism. We are not going to transform our fine FBI into a Gestapo secret police. That is what some people would like to do. We are not going to try to control what our people read and say and think. We are not going to turn the United States into a right-wing totalitarian country in order to deal with a left-wing totalitarian threat."   ---Harry S. Truman

WHEN JOEL ARRIVED AT THE NEXT SCHEDULED meeting with Boris Pronin in late October, he passed the last three rolls of film from Sperry. He concluded the story of his firing, "I don't know where to apply next; it almost has to be government work, and what are the chances I'll get more of the same reaction?"

"Nothing you or I say can alter the fact that your life is about to change." Pronin spoke without looking at Joel, "You're not going to be able to work in your field. Not in this country."

"I'm now one of the most experienced in the field. People with thorough feed-back credentials, who see the possibilities of digital controls should be in demand."

Archie waited patiently, watching Joel in quick glances. Joel's large deep brown eyes, magnified behind his glasses, moved about restlessly. "I'll soon have a patent on my light transmitter—"

"—You must give all that up, at least for now."

"Then it's not easy to imagine what I'd be doing…"

"Study in Europe. Isn't that still a possibility? What about a career in music?"

"Well, you know, I'm no longer a kid. I'm thirty-one now.

I have a serious girlfriend you might say, and I—"

"—Take her with you... Look, my friend, your reason for thinking seriously about Europe is not only that there is no work here for you. Or that you like the idea of studying music in Paris. Or Hieroglyphics. There are worse things here than losing your job. The United States is a war factory looking for targets. Things will get worse before they get better. Take along your girl, she too doesn't need to be around for what may come."

"So what if I really did want to forget all this and begin a life in music, studying serious classical composition with a famous composer? Are you sure the higher-ups will support that? And for how long?"

"Meter, you have been very valuable to our cause. Your intentions have never waivered. Of course we will help you in whatever way we can." 'Archie' allowed himself a twinkle-eyed wink at Joel, "You don't need us to supply willing women; you take care of that for yourself. You've never wanted money, so what can we do but help with your education and, make sure you are safe?"

Joel stared down at the second half of his sandwich on the heavy plate. He picked up the dill pickle and ate it slowly. *Apparently, they are serious, so why shouldn't I be? It could be a wonderful thing...I might some day have a chance to visit the Soviet Union to see a true Communist society. Vivian will find something to do anywhere she goes.*

"You don't have to decide this minute," Archie eased off a little, "there is no immediate problem. But you will not be safe here. So think about a life in Europe, and think about it with the assurance that you have our support in whatever keeps you out of harm's way."

Though Joel did think about Archie's proposal, Europe was not the attractive spot it would later become. Following the riots in French cities over severe bread rationing, the arrest of steel workers in Marseille on November 10 had started a Communist-led riot that spread to Paris. On November 16, in Brussels, 15,000 people demonstrated against the short sentences meted out to Nazi war criminals.

Meeting Julius again just after Thanksgiving at the Blue Mill restaurant, Joel expected a conversation of commiseration, now that they were both blacklisted. But Julius was cheerful and bursting with energy. After Joel related getting fired, the KGB's generous offer and his own doubts about war-torn Europe, Julius said, "Yes, why rush off; things are in flux. As you know, our friends have also given me several warnings and offers to get out, but why draw attention by making a dash for the exit?"

"I might go if Vivian were to come with me. She probably won't leave her family."

"That's easy. Marry her."

"I guess that's what my parents did, coming here. Maybe hers, too. Only, we'd be going the other way."

"So stay; there's plenty to do."

"Like what? I'll never have access to the good stuff again. Just as technology really takes the big leaps, I'm out of it. Two, three years from now, I'll be left behind and will know nothing worth knowing."

"Hey, it's not over," Julie's smile was his whole face, gray-blue eyes twinkling, "Want to know what, Mort, Bill, Neal and I did last weekend?"

"From what Bill told me. He's living with me on Morton Street, you know. You copied what's his name's entire files."

"The files on every bit of advance avionic research and design being done anywhere," Julius said.

"The balls on those guys! Mort's are getting bigger by the month. Perl doesn't need balls. He thinks he has a divine right." Joel's gaze rested on Julie. *Are you caught up in a religious trance?* "What do you think of Neal?"

"He's alright." Julius looked away. "My point is, there are other things to do."

"You mean dangerous brazen acts? How do you get out of bed without a wheelbarrow to transport those testicles?"

"It took us all weekend, using two Leicas, going around the clock. We barely slept."

"Where'd you get all the film?

"Archie gave it to Bill."

"It sounds like it would've taken hundreds of rolls."

"You'd have wanted to be in on it? Feeling left out?"

"Those guys grew up together; they were tight before they

even went to high school. I wonder whether to go or stay. If I stay I'm lucky to land a job in a Woolworth's, hoping to make manager before I'm forty."

"All this crap will blow over in a year or so. For a genius like you? Hey."

"What'd they do with all that film?" Joel asked.

"Neal met Archie at some train station on Long Island. Archie was supposedly on a camping trip with his family. They traded big duffle bags. Neal got camping gear and Archie got advanced avionics."

"We shouldn't be talking about this."

"Yeah, the film might not even be out of the country yet."

A FEW DAYS LATER, ON NOVEMBER 24, JOEL, Vivian, Julius, Ethel, Mort, Bill and their friends could not help being alarmed by the House vote in Washington, 346-17, approving contempt citations against ten leading Hollywood screenwriters. These men had refused to confirm or deny HUAC's allegations of Communist influence in the movie industry or to admit their own political affiliations. They were fired by Hollywood movie studios the next day, the first of thousands of Hollywood workers to be blacklisted for membership in the CPUSA, or through grudge slander by American fascist vigilantes for views aired in public or even for *alleged former* membership in the Communist Party.

The 346-17 House vote welcomed in a decade of romping, stomping American shoot-first-and-ask-questions-later witch-hunts that ruined lives, aborted talent, suppressed free speech, condoned fascism and violated the United States Constitution. It was to be the scoundrel times of J. Edgar Hoover, Joe McCarthy, Roy Cohn and Dick Nixon.

Joel accepted being fired twice, being blacklisted and being under continued FBI scrutiny as part of his chosen lot. None of that had eroded his strong self-esteem and rebounding confidence. But he became part of the unemployed. Shame dogged him as he became more destitute. His childhood fear of hunger and poverty outweighed his fears of discovery and prosecution. Within weeks of leaving Sperry, he had called contacts and applied for work often enough to know that there were new rules, new questions. He was not going to find meaningful employment anywhere in the United States, not for a long, long time, not doing anything he knew how to do. Joel knew a revolution in electronic feed-back system control was about to happen, exactly when he was one of a few in the world in a perfect position to take advantage of the post-war technology boom. *I'm going to miss it. No matter how much it needs me,* he thought and he began to consider Archie's proposals more seriously. Vivian's love and affection, though neither careless nor boundless, became a considerable comfort as the days grew shorter and cooler and Joel's bank account dwindled. Vivian was still working for the Army Signal Corps, and was not afraid to do better than pay her way in whatever they did together.

Joel began playing the piano more often, something Rebecca had taught him as a child. He imagined he might make a living at it. His brilliant career as a mainstream engineer, inventor and scientist seemed over. He dreamed of inventing a musical instrument based on electronically generated tones. *I've always loved music more, anyway,* he told himself. One day in early December while strolling hand-in-hand with Vivian, window shopping and watching people on a West 4th Street sidewalk, Joel told her again, "Our friends keep telling me to take some time off and study in Europe for a while. Archie believes just being an avowed Communist could land one in jail."

"Let alone any of our other activities," Vivian said.

She called it 'our activities'. Would she go with me?

"I'm not going to find work here," he said, "unless I want to floor manage a five-and-ten, or run a soda fountain. Even then, I'd have to work my way up."

"I just got a raise and I don't mind sharing."

"Believe me, I appreciate you now more than ever, but I need a solid plan. I'm a scientist. I need a laboratory. As I see it, either I make it here playing music and forget engineering or I work in Europe. They'll need to rebuild everything from the ground up. There's bound to be work in the midst of all that."

"You don't speak those languages."

"I'll learn them."

"When you say playing music here…?"

"Well, that's just it. The most I could hope for is picking up a few nights playing in a bar. Right now I'm not good enough. When it comes to *studying* music, I'd be better off in Europe where there are great masters looking for students."

"You'd look for work there as an engineer? I understand the wages are very low."

"You know me. What do I need? It could be fantastic!"

Vivian looked at her lover's rail-thin body, up and down, then smiled, taking his arm. "So your idea is to go to Paris?"

"Or Stockholm, or Helsinki…or Copenhagen. There are music masters in all those places."

"Working as an engineer, while studying with one of the great masters?" She was dubious, but not disapproving.

"I could pick up enough playing in bars and doing odd jobs to make it work, while concentrating on music."

"So, you're saying you're going? Let's get a coffee? Sit somewhere."

"Ah, sure, what about Jimmy's here?"

Vivian wasn't crazy about the Italian bar and its aromas. She ordered a hot chocolate. "Are you telling me you're going?"

"There's not much that's new in what I'm saying, but *if* I go, would you come with me?" As Joel uttered these words, he thought, *I should have waited until we were in bed, after doing the business, or after a good meal. I've bungled it.*

Vivian studied him with an appraising smile, not without grateful recognition of his offer, though she clearly heard her mother's voice: *Make sure you are married before you go off on some risky adventure.* But she heard, too, her own inner voice: *A good and generous Communist does not stand on the bourgeois ceremony of marriage.* "Well," she said, "I suppose the answer is that I'd love to go with you. But I have to wonder: Will you go without me, if I don't go?"

"My going is still a big if, so how can I answer that question now?"

"I'd like to know."

"You're saying you don't want to run off to Europe with a guy who'd be willing to go without you?"

"I suppose maybe I am."

"Come with me. We'll have a great adventure until all this crackdown blows over. Our friends have promised to help any way they can."

"Supporting your music, unrelated to their own interests?"

"Apparently so."

"Think what that means about how important you have been to them. And think what Hoover would do if he finds you."

"Exactly why our friends want me out of harm's way."

"Much for their own sake, I'm sure. Afraid you'll talk."

"For the sake of everyone who believes in socialism…"

"So what do they know about me?" she asked.

"Knowing how much happier I'll be, of course they'd like it if you went with me. So we're both out of harm's way."

"*What* do they know about me? What have you told them?"

"Nothing, but of course they know about you."

"What is there to know, if you've told them nothing?"

"Look, Vivie, they have a traditional fear of pillow talk, the ruin of many a secret, down through the ages."

"Oh, I'm sure it's all very classical."

"Probably they assume you're helping me. You're a Party member. It wouldn't defy logic that you'd know all about me and what I do. What I was doing."

"You're saying that I might be in danger here, if I stay?"

"That wasn't the basis of my suggestion. As fond of you as I am, I miss you when I imagine life in Paris, studying music, learning French, meeting the Party members over there."

Vivian took his hand. "It sounds like a great adventure and I agree with you that the climate here, even for the merely sympathetic and uninvolved, is dangerous."

"Then, you'd go?"

"I need time to think about it. I'll want to talk with you much more about it as I think about it, too, okay?"

"Sure."

"You'd work and study, let things settle down then come back?"

"Something like that."

"Right now, let's get to the show."

"What show? *Out of the Past?*"

"What about *Gentleman's Agreement?* Or *Unconquered?*"

"No, let's see *Gentleman's Agreement,* but Viv, let's take a little vacation, maybe down to Florida, somewhere warm."

"Yes! I don't have to think about that."

"Wonderful! What's *Unconquered* about?"

"We're going to *Gentleman's Agreement.*" She took his arm.

IN DECEMBER, AMID NEWS OF THE PARIS police seizing the offices of Communist newspapers, Archie agreed to Joel studying in Europe. He knew but didn't tell Joel that Moscow saw a future for Joel as an 'illegal' in Europe, to live under a new identity. After leaving the meeting with Archie, Joel applied for a US passport. Thinking Vivian would go with him, he was now pretty sure he wanted to go, but he steeled himself to act alone if she didn't go. He abided his nervous wait for the passport by reading everything he could about France. French Communist strikers had derailed the Paris-Tourcoing Express killing twenty-one innocent civilians. On December 8, Joel went to pick up his passport. The following day, Communist French unions called off their general strike to negotiate with the government. On December 15, Joel took Vivian to St. Petersburg, Florida. They drove south in his 1941 Dodge. It was the eighth day of Hannukah, the earliest she would leave her family. He could not remember her attaching such importance to family holidays in the past. Maybe it was because she was planning to leave them for Europe with him?

Once settled in a modest hotel, little more than a rooming house, but not far from the beach, they continued their love making and their discussion of possible futures.

"So, you're really going with me?" Joel asked.

Vivian was removing her clothes, watching him. "I think I just might," she said. "Why not, my persuasive friend?"

He loved watching her, enjoyed seeing the comfort she felt in her own body as well as her magnificent feminine beauty. "Fantastic, Viv. Think of it: maybe we'll visit the Soviet Union, Czechoslovakia, Poland." He embraced her, kissing her, and felt a stiff shiver run up her spine. "My darling, what a wonderful adventure awaits us."

"Away from all the perils and familiarity of our circle, here?" she asked.

"Of course, that too," he said.

On December 23, romantic in St. Peterburg, still in love after a week, Joel was hit by the news that Bell Laboratories in Murray Hill, New Jersey, had successfully demonstrated a practical working transistor. Joel knew the three credited inventors would be famous and untouchable. He knew it was the beginning of the end of the vacuum tube, which had been *the* electronic device for the last half century. He knew what it was and what it meant; it was going to open a whole new world. It was more than the pieces he'd wanted when he told his brother Artie he needed better components to make the radio transmitter he had in mind. He was thrilled; he had imagined it, dreamed about it; Bell Labs had done it. But then he felt the abrupt new distance between himself and the leading edge in electronics. It confirmed his gloomy prospects in America, where it was all going to happen, just as he had imagined, exactly when he could no longer take part.

By the end of 1947, the Loyalty program had begun its investigation of all federal employees: three million government workers. Attorney General J. Howard McGrath believed there were 'many Communists in America.' But only 300 people were dismissed as security risks, one in a thousand, no charges filed.

As a result of the Canadian Gouzenko arrests in 1946, FBI investigators discovered in professor Halperin's notebook both Klaus Fuchs's and his sister Kristel's contact information. She was placed promptly under FBI surveillance and investigators soon established that in 1945 an unknown American had come twice looking for Klaus. The first time, he had asked the building superintendent for information and the second time the Heinemann housemaid had seen him. It was Harry Gold, but the descriptions of a complete stranger were as yet useless to the FBI.

THREE

"Live as if you were to die tomorrow. Learn as if you were to live forever."   *--Mahatma Gandhi*

TO START WITH, ON NEW YEAR'S DAY, 1948, BRITAIN nationalized railways and Arab militants laid siege to the Jewish quarter of Jerusalem. A few days later, there was a news bulletin that sent a chill down Vivian Glassman's back. From a place called Darovskoye, Russia, a name roughly glossed as 'healthy place', the news was not fascist propaganda of slave labor camps, summary executions or severe food shortages in the land of Socialism. This was akin to the stray dog crossing the cheerful village square with a human hand in its mouth while the band played on. In Darovskoye, forty young children were killed and eaten by a pack of wolves. Vivian mentioned this to Joel and they imagined the terrible hunger of a northern Russian winter that would drive wolves to overpower several teachers and kill perhaps all the children of an entire village. *If this was at a New Years party for the children, imagine how hungry those wolves would have been by March or April...* But as they had agreed on the drive back from Florida, they would go to Europe together, not independently, as Vivian had sometimes suggested when Joel seemed reluctant to make her any serious promises about coming back and building a life together in New York. They purchased tickets on the SS *America*, to sail on January 21. On January 6, Vivian applied for a US passport, showing her steamship ticket. She was assured that she would have her passport in plenty of time.

On Friday, January 16, Vivian took the day off from work at Fort Monmouth. It was the day her passport was to be delivered. The SS *America* was to depart for *Le Havre* the following Wednesday. Joel was with her in her apartment, not so much because of the expected passport, but because he looked forward to the long weekend, thinking how they would 'do the business' and talk about their future together. When he was out shopping for supper, Vivian's passport was delivered, but, in a moment of anxiety, she refused to accept it. When he returned, she told him only that it had not come. She was not sure why she'd refused it or why she had lied. On Sunday, she told him, "I lied. I didn't accept the passport when it was delivered. I still don't know why."

Joel was surprised, but he said. "Because you don't want to jump off the edge of the world with a possible fugitive?"

"I suppose it has to be something like that."

"So you're not coming with me?"

"It seems I'm not."

"Oh, I see."

"You're going anyway?" she asked, barely a question.

"I feel pretty well set on it. ...Once I make real plans..."

It was an icy moment, but they soon talked about her coming when he got settled. It wasn't long before they were intimate again, though there was a shutter closing sluggishly in Joel's heart, and mind.

On Wednesday morning, very early, Joel began to come awake in Vivian's bed. For a moment he remembered only their sexual union before falling asleep and the strange melancholy he'd felt. There'd been pleasure, relief, assurance, but unusual feelings of woe, even fear of her and for her. After that first waking second or two, it swept in on him: *Last night was the last time...I'm sailing for Europe in a few hours! Alone...* Still shy of the light from her window, he felt a fine cold sweat and his nerves firing. His heart dropped to the pit of his stomach then pounded in his chest. His mind reached for the now familiar thrill, the excitement, the delicious challenge of changing his dreams into a reality that did not make him afraid and heartsick.

Vivian was up; he heard her in the kitchen. It was nearly 7 o'clock. *The ship sails at two...gotta be there by twelve. Five hours. Will I be stopped? They gave me the passport, but I could be flagged...Archie says to be ready for anything.* Seeing that Vivian was not naked, nor wearing a dressing gown but was fully dressed stopped Joel's breath. He studied her as she moved about the kitchen, fixing him a generous breakfast, Joel's favorites of toast, eggs and potatoes. *She's bracing herself, for missing me openly admiring her while she cooks.*

Vivian was thinking: *stark naked; that's the only time I have his complete attention…with my clothes on, he never comes close. But no, it's not all about him, but about how I feel…when his eyes are on me.*

They said very little while eating, only polite things meant to slow the hammer of time and any rush of strong feelings. The awkward mood that had re-echoed between them after she'd said she wasn't going returned. She said again, "Let me know right away where I can write to you. I'll write you every time you write me. Maybe more often." She smiled then frowned.

"Of course, I'll let you know how I'm doing, where I am." But Joel wondered if he would. "They could be watching my mail, reading it even. Not that there's much reason to worry so far."

"I hope we stay in touch." She reached for his hand, which he neither withdrew nor pressed to hers. "Once you're set up, you'll invite me to come over?"

"We'll see each other again soon." He squeezed her hand quickly then looked at his plate.

"You're determined to be unhappy because I'm not going, aren't you?"

"How can I be? Look at this beautiful breakfast. I still hope you will join me."

But Joel ate little. He had not stopped loving her or admiring her, but her decision was diverting his attention. His mind told him her general hesitation was enough reason to let her go. Her on-the-brink cancellation had brought disappointment, but he thought about a life of music with people who played music; a life of writing and playing music! Performing music even. *A good new life. Not feeling bitter and sad.*

Vivian was still filled with doubt, tempted to join him, to throw over her strong attachment to her family, her feeling of responsibility about her work and her Party ties. She told herself he would write, missing her, then she'd go. She now feared he'd never come back, never again have a security clearance; there'd be no work for him; he'd never be safe here. They both knew that the advances in electronics, the leading edges of research and experimentation in their field, were going to be US Defense Department controlled and coordinated by the new Pentagon. As an electrical engineer, Vivian understood all this as few people could have; she could not indulge herself in sentimental yearnings for Joel to stay. What they'd done could have serious consequences in the growing national hysteria. Even so, she did not want to risk losing America.

On this cold, bitter day, through flurries of snow driven by gusty winds, Vivian drove the '41 Dodge, Joel's old car, now Artie's—who'd promised to wire installment payments through American Express in Paris. They reached the passenger piers around 10:30. Neither Vivian nor Joel knew why they had come so early. *To face it bravely? To get it over with?*

The 34,000 ton *SS America* was the largest, fanciest passenger liner under an American flag and, looming above Manhattan's West Side piers, smoke wafting from her twin funnels, steam rising from vents, lights pricking the winter darkness, the *SS America* dwarfed several other ships up and down the eastern bank of the wide Hudson. With one glance, Joel felt confident that the ship could make it across the vast, deep ocean, but seeing the gangplank and the officials around the open embarkment port gave him pause.

Passengers were already boarding, passports and tickets were being checked. For a moment it seemed to Joel impossible that he could walk through that opening into adventure and glory. *And Freedom! They'll stop me somehow. Or do I not feel right about leaving Vivian…and Julie and Ethel, Mort and Bill, the whole crowd. But they can still work, so of course they want to stay.*

"Park and we'll go in this restaurant right here," Joel suggested as they passed the huge liner. Vivian was surprised. She'd thought he would kiss her goodbye and go on the ship. Was he having second thoughts about going…?

"You're hungry?" She asked. "You were telling me how you wanted to get on board and get settled. You're not ready to…"

"No. Well, I will be, by the time the food comes…"

She started to say they had just had breakfast, but she remembered he'd eaten little. After parking farther down the block, they walked back to the restaurant. After ordering and beginning to eat, Joel stood up, leaving his overcoat thrown over a chair. Slender as a greyhound, he looked out from the front window toward the *SS America*. Her gangplank and freight ramp were in plain view. All heavy baggage and ship's supplies were on board; the loading ramp was being hauled in. Passengers streamed up the busy gangplank, a few tourists, but mostly US servicemen accompanied by family and friends, businessmen with porters and government men setting about the nation's tasks in foreign lands. As Vivian watched, Joel moved from the window to the pay phone, dropped a coin, dialed, and waited.

Joel heard two long rings before a careful woman's voice answered. "Hello Ethel, I just called to say good-bye, before boarding, over here…"

"Oh," she said, "I was just playing the piano. Michael was singing…Joel, are you—is everything…alright?"

"I hope so, I'm just about to go over there, to the ship I mean—Is Julie there?"

"We were just talking about you, earlier. He doesn't think you should go—Oh, just a minute, he's right here—"

Ethel, don't you understand, if we stay, we could be arrested? Paris, he told himself. *They are rebuilding Europe over there; I'll find work.*

"You alright?" Julie asked. "It's not too late to forget the whole thing. Later if there's a problem—"

"—No, this is it." Joel lowered his voice, "I'm across the street; there's no sign of anybody from the hut (the FBI). I just wanted, you know, to say good-bye."

"Sure, sure Joel. I just wish you weren't going—"

"—But Julie, you know I want to study and play music."—*he's never been into music like me or Al*—"maybe visit a real Communist society—"

"—I was just going to say, now that I can see there is no doubt in your mind, that it may be for the best, all things considered."

"Yeah, maybe I'm lucky to go now, when I can," Joel wished Julie wasn't so solemn. He looked at beautiful Vivian.

"No, I have to say the coast looks clear."

"Joel, we're going to miss you. Thanks for calling like this. Please, write somehow, will you? We miss you already, you know?"

"Of course I'll write, but it may be a while before we see each other. Take care of Ethel and the boys. I couldn't reach the others—I tried a few times."

"I'll tell them. They'll understand and they'll miss your musicales."

"Tell them that, without a job—a position I should say—I can't be of much use to our friends anyway, I'm out of the running. Julie, will you be alright? Aren't things completely…"

"It'll blow over. If not, I've been prepared, for years already. Joel, really."

"Bye Julie." Joel wiped away tears. "See you soon, I hope."

"Ethel says *bon voyage.*"

Sitting down again, Joel looked at the duffel bag propped against the wall and then at Vivian. She knew Joel's coming to the restaurant had been about the telephone call as much as watching the gangplank. He did not look at his plate again. She guessed the call had been to Julius. They'd all become closer; their deeds during the war had joined them more permanently, not less so, as political repression grew.

Joel thought of Al Sarant: *married-with-children in Ithaca. I've barely seen him lately, but I'm going to miss him even more now.* Seeing Vivian sitting there thinking about him, wanting to know his mind, Joel thought, *If I feel this lonely now, how am I going to feel from now on, surrounded by strangers? I'm thirty-two, no job, little money and with only murky plans to play the piano for a living. To study with a great French composer—Do I even want to study engineering in Stockholm? I agreed to it, with Archie. He said registration would all be done when I go there.*

He took up the strap of the duffel bag. They walked several blocks, joking that Joel should get the feel of solid ground while he could. By the time they came back to the gangplank, it was nearly one o'clock. He could hang back no longer. There was no sign of any FBI or police officials—not even a uniformed patrolmen. *The policeman's union should be ashamed of themselves for not insisting on a paid detail.*

The purser's steward said to them: "Only those with tickets and passport can come aboard now. Any moment, you'll hear the warning whistle for visitors to go ashore."

Joel kissed Vivian quickly, ignoring the tears in her eyes and his own, "See you soon, Vivie." He shouldered the bag and walked up the slatted ramp.

Soon, momentarily alone in the cabin he was to share with three other young men, he heard the call rolling through the ship, "All ashore going ashore. Passengers only on board… All ashore who belong ashore!"

BUNDLED IN A SWEATER AND HIS OVERCOAT, Joel went on deck near the rail as the great vessel was pulled from its berth by harbor tugs. Peering down at the docks, he did not see Vivian. *Probably she went to see Ethel and Julie. Tomorrow morning she'll be back at work.* He wondered for a moment what she would do over the coming weekend while he was in the middle of the ocean. *How long will it be before she's with someone else? But she won't forget me. She and I have the real thing. But she decided to end it. No use kidding myself.*

For them both it had been the longed-for first coupling with an equal. Joel had been truly awed by a woman for the first time and he would bring some of that awe to all the women to come. He felt proud that neither he nor she had let her coming along depend on marriage. Placing love, respect and courage second to society's conventions and a sense of security rooted in the same wounded, suffering society they wanted so much to change; it would have been shameful to make marriage the issue.

Once the massive ship was underway, it did not take Joel long to realize that out of the nine hundred passengers, there were few attractive young women, and even fewer—if any— single women. Flirting with soldiers' wives when the soldiers were around did not tempt him. Venturing on deck for any reason was akin to putting one's life at risk: it was cold, windy, wet, stinging, slippery and forbidding. There was only one clear day with little wind. Except for the boring, meager meals at third sitting—which nevertheless quickly became the high points of the day—Joel stayed mostly in his bunk, reading and largely ignoring his three cabin mates who were going back to army bases in Germany and France. They came and went to card games and dances and other shipboard diversions with no more than a nod to Joel. He studied a Swedish language text, using his excellent memory and considerable skill at learning to think anew. He was already enrolled by Anatoly Yatskov in the Royal Swedish academy in Stockholm. He followed world news from printed transcripts of radio dispatches. British foreign secretary Bevin proposed a Western alliance against the USSR.

Archie's plan, no doubt vetted by Yatskov, was for Joel to take local trains and buses to Delft, in Holland, to register there for an engineering course at the Delft Institute of Technology, DIT, a leading engineering center in Europe. Credentials from a recognized European center might be helpful in securing employment. He would then go to Paris for the meeting with Yatskov. In Paris, maybe he'd forget the engineering courses in both Holland and Sweden, and pursue his musical career. *I'll start by going to live performances. I'll hear St. Mathew's Passion again.*

FOUR

"...the most important new idea today is socialism, and not only because this idea has created a Communist country! It is these beliefs, this philosophy that defeated Fascism. Without these ideas at work around the world, we might live under Hitler or someone like him."

--Joel Barr to Vivian Glassman, December 1947

DEBARKING THE *SS AMERICA* IN LE HAVRE, JOEL was at first tempted to exchange some of his dollars for local francs, but decided dollars would be welcome throughout Europe. *I will learn to dicker the exchange rate on any given transaction.* He opened his map of northern Europe. He studied apparent routes from Le Havre to Delft, Holland. He intended to follow Archie's instructions: to travel slowly by local transportation, changing buses and trains often to lose any possible followers and, more important, Archie had emphasized, to leave no trail of his passport along the way, so there could be no record of him for US agents to find. He thought of 'Archie', knowing he probably would never see him again, *Archie was a perfect name for that guy, he looked like an Archie, at ease amongst working class Americans. The KGB is a clever outfit, no doubt about that.*

Studying the map, he saw there were a number of roads going northeast to towns and cities of the coastal countries. The routes and roads don't matter: *I have only to select a nearby destination, in the general direction of Delft. Amiens, for example. A bus to AMIENS is what I want.* He pronounced it full and French in his mind as he wrote it in large capital letters on a blank page in his notebook. *I'll show this to people and I'll find a bus depot.* He refolded his map and put it back in his overcoat pocket.

Using his forthright friendly approach, inherited from Benjamin's engaging ways, Joel soon found a young man who offered to drive him there, for twenty dollars. He was barely tempted. He must remain anonymous. "Bus," he said.

"*Ah vous etes Americain*," the man said.

"I need to find the bus station," Joel said and made a move to walk toward what appeared to be a central square of some kind.

"Ah," the man said, and pointed in the direction Joel was already facing. Joel moved on holding the word AMIENS in his hand. After twenty minutes of stop-and-ask he found the bus station. It was a ten minute walk from passport control at Le Havre and the docks. He also discovered there was a local bus to and from the port of Le Havre.

Ten minutes later, he had succeeded in buying a ticket to leave in just over and hour for Amiens. Finding a spot to sit and wait, he saw and felt the poverty and privation of the people around him. Here, it was what he'd lived through growing up during the 1930s in Brooklyn. Even worse: people were not only poor but many were injured.

The bus, half full of local people, was destined to make a number of stops. Knowing the next bus would be three hours later, Joel decided not to get off and wait for it. He did not feel that he was being followed or observed beyond the natural curiosity about a stranger. *Changing too often might attract more attention than simply sitting in back all the way to Amiens.*

In observing the passing towns and the people dwelling in them, Joel saw their destitution and felt their dread and their hunger. The injured and crippled by war were ever present. Even older men who had lost an arm, a leg or an eye. *The old ones were injured in World War I,* he realized. *Europe was barely recovering when the Nazis struck.*

Arriving in Amiens after dark, he scanned the debarking passengers and felt sure no one who had boarded in Le Havre was following him. In his own sign language, using joined hands, head resting upon them, eyes closed, he conveyed that he needed a place to sleep. Thus he learned a phrase, *a fait dodo.* To go to sleep?

Joel secured a humble room for the night. For his one dollar, it included a morning coffee and a heavy roll. He set out early in the morning and made his way back to the bus depot. Using his map and note pad, he decided on the city of Ghent in Belgium as his next destination. *I'll get off the bus and take later ones to sift out any possible followers.*

As the bus moved through French countryside, Joel studied the people as they got on and off, struck by the fatigue they showed, the exhaustion. *Even two and a half years after the war, those at the bottom of the ladder haven't recovered. They are worn and weary. Socialist government is the only solution for France.*

He stepped down at some small town still in France and strolled about, drawing some attention, but was not accosted or stopped. He found a small shop that sold fresh bread and purchased a baguette and a piece of cheese, both delicious. On the outskirts of the village he found a wooded area to relieve himself, apparently unnoticed.

In Ghent, on a Belgian bus, after presenting his passport at the Belgium border, noting that apparently no record was made of his passport number, he decided to push on toward Delft, perhaps to stay overnight at some place along the way. He arrived in Antwerp at nightfall and was guided to a *pension*. He had learned that the word *pension* was one way to ask for a place with inexpensive rooms.

As Joel continued to see the war's destruction, his mood began to change from discouragement at the challenge it presented to a feeling that here was an opportunity to help and learn, to open new prospects. *They can use a guy like me around here.*

DELFT WAS A ANCIENT CITY OF EARLY CHRISTIAN churches, libraries and cultural landmarks just a short bus ride from the train depot in Rotterdam. To Joel it represented the medieval world of religious superstitions. He found nothing that appealed to him, nor he realized, did further engineering studies appeal to him. It seemed highly unlikely that any course available on this war-torn continent would approach what he'd already learned at Columbia, at Sperry Gyroscope and throughout the war. Developing computer controlled advanced guidance systems would have been next. But not here and not now. Instead, without regret, he began to look forward to a career in music, whether it was playing the piano in a bar or writing symphonies as he had often dreamed of doing. He'd write pieces for the piano and viola, pieces he could play himself. *To an endless audience of attractive young women.*

Joel did his best to hide from himself how much he missed Vivian. He kept in mind that it had been truly wonderful with her, that he'd always have that, even if he never saw her again. But he'd learned valuable lessons from Elie Siegmeister. His future was in music, playing music, even writing symphonies. To pursue such dreams, he would become a student of the famous Finnish composer Jean Sibelius. *If 'our friends' are serious about their offer...* Archie had insisted it wasn't only his idea; it was the 'gratitude of the Soviet people'.

Upon seeing newspapers with large headlines and pictures, the news struck Joel that Mohandas Gandhi had been assassinated. The murder by a Hindu nationalist fanatic seemed much more shocking here in Europe than it would have been in New York. He felt clearly the insular nature of his past life and guided himself to think about the changes he was about to experience. He had come to admire Gandhi just in time to feel his loss.

Joel understood that his low profile travel to Delft from Le Havre had the dual purpose of losing any pursuers and registering for engineering courses, but he did not want to study engineering or live in dreary ancient Delft. He decided, after exploring the grounds and the offerings of the Delft Institute of Technology, to move on to his meeting with Anatoly Yatskov in Paris, earlier than arranged. He'd looked forward eagerly to Paris for many weeks.

IN PARIS, SPEAKING HIS FEW WORDS OF French, especially *pension*, Joel found a small room on the fifth *etage* of a *pension* on the Rue Claude Bernard on *la rive gauche,* the left bank of the river Seine. This fifth *etage* was, from Joel's point of view, *the fifth floor only if you didn't count the ground as a floor.* For three days Joel wandered, mostly in the Latin quarter on the left bank, near his lodging. He learned to use the Metro underground railway, and visited bars and night spots looking for places that had live music, that might hire piano players. By stretching his optimism considerably, he thought he could find employment among them, perhaps only for a meal and tips, to start.

Joel appeared at the Luxembourg Gardens to meet Anatoly Yatskov on January 30, It was a cold, grey day but with almost no wind. Joel knew Yatskov would recognize him and approach with the password, *Bernadette*. The plan was that Anatoly would then introduce Joel's new Soviet contact, someone to provide help with tuition, lessons in musical composition, or further engineering studies. Yatskov was going to expect that he would study at the Royal Academy in Stockholm as already planned and paid for by the Soviets. Joel did not look forward to the idea, but was determined to keep that promise nevertheless.

Yatskov greeted him and led him away to a café, out of the cold. Joel did not know Yatskov but knew the KGB man was familiar with his case and was a close associate of Aleks Feklisov.

Anatoly inquired, "So you are all set up at DIT? What kind of courses will you be taking, advanced stuff, no doubt?"

"…Well," Joel said, "I doubt there'd be much to learn there. I've been at the forefront of developments and discovery. Until recently."

"Still," Anatoly said, "being a student there would bring you in touch with the future of Europe's scientific circles, you'll make important contacts with those who will build the new technology."

"The other consideration," Joel said, "is that the city itself is dreary, ancient and without any progressive society."

"But then you will be studying at the Kungliga Tekniska Högskolan Royal Institute of Technology in Stockholm will you not? You were registered at KTH classes for this August and the tuition has been paid…"

"I'll complete the year in Stockholm. But again, I doubt I'll learn much." Joel did not hide the fact that he did not look forward to this prospect even though he'd be learning Swedish.

"Well, if your purpose was to gather vital contacts from

scientific seminars and forums there, would that hardly matter?"

"You're suggesting that I study at a major university not in order to learn but to…spy, in effect?"

"You could put it that way, I suppose, Yatskov said agreeably.

"I'm saying that I want also to pursue a music career."

"We need to keep up with important scientific developments. Trends even. What better way than cultivating future scientific leaders?"

"What I had in mind was to study music with one of the great composers, Jean Sibilius for example. By the way I thought I'd be meeting a new contact."

"I decided to postpone that meeting so that I could get to know you better; we'll do that next time."

"There's to be a stipend as well as tuition and fees?"

"What you talked about with Aleks and Archie in New York," Yatskov said evenly, "some tuition, a small subsistence allowance." Yatskov caught Joel's eyes and Joel nodded to acknowledge that he was reassured. "Well," Anatoly said, "that was then and this is now. Now there are other possibilities…including the dedicated study of music. But more…fruitful options, I think."

Joel said nothing, but looked thoughtful.

"There is a lot for both of us to think about," Anatoly said. "I believe we best meet again, in a week, right here in this café. I'll take you to your new contact."

Though Joel had expected to see Yatskov only once and to be passed on, his lack of response to Yatskov's "illegal" agent idea seemed to somehow encourage the Soviet agent to arrange the second meeting.

Joel wondered, *Is there a new contact? Someone who I will see every month or so, to get what I need?*

Despite Yatskov's strange behavior, Joel found himself happy in Paris. Though even paying less than a dollar a day for his small room –in a poor pension on the left bank, well off the Boulevard St. Michel—his little New York money would soon dwindle to nothing. And he wasn't sure he could count on Artie to send his car payments to American Express. But he felt confident, buoyant even. *I'm a highly trained engineer from the streets of Brooklyn. I can fix anything that plugs into a wall.* For a moment, he felt born to land here in Paris with his full wits about him.

When Joel went to meet Yatskov at the café a week later, Yatskov intercepted him on his way. With a nod, Joel followed Anatoly circuitously to another bistro. There was no replacement for "Archie" or Aleks waiting for them, and Yatskov said to Joel once they were seated.

"There'll be time for arranging your contact. 'Pierre' is out of town, *au ce moment.* We still have things to discuss, *Je crois.*" Yatskov spoke French fluently and wanted Joel to know it, maybe as a suggestion that he learn to speak French.

Joel needed no urging; learning any language presented a welcome challenge, keeping his brain alive and nimble. He wondered if there really was an agent with the handle 'Pierre'. If there was not, perhaps Yatskove was planning to be his direct contact? Even less likely, was he being dropped? No, more likely than they would eliminate him if he showed signs of too much independence. He felt no fear, a reality check lacking apprehension. He had no intention of *betraying* anybody.

"Well," Joel said, "you mentioned last time I had options, including music study. But then too, you had a more specific suggestion. I'm not sure I heard you right. Maybe I misunderstood?"

"What I'm *suggesting* would make Joel Barr disappear. No more worries about FBI kidnap teams. Joel Barr? Gone!! Live where you like, get married, have a full life."

"Well," Joel said, "back in New York, supplying the information that came across my desk, though important to you and our cause, it was, I have to say, incidental to my very interesting work."

"Would what I propose be some much harder? Or so different really?"

What you propose is entirely different; the by-product becomes dominant while the intellectual rewards disappear."

"I could make you a full time agent, with a good salary, officially part of the committee." He meant the Committee for State Security, the KGB.

"That is very flattering, an honor, I'm sure, but much further from what I'd most like to be doing. I need to either continue to work as a scientist, an engineer, or pursue my dream of music."

"So you are saying what? That you don't want to attend the Delft institute or even KTH in Stockholm? That if you go, you will ignore all opportunities to make contacts? Still receiving only a bread and beans living allowance?"

"As I discussed with Aleks and Archie, in New York, I want to pursue music. They assured me that the higher ups were willing to support whatever I wanted to do, once I was safely out of harm's way. We even discussed my studying in Paris with a recognized composer."

"Becoming known as a musician is not going to make your potential FBI problems disappear. Whereas, a complete change of history would do just that."

"Maybe all of America's anti-Soviet nonsense will blow over?"

"I'd say that is very unlikely. Not while Comrade Stalin is in power." Anatoly seemed confident of a good, long time.

"Will you be able to help me with additional tutoring costs when I find a composer?"

"So be it. I can see you're determined to give this a try. Good luck with it. Your new sponsor will see to the details." Anatoly passed him a small white card. "Everything you need, to arrange your first meeting with "Pierre' is on this card. When you've memorized it, burn it."

Thus, Anatoly Yatskov seemed to wash his hands of Joel, frustrated but not angry or unyielding. Yatskov had plenty to worry about, what with his old friend Aleksandr Feklisov handling Klaus Fuchs's nuclear bomb information under increasing scrutiny and heavy consequence in England. Yatskov worried about the deciphered cables with information about the Rosenberg group. He knew the FBI was searching for the mystery man who was Harry Gold. There were other problems he'd left behind in New York, problems that might consume him. Joel Barr was only Joel Barr.

FIVE

"I believe in only one thing, the power of human will."
— Joseph Stalin

ON FEBRUARY 1 1948, THE SOVIET UNION BEGAN jamming the *Voice of America* broadcasts into the USSR, just short of a year after they started. On February 5, J. Edgar Hoover submitted an 1800 page document to Attorney General Tom Clark entitled, "Brief to Establish the Illegal Status of the Communist Party of the United States of America." It was marked *Strictly Confidential* and covered the origin, history and ideology of the Communist Party—as interpreted by Hoover. Like those whose sole interest in literature was to search for erotic passages, the FBI historians had combed the works of Marx, Engels, Lenin, Stalin and lesser Marxists for every mention of forceful overthrow. They could not cite a single instance of advocating violence on the part of the CPUSA. On February 18, the KGB, having reactivated agent William Weisband, received confirmation that the Army Signal Corps was successfully decrypting KGB coded messages concerning the Rosenberg spy ring, which of course included Joel, Russell McNutt, Al Sarant, Morton Sobell, Bill Perl and several others. Julie's innocent, clear-eyed idealism had recruited over a dozen people.

In Paris, Joel traded on his ingenuity, charm and wit. He played the piano increasingly well, but when new KGB contact, Andrey Yuriev, trade name 'Pierre', suggested he attend the Conservatoire in Paris, he demurred. He had his own theory of music and a system for learning it without any deadening practice of scales or studying harmonic progressions. He told Yuriev:

"I am hunting for a recognized composer who will take me on as a student and an assistant."

In Paris, there was free love and plenty of it! *Who needs*

money? Joel told himself. *After all, I'm a Communist!* His willingness to explore any subject, to play any melody he heard, on any instrument, became his entrée into the cultural heart of Paris; he supplemented his Soviet stipend with restaurant meals and spare change earned playing the viola or piano. Though Joel, leading a bohemian existence, could be called, by later standards, a fun loving playboy, in Paris, in 1948, he followed no trend or style but his own.

On March 17, the Treaty of Brussels was signed forming an anti-Soviet military pact, a predecessor of NATO and a further sign of increasing hostilities.

Telling Andrey Yuriev that he wanted to become familiar with Stockholm and the Royal Technical Institute before studying there, Joel arrived in Stockholm on March 27. The cold weather and completely foreign language and culture did not whet his appetite for spending a year there. He soon departed for Helsinki to seek a position as a student of composer Jean Sibelius who he'd worshipped via radio broadcasts as a child. Sibelius, who had not published any new works in decades, was now eighty-two-years-old and a recluse. Joel went so far as to visit Sebelius's country retreat, laid siege, but was not permitted to meet the great man and was politely informed that Sebelius was not taking students.

The Soviet Union walked out of the allied council governing Berlin and on April 1 and began interfering with truck and rail traffic bringing supplies into West Berlin. The allies countered with the beginnings of the Berlin air lift. On April 3, Harry Truman signed the Marshall Plan, authorizing $5 billion in aid for sixteen countries 'endangered by Communist influence'. In America, the hunt for Communists produced dozens of arrests and indictments for conspiracy to overthrow the US government. Joel's thoughts of eventually returning to New York withered. He had written twice to Vivian, defying Pierre's instruction, but he had not mailed either letter. The possibility of Vivian joining him no longer seemed likely He missed her terribly, but the break had been made.

On May 15, Britain terminated the Mandate of Palestine. Immediately, Egypt, Transjordan, Lebanon, Syria, Iraq and Saudi

Arabia invaded Palestine and attacked nascent Israel.

In early June 1948, FBI special agent Robert Lamphere sent a serial letter to FBI field offices requesting help tracking Joel Barr.

On June 24, the Berlin Blockade began in earnest and the allies ramped up the airlift which would eventually deliver more goods to West Berlin than rail and trucks had been doing.

On June 26, William Shockley filed a patent for a bipolar junction transistor. Joel knew he'd built operational versions by copying 1925 patents held by Canadian physicist Julius Edgar Lilienfeld, and that Shockley gave no credit to the original patent holder.

On June 30, Max Elitcher drove Morton Sobell to Catherine Slip in Manhattan where Sobell met with Julius to exchange microfilm. Julius had been re-activated by the KGB. His new case officer, Gavril Panchenko, gave him the necessary funds and instructions to help David Greenglass get a tourist pass for Mexico, a document which would allow him to escape.

On July 20, President Truman issued a peacetime military draft, spurred by the constantly increasing tensions with the Soviet Union. The next day, the *New York World Telegram* broke the story of Elizabeth Bentley across its front page with a huge headline:

RED RING BARED BY BLOND QUEEN

Though Bentley was not blonde and went unnamed in the long article, it was a lurid and fanciful description of her and her sensational revelations of widespread Soviet infiltration. The next day, July 22, Gus Hall, Gil Green and nine other US Communist Party leaders were indicted under the Smith Act on charges of "conspiracy to teach and advocate the overthrow of the US government by force and violence."

On July 30, the FBI, having gleaned Max Elitcher's name from decoded telegrams in early July, started tailing him. On July 31, HUAC convened, aiming to name names and make political hay out of Bentley's testimony. At about the same time, France's counterespionage force, DST, received a communication from Britain's MI5 stating that Anatoly Yakovlev (Yatskov), officially on the staff of the Soviet embassy in Paris, was a KGB spy.

On August 3, Whittaker Chambers, a former Communist Party member, testified under subpoena before HUAC that US diplomat Alger Hiss had secretly been a Communist while in federal service. Chambers had previously testified just the opposite, under oath. Called before HUAC, Alger Hiss denied the charge, but a federal grand jury would eventually indict Hiss on two counts of perjury. On August 25, HUAC held its first televised congressional hearing called 'Confrontation Day,' Whittaker Chambers versus Alger Hiss.

After staying in Helsinki, playing the piano in bars and playing his viola on the streets, Joel left in early August to travel by bicycle to Stockholm, arriving in time for the start of the school year at the Royal Institute on August 25.

At the end of August, the first decryptions of telegrams (codenamed *Venona*) between the New York KGB and Moscow Center in the Lubyanka began to emerge. By year end, whole paragraphs and some names, Joel's among them, would be revealed. FBI agent Robert Lamphere came across Barr's name and agent Miller called Rebecca Barr, Joel's mother who told him Joel was in Europe.

In Stockholm, Joel was enrolled at KTH and making an effort to learn Swedish. Though Andrey Yuriev had strongly suggested he break off all contact with family and friends, he did not heed this advice and received a letter from Julius at American Express in Paris:

> *"...I will never stop trying to help the Soviet people, who bore the brunt of the suffering in the war, while Roosevelt, and now Truman withhold even our mundane tools and most routine discoveries. Why should any of us, as engineers, continue to develop new ideas just to serve capitalism, to create profits for the rich, while they who fought for human freedom lost 30 million, maybe 40 million people, defeating those who killed six million Jews?"*

Joel wrote back:

> *"...though I have been side-lined by circumstances. I am now pursuing a career in classical*

music."

As Elizabeth Bentley began her testimony before congressional committees, Hoover and the FBI leaked her confessions to Republican members of Congress. J. Edgar meant to sway the 1948 elections in favor of the Republican Party by citing traitor Communists high-up in the Truman administration and in the Democratic Party. Hoover supplied his dirt directly to Truman's opponent, Thomas Dewey.

On September 9, the Democratic People's Republic of Korea was formally declared, with Kim Il-Sung as prime minister.

Even by October 1948, the FBI still thought Barr might be 'antenna' of the *Venona* cable decryptions, Julius's first codename.

Despite J. Edgar Hoover's best efforts, on November 2, Democratic incumbent Harry S. Truman defeated Dewey. At around the same time, Hoover turned over a copy of the FBI file on Joel Barr to the CIA, which knew nothing about the *Venona* decryptions. The file contained the less than accurate information that Barr had traveled to Sweden in January 1948.

On November 12, in Tokyo, an international war crimes tribunal sentenced seven Japanese military and government officials to death, including General Hideki Tojo.

In early December, a note was added to Barr's FBI file: Barr might be passing along nuclear secrets to the KGB. At the same time, the KGB in Moscow Center warned the New York KGB resident of FBI wiretapping and increased scrutiny.

On December 26, the last Soviet troops withdrew from North Korea. On December 31, Israeli troops drove the Egyptian forces from Negev.

Sensing that the FBI's interest in Harry Gold had abated, the Lubyanka ordered the New York Rezidentura to find him and get him out of the United States.

Joel Barr that fall, unaware of both FBI and KGB activities, did his best to attend and pass his courses at the Swedish Royal Institute, all taught in Swedish. Not particularly interested in the course work, Joel applied himself to learning the Swedish language more to engage in casual conversations with Swedish contemporaries—especially the young women—than to follow the uninspiring professors and instructors. He wanted to learn how to say, *lets go somewhere together and get to know each other.* He didn't see the point in learning the terms for advanced engineering, which he already knew in English. He didn't want to study engineering at all in any language. He wanted to pursue music at a higher level than his current street and barroom performances. Using his dearest possession, a bicycle he'd put together from parts acquired while repairing bikes for other people, he explored Stockholm and the Swedish countryside. It did not surprise him that young women he met were attracted to his music-making, a natural way to get comfortably acquainted. Joel was leery enough of Soviet motives not to entirely throw over the paid for tuition and engineering direction the KGB had provided, but he had come across the name Olivier Messiaen, one of the best known classical composers in Europe who might accept him as a student.

Though Olivier Messiaen was to become one of the major composers of the twentieth century, he had been held as a prisoner of war temporarily by the Nazis and was still a relatively young man, not yet forty and just over seven years older than Joel, with much of his achievements and fame still to come.

SIX

*"My faith is the grand drama of my life. I'm a believer,
so I sing words of God to those who have no faith."*
                                        --Olivier Messiaen

CHINESE COMMUNIST PARTY FORCES ENTERED
Beijing on January 25 1949, to declare victory over Chaing Kai
Chek. American-born Nazi broadcaster Mildred Gillars, aka Axis
Sally, went on trial for a sensational six-weeks before being
convicted of treason for her 'Vision of Invasion' broadcast. She
was sentenced to 10-to-30 years in prison.

On February 1, rationing of clothes ended in Britain. On
March 2, the US Air Force B-50 Superfortress "Lucky Lady II"
was refueled in the air four times for the first non-stop flight
around the world. The message to the USSR was clear: *We're
America! Our bombers can reach you wherever and whoever you are.*

Beginning on March 25, the Soviet Union began
deporting nearly 100,000 "enemies of the people" from Estonia,
Latvia and Lithuania to remote areas of Siberia. The sudden
move was meant to weaken resistance to mass agricultural
collectivization. On April 4, the North Atlantic Treaty was signed
in Washington to establish NATO, for mutual defense, to
respond to attack by any external party, and to be headquartered
in Brussels, Belgium, the Cold Warrior of Europe.

On April 9, J. Edgar Hoover, despite his non-partisan
office as the nation's chief policeman, used the US Senate radio
room to record a campaign endorsement of Senator Joseph
McCarthy. Though familiar with McCarthy's record, Edgar's
praise of the Senator's service as a judge had to be deleted
because McCarthy had been censured and nearly disbarred.

KGB NY resident Ivan Kamenev met Harry Gold on

April 10 1949. Gold assured Kamenev that he hadn't told the FBI anything, but he hid the fact that agents had searched his apartment in 1947 and again in 1948. Kamenev told Gold that the FBI was on to him and he should immediately leave the United States, to stay away, indefinitely. Gold stressed that his biggest problem was securing a good job. Though Kamenev gave Harry some money and warned him not to contact Abe Brothman again, when the meeting was over Kamenev knew Gold was not going to leave the country or steer clear of Brothman.

In May, after a poor and distracted performance at the Swedish engineering institute, but with passing grades, Joel began a leisurely bicycle trip to Paris, now determined to pursue a music career. He had mastered the viola which he took with him wherever he went. But making a living as he traveled by playing the piano and the viola was not his goal; he wanted to study in Paris with Olivier Messiaen.

At about the same time, in May 1949, an FBI audit revealed that the NYC office had dropped the ball on investigating Barr.

As Joel cycled toward Paris he traveled with other college students, most younger than he. They often ate together, played music, and watched out for each other. One of his road companions was a blonde Swede named Helga Jorgansson, who made no secret of admiring Joel as he played the piano in bars along the way and pulled sweet music from his viola at roadside stops. She was five foot six and sturdy and quite lovely. She spoke almost no English, but Joel's firm but small hold on the Swedish language provided reasonable acquaintanceship.

Just as Joel read of Israel being admitted to the UN, and that the Soviet Union had lifted its Blockade of Berlin to establish the Federal Republic of Germany, he also learned that EDSAC, the first stored-program computer, began operation at Cambridge University. Joel's professional trajectory seemed to be ongoing without him.

On June 8 1949, even as George Orwell's *1984* was published, such celebrities as Helen Keller, Dorothy Parker, Danny Kaye, Fredric March, John Garfield, Paul Muni and

Edward G. Robinson were named as 'card carrying' Communist Party members by the FBI. Then, as Judith Coplon, a Soviet spy in the US state department was tried for espionage, it was discovered that the FBI had wiretapped her phone. A *Venona* decryption had brought her code name 'SIMA' to the FBI in late 1948 and she was the first person tried as a result of *Venona*— although, to keep *Venona* secret the decrypted information was not revealed at her trial.

Joel and Helga had become friendly on the bicycle trip through northern Europe and arrived in Paris together on July 4 1949. Helga told him she was planning to study French cooking and said she had already arranged for a room in the Paris suburb of Neuilly Plaisance. Following her lead, Joel found a room nearby in the home of a friendly landlady who would enjoy hearing him play his viola. She would allow him to keep his quickly acquired motorbike under her porch roof. Later, she would also hope he might marry her daughter.

Joel and Helga were lovers, but he rarely brought her to his room. He seemed always welcome where she was staying. They made no commitments, but kept in steady touch and enjoyable contact.

The CIA and the FBI were now sharing information on suspected Soviet spies and the CIA informed the FBI in July that Barr was in Sweden. In reality, he had secured an interview with Olivier Messiaen in Paris, who found in Joel a talented and skilled self-taught musician who soon became his avid student. Joel had no imposed disciplines or preconceptions and was open to creative innovation. Messiaen was pleased. 'Pierre' began paying Messiaen's quite reasonable fees and Joel began his apprenticeship with the hope that engineering and espionage were both behind him as he looked forward to a creative future as a musician and composer.

By this time, over 140 leaders of the CPUSA were facing prosecutions and trials. Eleven Communist Party leaders were charged under the Smith Act in 1949: 'they conspired to organize as the Communist Party and willfully to advocate and teach the principles of Marxism-Leninism', which was equated with 'overthrowing and destroying the government of the United

States by force and violence' at some unspecified future time. They were also accused of conspiring to 'publish and circulate books, articles, magazines and newspapers advocating the principles of Marxism-Leninism.' *The Communist Manifesto* by Marx and Engels, Lenin's *State and Revolution*, and Stalin's *Foundation of Leninism* were introduced as evidence for the prosecution. The trial took nine months. Among those charged were Party leaders Eugene Dennis, Gil Green, Henry Winston, leader of the national organization; John Gates, editor of the *Daily Worker* and Gus Hall, leader of the Party in Ohio. Ten defendants were given sentences of five years and fined $10,000. Robert G. Thompson—a distinguished military hero of the Second World War—was sentenced to only three years as an act of gratitude. All of their defense attorneys were cited for contempt of court and given prison sentences as well.

On August 29, the USSR secretly tested its first atomic bomb, code named 'Joe One'. It was a copy of the US plutonium bomb detonated over Nagasaki. A US VB-29 spy plane gathered radioactive particles in the atmosphere east of the Kamchatka Peninsula to confirm American suspicions. The Truman administration and the Attlee government in Britain each held a secret meeting and came to the same conclusion: the Russians had stolen the secrets of the bomb. Anyone who'd worked on the Manhattan project, especially at Los Alamos, was to be carefully scrutinized. About the same time, Gestapo archives, retrieved after V-E day, turned up a document that listed Klaus Fuchs among a few hundred persons who were to be sent to German intel headquarters if they were captured by SS units. His *valuable prey* status did not surprise the British, who were aware of Fuch's Communist past and had risked giving him a mid-war security clearance, but to the Americans, in the throes of an anti-Communist frenzy, it was sensational. The FBI opened a criminal file on Klaus Fuchs under a code name.

On September 7, the Federal Republic of Germany was founded with Konrad Adenauer as the first chancellor, pledging allegiance to US interests.

On September 23, President Truman announced to his nation that the USSR now had the atomic bomb. Popular fear of

Communism blazed like a fire doused with gasoline.

On September 29, Mrs. Iva Toguri D'Aquino, dubbed 'Tokyo Rose,' was found guilty of treason for broadcasting Japanese propaganda during the war. She was prosecuted amidst hysteria whipped up by Walter Winchell and the American Legion. She would do seven years. On the same day, also taking place amidst Commie hysteria, Ivan Kamenev met Harry Gold who naively mentioned that the FBI was occasionally following him and that he knew this from Brothman. He still did not mention that agents had twice searched his house. Gold had ignored orders to stop seeing Brothman for the second time. Kamenev ordered him to leave the country immediately. Following this meeting, the KGB began to suspect incorrectly that Gold was now working for the FBI.

On October 1, the People's Republic of China was founded, adding to even greater American fear of Communists.

In October 1949, Kim Philby, not yet Britain's sensationally infamous Soviet spy, was posted in Washington as British Intelligence's contact with the FBI. Philby began receiving weekly briefings from special agent Robert Lamphere about the *Venona* decryptions including a tour of Arlington Hall, the US Army's Signal Intelligence Service (SIS) cryptography center. Though Hoover made sure Philby didn't tell the CIA, he missed Philby's weekly reports to the Lubyanka.

In October, as the KGB ordered Harry Gold to flee, Joel mailed a letter to his mother from his Paris address, proudly telling her he was at last pursuing a musical career, thanking her for teaching him how to play the piano.

On October 16, the civil war ended in Greece with a Communist surrender, an early Marshall plan success using American dollars and US secret agents to defeat the "Bolshevism" that Hitler had warned the world about.

Though the FBI got Barr's Paris address from his letter to his mother, they never asked for help from the CIA in France, who didn't yet know why Joel Barr was of interest to the FBI, nor did Hoover ask for help from the US embassy in Paris. Continuing to bungle Joel Barr, J. Edgar decided to wait until Barr returned to the US. Meanwhile, Kim Philby was relaying both CIA and FBI files to the KGB which moved up their plans to get Rosenberg and his associates out of harm's way. But Julius told the KGB that his brother-in-law David Greenglass could neither leave nor take along his pregnant wife, Ruth, and that he, Julius, could not leave them behind. All the while, Elizabeth Bentley was testifying to committees and grand juries as the FBI followed up her leads.

In November 1949, having been given no reason not to, the US embassy in Paris renewed Joel's passport. On December 12, even as the KGB laid out cash for Julius and his escape plans, Stalin launched a savage verbal attack on Soviet Jews, accusing them of being pro-West and anti-socialist. At the same time, a British investigation of Klaus Fuchs was proceeding. Rather than ordering Fuchs to London, MI-5 Special Branch interrogator William James Skardon went to the nuclear research center at Harwell on December 21 to speak to Fuchs in his office. Skardon asked Fuchs questions about his family and himself. When Fuchs talked about his work in New York, Skardon asked him point-blank: "During your stay over there, were you ever in contact with a Russian to whom you gave information about your work?" The question took Fuchs by surprise and he indignantly denied any such thing. Skardon became even more aggressive after lunch, repeating several times that Fuchs had passed along secrets to the Soviets. Skardon knew Fuchs was guilty, but decided to let his psychological crisis take a natural course. At Harwell, Fuchs's position became more and more strained. On December 29, he celebrated his thirty-eighth birthday. He was one of the main research scientists there. The next day, Skardon resumed hostile interrogation, but told Fuchs that the matter was not as serious as it might appear and that if Fuchs admitted his espionage activity, he would simply be fired for security reasons. Fuchs continued to deny everything.

Though much of Joel's time in Paris seemed carefree, he felt his old circle of friends in New York being drawn closer only by fear. Their original efforts, just out of college, a source of pride under the German onslaught, their delicious secret patriotism they'd shared while hundreds of thousands died at Moscow, Leningrad and Stalingrad, now appeared through a dark lens. They'd become the arch-enemies of the new prosperous solidarity of a victorious nation. US Public opinion against Communists was a fury, with hero cops hunting spies with murderous intent. Joel Barr, the most gregarious of the CCNY circle, was now an FBI target, but was not being watched as he began to suspect he was. Needing to feel free, Joel left Paris, convincing Helga Jorgansson to come along. They traveled around Europe with students, staying in youth hostels. They skied during the winter in Switzerland and she returned with him to Paris in the Spring of 1950. They grew closer.

Joel's life as a musician, a student of the soon famous composer, and as an affable wizard seemed enviable. But Joel's new friends did not see, as Helga did, his sudden worried frowns, the occasional panic as he read of political developments at home. Helga knew she was living with a troubled man and she knew whatever it was that troubled him, he wasn't going to tell her about it.

SEVEN

"Today we are engaged in a final, all-out battle between Communistic atheism and Christianity. The modern champions of Communism have selected this as the time, and ladies and gentlemen, the chips are down—they are truly down."
                    --Senator Joseph McCarthy

JANUARY 1 1950 WAS, JOEL'S 34th BIRTHDAY. Interpol was formed the same day. On January 4, J. Edgar Hoover tried to block the formation of the Kefauver Committee to Investigate Organized Crime. The next day, US Senator Estes Kefauver introduced a resolution calling for an investigation of organized crime in the US. When the Committee proved organized crime did exist, Edgar claimed it did not. Hoover and the mafia families had an understanding: they took care of him, especially at the race tracks, and turned over any juicy information to Hoover that did not hurt them. Meyer Lansky's expertise with the homosexual photos of Edgar guaranteed the FBI would never interfere with Lansky's people or businesses. And Lansky was not the only one to have explicit pictures of J. Edgar Hoover's homosexual activity. CIA counter intelligence chief James Angleton had similar photographs and may have gotten them from Lansky. Whatever their origins, the Hoover fellatio pictures were used against him for the rest of his life as he continued to deny that the Mafia existed and puffed up the threat from the Communist Party until long after its membership had dwindled to insignificance.

On January 6, the United Kingdom recognized the People's Republic of China. Chiang Kai-Shek's Republic of China severed diplomatic relations with Britain in response.

On January 7, after having illegally tapped author Max Lowenthal's phone for over thirty years, Hoover ordered his agents to burglarize Lowenthal's home. In doing so, he discovered Lowenthal's intention to publish an exposé of the FBI. What followed was a massive campaign by Hoover to terrify Lowenthal and intimidate booksellers. The book, eventually published, revealed some of Hoover's worst crimes.

On January 9, John Cockcroft, the director of Harwell, was finally informed of the Fuchs investigation's progress. He was deeply shocked and explained to his old friend Fuchs that it would be best if he resigned. He even promised to keep him on as a consultant. By now everyone at Harwell knew that Fuchs was a suspect and many of his colleagues ignored him, leaving Fuchs in what he later called 'a kind of soft emptiness, among shadows I couldn't touch.'

On January 14 1950, the FBI asked CCNY for a list of all its 1938 engineering graduates. On January 17, David Greenglass was questioned about balls of Uranium missing from Los Alamos, an item purloined by some technicians there as a sort of souvenir. David had expected questions about spying. He had stolen two such Uranium samples, one he gave to someone and one was going through slow radioactive decay in a closet next to where he was being questioned. He denied any knowledge of the missing Uranium golf-ball-sized pieces.

On January 21, accused Communist spy Alger Hiss was convicted of perjury for denying under oath that he'd passed secrets to Whittaker Chambers.

On January 24, Fuchs told Jim Skardon the whole story of his eight years of collaboration with Soviet intelligence. But he said that he did not know the identity of the agents he worked with. He was still not taken into custody and even allowed to remain free after the next interrogation on January 26. The next day, he went to London on his own and Skardon was waiting for him at Paddington Station. They walked to the War Ministry where Fuchs signed his confession. In a strange twist, Fuchs refused to describe in detail what information he'd given the KGB because Skardon didn't have a high enough security clearance. Three days later, he met Michael Perrin, the inspector for the State Commission for Atomic Energy, whom he had known since 1942. Perrin was quite knowledgeable and Fuchs related to him the amount and nature of the information he'd given the Soviets. He then returned to Harwell alone, once again.

On January 31, in response to the detonation of the Soviet Union's first atomic bomb in 1949, President Harry S. Truman ordered the development of the hydrogen bomb. On February 2, Klaus Fuchs was asked back to inspector Perrin's office to 'clear up some details,' and he was at last arrested by Scotland Yard. The following day at the Bow Street court, public prosecutor Humphreys read the charges to a very small audience. Despite the spy craze and the headlines that exploded when the charges were read, the wording was very objective, stating that at least four times, between 1943 and 1947, Fuchs had passed information on atomic studies that could benefit the enemy. Soviet agents took this to mean that Klaus had not confessed everything he knew. British courts wished to limit the public furor and damage to the country's image. The prosecution presented Fuchs as a most brilliant specialist in theoretical physics and it was even mentioned that his supervisors were so impressed by his scrupulous adherence to security rules that they'd given him the highest security clearance. Then too, it was mentioned that his acts of premeditated treason had not been motivated by personal gain.

Fuchs's situation caused anxiety among nuclear scientists many of whom had wanted to share nuclear secrets with the USSR. Niels Bohr had tried in 1944 to convince President Roosevelt and Churchill to share Manhattan Project information with Stalin. Albert Einstein, Bertrand Russell, Leo Szilard and Joseph Rotblat had all made public statements against an American A-bomb monopoly. Fuchs had done only what most of the Los Alamos scientists at one time or another had thought right. Though headlines screamed that Fuchs had turned over dozens of collaborators and Soviet agents, he'd only described Harry Gold who he knew only as 'Raymond'. Hoover begrudged Fuchs credit for breaking the case and insisted the FBI was already pursuing Gold.

Anatoly Yatskov and the KGB, knowing Fuchs was

connected to Rosenberg through Gold, stepped-up efforts to extricate Rosenberg and Greenglass. On February 4 1950, Julius, to encourage David to escape with his family, told him that Joel Barr was far more involved than he, David, was, and yet Joel got a passport out. Greenglass did nothing and on February 7, the FBI started investigating possible spies at Los Alamos.

On February 9, at the Republican Women's Club in Wheeling, West Virginia, Senator Joseph McCarthy delivered his sensational claim that the Truman State Department was consciously harboring 205 card carrying Communists. His speech was based on information Hoover had secretly given him though he claimed he had nothing to do with McCarthy, even as Joe dined regularly with Edgar and Clyde in public and joined the couple at the horse races, the only elected official allowed to use Edgar's private box at the racetrack. Later, it was Hoover who created the infamous McCarthy hearings.

On February 12 1950, pro-Communist riots erupted in Paris. Albert Einstein warned that nuclear war would lead to mutual destruction. The following day, the US Army began deployment of anti-aircraft artillery to protect nuclear installations and military targets, even as the US Air Force lost a bomber carrying an atomic bomb off Canada's west coast, scaring the shit out of everybody.

On February 14, pregnant Ruth Greenglass stepped too close to the gas flame in her kitchen and her gown went up in flames. She was rushed to the hospital badly burned. It was the same day the USSR and Mao's People's Republic of China signed a mutual defense treaty, further feeding US anti-Communist fear and frenzy.

On March 1, Klaus Fuchs was convicted in London of spying against Britain and the United States for the Soviet Union. On March 6, Prime Minister Attlee attempted to ameliorate the catastrophe:

"It was only in the fall of 1949 that Great Britain learned from the Americans that secrets had been revealed during the war. MI5 quickly established that Fuchs was responsible and placed him under

arrest."

The FBI disagreed: Why hadn't MI5 caught Fuchs passing classified documents to his Soviet handler? Did Soviet moles in the upper levels of British counterespionage help him?

For Joel, the conviction of Klaus Fuchs, in just under one month, was a dire warning and Andrey Yuriev told Joel that Fuchs was somehow connected to Julius and Greenglass and again forbid him to correspond with family or friends. "Be ready to flee at a moment's notice," he said. During times with his music teacher, Olivier Messiaen, Joel seemed so distracted that Messiaen asked, "So are you losing interest? Are you beginning to think of giving up on a career in music?

"No," Joel said. "I've a few family problems back home."

"You needn't be discouraged, you know. Though you've had a late start, the talent is there. Music is in you, part of you. There is no reason to give it up now."

Joel reddened, ashamed that he was not worthy.

"I mean it. You think I need your monthly fee? You now have the basic tools to write complex musical scores. What you hear in your mind, you can now write down, no?"

"I'm beginning to catch on."

"If you're not quitting, I can only say I hope your family problems will clear up and not interfere with your progress."

"Unfortunately, it doesn't look that way at the moment."

"You have a great future in music, don't let the past destroy that future."

EIGHT

"Leadership is the art of getting someone else to do something you want done because he wants to do it."
--Dwight Eisenhower

ON MARCH 8 1950, THE SOVIET UNION publicly claimed to have an atomic bomb. The following day a special subcommittee of the US National Security Council recommended Truman speed up development of the hydrogen bomb and the President made it a national priority. *The New York Times* estimated that Fuchs had shortened Soviet research time by as much as ten years. The Soviet H-bomb would follow the US test by only one year.

In early April, Aleksandr Feklisov met his old friend Anatoly Yakovlev (a.k.a. Yatskov) in Moscow. Yakovlev brought him up to date on Joel Barr and his studies with Olivier Messiaen in Paris. Yakovlev suggested, "It may finally be time to take him out of circulation and make an illegal agent of him. He'd be ideal at infiltrating scientific circles in Europe."

"I think it's too late for that," Feklisov said calmly. "Besides, he seems quite serious about his music."

Anatoly then described his meeting with David Greenglass. "He's a pudgy, dumb kid, way over his head, a person without backbone. He supplied only useless information."

Days later, when Ruth Greenglass got out of the hospital, now eight months pregnant, Moscow Center again strongly urged that David get his family out of the country. On April 18 1950, FBI agents in Albuquerque notified headquarters they'd identified six individuals who matched what was known of 'the Los Alamos spy'. One of the six was Greenglass. On April 24, FBI agents went to Joel Barr's Morton Street apartment and interviewed the building super who told them, "That guy? He went to Europe to study medicine Wants to become a doctor."

On or about May 3, Al Sarant and Carol Dayton confessed to Bruce Dayton and Louise Sarant that they were committing adultery. Both the jilted partners took the news without violent reaction or immediate plans for divorce, hoping passions would die down. There were four children involved; both the Daytons and the Sarants had two children each.

On May 9, J. Edgar Hoover ordered an intensive search for Harry Gold, now suspected of being Fuchs's courier, 'Raymond'.

Shortly after Victory Day, May 9, Aleksandr Feklisov visited Anatoly Yakovlev/Yatskov at his Moscow office. Anatoly, clearly troubled and depressed, took Feklisov into his private office and closed the door. "There's a traitor in our American networks," he said. "It's Gold, that strange bird!" Anatoly then confessed to Feklisov that he'd crossed two networks in using Gold as a courier for both Fuchs and Greenglass.

On May 11, the Kefauver Committee to investigate US organized crime began its hearings. Hoover was livid, doing everything he could to discredit their findings.

By May 12, the FBI agents who were assigned to investigate Joel Barr were too busy hunting Harry Gold to focus on Barr. Julius, though caught up in his growing role as the family protector and leader, unable to contemplate his own safety in isolation, did take Soviet warnings seriously enough to visit his doctor and ask what kind of inoculations were needed for a trip to Mexico. He also obtained passport photos for himself, Ethel, Michael and Robert.

On May 15, FBI agents discovered Harry Gold was living with his father and brother in Philadelphia. A week later, they searched Gold's house and found a map of Santa Fe. Gold was taken into custody, confessed and was arrested the next day, the same day Ruth Greenglass came home from the hospital with a new baby. FBI agents Lamphere and Clegg were still interrogating Klaus Fuchs in London, asking specifically what kind of information he'd given to Harry Gold. Fuchs told them it was the complete plans for the plutonium bomb, plus the starter notes on the hydrogen bomb.

On May 24, newspaper headlines across the United States shouted the news of Gold's **'ATOMIC SPY'** arrest. Julius came to the Greenglass apartment with a copy of the *Herald Tribune* featuring Harry's picture large on the front page. He asked Ruth, "Is this the guy that knows you and David from Albuquerque?"

"Yes," Ruth said.

"You've got to get out right away, for sure by Sunday June 11, at the latest. Or else!" He knew it would take a few days to arrange their escape with the Soviet handlers.

"What about you, Ethel and the kids?" Ruth asked.

"We're almost ready, but we won't leave you behind."

At the same time, KGB headquarters in Moscow at the Lubyanka notified the New York *Rezidentura* that Greenglass's escape was now imperative and that Rosenberg, too, should be rescued immediately. The Moscow center authorized $10,000 in cash as a first installment.

On June 2 1950, Joel Barr ran into Sam Perl, Bill Perl's brother, on a Paris street corner. When Sam asked how they could stay in touch, Joel told him, "I'll be gone, you won't see me around, better you don't know where." Joel knew what was coming; he was afraid, but he was ready. It was the same day Lamphere and Clegg returned to the United States to headlines screaming that Fuchs had "named over one hundred red spies." With that nonsense, the problem for Hoover of how to hide the FBI's true sources had been solved; new arrests would be seen as significant results of Fuchs's FBI confession. For the press and the public, the original source that doomed Communist spy rings in the United States was Klaus Fuchs, not Harry Gold betraying Fuchs. It was also on June 2 that David Greenglass accepted $4,000 from Julius, though he had no intention of fleeing.

LESS THAN TWO WEEKS FOLLOWING THE anxious meeting between Feklisov and Yakovlev, the dreadful premonition became reality; the Lubyanka bent all efforts to save its US agents, but all that could be done had already been done. What chance did they have against the wave of anti-Communist atomic spy hysteria engulfing America? They recognized that their efforts might even further endanger Rosenberg, Barr,

Greenglass, Perl, Sobell, McNutt and Sarant. KGB paralysis set in as US arrests followed each other like bullets from a gun and each individual was labeled, 'a member of the atom spy ring'. After Harry Gold, Alfred Dean Slack was arrested on June 15 for spying at the Oak Ridge laboratories in Tennessee. He had been Joel's and Elaine Goldfarb's one time house mate in Fort Monmouth New Jersey.

On Monday, June 5, David Greenglass went to his job to secure a six-week leave from work to take care of Ruth and the new baby. When he returned home, he was being watched from a van across from their front door. When he pointed the "Acme Construction" van out to Ruth, she found there was no telephone listing for an Acme Construction Company. On June 7, Julius saw men in a van and in a car and on street corners around the Greenglass apartment. When he met his KGB case officer two days later, he was told not to go near his brother-in-law again.

On June 10, at last wanting to escape, David took a bus upstate, as if losing the FBI was like ducking a bill collector. When he got off the bus, he saw he'd been followed. Badly shaken, he took the next bus back to New York. On June 11, when the deadline Julius had given Ruth and David to leave town passed without incident, David took this as a good sign and told Ruth, "They didn't come knocking. It'll probably all blow over." Two days later, on June 15, the FBI knocked on their door and confronted David. By ten o'clock that night, he'd broken all his promises and betrayed his sister, brother-in-law, Joel Barr and everyone Julius had ever mentioned to him. Had he kept his mouth shut, he could well have saved himself and several others from decades in prison and his sister and brother-in-law from the electric chair. Newspapers headlined the arrest the following evening, June 16. The FBI visited Julius that day.

Joel, in close contact with Andrey Yuriev, had been constantly warned about the revelations of Klaus Fuchs and Harry Gold. With the arrest of David Greenglass, it became clear that Joel could be next. He must escape. On that evening of June 16 he met Yuriev in Paris who told him, "You can not waste another day. You must get out now."

"Where to? I'd love to visit Moscow."

"You must go to Prague."

"Czechoslovakia?"

"You must get a visa, but France is in the US sphere, so don't apply for it here."

"Where then?"

"We'll arrange everything from Zurich. You must go there first."

For the moment, Czechoslovakia was a rare common ground between Western and Eastern Europe, easily accessible to Westerners, but part of the Soviet bloc. Joel hoped that it might be only a stepping stone on his way to Moscow and his long dreamed of visit to the land of Socialism.

The next morning, Joel told his friendly Paris landlady he'd be back for dinner and he left with his viola and a briefcase, leaving behind all his clothes and his motorbike. He did not say goodbye to Helga. Later, when he did not turn up at her pension, she merely suspected he had grown tired of her and, when questioned later, she knew nothing. Joel had left no hint of his destination with anyone. On his way to the train station, he read in the *Herald Tribune* about the Greenglass arrest and how the accused was facing the death penalty for treason in time of war. *I warned Julie that sniveling brat could not be trusted.*

Joel took the train to Zurich and was instructed to wait while the KGB studied the situation. Shortly, he was issued a Czech visa on his US passport at the Russian Embassy. From Zurich, traveling through Austria, he feared he would be caught at the Czech border, but he passed border control and arrived in Prague on June 22 1950. He descended to the platform with tears of joy and hugged the KGB agents who greeted him like a long lost brother. Fully emotional, without any attempt at conversation, they took Joel to a modest hotel near the rail station and explained that this would be his temporary lodging. In addition to two young local KGB men, there was a tall, handsome, sharp-featured man, with clear blue eyes: Lieutenant Viktor Taroikin from the Lubyanka. As their meeting progressed, Joel noticed that Lieutenant Taroikin was studying him with careful interest. Taroikin seemed to know the other men fairly well and Joel guessed that he was their superior, alert, watchful and in charge.

With the two younger agents doing most of the talking, translated and supplemented by Taroikin, they explained to Joel that though he was now safe, it would be best for him to remain anonymous in order to avoid a US attempt to kidnap him and return him to the United States. After impressing this danger upon him and securing his renewed promise that he would not try to contact friends or family, they strongly suggested a complete identity change. The KGB would provide a new legend and an entire documented lifetime that he had not lived. He agreed. Lieutenant Taroikin liked what he saw in Joel, the openness of this tall thin man, his brief flashes of fear and panic, his clearly heartfelt smiles of gratitude, relief and sincere enthusiasm. This was a true believer who had, naïvely, taken every risk for his belief in the justice of socialism, risks and travails which had not discouraged him. He expressed no remorse, shame or guilt; he did not feel unlucky, betrayed or foolish. Taroikin sensed Joel had a good sense of humor and was glad for him. He hoped he would not stagnate and die in their care, as had other escaped Western spies.

"What about eventually moving me to Moscow or Leningrad?" Joel asked, instinctively looking to Taroikin, "I've always dreamed of living in the Soviet Union, seeing real Communism at work."

Taroikin understood this was no idle gesture of devotion. He shook his head slightly, saying evenly, "I doubt that'll be possible immediately." He did not want to tell this affable young man, his contemporary, bubbling with enthusiasm even in this adverse situation, that the higher-ups needed to know Barr was not an FBI plant, ready to become a double agent for the land of his birth. Taroikin intended to emphasize in his report that he felt sure this was not the case, but he was not yet ready to stake his career on it. He also did not want to explain to Barr that now was not a good time to introduce a Jew, especially a high-level-American-source-and-possible-counter-spy Jew, into the higher circles of scientific and technological development in the USSR, which seemed to be what Barr had in mind, repeating his role in developing high level radar and radar controlled devices in the United States. And Viktor Taroikin dared not mention, even had he wanted to, that an anti-Semitic storm was brewing in the land where anti-Semitism was so famously a serious state crime.

On June 22, as Joel was arriving in Prague, Morton Sobell and family flew from LaGuardia airport in New York City to Mexico City, as instructed by his KGB case officer. Fully aware of what was happening, Mort was terrified. He felt they were out to kill him.

NINE

"Greetings to you, beloved Comrade Stalin!
You and Lenin have thrown open to us
Boundless sunny expanses,
And filled us with hope and joy...
Following in the footsteps of Lenin,
And learning our lessens from your works,
We have built a mighty power
That makes us rejoice, and puts fear into
Our enemies hearts."

--A poem for Czech school children

AS JOEL'S WELCOMING DELEGATION DEPARTED his hotel room, they told him they would contact him, not the other way around. Though less intense than the secrecy practiced in New York, tradecraft protocols were to continue for Joel's protection. While waiting for further contact and instruction, Joel roamed the streets of Prague. He discovered art galleries, museums, an opera house, a concert hall and symphony orchestras. Within days he received the signal at his hotel to go to an office in Old Town Square where he met Lieutenant Taroikin who presented him with a Union of South Africa birth certificate, a British passport and various identity and membership documents, all forged well-enough to pass inspection by Czechoslovak police and the *Statni Becpecnost* (StB), Czech state security. His US passport, driver's license and all other identification from his former life were taken from him; he must become Johan Burgh, a citizen of the Union of South Africa, a British dominion.

"You're not likely to run into a real South African here in the streets of Prague," Taroikin told him, "and South Africa explains your European appearance, knowledge of English and why you don't speak Czech. The Afrikaans name in Czech is Dzhosef Berg, which sounds natural here. We've taken twenty months off your age by using the date you gave me as one you will remember." It was Arthur Barr's birthday, October 7 1917. "Here is your history of traveling and moving about the world. Learn it thoroughly and destroy the paper." You emigrated here to escape strife and hostility. The people you'll meet in Prague do not know Americans and won't recognize your Brooklyn accent. Soon, I trust, you'll learn Czech and Russian. You're an electrical engineer who loves music, eager to become a citizen of Czechoslovakia. Above all, you must absolutely never contact any family or friends. Such a mistake would endanger you, me and many others." Dzhosef Berg nodded solemnly. As far as the world was concerned, Joel Barr had vanished.

On June 25, 90,000 North Korean troops armed by the USSR crossed the 38th parallel and attacked South Korea. Without the bomb, newspapers proclaimed, Stalin would never have dared make such a move! Those who'd given the USSR the bomb, they decried, should be held responsible for the loss of American lives. Two days later, Truman ordered American military forces to defend South Korea. The following day, North Korean forces captured Seoul.

AT THE SAME TIME, THE ARLINGTON HALL codebreakers informed the FBI that New York KGB had named Alfred Sarant as their spy in a decoded telegram from May 5 1944. With Gold on trial in Philadelphia, the press began speculation that Greenglass would turn government witness and indeed on July 17 David told the FBI that Rosenberg started spying when he became an inspector at ASC and that Julius had implicated Barr as joining him at that time. Greenglass recalled Julius urging him to flee to Mexico. The next day, July 18, Rosenberg was taken into custody and the FBI asked the US embassy in Paris to find Barr.

On July 19, the FBI visited Al Sarant in Ithaca. He had no one to turn to, no Joel, no Julius, no KGB officer and he admitted that Joel was a Communist. When he said he barely knew Vivian Glassman, the FBI showed him pictures of himself with Vivian and Joel. At the same time, in Paris, the embassy attaché reported that Joel Barr had 'suddenly disappeared'. On July 20, FBI agents arrived at Reeves Corporation in upstate New York to question Max Elitcher, only two days after Julius' arrest, which mistakenly suggested to Elitcher that Julius had talked. Max told them Julius had tried to recruit him unsuccessfully in 1944 and 1945. Max also gave up Joel Barr's name.

In Prague, Joel was reading the headlines in anus-quivering, spine-freezing horror. Then, unknown to him, on July 21, the New York KGB used another American spy to contact his sweetheart, Vivian Glassman. She was asked to visit Bill Perl in Cleveland, to urge him to flee and to give him $2,000, as supplied by the KGB messenger.

On July 22, FBI agents took Sarant in to the local sheriff's office for further interrogation. At the same time, Morton Sobell, in Mexico City, cashed in his return tickets to New York. He knew nothing of Max's interviews with the FBI. Though Mort had not yet found a Soviet contact or any other help, he had no intention of turning back.

On July 23, Vivian reached Perl's home in Cleveland. She was obviously terrified as she warned Bill of the rapidly growing dangers. "Here's $2000, there'll be more if you need it but you've got to get out."

"What are you doing here and what are you talking about?" Perl exclaimed, "I don't know anything about those people."

"Just take this and get moving, really Bill."

"This is my home; get out! And take that filthy money with you."

"But Bill…"

"Get out!"

The next day, Perl phoned the FBI in Cleveland to report the strange visit of Vivian Glassman and, in effect, he betrayed her. At the same time, the interrogation of Sarant continued briefly, as if the FBI was about to make an arrest. On July 25, Hoover sent an urgent message to the Paris embassy demanding that Barr be found.

Sarant had had enough; he wanted out. He took his wife, Louise, next door to the Dayton's and told them he had to get away, but that he needed someone to help with the driving, to Mexico.

"I certainly can't do it, Al," Louise said, I've got your two kids to look after."

"Don't look at me," Bruce said. "I can't drop work on my Ph.D. thesis. You're talking about a week or more, all told."

For a moment, no one spoke then "I could at least drive you to a bus station, Carol said quietly to her lover as she felt Bruce's eyes on her. "In New York City, or maybe even Philadelphia," she added.

To her surprise and to Al's, Bruce looked at both of them and said, "It's up to you." His look said, *Get rid of him! Maybe I'll forgive you.*

Al saw how certain Bruce was that Carol would come back: *After giving a neighbor a ride to the bus station. His way of being permanently rid of his rival.*

"Well, Bruce said, "how are you going to do it? When?"

They made plans for Al's escape, careful plans.

On July 26, Bill Perl gave the FBI a written statement claiming he had no idea why Vivian Glassman showed up with $2,000.

Vivian returned the cash to the KGB agent who sent her to Cleveland and related how Bill had ordered her out of his apartment. "A fool's errand," she called it.

At the same time, Sarant told the FBI he was going to Long Island to visit family. When he set out, he was tailed to his father's house.

On July 27, the US Attorney General issued a warrant for Joel Barr's arrest, charging him with espionage. FBI agent Robert Lamphere was assigned to the world-wide search for Barr.

On July 28, the New York City FBI was responsible for watching Sarant while he was on Long Island. They even brought him into their Manhattan office for questioning and to show him, through a one-way mirror, to the superintendent of 65 Morton Street and to the super of Vivian Glassman's building. They both recognized him.

In Prague, Lieutenant Viktor Taroikin told Dzhosef Berg, "Your friend Sarant is being thoroughly grilled. They asked whether you had introduced Julius and Ethel to us. They asked about several others, but there were a lot of questions about you. No doubt Sarant told them what a great guy you are, a scientist, a music man, bragging about you."

Joel, pale, trembled as he asked, "And the US attorney general has a world-wide warrant out for my arrest?"

"They're after Joel Barr. You're Joe Berg from Jo'berg, and we're keeping an eye on you. Finding you won't be easy."

"I wish it were only me."

"Greenglass has betrayed everyone. That's why Rosenberg was arrested!"

"That louse," Joe exclaimed. "A half-wit, who can't handle a simple conversation. He's probably dreamed up lies about his own sister."

"It was a mistake between Julius and Feklisov to recruit him. We did not take the care we should have. What can I say?"

"I told Julius at the time it was a bad idea. The kid was a stuffed shirt. Ratting his own sister."

"They haven't arrested Ethel. Probably they won't."

"Imagine that! While she's busy rattling clean dishes, making the best apple strudel in Manhattan."

"I've heard about her strudel, from your friend Aleks."

"But damn! Poor Sarant. And I got him into it."

Taroikin's eyes studied Joel as he said, "But Dzho, he's not stupid. We can help him." Viktor made a conscious decision to confide in Berg beyond what he had been outlined to do. He said, "What I want to tell you should remain strictly between us."

Joel studied the pleasant open expression on Viktor's face and met his eyes, "Of course,' he said, "we're having a private conversation."

Then Taroikin related in greater detail facts not in the newspapers about Fuchs and Gold and he concluded, "So you see, all of these disasters are from Gold giving up Greenglass."

Joel was appalled and asked, "But Vivie? What about Vivian? You started to say?"

"They'll question her. She has not been arrested. Perl was

very stupid. For such a brilliant fellow, I have to say—"

"—No, he's always been that way! Since he knows avionics better than anyone in the world, he thinks everything else must be simple stuff, nothing his casual impressions can't handle."

Viktor nodded, "Clearly he's not well prepared for what's to come. But Vivian? What can you recall about what she knows? Tell me. It would be useful to know, in case she talks."

Joel understood that Taroikin was not being malicious or blaming him, but that his quest was urgent and reasonable. He said, "We lived together like man and wife." He hung his head, "Better figure she knows everything." Then he looked Taroikin in the eyes: "But she'll never talk."

"Oh?"

"It's in her nature. She has a stainless steel will: bright, shiny and hard. Not about protecting me or our cause; she won't do what she knows is wrong. No one is going to force her short of harsh torture."

"Your faith is reassuring, despite your likely subjectivity."

"Listen," Joe Berg said, "your side over-reached. She was not your agent. You involved Vivie because of me."

"…I agree. But she was the only one who knew Perl, the only one who he might trust."

"You blew her safety over that idiot." Even as Joe said this, he knew sending her had been an attempt to save everyone else, thinking Perl might talk. Even so, Joe remembered Bill fondly, Perl's sweet nature, his great pleasure in being included. Joe concluded, "To me, now, it seems to be a big mistake."

"I have to admit," Viktor conceded, "I do not disagree with you. Though it's perhaps understandable."

Though not remorseful for his own deeds, Joel saw for perhaps the first time, with the rapid arrests, the headlines, the trials and now the ensnarling of Vivian, that everyone he knew was desperately fleeing the flames of anti-Communism. *I'm safe but when they can't find me, they'll go after my family. That I'm gone will further condemn Julius and Ethel! I'm not really safe here, either, uncertain at best, and who will ever love a man who forsakes his friends?*

Far from starting afresh, Joe now saw that pursuit and

recrimination would never be over. *But I've never been one to sulk. I must learn Czech and live in the city of Prague, with its vistas and skyline of bridges, churches, castles, statues and its ancient drinking establishments all monuments to a decayed past.*

Hradcany Castle still watched over Prague where Czech rulers had lived for nearly 1000 years. Old Town Square was dominated by the statue of religious dissident, Jan Hus, who was burned at the stake by the Roman church in 1415 for refusing to give up his truth. At the base of the statue were the words:

SEEK THE TRUTH, LISTEN TO
THE TRUTH,
TEACH THE TRUTH, LOVE THE
TRUTH,
ABIDE BY THE TRUTH
AND DEFEND THE TRUTH UNTO
DEATH.

TEN

"The Communist threat from without must not blind us to the Communist threat from within. The latter is reaching into the very heart of America through its espionage agents and a cunning, defiant and lawless communist party, which is fanatically dedicated to the Marxist cause of world enslavement and destruction of the foundations of our republic."

--J. Edgar Hoover

JOE FELT PROPELLED BY THE CATASTROPHES behind him, but was still driven by dreams of Communist utopias and hope for a chance to invent the future's beneficial technologies. His situation molded his view of the fabled medieval antiquity of Prague, which he saw as an example of mankind's failures and mistaken pursuit of capitalism and religious dogma. On dry, clear days his footsteps rang with hollow sounds on the cobblestone streets as he studied the faces and gestures of Prague's people, their clothes and above all the sound of their voices which he imitated quietly as he strolled among them. When it rained, sounds were muted and the city's cobblestones showed hues of pure white, blue and pink. He breathed in the smells of sauerkraut, simmering cabbage and the bitter smell of beer as he passed open pub doorways. Delicious odors drew him to a bakery where he found warm rye bread and long rolls sprinkled with caraway seeds and coarse salt. For a pittance, he could buy several rolls, tearing off pieces to munch on as he walked. He was surprised at the reassurance he felt, simply because of this easily obtainable sustenance. *I can live here!* He sampled the street stands selling fat sizzling sausages served with strong mustard. He tasted cream and chocolate covered cakes from pastry shops. With everyone carrying their groceries in net bags, Joe could see what they were buying and often where they'd found it.

Downtown, there were huge signs on building walls:
THE SOVIET UNION FOR ETERNITY
THE PROLETARIANS OF THE WORLD UNITE
There were banners with pictures of Stalin and Lenin. The city's billboards, instead of advertising consumer goods carried ideological messages:
KARL MARX AND FRIEDRICH ENGELS ARE
THE LIVING TEACHERS OF COMMUNISM
OUR DEAREST COMRADE LENIN IS NOT DEAD
HE LIVES FOREVER IN OUR HEARTS!
GREETINGS TO YOU BELOVED COMRADE STALIN!

Joe had no tourist guide. He learned the Czech of those signs because the slogans were familiar in English and French. There were no ready captions for the views and vistas in this ancient city, but as he explored, he felt the impact of the abrupt transition Prague was experiencing since the Czech Communist Party's takeover in 1948. Many shops had been closed and the newly nationalized state stores, with sparse or depleted shelves, caused many customers to shrug their shoulders and hurry off to look elsewhere. One woman asked for things that weren't there, declaring her certainty that they always had been available. She even persisted before leaving the store, saying that they *should* be there still, and *must be* soon again.

BY AUGUST 3, THE FBI WAS CAREFULLY studying the discrepancies in Sarant's testimony compared to what they knew from *Venona* decryptions. On the same day, Vivian was confronted by FBI agents at her door. Though surprised, she maintained that she knew nothing about the stranger who'd given her the $2000. Only thinking Perl was in some kind of trouble, she'd gone to him. She told the FBI nothing else.

On August 4, Carol Dayton, Bruce Dayton's wife, very much in love with Sarant, packed a small suitcase, enough for a few days, and went to meet Al at a bus station in Manhattan. The

FBI followed Al every step of the way, but that evening the couple went to Roosevelt Raceway with Al's sister and brother-in-law who had parked Al's 1936 Dodge sedan in a lane near the racetrack. Al's sister had horses and paddock privileges at Roosevelt. The place was packed with an excited crowd. At the height of the featured race, Carol and Al slipped away from multiple FBI agents through the horse paddocks, to make a run for his life. As Al and Carol ducked away, an arrest warrant was issued in Manhattan for Morton Sobell, who was in Mexico with his family, trying to contact the KGB.

Al and Carol didn't even mention a bus station. They had made their own plans. They drove constantly southwest, taking turns at the wheel. They were headed for Carol's cousin's house in Tuscon Arizona. As Carol drove, Al scanned the radio news stations. They expected to hear a 'Wanted' all points bulletin for Alfred Sarant. The news was full of Florence Chadwick swimming the English Channel in thirteen hours, twenty-two minutes. Then too, a bomb-laden B-29 Superfortress had crashed into a residential neighborhood in California killing 17 people, injuring 68 and infuriating many more. The radio was full of the FBI's hot campaign against 'Atom Spies'. Carol and Al were amazed that the campaign did not include a sensational bulletin about them.

When Al and Carol reached Donald's house in Tuscon on August 8 1950, there was still no hue-and-cry. Even that seemed somehow ominous. Donald and his wife were hospitable, knowing nothing of Carol beyond her lefty days in college, though Donald suspected that both Carol and her boyfriend might be Communists. After another day of much needed rest, there was still nothing in the news about their escape. Donald bought Al's grey Dodge and, as he drove them to the border, they heard the news of Ethel Rosenberg's arrest.

Nervously they crossed into Mexico as Mr. & Mrs. Bruce Dayton. Neither had a passport or birth certificate. Donald drove them more than 100 miles south into Mexico.

IN PRAGUE, JOE BERG REALIZED QUICKLY that imitating Czech sounds and picking up phrases only scratched the surface. Czech grammar was unlike English and learning it was going to be much more difficult than Swedish or French which he had learned quickly and spoke fluently though with a Brooklyn accent. A highly inflected language like Russian or Czech required a knowledge of masculine, feminine or neuter, formal or informal, nominative or accusative. There were numerous prefixes which changed the meaning of the root word. And, like Russian, Czech required not only grammatical endings, but the correct inflected noun ending depending on what preposition was meant. Viktor Taroikin gave Joe two dictionaries and a grammar with a pronunciation guide, but Taroikin could see that Joe's Brooklyn accent was not going to be lost in Czech. He also saw that, unlike many American Communists escaping the Smith Act in Prague—who disdained learning the language— Joe was quickly gaining the ability to communicate. Neither his Brooklyn accent nor his fumbling, inconsistent grammar would keep him from talking to whoever was willing to listen. Soon, Viktor was able to tell Joe the news of his dear old friend, Al Sarant:

"Sarant didn't wait; he disappeared in the middle of the night with his next door neighbor's wife. Her husband says she told him she would drive Sarant to the bus station in New York or Philadelphia, as a neighborly thing to do."

"He hasn't been caught?"

"Fortunately, the FBI was asleep: the Albany office thought he was on Long Island; the Manhattan office assumed he'd gone back to Ithaca. They thought Carol Dayton was in Boston. None of them dreamed Sarant would leave a house he'd just built, a wife and two kids. They left four kids behind between them."

"Are you sure he hasn't been caught?" Joel was pale with desperate hope.

"If he has been, we don't know about it. Normally, we would."

Joe managed to say, "I'll be damned. Good old Al. The ladies never could resist him. But what are their chances now, I wonder? Will she stick with him?"

"She might as well; she's aiding a major fugitive."

"Damn. Unless she says he forced her."

"The FBI may still have no idea where they are. But then, neither do we."

"No word from them?"

"None," Taroikin seemed truly gloomy, though his meetings with Joe were nurturing a growing mutual respect.

ETHEL ROSENBERG WAS ABOUT TO ENTER the subway after testifying before a grand jury on August 11 when she was arrested and was not allowed to return home to take care of her two young children or to arrange a place for them to stay.

On August 12, Al and Carol flew from Guadalajara to Mexico City under Bruce Dayton's married names. They were not safe. Four days later, on the evening of August 16, Morton Sobell was kidnapped in Mexico City, sped to Nuevo Loredo and turned over to the FBI. The following morning, Ethel Rosenberg was charged with conspiracy to secure information relating to national defense for the USSR. On the same day the same charges were issued against former vice-consul of the USSR Anatoly Yakovlev (Yatskov), in absentia. The FBI formally arrested Morton Sobell in Texas and Hoover announced it. The New *York Daily News* headlined:

FLEEING RADAR EXPERT NABBED AS ATOM SPY.

On August 22, Carol Dayton's friend Judy Bregman told the FBI a letter she'd received from Carol was post-marked in Tuscon. The next day, the FBI was at the home of Carol's cousin, Donald, and soon learned of their flight to Mexico.

As Joe Berg absorbed the constant shocks of each downfallen friend, lover, or Communist Party leader in the United States, he began to explore areas farther outside Prague, using his own newly homemade moped. No one followed him or seemed to take particular notice of him.

On September 12, Communist riots erupted in Berlin. Soon, the purging and arrests of Communist officials began there. On September 15, Allied troops under Douglas MacArthur landed at Inchon, Korea, in a counteroffensive.

On September 20, at what had become their regular

meetings, Joe Berg pointed out to Viktor Taroikin that his 60 day Czech visa was about to expire. The next day, with help from high-up Czech officials, Taroikin handed Joe his residency ID for Prague, but firmly informed him that his official request for permission to settle in the USSR had been refused. Taroikin knew he'd be safer in Prague than in Russia.

On September 30, an NSC report, signed by Truman, set the policy of containment for the Soviet bloc for forty years.

In October, after two months of wandering and hiding in Mexico, Al and Carol wandered into a Polish trade delegation and made a contact.

On November 1, Dzhosef Berg began a boring job at the Tesla plant in Prague designing vacuum tubes. There he overheard a rumor about the defection of Czech pilots who had taken an army plane and flown to England. There seemed to be an element of envy beneath the dogmatic condemnation of such daring treachery. But Joe took little notice.

As the spies and CPUSA leaders were being arrested and tried, on November 10, a US Air Force B-50 Superfortress bomber jettisoned and detonated a Mark 4 nuclear bomb over Quebec, Canada. Fortunately the bomb was not armed with it's plutonium core, but the serious accident added to the up ramping apocalyptic feel of the times.

On November 26, troops from the People's Republic of China moved into North Korea and launched a massive counterattack against South Korean and American forces at Chosin, dashing any hope for a quick end to the war. Three days later, the Communist troops forced a retreat of UN forces from North Korea. Douglas MacArthur threatened to use nuclear weapons against them.

By December 1950, Harry Gold's trial in Philadelphia was winding down; the first TV remote control, Zenith's *Lazy Bones*, was on sale; Australia was desperately trying to control their escalating rabbit population, and Harry Truman sent United States military advisers to Vietnam to aid struggling French colonial forces.

JOE WAS STRUCK BY PRAGUE'S FRANTIC

preparations for the coming Christmas celebrations. Bake shops offered special bear's paw cookies and little cakes in the shape of angels and Saint Nicholas wrapped in foil. There were delicate hand blown glass Christmas tree ornaments, each unique, which won Joe's admiration. These were highly sought after by customers who raced everywhere looking for just the ones they wanted, prized Christmas gifts. The usually long lines in the stores were now much longer. On the streets, women dressed in native hand-embroidered folk dresses and kerchiefs sold home-cured goat cheese and fresh eggs. People congregated around barrels on the sidewalk trying to decide which live carp swimming around in the barrel they wanted to take home and keep alive in their bathtub, fresh for Christmas dinner. To Joe, though all of it seemed polluted with religious superstition, it touched a human sentiment, giving flavor to his loneliness, not as if he was tempted by religion, but the beliefs seemed more tolerable to him here. He couldn't help being pleased by the happiness of his new milieu.

For the next twenty-seven years, FBI agents would speculate on Joel's disappearance and all but two would conclude that the KGB had eliminated a man who knew too much. Lamphere and Clegg would continue to hound Joel's family and friends for decades after the FBI gave up twenty seven years later.

ELEVEN

"The only sensible and courageous way to deal with Communists is to make membership in Communist organizations...a capital offense and shoot or otherwise put to death all persons convicted of such."
--Westbrook Pegler, Hearst columnist

IN 1951, BY A VOTE OF SIX TO TWO THE SUPREME Court upheld the 1949 convictions of the CPUSA leaders arrested in 1948. Justice William O. Douglas and justice Hugo Black dissented. Black called the government's indictments "a virulent form of prior censorship of speech and press." Soon after this US Supreme Court decision, twenty-three other CPUSA leaders were indicted under the Smith Act, including Elizabeth Gurley Flynn, a founding member of the American Civil Liberties Union. Joe Berg knew that some of those prosecuted were little more than ordinary workers who'd joined the party hoping for a better world, advocating what seemed a good idea at the time. None of those being arrested as Communists had given away major military secrets to the 'the enemy'. Joel thought of what he, Julie, Al, Bill and Mort had done. *If fairly ordinary Party members are being given ten year sentences, I'd get the chair, for sure. Mort and Julie, too. Al is probably already dead.*

Inside the cocoon of his new identity, getting used to it, Joe began to make friends at work. He took long walks to explore the countryside around Prague. He once again thought of women and his fondness for doing the business with them. Was he lonely? Of course. He missed Vivian doubly now that she was in danger. He missed Helga, too. They had never been serious, but she'd been a welcome companion. To be alive and free in the face of captivity and execution, to have even a menial job, merely to want a woman, all these were good medicine for the dread he felt for his friends.

As Joel settled into a routine of work, studying Czech and playing his viola, in chance meetings with other Western defectors, he noticed they were not so heavily disguised and protected as he was. Many were using their original American birth names. *They are not in the danger I am in,* he realized, *no one is out to kill them.*

On January 9 1951, the new United Nations headquarters officially opened in New York City, the 1951 version of hope for a better world. In Prague, after the Soviets had pressured the Czechs to cut trade ties with the West and had closed many restaurants and stores, Czech living standards fell. This spurred anti-Communist demonstrations and strikes. Czech leaders, under pressure from Moscow, reacted by arresting and torturing thousands of people and executing hundreds of loyal senior party officials in show trials. By the end of January, 169,000 members of the Czechoslovakian Communist Party—10% of the membership—had been arrested. Even so, guided by the KGB, the top officials in the Party were made aware of Dzhosef Berg and his importance to the Soviet Union.

Berg soon had a letter of recommendation to do classified work from Rudolf Slansky, the powerful General Secretary. He allowed himself to have hope that he would once again find interesting work at the leading edge of electronic technology. He now also had the personal support of Antonin Prchal, the Czech deputy interior minister. During the time Prchal sponsored Berg, he was in charge of fabricating evidence for the Czech show trials.

Taroikin said little about the trials, commenting only that it was true that they were taking place. As far as Berg's higher security clearance and the possibility of more interesting work, he said nothing.

Joe, partly because he himself had lived a double life, was willing to believe there were those who had worked in secret against the state. But even deeper within him, he could let nothing encroach on his admiration for Stalin, who had succeeded in making Communism work in the way Berg wanted and understood: scientifically, technologically and industrially. Stalin, for Joe, was also the man who'd defeated Hitler. Anti-Stalinism was lies. Stalin could do no wrong.

On January 31, a New York grand jury indicted Ethel and Julius Rosenberg, Morton Sobell, David Greenglass and Anatoly Yakolev (Yatskov). On February 1, the United Nations General Assembly declared that China was the aggressor in the Korean War. Due in part to the Korean War and because the US was constantly infiltrating the Soviet bloc with spies, Stalin was expecting a US invasion and a nuclear attack. He was well aware that the USA had all the machines and weap[ons for it.

On February 23-24, under constant pressure from federal prosecutors, who dangled lenient consideration, Ruth and David Greenglass changed their testimony to say that Ethel had typed up her brother's atom bomb notes.

Well before March 6 1951, when the trial of Rosenberg *et al* opened in federal court in Manhattan, J. Edgar Hoover, Chief Prosecutor Irving H Saypol, and trial judge Irving R. Kaufman met and colluded on how most certainly and sensationally to convict them as Atomic Spies. Above all, they counted on forcing the defendants to name others. The three men were sure with Ethel included there would be confessions.

Losses in the Korean War against a mighty new enemy, had whipped up a patriotic tidal wave in a nation accustomed to victory. The Communists had stolen the bomb, hastened the end of colonialism, seized power over the massive population of China and were killing 'our boys'. America saw itself in a life-or-death struggle with an evil incarnate that was rapidly spreading everywhere, even in the American heartland. Everything conceivable must be done to avoid losing even one more battle.

When the Rosenberg trial began, American society and its selected jury *knew* the Rosenbergs were guilty of the most heinous treason in US history. The day after the trial began, on March 7, United Nations troops began an assault against the Chinese army in South Korea. A week later, they recaptured Seoul.

As though the peril to Joel's old friends and the war's new acceleration of hatred for Communists were not enough, on March 15, Bill Perl was arrested and charged with espionage:

COLUMBIA TEACHER ARRESTED, LINKED TO ATOM SPIES

Hoover was sure Perl would break down, confess and strengthen the not so damning evidence against the Rosenbergs.

By March of 1951, Joel's oldest friends were facing execution; Sarant, his very best friend, was presumed dead and his sweetheart, Vivian, was now in the government's crosshairs. *She'll be locked up.* As a result, he was often desperate for any distraction. On March 28, the trial came to an end. The next day, the jury found Ethel Rosenberg, Julius Rosenberg, Morton Sobell David Greenglass and Anatoly Yakovlev guilty of conspiracy to commit espionage. It was the same day Rodgers and Hammerstein's *The King and I* opened on Broadway, to make Russian-born Yul Brynner a big star. On April 5, the swelling of anti-Communist rage that rose with the Rosenberg convictions was somewhat assuaged by Judge Kaufman's imposition of the death sentence on Julius and Ethel, parents of two young sons. Popular reaction was somewhat taken aback: *At least they're gonna get what they deserve.*

Sobell got thirty years, the maximum—short of execution—under the statute. Kaufman, Saypol and Hoover had agreed on the sentence before the trial began. The day after sentencing Julius, Ethel and Mort, Judge Kaufman surprised David Greenglass with fifteen years in federal prison. Poor stupid naïve David had expected that ratting out and lying about his sister would get him two or three years. Equally guilty, Ruth Greenglass was neither tried, convicted nor sentenced. That was part of David's deal to testify.

Joel was horrified and filled with terrible grief, but he, like so many others, could not conceive that this was the ultimate decision; there would be appeals and eventually the furor over communism would die down and things would change. Even in grieving horror at it all, Joel read about the delivery to the US Census Bureau of Remington Rand's first UNIVAC computer. He read everything he could about the inner workings of the world's most powerful calculating machine, seeing the dawn of a new age of technological advance.

On April 11, President Truman fired General Douglas MacArthur. Many asked, who but a Communist sympathizer would have disgraced the victorious hero of World War II?

By the spring of 1951, Dzhozef Berg had friends and co-workers at Tesla's Prague Electrical Research Institute who called him 'Joe'. In this design shop for a nearby factory where parts and instruments suitable to rockets or jet planes were being made, Joe needed surprisingly little Czech or Russian to design various devices to mathematical specifications. He attended concerts with special attention to the two most important Czech composers, Smetana and Dvorak, partly because he found co-workers willing to discuss them. With a hotel room and a job, though his hope of living and working in the USSR was discouraged, his fears for his life and freedom began to ebb. His job was tedious, but learning Czech and finding a girlfriend buoyed him.

May Day in Prague, Joe's first in the land of Communism, was a grand affair. School children had no classes. Joe was deceived by the regimented loyalty of crowds cheering along the parade route down Prague's main street, hailing the procession's various dignitaries. Pioneer youths in white shirts and red scarves were well trained to sing and cheer. There were banners with pictures of the heroes of labor, workers who had excelled in production achievement. Large banners proclaimed socialist credos:

MARCH FORWARD WITH BOUNDLESS LOVE FOR
THE SOVIET UNION, THE PROTECTOR OF OUR
FREEDOM, INDEPENDENCE AND SOCIALIST
DEVELOPMENT!
LIMITLESS LOVE FOR THE GREAT STALIN WHO
LEADS ALL THE WORKING PEOPLE OF THE
WORLD TOWARD THE VICTORY OF COMMUNISM!
LOVE FOR THE WORKING CLASS AND THE
COMMUNIST PARTY, THE FOREMOST FIGHTER
FOR A JOYFUL AND HAPPY TOMORROW!
REJECT ALL REMNANTS OF BOURGEOIS
THINKING AND BEHAVIOR!
LOVE OUR GLORIOUS COMMUNIST LEADERS!

To Joe, it all seemed real and idyllic. Children joined hands with factory workers, doctors, nurses, professors, journalists, store clerks, actors and artists beneath banners declaiming unity and equality. The songs they sang and slogans they chanted could be heard for miles. Joe felt the power of this celebration with renewed hope. And he noticed the sexual excitement of the parade as couples marched by in a state of bliss, hardly aware of their surroundings.

ON MAY 3, THE US SENATE ARMED SERVICES and Foreign Relations Committees began closed door hearings into the dismissal of General Douglas MacArthur. They concluded that Truman was within a president's constitutional rights, but his decision cost Truman his troubled popularity. He could not run again for President in 1952.

The Supreme Court's upholding of the Eugene Dennis convictions on June 4 1951 led to a new wave of anti-Communist indictments and FBI raids.

ON JUNE 15 1951, DZHOSEF BERG was visited at the Tesla plant by a Czech StB agent who told him to go home immediately. "Your days here at Tesla are over." It struck Joe as yet another rejection and failure. He was just settling in at the plant and was glad to be making new friends.

At his hotel, still his only home in Prague, Viktor Taroikin was waiting for him and gave Joe a ninety day Soviet visa and a ticket to Moscow.

"You're to work on a special project with another engineer," was all Taroikin would tell him. Joe felt he had little choice. But he was excited to accept this chance to visit the glorious land of Socialism. He was excited, but wary. Viktor Taroikin obviously knew a lot more than he was willing to tell him.

TWELVE

"Liberty, as it is conceived by current opinion, has nothing inherent about it; it is a sort of gift or trust bestowed on the individual by the state pending good behavior. ---*Joseph McCarthy, 1952*

THERE WERE NO FAMILIAR FACES IN MOSCOW to meet Joe at the airport. Those that did, announced that they would take him to the Moskva Hotel, near the Kremlin. The fear that he might be imprisoned or eliminated was scant and easily dismissed from his mind, but the two men who escorted him said nothing about what to expect. On the way in from the airport, Joel was thrilled to see the people, real citizens of Socialism. He hoped he would be able to meet some of them, be able to walk among them. He even hoped he might be able to stay. Was it possible he would be allowed to work in his field again? And to listen to their the music, a people renowned for the greatness of their symphonies and orchestras? He remembered that visit to the Russian baths with Al Sarant on the Lower East Side of Manhattan, the magic of seeing and hearing Sergei Rachmaninov conducting his choir, all of them naked but for white bath towels, a single harbinger of today, to be in the heart of it all at last. In short, Joe was agog with the sights, sounds and his hopes in the Capitol of Communism, a dream come true. Seeing the Kremlin, he imagined Stalin laboring tirelessly for the proletariat behind those high, red brick walls.

The young KGB agents accompanied Joe Berg through the lobby of the Moskva Hotel with a mere nod to the concierge. Arrangements had clearly been made. An elevator took them up, Joe and the two agents.

Upon opening the door to his hotel room, Joel saw a man

standing in the shadows on the other side of the room. Beside him was a stunningly beautiful blonde woman sitting on the bed. Joel could not take his eyes off of her until:

"Joel!" the man yelled.

"…Al?" Joe croaked. He had been almost sure Al Sarant was dead. They rushed to embrace with pounding hearts, tears streaming down their cheeks, squeezing each other's flesh with their hands in disbelief: *Oh, can it really be you!?*

The single agent who had come into the room with Joe stepped out silently to join his colleague in the corridor.

Joe made an effort to stem his tears, "When did you know?"

"I didn't know. They told me an old friend. But it's you, alive and well! I had no idea." Al glanced at the gorgeous blonde. "Let me introduce you to my sweetheart, the woman who saved my life, Carol Dorothy Dayton."

She stood and Joel turned to take her hand, still grasping that this was not another Soviet agent. Her full American persona struck him as she took his hand and she said, "Yes, I guess I tagged along with Mr. Sarant."

"I'm Joe Berg now," Joel introduced himself to Carol, "from Johannesburg South Africa. Joe Berg from Jo'burg. Who says the KGB doesn't have a sense of humor, eh?" He laughed.

Carol beamed, "So pleased to finally meet you. Al told me often, 'There's one person who cares about me, who at least will wonder what happened to me: my old pal, Joel Barr.'"

"I'm Phillip Soros," Al said. "They stuck with my obvious Greek profile when they picked my new name."

As she withdrew from embracing Joe, Carol said, winking at 'Phil', "I'm Mrs. Philip Staros now. Anya Petrovna Soros," she added, looking at Joe. "Call me Anne."

"Anne, a pleasure to meet you." It was dawning on Joe: *This is his neighbor's wife! Just like Taroikin said.*

"We're going to have a baby this spring," Anne said.

If Joe had been reeling from his first glimpse of Anne, this news bowled him over. Sarant was alive, in the full force of manhood, after what must have been a harrowing escape. *And you've captivated this lovely, charming creature! You old Romeo you.*

"Congratulations, to both of you."

"We are not unhappy," Anne said.

"The last news I had of you," Joel said to Al, "from Lieutenant Taroikin, was that you were in Mexico. Not even the KGB knew where you were, let alone the FBI."

"And all I knew of you is you were in Europe, studying music, maybe," Phil said. "We had a year long nightmare, after we got to Mexico City."

"I got out of Paris just in time; I've been in Prague ever since, until today."

It was mostly 'Anne' who described their "year long nightmare' in colorful detail, after 'Phil' had explained making contact with a Polish trade organization. She described their long trip through Mexico, hidden and protected by Polish agents, then wading through malarial swamps to cross a river into Guatemala, hidden in Guatemala, at last to reach a Polish freighter in the bay of St. Thomas, then the freighter from Puerto Barrio to Morocco. Another Polish ship to Spain. From Spain, a flight to Warsaw. Only days before had they come to Moscow from six months in Poland.

Anne had only concluded her account by the time they were seated in the hotel restaurant.

"So fantastic," Joe said. All of it, for all three of us. It's so utterly fantastic."

"So what about Vivian?" Phil asked.

"...She didn't come with me. Changed her mind at the last minute."

"Yeah, I see," Phil said.

There was an empty silence until Anne said, "They've given you two lucky fellows a wonderful reunion."

"But let's ask ourselves, why are we here?" Joe suggested. "Just for this reunion? Or what?"

"I think they've plans for us to work together," Phil said.

"They told me I'd work with an engineer," Joe said. "I never dreamed it would be you. This is all so utterly fantastic."

JOE AND PHIL STROLLED MOSCOW WITH ANNE, the warmest of best friends again, enjoying the wonders of the wide boulevards, beautiful parks and the "Peoples' Palaces" of the Moscow Metro, inspired by the world's greatest railway stations. Seeing poverty-stricken old women and ragged young children, they told themselves the workers' paradise was still caught in the inevitable aftermath of the terrible 'Great Patriotic War'. Every citizen they saw was a hero to Joel Barr and Alfred Sarant. Joe and Phil were new. It was their hance to start over.

As the warm days of July passed in a bubble of hope and wonder, the sponsoring Soviet agents watched and approved. Gradually the two Americans realized their relationship had changed. Joe was awed by Al's beautiful, intelligent and devoted wife. Joel's casual girlfriend, Helga, in Europe had not come close to what he'd had with Vivian. Anne had saved Al's life, taken him to Mexico and stayed with him from then on. Joe gathered, from what they told him, how it happened that they'd left their spouses and children behind. Joe admired the man who warranted such love, but another change in their relationship was set by the fact that Joel had recruited Al into stealing secret documents for the KGB and not the other way around. They were both alive and free, but the cost had been greater for Al. As Phillip Staros, Al did not voice any blame to Joe for what had happened, but he now considered Joe a dreamer whose dreams could be dangerous. Late in July, they agreed that the best thing that could happen was to work together again on scientific and engineering problems. "Advancing the science, inventing the future," Joe said.

"Working for the great Soviet experiment," Phil added. "But in the old days, it was you who led the way, you who had the senior positions and greater respect from our colleagues, but now that must change. Your judgements have not always been beneficial. To be clear, from now on, I'm the one to decide things if occasionally we don't agree. I will no longer follow your lead, blindly or otherwise. I hope you can accept that."

"Sure," Joe said. "I trust your judgement. I'm so delighted to see you, I have no problem with you taking the lead. It's a small price to pay to work with you again."

"I see better what's practical and advantageous than you do."

"You're the boss," Joe said smiling comfortably. It seemed a small concession to make, for such a friendship.

"Okay," Phil said. "Look, it seems to me, with this recent announcement by Shockley of a junction transistor, that electronics are about to get much smaller and more powerful."

"And, much, much more portable," Joel added

"So our job will be to bring all this into the USSR?"

"Of course! That'd be fantastic, my dream come true."

"Let's hope our hosts will agree and will facilitate some interesting work," Phil said."

TWELVE MORE US COMMUNIST LEADERS were arrested in August, in Pittsburgh, Baltimore and Cleveland. The anti-Communist furor in America was still building steam. J. Edgar Hoover hosted a Richard Nixon fundraiser and became close friends with two Texas oil men, Clint Murchison and Sid Richardson, very wealthy men whose circle of friends included a number of major organized crime figures and who provided financial support to American Nazi leader George Lincoln Rockwell. The two oil barons lavished Edgar with entertainment, hunting trips and vacations. They joined him in supporting Eisenhower and Nixon for the White House. Hoover dug up dirt on the Democratic nominee, Illinois Governor Adlai Stevenson, spreading the rumor that Stevenson was an active homosexual and a Communist. After they engineered the Eisenhower landslide, during Eisenhower's first term, sixty oil leases were granted on US land, compared with sixteen during the previous fifty-five years.

August 1951 was the start of the Rosenberg support movement. It followed *The National Guardian* article of August 15:
THE ROSENBERG CONVICTION—
IS THIS THE DREYFUS CASE OF COLD WAR AMERICA?

In October, Phil and Anne were sent to Prague. Joe followed them a week later. Phil and Joe were to begin work at the Army Technical Institute (VTU in Russian) under director Dr. Bedrich Goldschmied. Their urgent task would be to build an analogue computer to control anti-aircraft batteries, to further develop what they'd done in the US, even using plans they'd stolen which were to be made available to them in Prague. The Soviet leadership, the Politburo, expected a US attack at any moment. When Joe arrived back in Prague, he was taken to the VTU directly from the airport to meet the generals and big bosses.

On November 1, the first US military exercises for nuclear war, with infantry troops included, were held in the Nevada desert where a number of US soldiers were lethally radiated.

In Prague, on November 11, a dedicated Communist of Jewish descent, Chairman of the Czech Communist Party, Rudolf Slansky, a backer of Joe Berg, was arrested and began a year of torture and humiliating interrogation.

It was also in November that KGB agent Viktor Taroikin re-entered Joe Berg's life, one of the very few who knew who he really was. No officials he'd had any contact with since leaving Prague for Moscow had any idea who he was or that he was an American escapee. Most thought he was a Czech, only a few even knew he was South Afrikan.

THIRTEEN

*"An obscure senator from Wisconsin named Joseph R.
McCarthy stirred up anti-Communist hatred reaching
epidemic proportions. For many years that citadel of
pragmatic thinking and lucidity that was America
became a country in the grip of hysteria. The mere fact
of being, or having been, a Communist, was a crime,
not to mention engaging in any activities favorable to
the Soviet Union. Long before the [Rosenberg] trial
began, American society in general, and the jury most
notably, was convinced that the Rosenbergs were
guilty of "the most heinous crime in the history of this
country." The accumulation of evidence forged by the
FBI, which would have been rejected a thousand times
by an objective and detached jury, appeared rock solid
to a country in the grip of such fever."*
--Aleksandr Feklisov, *The Man Behind the Rosenbergs*

ON JANUARY 10 1952, THE ROSENBERG DEFENSE
filed an appeal before the United States Court of Appeals,
Second Circuit. Less than a week later, the Committee for Justice
for the Rosenbergs placed a major advertisement in the National
Guardian, its first public appeal for support. Though Joe grieved
and worried for his friends, he believed, even when pessimistic,
that the harsh sentences would be overturned. The appeals would
take time, the political mood would mellow and his dear friends
would not be killed and might eventually be free again.

Even though Joe and Phil had the help of Anton
Svoboda, the Czech computer genius who had worked at MIT
during the war, their assigned project of developing an anti-

aircraft computer was no easy task. Often the parts they needed did not exist in Czechoslovakia. Their project director did not have the budget for expensive electronics from Europe or the US. They had to make their own component parts or design their machine around such shortages. Sometimes, they even had to invent the machines to manufacture the needed parts. From the point-of-view of the Soviet military, expecting a US attack at any time, their progress was terribly slow. Only because their progress was steady, were they tolerated and supported.

On January 21, 1952, Anne and Phil's son Kolya was born, a third child for each of them. Joe shared their happiness in a lonely way; he hadn't had a satisfactory relationship with a woman since leaving Vivian in New York four years earlier. With Kolya's birth, Joe was now the bachelor family friend, to be called 'Uncle Joe'.

Joe saw clearly that by sentencing Ethel and Julius to death, especially Ethel, *less guilty than Morty or David, they're counting on a woman yielding her secrets rather than orphaning her children. They're even sure Julius will insist that she do so. A brutal act of extortion. They've got to beat this on appeal.*

On February 25, the US Second Circuit Court of Appeals admitted that procedural violations had taken place during the Rosenberg's trial, but denied them a new trial. "None of the accused has followed the path set by David Greenglass and Harry Gold," Judge Kaufman declared. "Their lips remained sealed." *As is their fate,* Joe thought, *He's telling them if they confess, they'll live.*

The Rosenbergs remained silent as Joe at first had hoped they would. But, as the danger grew, he thought of Julie. *I escaped and left you behind. Instead of agreeing with you over the phone that last day in New York, that the madness would blow over, telling you my main reason for leaving was to study music and seek interesting work, I should have warned you and begged you to join me. I should have told you the truth, that I was afraid. I might have convinced you to come to Warsaw or somewhere in Poland. I should have promised to prepare the way; I should have urged our friends in Paris every day to save you. I asked Pierre only once. Please forgive me. You must save yourself.*

Even after the Rosenbergs' appeal was denied there was hope in more appeals. The Soviet Union was launching a world-wide propaganda effort on their behalf. As his only choice, Joe let hope swell enough inside him to resist the all too reasonable grounds for despair.

On February 26, hours after the Rosenberg appeal was denied, British Prime Minister Winston Churchill announced that Britain now had the atomic bomb. The man who had given the bomb to the USSR and had helped the British develop it, Klaus Fuchs, was still in a British prison.

On April 15, the US introduced the B-52 Stratofortress, the giant eight-engine bomber capable of delivering a thirty-five ton bomb load anywhere in the world on a moment's notice. Eight days later, just such a nuclear bomb as the B-52 was designed to carry was detonated in the Nevada desert, as practice for nuclear war.

The turnout for the April Rosenberg support demonstrations sponsored by the Committee for Justice for the Rosenbergs was disappointing for those who believed in their innocence and for Joe who hoped such a mistaken belief might save them. Phil would only say, "He should have gotten out."

Joe said, "He was on some kick; why would anyone thinking straight have trusted David?"

It frightened Joe to realize *Deep down, Al thinks they almost deserve it...* By June, though his friendship with Phil was strong in their work on the air-defense computer, Phil and Anne spent much of their time with Kolya and less time with Joe. He told himself he wanted his own adoring wife and family. *Even if I'm going to be alone, I need to get away from them and think about my life.* After days of brooding, he booked a long weekend in a mountain resort well away from Prague.

ON THE TRAIN TO THE MOUNTAIN SPA, JOE shared a compartment with a farmer named Anton Krcmarov, his wife and their daughter, Vera. Polite exchanges revealed that they were all going to the same resort which, for Vera, relieved the prospect of a boring, unnecessary rest with her parents. Once they arrived, and after exploring the grounds of the retreat together then the resort town and the surrounding hills and forests, Vera and Joe stretched out side-by-side on the resort lawn. She listened as he made skillful use of his crude, ungrammatical Czech. She was 26 and beautiful. He was 35. They spent only three days together, but became inseparable. Vera's father hated Communists only slightly less than he hated Jews. His hatred for this pushy, sinister-foreigner-Jew-Communist reached ever greater fury with Vera's obvious attraction to Joe. The prospects were a hellish nightmare for the Catholic farmer. But he hated Joe even more after Joe tried cheerfully to convince him to give up his centuries-old family farm:

"People need to share everything is the idea, and sooner or later your farm will be collectivized. Why not join with the future?"

Krcmarov replied, "Those swine took my land but I will never leave my house or sign their papers. Only if they kill us will they ever get me out. I built that house when Vera was still small. You remember Vera."

"I think so, father," she said.

"We have only Vera," he said to make an obvious point then stared at Joe as if to sterilize evil.

DURING THE FOLLOWING SUMMER DAYS, the Diary of Anne Frank was published; the US Army Special Forces was created; the Marshall plan was ended. The Summer Olympics were held in Helsinki; a massive 7.5 earthquake shook California; Nasser seized power in Egypt. It was the summer Joe and Vera were together every minute they were not at their jobs, in love and already facing the main threat to their future happiness: Vera's father. He threatened police action, physical harm, disaffection and disinheritance. He did everything a strong old bull could do to keep his seed from being abducted by evil. But if anything could have driven Vera faster into Joe's arms, it was Anton Krcmarov's terrible anger.

Krcmarov was not the only threat to their betrothal. Her hometown authorities, un-re-educated Catholics, hated her marrying a Jew atheist. As Joe discovered when he sought legal redress, it was against the law for a non-Czech to wed a Czech. Becoming a Czech citizen was a formidable hurdle.

As to their anti-missile computer, their designed and

manufactured electronic components had come to the attention of the USSR defense establishment which was desperate to match the West in electronics. In August, a delegation from Moscow visited their lab armed with an offer signed by Stalin to put Staros and Berg in charge of a planned research and design bureau which would employ 50,000 people. At that moment, when their progress in their little Czech design shop was slow and perhaps faltering, the offer was more than just challenging. Phil saw innumerable ways failure was nearly certain. "I can barely lead and direct the fifty people we have. And we neither of us speak Russian."

Joe might have tried to persuade and encourage Phil. He knew if the offer had come before he met Vera, he would have been eager for them to accept. After sharing their reluctance, Viktor Taroikin reappeared and somewhat mysteriously advised, "I think you should stay in Prague. It is not a good idea to go there now."

"Why not?" They asked out of curiosity if nothing else.

"That advice is personal and confidential, as a friend, not shared by my superiors."

"What is our excuse for turning down such an offer?"

"You are duty bound to finish the anti-aircraft guidance system you've promised to do for the Czechs."

They took Taroikin's advice. With little regret on Joe's part, Phil gladly conveyed to Stalin's emissaries: *we must honor our word.* Realizing how unprepared he'd been for the Soviet offer, Phil vowed to be ready if such an offer came again. He realized their design shop staff's collective mentality erased individual responsibility and initiative. In September, he assigned specific tasks to each person in each work group, telling them, "You can't blame your failures on the group or on the other guy." As a result, various subordinates filed complaints against them to the StB, the Czech security police.

In America, J. Edgar Hoover gave Senator Joseph McCarthy use of his extensive illegal files conducted throughout the 1940's on Dashiel Hammet, Dorothy Parker, Lillian Hellman, Pearl Buck, Thomas Mann, Erskine Caldwell, Sinclair Lewis, William Saroyan, Carl Sandberg, Ernest Hemingway, John

Steinbeck, Irwin Shaw, Aldous Huxley, John O'Hara Arthur Miller, Tennessee Williams, Truman Capote, Rex Stout, E.B. White, artists Georgia O'Keeffe, Henry Moore and Pablo Picasso—who never set foot in the US—scientists Dr. Jonas Salk and Albert Einstein, not to mention Hoover's 1900 page file on Charlie Chaplin, one of the most adored men in America. McCarthy used this cornucopia of sex lives and indiscretions to smear reputations of the Left. Hoover's and McCarthy's criminal slanders and blackmail efforts used 40 per cent of FBI man hours to violate these private lives though no insurrection, espionage, or terrorism was discovered in any of them. Charlie Chaplin called it: "America's hate-beleaguered atmosphere of insults and moral pomposity."

On October 13 1952, by an eight to one vote, the US Supreme Court refused to grant a writ of *certiorari* in the Rosenberg case, and thus refused to review it, because of "insufficient cause to hear arguments." If even four of the nine justices had voted for *certiorari*, the case would have been reviewed. A few days later, Judge Kaufman set the date of execution for the first week of January 1953. Morton Sobell was sent to Alcatraz to begin his 30-year sentence. Aside from the final appeals, it seemed only public protest could stop the executions. Joel's optimism was taking a beating and he felt almost constant crushing stress.

On October 19, Bedrich Goldschmied, Phil's and Joe's Czech sponsor, mentor and friend, director of their institute, a Jew who was mentioned as seen leaving the Swiss Embassy in a filed denunciation against Joe and Phil, committed suicide by jumping out of his high office window.

On October 24, both Joe and Phil applied for Czech citizenship. Joe soon began pestering the authorities until it was done. Vera and Joe began to plan their wedding in spite of her father's frantic and bitter efforts to stop them.

On November 1 1952, the United States successfully detonated the first full scale hydrogen bomb at Enewetok Atoll in the Marshall Islands. Too large to be a deliverable weapon, it was 450 times more powerful than the Nagasaki bomb.

As the Rosenberg's execution date approached, support

swelled almost overnight for the Committee to Secure Justice in the Rosenberg Case. Due in part to a tremendous effort by the USSR, a wave of indignation grew world-wide. The young couple's plight disturbed millions. Hundreds of thousands, outraged by 'the injustice being perpetrated', took to the streets, demonstrated and organized picket lines in front of US embassies.

On November 20, in Czechoslovakia, the largely anti-Semitic show trial of Rudolf Slansky and thirteen others took place with front page headlines in the Czech Communist press which read:

TRIAL FOR ANTI-STATE CONSPIRACY OF RUDOLF SLANSKY

Eleven men, ten other Jews, were sentenced to death.

SLANSKY PLEADS GUILTY TO TREASON!

Vera's father, after an attempt to strangle his daughter to death, prevented only by the physical intervention of her mother, refused any part of their civil wedding. A few weeks later, at the mother's funeral, Krcmarov declared that his wife's death was God's punishment for her allowing Vera to marry a Jew.

On December 3, Rudolf Slansky and ten other leaders of the Czechoslovakian Communist Party were executed. In Czechoslovakia, Stalin's man, Gottwald, had won the struggle for power over Slansky. By this time, Stalin had arrested a number of Jewish doctors and loosed a fierce attack on Soviet Jews. Slansky's execution gave anti-Semitism throughout the Soviet bloc semi-official sanction. Anyone connected to Slansky with Jewish heritage or friends was suspect. Joe carried Slansky's high recommendation, was himself ethnically a Jew, and worked closely with Jews. He could survive in Prague only through the consistent influence of the Lubyanka at the upper levels of Czech bureaucracy. Anti-Semitism coupled with reactions to Phil's adoption of an incentive-and-consequences work ethic, brought attacks from all sides. They often needed the direct intervention of Viktor Taroikin who was now betting his career on them.

It was in the midst of all this that Joe and Vera found a modest apartment in a good neighborhood with a nice view and a large park nearby. As they set up housekeeping and met their neighbors, Joe could not help thinking that by marrying Vera, he had demonstrated his Communist atheism and disregard for Judaism. Vera, in turn, though very much in love, was additionally happy that she no longer had to visit an outhouse privy, draw water from a well or be told this had been good enough for her predecessors and should be good enough for her. Her man was going places and could provide a good life for her. His growing success sheltered her from family recriminations and chased away her own lingering ingrained doubts about marrying a Communist, atheist Jew.

On December 30, Judge Kaufman rejected a Rosenberg appeal for reduction of sentence. The following day, appellate Judge Thomas Swan rejected another appeal. The blunt refusals and crushed hopes were adding up. Joe was constantly haunted as Phil said things like, "Julius got us all in trouble. Try to be glad the feds got only those few. Hope none of them crack and start talking like Greenglass. What was Julius thinking?"

Joe's answer was, "Julie was thinking what he always thought: *Help our friends.*" But Joe remembered that in listening to Julie's sincere proposals for doing 'what was right', he'd often agreed just to make Julie happy.

FOURTEEN

"Ideas are more powerful than guns. We would not let our enemies have guns, why should we let them have ideas, or keep even their own?"   *--Joseph V. Stalin*

FROM 1953 ON, HOOVER AND TOLSON SPENT LONG summer vacations as guests at Clint Murchison's Del Charro hotel in La Jolla California, while enjoying the horse racing at Delmar. Hotel management made sure the couple wanted for nothing. Staying months, they accepted $300,000 in accommodations alone, not counting the can't-lose oil deals, which made them both rich. But wealthy oilmen were not the only sponsors of Edgar and Clyde's life of luxury. There were other vacations at US taxpayers' expense. Stoves, refrigerators, washing machines, dryers, air-conditioners, stereo equipment, tape-recorders, televisions and electric wiring installations were all supplied by unknowing American taxpayers, even a lawnmower, a snowblower, custom made furniture, fresh sodded lawns, fine shrubbery, a lavish deck, a redwood fence, a flagstone patio and sidewalks, all while Edgar kept files on US Senators and Congressmen, protecting those who took money from organized crime and smearing those who defied him. Each year he presented highly inflated and misleading data on the rate of criminal convictions—based on arrests often made by local police—to harvest ever greater funding from the US House Appropriations Committee.

On January 1 1953, Joel Barr's thirty-seventh birthday, Julius and Ethel learned that their second appeal was dismissed by the Circuit Court of Appeals. They began to lose hope of a legal salvation and turned their hopes to public pressure for clemency.

On January 7, President Truman announced that the United States had developed a hydrogen bomb. Less than two weeks later, Eisenhower took over as President, bringing Nixon along. On February 11, Ike, three weeks into the job, refused a clemency appeal for the Rosenbergs, going along with the plan hatched by Hoover, Saypol and Kaufman to make them talk.

As the Rosenberg defense fought for their lives, Joel read all the US news he could find, often with Viktor Taroikin's assistance. Browsing a two-week old New York paper, he said to Phil, "here's a sign of progress back there; Georgia has established a censorship board, first one in the country it says, to ban books and prevent people from reading them. While we read Czech classified documents, people in Atlanta can't read D.H Lawrence."

"Keep in mind," Phil said, "here we're of proven loyalty and scientific value."

"The use of vacuum tubes and separate components in a complex circuit will soon be a thing of the past," Joe said.

"I believe it: micro-electronics is the next wave."

Joe nodded, "That's what we want, that deal, if we want to have the real fun."

"Here in Prague, we're stuck out in the sticks," Staros said.

"Maybe we should have accepted Stalin's invitation," Joe said lightly.

Phil frowned, "We would have had membership in the Soviet Academy of Science and access to a much bigger client."

"The thought has crossed my mind," Joe joked, meaning to agree with Phil, that they may have made a mistake by staying in Prague.

"You'd have left Vera behind? Not something you were about to do."

"Wait a while," Joe said. "We decided that together. Not that Vera didn't have something to do with it, but we agreed we should finish the missile guidance system. I still think so. Think about it: the Soviet defense ministry offered us a job because they heard we'd designed a few scarce potentiometers. Think what they might do if we succeed in developing an effective air defense against NATO attack."

"Maybe," Phil said, "their offer had to do with Taroikin's unshakeable faith, in you especially."

"Then why did he steer us away from it?"

"Because he knows some things we don't know?"

"Even without the right tools and materials, we'll make it work," Joe gave Phil a look of confident reassurance. "American know-how," he said with his full smile, relishing a symphony of ironic thoughts.

ON MARCH 1, JOSEPH STALIN COLLAPSED

after an all-night, all-out dinner with Lavrenty Beria, Georgi Malenkov, Nikolai Bulganin and Nikita Khrushchev. He'd suffered a stroke and his right side was paralyzed. Four days later, the man who had ruled and led world Communism for more than three decades, almost the whole of Joe's lifetime, was dead. Normal activity in Prague came to a stop. Many citizens wore black bands on their sleeves as if Stalin had been a close family member. Buildings were draped in black, schools held memorial services and radio stations devoted every minute to the funeral arrangements and commemorations of Stalin's life. Joe Berg and Phil Staros were only two of millions who mourned the 'architect of Communism'. Joe would always remember his own warm feelings upon hearing Stalin's May Day announcements of lowered food prices, while capitalism drove inflation and food prices higher.

Very quickly, the Politburo promoted Georgi Malenkov as the new Premier and First Secretary of the CPUSSR.

Days later, when a Czech MiG-15 shot down a US F-84 Thunderjet, which had apparently violated Czech airspace, Joe remembered Bill Perl. *Maybe the MiG was faster because of Bill's wind tunnel data. Julie couldn't resist telling me about stealing it—pure Julie, so happy, so proud.* At the thought of Julius's plight and the imminent threat to his life, Joe did not feel so conflicted as he once might have at the thought of strangers from his adopted country in mortal air combat with those of his native land. There would be no relenting in America's steady march toward extracting confessions. In the rat-or-die threat was the popular hunger for harsh punishment. *They are the scapegoats for losing the bomb to the USSR. There'll be no comprehension or mercy. The taint of Communism affects every witness, every suspect and the two Irvings, Saypol and Kaufman*

On March 14, Nikita Khrushchev was selected First Secretary of the CPUSSR, placing him among the top five leaders who quickly killed Stalin's plan to deport all Soviet Jews to the isolated Jewish Autonomous Region in Eastern Siberia, though anti-Semitism did not die out with Stalin.

On March 17, US authorities allowed 1,620 spectators to witness a massive nuclear test in Nevada, two miles away. Scientists would then study the spectators for exposure to more than a dozen deadly radioactive molecules.

On April 11, Justice William O. Douglas voted against *certiorari* in the Rosenberg case, refusing to consider any review.

On April 13, Ian Fleming published *Casino Royale*, the first James Bond thriller, full of Cold War spies and secret agents, thus transforming disturbing Cold War headlines into palatable fantasy.

EARLY ONE MORNING IN SING SING PRISON in Ossining New York, Ethel Rosenberg, who was starting a menstrual cycle, asked a prison matron for sanitary napkins. The matron asked warden Wilfred L. Denno, "Mrs. Rosenberg would like to have some Kotex, should I get her some?"

Annoyed, warden Denno replied, "Who does she think she is? She can have the cornflakes, like everybody else." The sworn account of a prison trustee who was cleaning Warden Wilfred L. Denno's office at the time.

IN MID-APRIL, ROSENBERG SUPPORTERS took hope when the Committee for Justice announced that a console table, a significant item missing from the original trial evidence, had been found. Days later, the publication of memoranda stolen from Ruth Greenglass's attorney, quoted her as saying that her husband David was "given to fits of hysteria, making things up out of thin air." Also, there was growing conflict between Manny Bloch, the Rosenbergs' attorney, and other attorneys who thought Manny Bloch had made serious mistakes, and thought they knew better. In early May, the Ruth Greenglass quotations hit the American newspapers and radio bulletins. On May 11, the Committee called for a nationwide drive to press for clemency.

MAY 22, IN UNDER FIVE HOURS, BY A JURY of eleven, Bill Perl was found guilty on two counts of perjury in claiming not to know his own classmates, Julius Rosenberg and Morton Sobell.

On May 25, by a vote of 7 to 2, the US Supreme Court rejected a stay of execution for Julius and Ethel. Their death was set for 11 p.m. on June 17.

Everybody knew: only a full confession and collaboration would save their lives now. Hoover, Saypol and Kaufman were counting on the Rosenbergs to give in. But in Sing Sing the twists of American justice and the failure of their defense lawyers didn't break them. "No one will be able to separate us by the threat of death," Julius told his wife. "Whatever the final result may be, they shall see our victory."

"They picked the wrong people," Ethel said.

FIFTEEN

"What are our schools for if not indoctrination against Communism?"   ---*Richard M. Nixon*

ON MAY 31 1953, THE COMMUNIST GOVERNMENT of Czechoslovakia, after months of denying rumors, instituted a currency reform which amounted to a devaluation of savings in the ratio of 50:1, with salaries devalued by 5:1. Money which a day earlier was buying bread and groceries was being thrown in handfuls from windows, blowing through the air in clouds like confetti then swept from the streets into trash cans.

On June 1, Joe found a copy of *Time* magazine in a plain envelope on his desk, left, he assumed, by Viktor Taroikin. Joe read the article about his convicted roommate:

"Lean, black-browed William Perl of The Bronx came of age just in time to profit by an era in which young physicists are scouted almost as assiduously as young ballplayers. As a student at Manhattan's City College '38, he proved himself a veritable Mickey Mantle among rookie scientists. By 1944 he was in the big leagues at Cleveland's Lewis Flight Propulsion Laboratory and directed an Air Forces research project in supersonic-aircraft design. By 1950, the year he got his doctorate from Columbia with a 'secret' thesis on 'transonic flows past thin airfoils,' it began to look as though Perl was in league with people who wanted to throw the game. The federal grand jury which indicted Atom Spies Julius Rosenberg and Morton Sobell called Perl in and asked him if he hadn't been palling around

with them. He denied it. He denied it again last week in a New York federal court where he was tried for perjury. He repeated over & over, 'I do not lie.' But witnesses testified that Perl and the spies, classmates at City College, had been seen together dozens of times and that he had frequently attended meetings of the Young Communist League with them in New York.

A jury found him guilty on two counts of perjury, acquitted him on two others, and recommended clemency. But immediately after the verdict, an assistant US attorney rose and suggested that Perl's troubles were only beginning: the FBI, he said, had information 'directly' tying Perl to the Rosenberg spy ring. Perl's $20,000 bail was revoked and he was led off to jail to await further judgment."

So far he hasn't cooperated, Joe thought, *maybe he won't.* But news of his old roommate and friend was one more blow against the past, leaving him only the road ahead.

Evidence of Perl's espionage activities was largely circumstantial while there was massive evidence of Perl's close friendship with the defendants. Hoover, Saypol and Kaufman settled for perjury. Later evidence would show that Perl had given the USSR designs that were incorporated into the MiG aircraft which shot down American airmen over Korea.

On June 4, there were more announcements from the Committee for the Rosenbergs and a release of the purloined Ruth Greenglass documents. On June 5, Bill Perl was sentenced to five years in federal prison, knowing full well that if he testified against others, his sentence would be reduced. He didn't talk. On June 6, Rosenberg defense attorney Bloch submitted new evidence to Judge Kaufman to show that David Greenglass had lied. Kaufman answered him on June 8: "The guilt of the accused has been proven and new testimony will not reduce the strength of the proof introduced by the prosecution." On June 10, the US Court of Appeals confirmed Kaufman's decision. Bloch immediately asked the Supreme Court for a stay of execution to allow time to submit a request for a new trial.

As Joe suffered each tightening of the screws on his friends, on June 12, night shift workers at the Škoda defense plant in Plzeň, Czechoslovakia, went on strike. They sabotaged machinery and marched to the city center. Around noon, the angry crowd, now including thousands of students, attacked city hall, built street barricades, trashed Communist Party signs and posted slogans demanding an end to single party rule. The government sent 8000 police, 2500 soldiers and eighty tanks to suppress the rebellion. Over 200 rioters were injured and more than 2000 were arrested. Martial law and long prison sentences were imposed.

On June 13, the US Supreme Court denied a stay of execution for the Rosenbergs. By this time, 22,000 telegrams a week were pouring in demanding that they be spared. A petition signed by 2300 scientists was published. On June 15, famous defense attorney, John H. Finerty, appealed to the Supreme court and two days later, on June 17, Supreme Court Justice William O. Douglas granted the Rosenbergs a stay of execution. The next day, Joel, somewhat heartened by this news and momentarily expansive, encountered a Czech colleague who was angry at harsh punishments for the Plzeň strikers. The man said to Joe:

"I suppose we're not allowed to complain about the cut in salary, the fact that the government is stealing our money?"

Joe answered, "If you're asking about a raise to compensate, of course it should be brought up. As Czech citizens, it's our constitutional right, to speak our minds, isn't it?" With a puzzled, suspicious look on his face, the man said nothing further. He was afraid of a trap which would lead to denunciations, loss of his job and his party membership. "Look," Joe said, "of course the currency reform was a dumb move, only making things worse. They should have worried more about what makes people want to work, a way to improve their lives. When there's nothing you'd be happy to buy, why work your ass off, right?"

Perhaps it was this very colleague who denounced Joe to the StB, so that instead of demonstrating patriotic belief in the Czech constitution, Joe seemed to be part of the Plzeň rebellion in openly denouncing the government. Unaware of the danger to himself, he soon had very bad news. Taroikin had left him a fresh New York newspaper: On June 19, the Supreme Court, in special session, had vacated Justice Douglas's stay of execution.

TWO AGONIZING DAYS LATER, HAVING HEARD no further news, Joe arrived at work to see the Czech newspaper, *Rude Pravo*, with a picture of Julius and Ethel on the front page. The headlines told him they'd been killed. They were gone. Trembling, Joe closed the door of his office and wept, still clutching the newspaper. *The Supreme Court came back from vacation to make sure they were murdered on a Sabbath evening? They couldn't wait till Monday to hear their plea? I will never go back there. Never. The US government is the enemy of peace and freedom.* Joe wept in an agony of anger, sorrow and self-reproach.

When Joe could, he read about the funeral, attended by 8000 people, mostly people who believed the US government had fabricated the evidence and that Julius and Ethel were innocent. *My brother and sister. I've remembered Michael's and Robert's birthdays every year. I was their uncle Joel.*

When Joe read how the FBI had had a six man team located above the death chamber at Sing Sing, counting on the Rosenbergs to confess, even from the electric chair itself, he thought, *You stood fast; just what they couldn't believe. That you would never be a traitor to your ideals.* Tears streamed from his eyes as he whispered, "They counted on getting Barr, Perl and Sarant, but old Julie wouldn't let them."

Joe had no way of knowing that Julius, during his stay in the New York House of Detention had confessed many of his proud secrets to another inmate who had professed socialist beliefs, but who was an FBI informant whose reports went directly to Hoover. While the defense lawyers pleaded their innocence, pleading for justice, for mercy, the executioners were learning of additional crimes and of Julius's pride in committing them. Nor did Joe know that some prosecutors did not want to deprive Ethel's children of their mother, nor that Hoover saw killing Ethel as bad publicity for the Bureau. Joe's alienation from America seemed complete and final.

The Soviet Union touted the gross injustice as a frame-up

and part of a hypocritical US anti-Jewish plot. The propaganda campaign continued for days. As Joel remained in sorrow and remorse and was clearly distracted, Staros lost patience and spoke one day in a raised voice, not in Czech as was their usual careful practice, but in English:

"What did you expect? Did you count on a miracle?"

"I loved them as I do you. I—"

"A vaunted atheist like yourself? What about being glad you and I are both alive? They could have gotten out—they could be here now, with us. But no, after we all went along with him, he had to tell his snot-nosed idiot brother-in-law all about us. It was purely foolish, even suicidal."

"I should have stayed and made sure they got out, at least found them a good lawyer. From what I understand, this Manny Bloch botched it."

"Be happy he didn't kill us along with himself."

"Poor Julie," Joe said. "I'll never go back there now, ever! I will bend every effort to thwart them and their treacherous capitalist schemes!"

"Oh, so now it's revenge? You versus America?"

Joe held back tears. Al's familiar voice, though it seemed like cruelty itself, was the hard truth, told by a dear friend when he least wanted to hear it, but needed most to listen.

"...No," Joe said, though at that moment he wanted the chance to wreak havoc. "No, but I will never doubt that we are doing the right thing. Julie and Ethel never said a word about any of us."

"Yeah, except to David Fucking Moron Greenglass, who you've called a 'sniveling gutless brat,' more than once. And well before any of this happened."

"I knew he'd be trouble," Joe said. "He could barely form a sentence."

Staros, hearing something outside their office, admonished their loud voices by tapping his finger across his lips, "If you had stayed, you'd've ended up dying for nothing," he said quietly in Czech to set the example, "Joe, stop your crying; what's done is done. Be happy it wasn't us."

"They were murdered!"

"We're not exactly safe and sound right here," Phil said.

Staros was right: they had plenty to worry about. Complaints from their own department were piling up at the StB about Staros criticizing the drop in living standards and Joe's condemnation of the currency reform.

Now it was going to be about loud arguments in English, behind closed doors. The StB began an investigation of them in July, but under Viktor Taroikin's watchful eye it wasn't long before the KGB in Moscow squashed the investigation from the top. One Czech investigator though, by the name of Ivan Burda, felt challenged by the sudden cancellation of his mission and decided to go it on his own, against orders. He found that Berg and Staros had been placed in their sensitive classified positions by the recently executed 'traitor', Rudolf Slansky.

JULY 9, THE NEW YORK *WORLD TELEGRAM* speculated that William Perl had passed on files to the KGB which inspired the high-tailed MiG fighters used against 'our boys' in Korea.

On July 10, *Pravda* announced that Lavrenty Beria had been fired as head of the KGB. Viktor Taroikin was soon promoted to Captain. Joe and Phil congratulated him.

With an armistice agreement, the Korean War was over at the end of July and it seemed the anti-Communist hysteria in America might begin to ebb. Two weeks after the armistice was signed, POWs were exchanged. Then Malenkov, Soviet Premier, announced that the USSR also had the hydrogen bomb.

On September 7, Nikita Khrushchev became Chairman of the Soviet Central Committee which began to arrange for the first German World War II POWs to be sent back from Soviet slave labor camps.

In October, Joe read about the US release of the UNIVAC 1103, the first commercial computer to use random access memory and reusable data storage. He also read that the US was testing another "H-Bomb." It was obvious why Staros was getting calls from the higher-ups inquiring about their progress on the anti-aircraft system. In late October, Berg and Staros proposed in a letter to the Czech deputy minister of defense to create a new central anti-aircraft defense research institute, which of course they would lead and direct. They promised to make Czechoslovakia the leading microelectronics and computer center of Europe and to surpass the West in advanced technology. But there was no bureaucracy that could comprehend or judge their proposals and no money to invest in such speculation.

In early November, Staros began to study Russian in earnest, and as his Czech colleagues noted and reported to the StB, he was making rapid progress. Response from the Czech defense ministry was a forgone conclusion. The two American engineers wrote to Khrushchev for permission to come to USSR to pursue microelectronics. Meanwhile StB agent Ivan Burda was pressing his superiors to take action against the two mysterious 'foreign spies'. He was soon reassigned and sidetracked but this only whetted his appetite to discover whose power lurked behind them.

By the end of 1953, Max Elitcher, who almost single handedly had convicted Morton Sobell to 30 years and was perhaps the strongest witness to doom Julius and Ethel, had become a pet government mouthpiece, naming names to HUAC and any other agency or grand jury tribunal that cared to invite him. He repeatedly recounted Rosenberg's attempts to recruit him and his own 'steadfast refusals' to become a spy. He never mentioned Julius's answer to his question as to whether Julius was satisfied with having helped the Soviets and Max never explained why he had not come forward earlier.

On December 8, President Eisenhower delivered his Atoms for Peace speech to the UN General Assembly in New York City. The atom would remain under civilian control and would be used to generate electricity, he claimed.

On December 23, the USSR announced Lavrenty Beria's execution, done in a hail of bullets much earlier. On December 30, the first color television sets went on sale in the US for nearly $1200, far beyond the budget of most American families. As yet, there was no color television or black and white in Czechoslovakia.

SIXTEEN

"When public men indulge themselves in abuse, when they deny others a fair trial, when they resort to innuendo and insinuation, to libel, scandal, and suspicion, then our democratic society is outraged, and democracy is baffled. It has no apparatus to deal with the boor, the liar, the lout, and the antidemocrat..."
--Senator William Fulbright

BY JANUARY 1954 IDEALISTIC SPIES WERE GONE, tragically like the Rosenbergs, dramatically like Fuchs or Sobell, bitterly like Maclean, Burgess and Philby, energetically like Barr or Sarant, or undetected and inactive like so many more.

On January 14, Marilyn Monroe married Joe DiMaggio. A week later, the first nuclear-powered submarine, the USS Nautilus, was launched in Groton, Connecticut, by Mamie Eisenhower. It was whispered that she hated to waste a good bottle of champagne on its bow.

On January 30, Emanuel Bloch, hounded by the press and public, worn out physically by the Rosenberg trial. a nervous wreck from fear of FBI retribution, died at 53.

On March 9, Edward R. Murrow and Fred W. Friendly aired a 30-minute *See It Now* program, entitled *A Report on Senator Joseph McCarthy*. In summation Murrow said:

No one familiar with the history of his country can deny that Congressional committees are useful; it is necessary to investigate before legislating. But the line between investigating and persecuting is a very fine one, and the junior senator from Wisconsin has stepped over it repeatedly. His primary achievement has been in confusing the public mind as between the internal

*and the external threats of communism. We must not
confuse dissent with disloyalty; we must remember
always that accusation is not proof, and that
conviction depends upon evidence and due process of
the law.*

In Prague, rogue StB investigator Ivan Burda pressed his
inquiries into Staros and Berg to the point that StB officers
started asking VTU management about them as possible spies.
The investigation was halted again in May by Interior Minister
Rudolf Barak and First Secretary of the Czech Communist
Party's Central Committee, Antonin Novotny, who both cleared
the engineers for advanced defense research, something they
would not have done, considering the constant Soviet Bloc
paranoia of Western spies, without orders from Moscow. But,
though the most top secret Czech files on the American
engineers had been reviewed and approved by Minister of
Defense Alexey Cepicka, there was no hint in those files of their
true origins or their connection with the Rosenbergs. It did say
that they had designed a potentiometer winding machine of a
precision needed to produce a highly accurate anti-aircraft missile
guidance system.

On April 7, Eisenhower introduced his 'domino theory'
that if one country fell to Communism, the rest would fall like a
row of dominoes. Soon, vice-president Nixon announced, "We
may be putting our own boys in Indochina regardless of Allied
support." Days later, Senator Joseph McCarthy accused the US
Army of being 'soft on Communism'.

On May 7 1954, when the Viet Minh won the Battle of
Dien Bien Phu, which the French had started two months earlier,
US politicians kept talking about dominoes and 'our boys going
in'. Ten days later, in Brown versus the Board of Education, the
Supreme Court ruled segregated schools were unconstitutional,
that 'separate but equal' was a lie.

On June 9, the 30th day of Joe McCarthy's Army hearings,
he attacked the reputation of a young lawyer in the Boston office
of the army's chief lawyer, Joseph Welch. Welch struck back:

"Until this moment, Senator, I never really

gauged your cruelty or your recklessness. Let us not assassinate this lad further, Senator. You've done enough. Have you no sense of decency, sir, at long last?"

The audience in the gallery and much of the nation, cheered Joseph Welch.

On June 14, as a part of America's growing holier-than-thou-we're-on-a-mission-from-God hubris, the words "under God" were inserted into the US Pledge of Allegiance, violating the US Constitution by joining religion and state.

ON JULY 4, AS AMERICANS ENJOYED THEIR backyard barbeques, British meat rationing ended and only then could Brits buy meat again without restriction, eight years after the war's end.

On July 23 1954, Vera Bergova, Joe's wife, gave birth to a daughter, Vivian, named after Joe's sweetheart, Vivian Glassman. Fond of children, Joe was delighted with Vivian and would remain so for the rest of his life. With her, he began a deeper commitment to life in Communist society and to a larger family. He watched Vivian constantly in her first days, weeks and months, fascinated and in love. As Vera watched Joe with their tiny baby girl, her heart softened for him and he felt this in her. Grateful, Joe said to her, "It's a dream come true, you have given me the best part of my life," and he put his arms around her and drew her close.

"But you'd wished for a boy?" she turned her head up, and around, to look into his eyes.

"Well," he said fondly, "we have plenty of time, don't we, to keep trying?"

She turned shyly away, saying, "Yes we do, Joe."

"I'm willing to try many times" Joe joked, "if we can have another baby like this one. Boy or girl."

She snuggled a little closer, "I am also," she said modestly.

Joe stared down into the crib where Vivian slept, "Look how beautiful she is," he said.

"So you are not disappointed, she is not a boy?" Vera teased and taunted gently.

"Absolutely not," Joe said, turning her and kissing her.

Vera knew he meant it and she enjoyed their kiss.

"We need to line up some baby sitters, so that we can..."

"I will," she said, not moving, feeling his mood from his enclosing thin frame.

In October, shortly after the Viet Minh took control of North Vietnam, the Texas Instruments company announced the development of the first transistor radio, which was to be, for many world-wide consumers, the first hint of a whole new age of smaller, portable electronic products. For Joe and Phil, it was confirmation of their current thinking about the direction they should take.

Time's passing was impressed on Joe in Prague when he read in a copy of a New York newspaper that on November 12, Ellis Island was closed. *Nearly fifty years since Rebecca and Benjamin passed through with their new name, after that long journey from...Lubny, wasn't it? Walking, riding in carts, on crowded trains, sneaking across boarders. I've come back to where we came from. Like the reactionaries always tell you: 'You don't like it here? Go back to where you came from! Lubny is not so far from Prague. We could go there...some day.*

After Gamal Abdel Nasser took over Egypt, the Dow Jones closed at an all-time high of 382.74, passing its 1929 peak. When Joe read that in rural Alabama a ten pound meteorite crashed through the roof of a house and badly bruised a sleeping woman, he said to Phil: "Imagine! There you are; what's the last thing you expect?"

Phil smiled, glad to hear Joe's expansive tones, "Quite a shock," he said.

"You call in to work," Joe said, "Sorry, can't come in today. Got hit by a rock from outer space. Don't believe me? Read your newspaper, boss."

To bring an end to Joseph McCarthy's reign of terror, a US Senate committee waited until after the Congressional elections of November 2, in which, for the first time since McCarthy's rapid rise, pro-McCarthy candidates were defeated. Then, six days later, the committee unanimously recommended McCarthy's censure. McCarthy refused to admit he was licked and delivered another diatribe, quoting as proof of a Communist conspiracy the *Daily Worker*'s headline, 'THROW THE BUM OUT. On December 2 1954, by a vote of 62 to 22, McCarthy was officially censured for "conduct that tends to bring the Senate into dishonor and disrepute." His political death followed quickly and alcohol brought corporeal death at 48, making him history's ugly, polluting, flash-in-the-pan.

ON JANUARY 22 1955, THE PENTAGON announced its plan to develop intercontinental ballistic missiles armed with nuclear warheads. On May 14, eight Communist countries including the Soviet Union, in response to the encircling NATO alliance, signed a mutual defense treaty, the Warsaw Pact.

On July 1, Joe and Phil's VTU anti-aircraft missile system was tested. Combining all they had learned in US defense laboratories and all they had invented in Prague, the demonstration missiles hit all targets, fast moving and slow, low flying and high, with deadly accuracy. The Czech defense establishment and observers from the Soviet Union were greatly impressed. As soon as the two American engineers were awarded state prizes a month or so later, they asked for large research and design facilities in the USSR. They insisted that if they could accomplish such success in small and limited Czechoslovakia, the possibilities would be nearly unlimited using the full resources of the Soviet Union. Response was not long in coming, beginning with a visit in September from their old friend, Aleksandr Feklisov, now a top KGB liaison officer in Prague, along with Captain Viktor Taroikin. Though Joe came to the meeting without Vera, Phil brought Anna along. During the war, Joel had always handled all the secret data from Sarant going to the KGB, so it was the first time Feklisov met Sarant.

Aleks treated them to one of Prague's best restaurants and after pouring everyone a vodka, Aleks proposed a toast to Julius and Ethel. It wasn't only the bite of strong, raw vodka that sent tears down Joe's cheeks.

"Look," big, blond Aleks said, "I understand you are interested in transistors. But let me assure you, these Czech scientists are just as enthusiastic as you are about miniature electronics."

"Unfortunately," Phil said, "enthusiasm is not enough. Miniaturization of the components for increasingly complex circuits will require enormous investments to create new research centers and new production facilities. A whole new industry must be created and Czechoslovakia does not have the resources to do that." He went on to explain the kind of research and delicate production that would be needed.

"How inevitable is this...direction and how immediate?" Fekliosov asked.

"It's the most important technological development in half a century, at least," Phil said.

Aleks kept looking to Joe, who he knew very well, and liked quite well, though he was not as fond of Joe as he had been of Julius, 'Libby' he called Julius, a nick name for Rosenberg's code name, 'Liberal'.

Joe reassured Aleks in their old way: a quick sharp look directly into Feklisov's eyes with a strong affirmative nod. It was all Aleks needed. He said to Phil:

"I don't suppose sponsorship by the Soviet Politburo while you remain here in Prague would suit you?"

Joe and Phil exchanged a look and both looked at Anna. Joe wasn't sure how Anna would feel, but he was pretty sure Vera would not want to relocate to Moscow or anywhere in the USSR.

Without missing more than a single beat, Phil said, "What makes you think the Soviet Politburo would want to finance a top secret laboratory in Prague?" *Only too open and vulnerable to the West...*

Aleks showed no surprise at this, but nodded congenially, "I believe you are correct about that, and about all that your are saying. I understand. Let me see what I can do to forward your message." Again he looked to Joe to see that he was comfortable with that.

On November 7 1955, Pyotr V. Dementyev General Director of the USSR State Committee of Aviation Technology (GKAT) came to Prague to extend his personal invitation to Phil and Joe to come to Leningrad to work. I think we can set you up very nicely there, everything you have here and much more of what you need there."

"Of course that sounds good," Phil said, but, catching a panicky look from Joe, "he added, "we'll just need some time to think it over..." Joe gave Phil a relieved look.

"To think about moving our families," Joe added.

After their meeting with Dementyev they discussed the invitation:

"We'll go of course," Phil left no trace of a question.

"Absolutely," Joe agreed.

"If so, why did we ask for time to think it over?"

"Yes, we did ask, but I think Taroikin and Dementyev both believe we agreed to go."

"We asked for time to think about moving the families. Let's talk about that." Phil and Anna were having another baby within weeks.

"I don't know about Anne," Joe said, "but Vera is not going to be happy about moving to Russia, especially northern Russia."

"Anna will be twice as 'unhappy'. She's buried, even here. She hasn't yet learned Czech, and now Russian?"

Joe couldn't help thinking, *If that beautiful woman is buried, you buried her!* "You're the one giving her kids, one after another. When has she had time to learn more Czech than she needs to feed them?"

"I know, don't tell me."

"And you better bet she knows about your other women."

"Let's not get too far off the subject, okay?" Phil was stern.

"But this *is the subject*: What am I going to tell Vera?"

"We won't go until the middle of January, February maybe. Tell Vera we're just going for a visit. I'll tell Anna the same thing."

"I suppose we can't put it off till March..."

"Let's not kid ourselves. It's what we both want."

"It's not like we'll leave them here and take up with Russian women," Joe said.

Phil said modestly but with an appreciative smile, "*Leningradskaya zhenshiniia.*" Leningrad women. His Russian pronunciation was nearly perfect.

"Probably you already know about them," Joe said.

"Better make it a good Christmas, Joe. And tell her now, why don't you?"

Joe gave a humorous sigh, "We're going to Leningrad in January or February just to help them out for a week or so. How's that?"

"Precisely," Phil said. "I'll say the same.

They'd concocted a lie designed to assure domestic tranquility, plus freedom and convenience for themselves. They agreed to let Viktor Taroikin know he could arrange travel plans for Leningrad."

That evening, when Joe came home from their lab, he was greeted by seventeen-month-old Vivian, racing to jump into his arms with a happy cry. He hugged her and kissed her more fondly than usual, relieved to feel sure that their love for each other would survive a move to Leningrad, even thinking it might help with getting Vera used to the idea. He played with Vivian all evening until her bedtime, reading her a story as she went to sleep about a girl and her pet bird.

Vera watched him, catching him glancing at her from time to time so that he seemed to look away when she noticed. When in bed as he took her in his arms and began whispering endearing pleasantries, she asked, "What's going on Joe? You have been odd all evening."

"Odd, what do you mean?"

"Looking at me like you have something to say, but can't say it."

"No, it's just that Phil and I have to go up to Leningrad to consult on some things." He stroked her thigh in a tentative conditional sort of way. She drew herself closer, letting his hand ride higher.

Kissing his chin she asked, "When will you go and how long will you be gone?"

"Late January, February maybe. Not long, a few days, a week maybe."

The next day, Phil asked, "How did it go? You told Vera?"

"So far, she only asked, how long we'd be gone."

"Yeah, so far. Couple of weeks, I told Anna."

"That's good, I guess."

ON DECEMBER 21, JOE AND VERA JOINED nearly one million Czech citizens in nearby Letna Park for dedication of a gigantic statue of Joseph Stalin on the 76th anniversary of his birth. The largest statue of the powerful dictator in all the Stalinized worldm among many thousands, had taken years to build. Behind Stalin's towering figure were sculpted the workers of Czechoslovakia and of the USSR, clearly following together in the brotherhood of the international proletariat. Joe was enthralled and listened to the speeches of commemoration in awe of Stalin's achievements, but also awed that he'd brought part of the Zbarskii family back to see their socialist dreams come true in the land of the Tsars.

Vera was not so thrilled; she'd not left her anti-Communist, anti-Semitic father in defiance and pain without bringing along a few doubts. Soviet Communism seemed to have more than its share of inconveniences, inconsistencies and even absurdities. So far, her love for Joe had all but cured her ingrained anti-Semitism. But standing hour after hour in the park listening to praise of the great Stalin, Vera felt the December cold and was weary of the droning voices. Though tired of exchanging comments with Joe and translating any Czech he didn't quite catch, she showed no sign of discontent that Joe noticed, even her scowl and groan when Stalin's motto was quoted: "A little better ever day, each day a greater joy."

On December 23, amidst the bustling of Christmas shopping in Old Town Square, Joe and Phil met discreetly with Captain Taroikin who gave them one-way plane tickets to Leningrad dated January 9 1956. They did not try to explain to Taroikin their less than enthusiastic reaction to the date on the tickets. Instead, they thanked him with unsmiling faces. Joe dreaded Vera's reaction and wished he'd never mentioned February.

SEVENTEEN

"They say that Soviet delegates smile. That smile is genuine. It is not artificial. We wish to live in peace, tranquility. But if anyone believes that our smiles involve abandonment of the teaching of Marx, Engels and Lenin he deceives himself poorly. Those who wait for that must wait until a shrimp learns to whistle.
                                              --Nikita Khrushchev

AT DAWN ON JANUARY 9 1956, JOE AND PHIL ARRIVED at Prague's Ruzyne, airport, the pride of Czech aviation. The rectangular two-story terminal building with an adjoining tower a few stories higher had won architectural commendations back in its virgin days of 1937. The hour was not only early, but cold and windy. There were guards, mechanics and necessary workers, but no other travelers. Met inside by a two man Czech security detail, they were escorted to a waiting Ilyushin Il-14, an upgraded DC-3 copy. Captain Taroikin and his adjutant, a lieutenant with a Ukrainian name, were waiting on board. The adjutant was seated ten rows away, not meant to hear their conversation.

Joe and Phil had not yet taken seats when the embarkation door was closed and sealed. The twin 1900 horsepower Shvetsov ASh-82T-7 radial piston engines started within a few seconds of each other, sending stirrings of powerful thrust down the fuselage. The loud engines dominated the wind-buffeted take-off and they were silent until aloft, when Joe asked Viktor:

"How long to Leningrad?"

"I'll let you know when we get much closer," Viktor said. Then, thinking they might wish to discuss things between them, "Let me check with our pilot."

Though clearly the flight was being made especially for

them, it seemed *special* only in a furtive sort of way. Joe decided, *We are not so not much being honored but kept secret.*

"When we first met, did you ever imagine anything like this?" Joe joked.

"Of course!" Phil was benevolently sarcastic. "I pictured this very moment."

"If only Julie could see us now!"

"…Tell me, how's Vera taking it at this point?"

"When are we coming back, is all she asked."

"She didn't ask to see the return tickets?"

"It didn't come up."

Joe already missed Vera, and little Vivian, even more. The night before he had spent nearly an hour with her playing the piano for her and letting her sound the keys.

Their landing was smooth amidst a light snow at Rzhevka airport, near Leningrad. Again there was little activity. When Joe looked around he was surprised that this late in the morning, there were still so few people there, besides the guards.

"Only special flights still use Rzhevka," Taroikin told them. "Most Leningrad air traffic uses Pulkovo."

Outside the terminal, a bitterly cold wind whipped sparse, icy snow needles into their faces. Taroikin, seeing the Americans cringe, told them, "I know you're anxious to see the new lab site, but let me suggest we go first to your hotel."

"The hotel can wait," Phil said.

"Preparations have been made there for you," Taroikin insisted gently. "There will be warmer clothing, perhaps."

AT A MODEST HOTEL IN THE CITY CENTER, they checked into ample rooms adjoining each other on an upper floor. Upon quickly unpacking, as Viktor waited in the lobby, they found an envelope with 400 rubles, a selection of Russian and Western-made winter clothes, city maps, bus and tram routes with schedules, bulletins about the new Metro line, dictionaries and even theatre and concert tickets.

Donning heavier winter coats, they returned to the lobby and accompanied Taroikin and his adjutant to a grey brick building at number 12 Volkovskaya Street. Inside, in a sort of lobby, there was a guard detail, not the run of the mill KGB cubs. They saluted Taroikin and stood straight. Taroikin gave them a brief introduction as the two men nodded.

After trudging up four flights to an attic under a hip roof, they found a single large empty space of some 200 square meters. The several iron radiators were cold, but the room temperature was above freezing. Their stunned silence seemed to prompt Viktor:

"You'll be working with certain departments of Pyotr Dementyev's State Committee of Aviation Technology, (GKAT) for purchasing requests and accounting; otherwise you should be largely undisturbed. But at no time should you write or print this street address, nor should you ever describe the location to anyone. This place must be a secret laboratory. It will be designated in official circles as Special Laboratory Eleven (SL-11) under the Experimental Design Bureau, OKB-998. Your official name and titles, Filip Georgievich Staros, Chief Designer, Dzhosef Veniaminovich Berg, Chief Engineer."

"Let me ask you," Joe said, "who occupies the three floors below us?"

"Just as you are of no concern to anyone else, should there happen to be others in this building, so they are no concern of yours. However, I believe your guard detail regiment will occupy some space in the building. But not so you'd notice, I think. You understand, there will be very careful precautions to assure that no one discovers you here."

"I need the men's room," Joe said, "and I think I see it over there," he disappeared through the doorway, came out and went through the adjacent door, the women's lavatory then out again and back to the men's.

"That assurance of privacy is appreciated," Phil said to Viktor, "but I'm more concerned with getting this place cleaned up and painted. Soon we'll need machinery and furniture, but how about fifty liters of flat white paint and some large brushes? —We'll paint this place this afternoon. I doubt you have paint rollers or spray equipment…?" Al Sarant had had a house painting and home improvement business in Ithaca.

"I believe there may only be gray paint," Viktor said, "but

look, it's only Monday. We have all week." His expression seemed to imply: *Try to act like a Soviet scientist; maintain your dignity.*

Both Phil and Joe looked disappointed

"No doubt you're tired," Viktor insisted, "I'll introduce you tomorrow to the person who can handle purchases, along with a translator who will accompany you ten or twelve hours each day."

Joe, who'd found the two lavatories—one for each gender, both still more or less functional—emerged from the men's room to say, "I'm not tired, but anxious to get started."

"Maybe there's a store where we can buy some white paint," Phil stroked and exercised his thick black mustache to the left then to the right to demonstrate his ready energy, and a hint of impatience.

"All in good time, my friends. Tomorrow is another day. Let's walk you back to the hotel so you can have a good rest. I'll leave one of our officers with you, in case you need anything. We can resume preparations at nine tomorrow, I promise you."

On the walk back to the hotel, several hundred meters, Phil looked about for a supply store that might sell paint, but he was forced to agree with Joe that probably private citizens had no need for paint, in that all property belonged to the collective and was maintained by state employees.

"I'm going to intensify my Russian studies so we can soon get rid of this translator they're giving us." Phil clearly implied that Joe should get cracking on his Russian.

"Russian is first cousins with Czech," Joe said, "but uses the kyrillic alphabet instead. Once you know the alphabet, it'll be easy."

Phil looked at Joe somewhat fondly, "I'm going to learn Russian down to the last jot. You don't think we're going to get anywhere in this country without speaking and writing perfect Russian do you?"

"It won't hurt, that's for sure."

"If your Russian turns out to be anything like your Czech, Joe, you'd better let me do all the talking."

"You could sell a polar bear warm chocolate ice cream and make him believe it was fresh Cod, in any language."

Short, dark, muscular and handsome Phil shifted his mustache from side to side as if checking the blade of a dagger. "Your faith is reassuring," he said without further expression.

TO THEIR SURPRISE, NOT ONLY TAROIKIN and the purchase agent, but Svetlana Mirovova, an attractive young blonde woman arrived at SL-11 at nine o'clock the next morning. Svetlana introduced herself in perfect lightly accented Czech, offering her hand, saying as she shook hands with both men, "Yes, I am Svetlana, I will be your translator, for whenever you need me."

Joe watched the wheels turning in Phil's head as they both took Svetlana in, a perhaps complex and mysterious surprise.

The purchasing agent was apparently ready, willing and able, even eager, to write down their long list of requirements: two German-made turning lathes, a small furnace for heating metals, a dozen soldering stations, drafting equipment, various beakers and burners, substrate materials and so on.

There was a brief visit from Pyotr Dementyev, from GKAT,. Cordial, charming, perceptive, Dementyev nodded consistently as they spoke of needs and plans, glancing constantly at his own young, blonde and blue-eyed assistant to make sure she was writing it all down. In short, he swept away the last of their concerns

Svetlana translated everything that was said in Russian to Czech. Phil was catching much of the Russian without her translation.

"Well," Dementyev said, "what good are all these tools and materials without a project to work on, eh?" Phil and Joe were all attention as he continued, "It may take a few days, even weeks to get you everything you've asked for, but I can now give you your first assignment, from your first client, the much respected Admiral Aksel Berg. He will have a contract for you in the next few days, I believe. "Are you familiar with helipots? Because that's what he wants you to produce."

"We know what they are," Phil assured him.

"But we've never made any," Joe added.

"Well, this is your chance to make some new friends and

impress potential clients. Do you foresee any problem with that?"

"No," Phil said. "We'll get it done as soon as possible."

"I'll introduce you to Admiral Berg once you're underway. I'm sure you'll have much to discuss."

"Well," Phil said, "we need to recruit and hire a crew, somewhere between thirty and fifty people initially. We'll need to do some extensive training."

"Right you are."

They did not know at the time that Admiral Aksel Berg was the man in charge of Soviet radar development and air defense of Moscow. During the war, he had gratefully received their purloined documentation of the US Army Signal Corps advanced microwave radars. So they didn't know that Admiral Berg was predisposed to appreciate working with them.

Shortly after ten, to their pleasant surprise, a crew arrived, bleary-eyed, no doubt from an unusual deprivation of their long winter sleep, but who began to set up ladders and drop cloths. Thirty minutes later, they were at work. When Phil saw the gray paint, he pleaded with the burly foreman to lighten it by adding white pigment. The foreman shrugged obligingly, but immediately asked Captain Taroikin, "Can the radiators be connected to the main valve? The paint will dry if it's not so cold."

When Dementyev and entourage had departed, "Well," Taroikin said still speaking Czech, "perhaps we should have some dinner at the restaurant in the Hotel Evropeyskaya, on our famous Nevsky Prospect, a short drive from here."

Joe and Phil readily agreed. Taroikin released his adjutant, Koronenko, for the remainder of the day. He might well have done the same for Svetlana, except that she and Phil were busy flirting in a refined but concentrated fashion. Viktor, alert to the inner workings of his charges, decided to invite her along. *It is perfectly reasonable to bring her; but she mustn't know I speak English with the two scientists.*

THE EVROPEYSKAYA, A HUGE NINETEENTH

century baroque building with lush art nouveau interiors, was one of the few places in Leningrad that catered exclusively to foreign guests. It was a place where the average Russian could never go. The hotel's premiere restaurant made a valiant stab at maintaining the highest Western standards of service and cuisine. During a most pleasant dinner, over several glasses of Georgian wine, Joe and Viktor, speaking Czech, discussed some of the great fictional characters in both Russian and English language novels. Phil and their translator were speaking mostly Russian. Joe, after extolling the fun he'd had reading Henry Fielding's *Tom Jones*, and upon then hearing Viktor's views on Roskolnikov in *Crime and Punishment*, told Viktor about his youthful reading *Of Human Bondage*, how it had cemented his disbelief in God.

"Religion never interested me," Viktor said reflectively, "but I understand that people depend on it and I suppose there are worse things." As they drank together, Joe found this relative sympathy for religious devotion an overture of friendship. Such sharing of views seemed unusual for an ambitious young KGB officer.

Phil and Svetlana were paying attention only to each other. For the sake of Soviet decorum, Viktor consulted Phil from time-to-time on the names of secondary characters in the great novels, each of which Phil supplied instantly, but without elaboration before re-engaging the pretty young translator. Phil had started the conversation with Svetlana by asking a series of questions about the Russian language and had managed a conversation of sorts in Russian, but he'd soon steered back to whatever interests and thoughts Svetlana wanted to share in Czech. Joe had seen his friend work like this for years. He noticed she was no longer addressing him as Philip Georgievich but as 'Pheel'. Sharing eye contact with Viktor, Joe knew Viktor was aware of growing tradecraft bruises.

"So, your family has a place in the country, Lana?" Phil asked.

"Yes," Svetlana said. "We'll go in May. Phil," she added in careful Russian, "you can also call me Veta. (Vayta) if you like it better; I have many little names."

"I'll call you Lana," Phil smiled with pleasure in using her personal name.

"Well," she said, "different people use different ones for

us Russians." *Only one other person calls me Lana.*

Joe, looking at his old friend and this lovely young woman, thought, *I can't really blame either one of them.* But Joe suspected Phil's philandering might get them in trouble, not only with their wives.

"Joe," Phil said abruptly, perhaps aware that Joe was focusing on his flirtations, "Lana wants to know what a helipot is, the ones we will soon produce, and I told her you'd explain it to her."

Joe guessed that this was Phil's way of informing Taroikin that he would need to share professional interests with Svetlana. Taroikin did not blink or change expression.

Finding Svetlana very quick to comprehend, Joe explained that a helipot was a device for precise control of electrical impulses by varying resistance values. On a helical shaped insulator, a thin resistance wire was wound on the insulator's full length, providing a contact point at each end: A and B. When the knob of the device was turned, a third contact, C, attached to a second wire moved along the helical winding and thus varied the resistance between contacts A, or B, and C. "Helipots allow for a very wide range of precise tuning in a miniature component," Joe concluded.

The helipot, invented in California years earlier, was another technology never shared with the Soviet Union during the war, and which had been prohibited for sale to Communist bloc countries after the war. Soviet military engineers clearly understood the necessity of these devices in everything from radar to rockets, including computers and missile guidance systems.

Demonstrating an advantage of the Soviet system of centralized command over that of Western democracies, materials, furniture and tools began to arrive at SL-11's loft by the end of the first week.

EIGHTEEN

"Comrades! The cult of the individual brought about rude violations of party democracy, sterile administration, deviations of all sorts, cover-ups of shortcomings and varnishings of reality. Our nation bore forth many flatterers and specialists in false optimism and deceit.
--Nikita Khrsushchev, the Secret Speech

IN EARLY FEBRUARY 1956, BRITISH KGB SPIES Guy Burgess and Donald Maclean resurfaced in Moscow after disappearing five years earlier in an escape from London.

On February 14, the 20th Congress of the CPUSSR opened and on February 25 Nikita Khrushchev, in a long speech, denounced the cult of Stalin as the "source of severe perversions of party principles, of party democracy, of revolutionary legality." After extolling and holding Lenin up as the shining example of Communist leadership, Khrushchev laid before the 20th Congress personal letters of Lenin's clearly expressing his dislike of Stalin and Stalin's rude, cruel manner. Khrushchev told the breathless party gathering:

"...Stalin originated the concept "enemy of the people", a term which made possible the use of the cruelest repression against anyone who in any way disagreed with Stalin, against those who were only suspected, or who merely had bad reputations."

Khrushchev went on at great length and left little meat on the bones for later critics of Stalin: Stalin was a monster of depravity, a sick man who murdered anyone who stood against him, a leader whose incompetence caused the great suffering and massive Russian deaths at the hands of the Nazis, a liar and a coward who murdered millions more. The stunned delegates now understood why this speech was given in an unprecedented closed session. They went home the next day still in shock, with a radically changed future to consider.

Joe and Phil at first heard nothing of Khrushchev's speech, but as they set up their lab, the consequences began to appear in Soviet policy. Vast numbers of people were soon released from the Gulags, many of whom, having spent decades in the most humiliating circumstances, came out still praising Stalin, still sure, if indeed they had been done an injustice, it was the fault of those under Stalin who had deceived him. Some who rejoined their families after decades were convinced of their own guilt. *Who has not thought bad thoughts?* But whether or not Joe and Phil had any inkling of Stalin's fall from the Party pedestal, they were to be among its immediate beneficiaries. Their arrival in Leningrad could not have been better timed.

Viktor Taroikin understood without having heard Khrushchev's speech that his country was about to change and that it must change to survive. Viktor knew that Joe even more than Phil believed with every fiber of his being that socialism was the only bridge from capitalism to a good life on earth for the vast majority. Joe believed Stalin had created and led the USSR, the only people's state.

Viktor, alone among all the people in Joe's new world, understood that this innocence, this utter loyalty to his ideals was by no means a blind obedience. The KGB captain regarded Phil as much more calculated, and he noted that Phil's short stature was the perfect balancing element to his immense magnetic ego, charisma and charm. He was less physically overwhelming and even more appealing because of it.

By mid-February, the lies Joe and Phil had told their wives were transparent. They'd claimed their stay had been extended because new opportunities opened up. With great sentimental effort, Joe at last said to Vera on the telephone, "It's taken longer than I thought. Why don't you both come up? I miss you and Vivie terribly." This, at least, was no lie.

"I'll come, maybe only to turn around and come back?"

Joe pictured his neat attractive wife, her dark hair

encircling her pale face, her head cocked slightly as she held the phone. "Umm, well, no, it's going to be a while yet, I'm afraid. I miss you, Vera."

"I don't suppose you can come get me?"

"I can't leave now. Hire someone. Money's no problem. Spend whatever you need."

Viktor Taroikin saw the wives and children joining their husbands as a good thing, certainly for a favorable outcome of the helipot project. *Svetlana and Phil will both be better for it, in the long run,* he thought and set about finding ways to aid the families, starting with transportation and identity papers. He applied for apartments in a good central Leningrad neighborhood at a time when most Soviets lived in crowded communal apartments, one room for each family. Viktor relentlessly urged his superiors to pursue his drastic requests. He pointed out the great debt owed and the great promise the two scientists presented.

Phil, though less anxious for his wife's companionship than Joe, made Anna similar entreaties. By March 1, their large hotel rooms were home to both families. Naturally, Vera had a much easier time of it than Anna who was pregnant with their fourth child, her sixth. Anna was overwhelmed; she'd begun to suspect her husband's preoccupation with the young translator. Vera, as a native Czech speaker, with some grade-school Russian and with only one child to look after had time for her husband.

WHEN IT WAS TIME TO BEGIN HIRING ENGINEERS, in mid-March, Captain Taroikin offered what sounded like an official pronouncement: "You of course understand that here, in the Soviet Union, a confederacy of many nationalities, Jewish is considered to be only one of many national origins, not a religion." Neither Phil or Joe said anything and the young KGB officer continued, "A largely unspoken caution exists not to allow a concentration of any one nationality to develop a clique in any position vital to the interests of the nation. As the directors of a highly sensitive defense enterprise such as SL-11, you should understand that there is this unspoken quota on hiring Jews."

"A quota?" Joe said.

"Yes, two per cent. That's in proportion to the general

population." In the silence that followed Viktor added, "This quota can unfortunately at times be counterproductive to some extent, but the rule is: don't place too many eggs in one basket."

Phil could not help a quick look at Joe and both had studied Taroikin during this declaration, wondering how deeply he felt what he was saying. They had agreed back in Prague to hire only young engineering school graduates and not individuals who were already experienced in Soviet technology and thus inured to the Soviet ways of risk aversion and the political futility of innovation. But some positive response or agreement was clearly called for. Phil nodded as he prepared a reply while a smile tugged at the corners of Joe's mouth and before Phil could speak, Joe said: "So, doesn't this mean there will be a higher percentage of Jewish engineering graduates who can't find a job worthy of their talent and education?"

"You're supposing that qualified Jewish graduates form a larger group than is represented by their population?" Taroikin asked smartly.

"Jews are not prevented from studying and graduating from universities here, are they?" Phil interposed.

"Certainly not on all official levels."

"No," Joe said easily, "wait a while, I'm not saying Jews are smarter, better qualified or hold themselves to a higher standard. That may be true or may not be true, but that is not my point, which is: there'd be no quota unless it was necessary to prevent what would happen otherwise. Therefore, qualified individuals will be eliminated from the job market and will thus be available."

"…Yes, perhaps," Viktor conceded.

Joe turned to Phil, "That's where we'll get who we need, from a pool of eager, highly qualified Jewish engineers, Jews who are being under utilized." He said this with such humorous relish, it seemed he might be kidding, as he so often was. But Viktor, taking his cue from Phil, saw that Joe was quite serious and was merely amused by the idea of taking advantage of the rule, as if the state had made a special effort to find them a protected nest of talent. Viktor understood in a flash that there was nothing malicious or rebellious in this, that Joe's pure devotion to the ideals of Communism gave him the right, as he saw it, to correct the mistakes and misunderstandings of bureaucracy. Joe thought nothing of ignoring rules if they were not in tune with the common good, so clear was his vision of those ultimate goals. Viktor was not unsympathetic; he smiled at the cloud of formidable difficulties he saw lying ahead: He would always remember this moment. Joe would need careful guidance and protection, even now that Stalin was dead. Taroikin, who had helped forge Joel Barr's new identity, was aware of Joe's Jewish origins and that his new Russian passport gave his national origin as British, from South Africa. *I'll have to hope that Dzhosef Berg's desire to make things work will outweigh his lack of interest in being recognized as politically pure.*

"You should be aware of this quota," Taroikin said. "If you chose to ignore it. there can be adverse consequences."

Even as they spoke, Khrushchev was counseling Polish leaders to limit the number of Jews in high positions. Whereas, in America, 19 US Senators and 82 US Representatives, including the entire congressional delegations of Alabama, Arkansas, Georgia, Louisiana, Mississippi, South Carolina and Virginia signed the 'Southern Manifesto', to protest the 1954 decision desegregating public education. They said in part:

"This unwarranted exercise of power by the Court, contrary to the Constitution, is creating chaos and confusion in the States principally affected. It is destroying the amicable relations between the white and Negro races that have been created through 90 years of patient effort by the good people of both races. It has planted hatred and suspicion where there has been heretofore friendship and understanding."

Only 3 Southern Congressional Democrats refused to sign the Southern Manifesto: Albert Gore Sr., Estes Kefauver and Lyndon Johnson.

NINETEEN

"The Cold War isn't thawing; it is burning with a deadly heat. Communism isn't sleeping; it is, as always, plotting, scheming, working, fighting."
---Richard M. Nixon

IN LENINGRAD, JOE WAS PREPARED TO TAKE advantage of Soviet anti-Semitism as they set about recruiting thirty people, to be the germ of a broadly and vetically integrated company capable of solving each engineering design problem in-house. With Joe's advice, Phil hired a chemist, a physicist, computer engineers, memory specialists, system designers and techs. He assigned them to five separate departments, each responsible for solving specific problems.

Joe and Phil, because of their value as scientists, their past service and obvious loyalty were, from the start, given the highest clearance to use ranked and classified scientific libraries and thus to have access to all foreign publications. Their speculations about solid state microelectronics were spurred well beyond the helipot project by avid reading of western technical journals in these libraries where they could take notes but where photo-copying was forbidden.

Phil was learning Russian at a fierce pace, studying tables of verbs and listening to recordings. He knew that to sell their ideas to the Soviet defense establishment, he would need to speak flawlessly. By April, there was little excuse for retaining a translator and because his affair with Svetlana was impinging on his family life, Phil relinquished her professional services. Though Svetlana had been useful to Joe, he too, though his Brooklyn accented Russian was crude, was willing to let her go. He preferred direct contact and one-on-one exchanges. Unlike Phil, with language texts and grammars and tape recordings, Joe was learning his Russian from colleagues, SL-11 employees, taxi drivers and grocery clerks. Joe did not know that Phil continued to see Svetlana anyway.

In late April, after office and laboratory construction at SL-11 was sufficient for a start, after a staff of mostly young engineers were hired—just over ten per cent of whom had Jewish backgrounds—after furnaces, turning lathes, table and band saws had been shouldered up the four flights of stairs, and after irritation in their cramped rooms had grown to an edge, Viktor miraculously obtained, with the help of KGB generals and Pyotr Dementyev, an apartment with two rooms, a bath and a kitchen for the Bergs and three rooms, a bath and kitchen for the Staros family, both apartments in the same building on Kuznetsovskaya Street. It was an astounding offer at a time of extreme overcrowding. But, to Taroikin's dismay, his offer was not received with the unrestrained joy he expected. He gave them a questioning look of some disappointment.

Joe frowned and said, "I understand how difficult it must be to find such accommodation. Perhaps there are others who need this more than we do?"

As Taroikin suppressed consternation, Phil looked knowingly at Joe and said, "I'm afraid the time has come."

Viktor said, "I was sure you'd be delighted to move out of your hotel rooms."

"Oh, we are, *we* are." Phil said, also unenthusiastic.

"Eventually, sure," Joe said.

"Are you suggesting I must find someone else for these apartments?"

"I know it's a lot to ask," Joe said, "but could we hold off a month or so, at least a few weeks?"

Viktor, now showing rare signs of irritation, shook his head from side to side. "I suppose you don't need to move this week or next, but I will be a laughing stock if you delay much longer than that. And I don't mean anyone actually laughing."

"It's the wives," Phil told their mystified KGB officer. "Joe's afraid to tell Vera we're not going back to Prague. I'm forced to lie to Anna because he won't tell Vera the truth." Phil gave his thick mustache a sweeping skeptical side-to-side scan of the entire situation.

"But wouldn't having a place to live be somewhat persuasive?" Viktor's shoulders did not lift in his usual fraternal shrug. "Why Vera cannot be happy in Leningrad? After all, Joe, your salary is at least that of a deputy minister. Make her happy. Is Prague really so much better?"

"For her," Joe said, "Prague has family advantages."

"Such as—Well, it seems to me that sooner or later you'll have to come to terns with—"

"Make it two weeks then?" Joe asked.

They moved just short of two weeks later in mid-May. Vera's and Anna's sharp disappointment at the prospect of an indefinite stay in Leningrad was at least somewhat ameliorated by lodgings much superior to the hotel, but which were nevertheless no match for their larger and more pleasant accommodations in Prague. Neither Joe nor Phil revealed that they'd known since last December they would be moving permanently to northern Russia.

On June 1, there was another obvious sign of the USSR's de-Stalinization. Stalin henchman Vyacheslav Molotov resigned as Soviet foreign minister and was relegated to the ambassadorship in Mongolia. But on June 28, labor riots in Poznań, Poland, were crushed when Soviet troops killed 53 people by firing into a crowd of citizens protesting high prices.

In America, on June 29, Marilyn Monroe married playwright Arthur Miller. First the Italian stallion baseball star then the famous New York intellectual. When a girl can have whoever she wants, she can get lonely and Marilyn's incongruous loneliness would reign over the land for the next six years and then some.

On July 30, Eisenhower and the US Congress made 'In God We Trust' the US national motto, replacing *e pluribus unum*, the union of many. Whether many can ever be one or not, Joe Berg trusted the many far more than any notion of God.

ONE LISTLESS DAY IN AUGUST 1956, IVAN Prokherov, SL-11's highly skilled lathe operator was working on a bearing trace when Chief Engineer Dr. Dzhosef Veniaminovich Berg came into his shop.

"How can I be of assistance, Dzhosef Veniaminovich?" Ivan asked.

"Let me borrow your lathe for a while. You can give me a hand." Ordinarily Joe would've waited until the workers had gone home to tinker with prototypes, but he was anxious to test an idea. Ivan was surprised to see Dr. Berg roll up his white sleeves, take several rough chunks of metal from his pockets, slip into an apron and quickly fit the cutter with a selected chisel tip. As the seasoned mechanic watched, he was astonished to see Joe quickly set the machine's cutting parameters from memory then turn out the identical part from each sample alloy, without needing a 'hand' of assistance.

Sensing awe and interest in Ivan, Joe said, "It's nearly time to go anyway, maybe we could get some tea or coffee?"

"Sh-sure."

"Know of any place with fresh pumpernickel rolls?"

"In fact, I do." Ivan had enough sense not to question Dr. Berg as to how on Earth, as a Soviet scientist, he had ever learned how to use a metal turning lathe with such enviable skill.

Joe asked him: "As a young man at the top of your profession, how do you like working at SL-11? How could we make it better?" The fact that they were in a familiar bar made Joe's question seem casual.

"It's already better than the last place I worked," Ivan said.

"Oh yeah, how is that?" Dr. Berg seemed at least as interested in the sweet roll he was eating with his hot black tea.

"Dzhosef Veniaminovich, correct me if I'm wrong, but we've, that is *you* have, agreed to design and build something from raw materials, agreeing to deliver a product in a reasonable amount of time."

"You find the pressure uncomfortable?"

"Where I worked before was—"

"You needn't tell me where, but how was it different?"

"Before our manager would sign a contract to develop a component over a period of a five-year plan, he would make sure we had already produced it. So that there was no way he would fail to have it in time, and a bit earlier."

"Hmmm," Joe said, slowly chewing his roll and taking another swallow of tea from the glass held in a metal holder. "Sure, that'd be the safe way to do it. I hope we can do it without needing such elaborate precautions, eh?" *No wonder the USSR is behind in developing computers!*

"And of course," Ivan added, "I've never seen a senior scientist or manager operate machine tools."

Joe smiled engagingly, saying nothing further. Ivan was going to be his favorite mechanic for decades to come.

AUGUST 17, THE SOVIET COUNCIL OF MINISTERS authorized plans for an experimental facility for missile defense to be located at Sary Shagan, on the west bank of Lake Balkhash in Kazakhstan.

In September, when already discernable progress was being made in developing the helipots, Pyotr Dementyev introduced the two engineers to Admiral and Deputy Defense Minister Aksel Berg, who was in charge of Soviet air defense and development of a computerized missile defense system for Moscow against likely US and NATO attack.

Upon meeting Phil and Joe, encountering their American ways, Admiral Berg discounted their KGB legends and correctly surmised that the two 'Czechs' were in fact the Americans who had supplied complete files on numerous advanced US microwave radar systems, information vital to him in developing the leading edge of current Soviet radar. Once formal introductions were over, unable to resist the situation's humor, the former World War I submarine commander asked Joe, "Berg, eh? Are we truly related? What branch of the Berg family are you from? I myself am a genuine Russian Berg, from Finland."

Feeling a slight shiver of danger, Joe said, "I can only hope to live up to the name." They both knew he meant *as a scientist*, for Aksel Berg was renowned in the USSR's scientific fields of radio electronic communications and cybernetics.

"Well," Aksel said, "we have strong common interests." There was a fragile magic enjoyment to the moment, two men understanding that in each other they were meeting someone equally adept in a new scientific field, thus a potential true colleague.

Phil, ready to speak about the helipot project held off. Admiral Berg had a few questions related to radio propagation theory, which Joe was happy to address. When the time came to mention their progress on the helipots, the admiral waved Phil off, "I'm told you are making quite adequate progress. I have faith in you; you have my support. Once the helipots are in mass production, I think you will find yourselves working on some more interesting projects, with solid contracts. And not only from the Soviet Navy."

It's the same everywhere, Phil thought, *the interesting science is in defense, where the money is.*

In mid-October, on a visit to a special library, ostensibly to check for news of transistor developments, which might appear as auxiliaries to the articles about Shockley winning the Nobel Prize, Phil found Joe avidly reading the *New York Times* sports pages. "You won't find the latest transistor news in there," he said.

"It's amazing," Joe nodded benevolently, "this Yankee pitcher, Don Larsen, just pitched the only perfect game in World Series history. What can even the Dodgers do against that guy?"

ON OCTOBER 23, STUDENT DEMONSTRATORS were arrested in Budapest. When a crowd demanded the release of the detained students, they were fired upon by security police. One demonstrator was killed. This triggered a spontaneous nationwide Hungarian revolt. The rebels demanded civil rights and withdrawal from the Warsaw Pact. Three days later, Soviet troops invaded Hungary, but were unsuccessful in quelling the uprising as the rebels ousted the Communist government and began setting up a democratic process. On November 4, a much larger Soviet force invaded and crushed the rebellion, but not before 700 Soviet soldiers had been killed along with thousands of revolutionaries and even more civilians. By November 10, the armed conflict was over, but it had driven cracks into the Communist parties of Europe which would widen in years to come as nearly a quarter million Hungarians fled the country and told the world about what had happened there.

The Soviet press, taking its cues from *Pravda*, reported the uprising with some factual accuracy, but a skewed perspective:

"fascist, Hitlerite, reactionary, counter-revolutionary hooligans financed by the imperialist West in order to use student unrest to stage a counter-revolution. Hungarian patriots, with Soviet assistance, smashed the counter-revolution."

Joe and Phil, engrossed in developing the helipots, accepted the Soviet account of Hungarian events. They were more interested in news from the US announcing the birth of IBM's hard disk drive, capable of storing an amazing 5 megabytes of information.

Nikita Khrushchev threatened to attack London and Paris with missiles if Britain and France did not withdraw their forces from Egypt. On November 7, the UN General Assembly called for Britain, France and Israel to withdraw troops from Arab lands immediately, which they did, six weeks later, as petrol rationing took effect in Britain due to oil deliveries being halted in the Suez Canal.

On November 13, the US Supreme Court answered the 'Southern Manifesto' by declaring Alabama's segregated bus laws illegal, and thus ended the Montgomery Bus Boycott.

By the end of their first year in Leningrad, SL-11 was well established. Any doubts Joe might have had about Phil's ability to lead and promote their interests with the higher ups, if indeed he'd ever had any, were long gone. Phil understood that success depended on intimate relations with the right, powerful people, and that personal trust was the only road to dependable agreements. Increasing his Russian vocabulary by studying every day, Phil now spoke grammatical Russian and could write faultless letters without spelling mistakes. In chance encounters with Russians, he most often left no doubt that he was from an unfamiliar Russian-speaking land. Joe was comfortable tinkering his way out of every technical problem they encountered, ever the scientist, learning his Russian in the vernacular.

IN APRIL 1957, SHORTLY AFTER IBM BEGAN to sell the first compiler for the FORTRAN scientific programming language, GKAT head, Pyotr Dementyev came to see Staros and Berg. After sharing their excitement about the FORTRAN software, Dementyev urged them to accompany him. "There's somebody I want you to meet, someone who can be a big help in authorizing advanced projects. Perhaps you've heard of Dmitry Feodorovich Ustinov? Chairman of the Central Committee?"

"Not sure," Phil said.

"When the Germans attacked in 1941, Comrade Stalin appointed Comrade Ustinov Commissar of Armaments, but his job was to get the defense industry, the military factories, moved from Leningrad and Moscow quickly east to the Ural mountains. Stalin awarded him Hero of Socialist Labor in 1942. Shortly after Comrade Stalin's passing, the Soviet Ministry of Armaments was merged with the Ministry of Aviation Industry to become the Ministry of Defense Industry, headed by Dmitry Feodorovich. Though he carries a general's rank, he is above all an engineer and a very practical man. He makes it his business to know smart people. Those who know him call him Uncle Mitya, but not to his face, I'm pretty sure."

Flattered and impressed by these confidences, Joe and Phil soon found themselves at the offices of the well-known military engineer. He was a tall man with a high forehead and deep brown eyes that missed nothing. He wore glasses but the lenses did nothing to blunt the intensity of his gaze. Looking directly at them with a friendly smile, Ustinov shook hands, "Though I understand your progress on the project with Admiral Berg is already impressive, in designing the miniature helical potentiometers, which I believe are already being relied on in some important areas, I am also familiar with your achievements in Prague. Air defense is one of my strong interests."

"Well, we are very pleased to meet you," Phil said in his excellent Russian, "we will work to complete whatever projects we are fortunate enough to be trusted with."

When asked about miniaturization of electronic components, Phil explained that since all electronic systems were basically about controlling the flow of information, if this process could be achieved using less space and less electricity, there would be significant military advantages.

Ustinov's immediate comprehension, incisive questions and simple direct manner made a strong impression. When their brief meeting ended, Ustinov invited them to come visit again.

TWENTY

"The aggressor too should know that the preemptive use of nuclear weapons would not insure victory. With modern detection systems and the combat readiness of the Soviet Union's strategic nuclear forces, the United States would not be able to deal a crippling blow to the socialist countries. The aggressor will not be able to evade an all-crushing retaliatory strike."
---Dmitry Ustinov, Minister of Defense, USSR

JUNE 17 1957, IN YATES V. UNITED STATES, THE Smith Act was held unconstitutional in the convictions of numerous Communist Party leaders. The Supreme Court ruling distinguished between advocacy of an idea for incitement to violence and the teaching of an idea as a concept. The same day, the Court ruled 6-1 in Watkins v. United States that defendants could use the First Amendment as a defense against "abuses of the legislative process." The witch-hunt seemed to be easing, but not for actual Soviet spies. On June 21, Vilyam Genrikhovich Fisher was arrested. His assistant, Reino Häyhänen had defected to the CIA. The Soviet master spy, under the name, Colonel Rudolf Abel, had operated unchecked from 1947 on. His home, a hotel room and photo studio, contained state-of-the-art cameras for producing microdots, cipher pads, courier cuff links, the famous hollow nickels, cavitized shaving brushes and shortwave radios. J. Edgar Hoover made the arrest and claimed credit for the entire investigation.

On July 28, the 6th World Festival of Youth, part of Khrushchev's bold de-Stalinization, opened in Moscow to 34,000 people from 130 countries, the first to be held in the USSR, a gesture of openness to the world. Soviet youth met foreigners, albeit under supervision, but volunteer Russian foreign language students translated for new international friendships. However, it was the music that came to Russia which made the biggest impressions; Russian young people were dancing in the streets, holding hands with people from all over the world. The first Russian popular band, *Druzhba*, (friendship) began its three decade stardom as it won the festival's First Prize in popular music, thanks to its lead singer, Edyta Piecha.

Joe, always interested in musical events, was tempted to take the train to Moscow with his viola, hoping to find musicales like those he'd hosted in Greenwich Village. But when Joe suggested they go to the festival, Phil was unenthusiastic.

"Well," Joe said, "you, the lover of folk music? You'd get to hear Edyta Piecha who, together with *Druzhba* and Vladimir Troshin is performing *Moscow Nights*, with Americans and Frenchmen singing along."

"Edyta and *Druzhba*," Phil said, "are the most popular sound in Russia, which you'd know if you didn't listen only to Rachmaninov."

"I feel we know Rachmaninov, personally, but any music is better than no music, and to play with strangers could be fun…"

"Did you know *Moscow Nights*, a remake of *Leningrad Nights*, popular here before we arrived, was officially ordered over two years ago in preparation for this festival?"

Joe changed the subject: "The US is setting up an International Atomic Energy Agency. That would never happen if only the Americans had the bomb."

"Don't start in again about how Julius got blamed for doing very little, please. It will only make me think you were foolish enough to believe there would be justice from capitalism. Instead, let's worry about why some of our prototype helipots are dying after five hundred hours. Dementyev told us some are being put to use in advanced projects. He had a sparkle in his eyes. But not quite a friendly twinkle. We can't afford any fuck-ups."

"Well five hundred hours is not nothing," Joel said thoughtfully. "Tell them to make it a practice to replace them after four-hundred hours."

"We'll see. Go to the festival if you must."

"No need; I thought we might make some valuable contacts in Moscow."

"Dementyev says the real Berg is quite happy, that if all continues to go well, Ustinov may introduce us to the big bosses."

"Like who?"

"Deputy ministers, party higher-ups."

"The helipot wire must be breaking. Either the insulator isn't absorbing the heat, or there's too much friction at the contact point. Or, the winding is stretched too tight. It needs some thought."

On August 21, confident of US nuclear arsenals, Eisenhower announced a two year suspension of nuclear testing. *See, we're not the bad guys here. (But we're ready for nuclear war.)*

On September 4 1957, Arkansas Governor Orville Faubus called out the National Guard to prevent nine African-American students from enrolling in Little Rock's Central High School. Three weeks later, Eisenhower sent the 101st Airborne to Arkansas to sort it out, and to provide safe passage into Central High for the nine students.

ON OCTOBER 4 1957, THE USSR SURPRISED nearly everyone in the world by launching Sputnik 1, the first artificial satellite to orbit the earth. People around the world stood outside at night with binoculars and telescopes or simply used their naked eyes to see the little light moving across the sky. This startling event thrust the United States into a race to space. Joe and Phil were not quite as surprised as most. They were now pretty sure Soviet tracking radar was using SL-11 helipots.

One week after the launch of Sputnik, a group of amateur and professional telescope users in the United States, along with the MIT Computation Center, successfully calculated the orbit of Sputnik's R-7 Semyorka launching rocket on an IBM 704 computer. This news, in the *New York Times*, drew Joe's interest. *The 704 is a heavy, heat generating vacuum tube machine, but IBM uses a core memory for the first time and has expanded the registers. It's quite possible that this Harvard-MIT group can track the launch rocket. But solid state computers are what's needed for following and guiding these unmanned vehicles,* Joel knew. He could see the future as clear as day.

On November 3, in a stunning follow-up to the sensational Sputnik 1, the USSR launched Sputnik 2, with a dog on board. The Russian word *Laika* simply means *barker*, one who barks. It was the name of a breed or several breeds of northern Russia hunting dogs, but in world popular culture *Laika* became the name of that one dog: *'poor little Laika', 'brave Laika'*. Thus Sputnik 2 was not merely a confirming technological victory, but a magnificent propaganda success for Khrushchev as *Laika* won hearts and minds everywhere. No one talked about the fact that *Laika* died hours later from extreme heat. In a follow-up to the Sputnik triumphs, President Eisenhower's Science Advisory report called for more American missiles and fallout shelters. The USSR's ability to send rockets armed with nuclear warheads anywhere in the world was clear.

On November 14, in Apalachin, New York, after ticketing one Cadillac driver for speeding, a police officer wondered why there were so many Cadillac sedans parked around Joseph Barbara's estate. The major Cosa Nostra conference was soon to be investigated by an embarrassed J. Edgar Hoover who had long claimed organized crime did not exist.

On November 25, Eisenhower had a stroke.

On December 6, America's first desperate attempt to match the Soviet Sputniks failed; the Vanguard rocket rose four feet from the launch pad, lost thrust and fell back. The fuel tanks ruptured and exploded, badly damaging the launch pad. The TV3 satellite payload, a 1.36 kg aluminum sphere was damaged.

It was about this time that *Operation Dropshot* was considered by the US Defense Department, a plan hatched much earlier for a combination nuclear and conventional war with the Soviet Union in order to counter the anticipated Soviet takeover of Western Europe, the Near East and parts of Eastern Asia. Such a war was expected to start at any moment. *Operation Dropshot's* plan depended on bombers to deliver the nuclear arsenal and would use 300 nuclear bombs and 29,000 high-explosive bombs on 200 targets in 100 Soviet cities and towns to wipe out 85% of the Soviet Union's industrial potential at a single stroke. Nearly one third of the 300 nuclear weapons would be used to destroy Soviet combat aircraft.

IN LATE DECEMBER PYOTR DEMENTYEV arrived again at SL-11 with Viktor Taroikin intent on another visit to Dmitry Ustinov. "He's a Deputy Premier of the Soviet Union now," Taroikin said solemnly, "Did you know?"

"Yes," Phil said. "I heard a...rumor."

"Perhaps more important," Dementyev was deferential, "he was only two weeks ago made Chairman of the Voino Promishinaya Kommisia, VPK (War Industries Commission) whose job it will be to coordinate defense efforts and to make sure there is inter-agency cooperation and understanding. He has authority over all military industries, directly under the council of ministers."

"And," Taroikin said without added gravity, but firmly, "the VPK is a highly insulated body which even you are not authorized to know about or discuss."

"Let's go," Dementyev urged, "it is he who has asked to see us, not the other way around."

Ustinov's interest in them seemed more receptive. His pauses after ideas that Phil expressed were longer, meditative almost, without immediate sharp questions or challenges, as if in respectful appreciation. After several minutes of listening to Phil, Ustinov said quietly, "So, you are telling me that to achieve the complexity needed for fully automated processes, vacuum tubes must go?"

"Well, yes," Phil said. *Why was I afraid to put it just like that?*

"To process what needs now to be processed," Ustinov was now with the pointed question, "there must be so many more answers to so many yes or no questions, that it cannot be done with the vacuum tubes we are now using?"

Though Phil had not dared put it so simply, it was exactly what he believed and even he, so skilled at fast-on-his-feet improvised conversation, was stunned by Ustinov's rapid comprehension. "Yes," Phil managed, "the size and the heat, from a tube computer would preclude any valid functioning, not to mention geometrically increasing power requirements."

"Vacuum tubes won't do the job," Joel said quietly. Once again he had assumed the inevitability of what later became Large Scale Integrated circuits, LSIC, to achieve the necessary matrix, imagining circuits containing hundreds or even thousands of transistors in one single component. "There isn't one vacuum tube in existence that will be worth ten kopeks within a few years." He wasn't sorry he spoke though he'd agreed to let Phil do the talking. Ustinov looked at Joe and asked:

"Do you understand how few engineers would agree with you?"

"Even so," Joel said modestly, "it's inevitable, like the sun coming up."

There was more than enough weight to Ustinov's questions to counter any overconfidence on Phil's part, but, flashing a look at Joe, Phil answered with an appropriate sigh:

"It is natural that when technology reaches a dead-end that only a breakthrough can solve, it is difficult for anyone directly involved to see that an entirely new and untried direction must indeed be the solution."

"But transistors are hardly dependable enough to replace tubes at present," Ustinov offered a simple fact.

"Not yet," Phil replied, "but there may be engineering solutions to that problem, which could precede manufacturing solutions."

Joe was listening with swelling pride. He understood how brilliantly Phil was explaining it. Joe's feelings for his partner had never been more admiring and fond. *He is a real master.* Eager to congratulate Phil, Joe imagined what he would say when they were again back at the lab, using English behind closed doors.

Ustinov, the highly skilled and intelligent engineer in his own right, asked Phil, "What sort of engineering solutions?" The edge was back in his voice.

"Using redundancy. Once the problems of heat, size and power consumption are solved, doubling or tripling circuits should be possible. But I'm afraid our ideas here are still quite preliminary."

Seemingly unimpressed, Ustinov turned to Joe, "Speaking

of manufacturing solutions—let me first say that your helipots, even in their experimental iteration, have been instrumental in certain of our most significant achievements." Joe's gaze met Ustinov's deep intelligent eyes and he saw that look Phil had talked about in Dementyev's eyes, the not quite twinkle of secret understanding. Joel felt safe in assuming that all those present knew Ustinov meant the helipots had been used in guiding the orbiting Sputniks. Without a word, the four men paused to acknowledge the Sputnik triumphs, then Ustinov continued, "But, there has been, has there not, a problem of sustained performance over time?"

"The metal alloy," Joe said, "used for the resistance winding in our prototypes was too brittle. That's why the heat, friction and tension were breaking them after 500 hours."

"Sometimes a bit less than 500 hours?"

"Well, I've fixed that," Joe said, "with a new alloy which makes a less brittle wire, one that should provide 1500 to 2000 hours of operation without any sacrifice of precision."

"Hmm, this is new? But it's nothing I've heard about."

"That's because I only tested the wire over the weekend."

"That will be a welcome development, in several areas." Again that look. *Maybe that's why they call him Uncle Mitya?*

"We'll have the new prototypes within weeks," Phil said.

Ustinov looked at Joel who met his gaze and smiled confidently.

THE NOBEL PRIZE FOR THE TRANSISTOR was now two years old and though semiconductor theories were therefore well known to Soviet engineers, it was true that virtually none of them believed transistors had any defense applications. Even Phil and Joe were not sure enough yet that solid state electronics was the only path to the future, to actively seek high-level advocates beyond what they had spoken about with Dmitry Ustinov.

On January 4 1958, Sputnik 1, the man-made satellite that began the space race, burned up as it fell from Earth orbit. It had flown for 92 days. Its beeps were monitored by radio listeners throughout the world. Though it stopped beeping after 22 days, the shiny sphere, less than two feet in diameter, passed overhead every ninety-six minutes. It was seen by millions. It had changed humanity's thinking and its future. Significantly for Joe Berg and Phil Staros, they learned that Sputnik's inception had begun when rocket engineer Sergei Korolev gave Dmitry Ustinov a report by a leading theorist, Mikhail Tikhonravov, who explained that other countries were working on creating Earth satellites and that this was a necessary step in developing inter-continental ballistic missiles. Sputnik had been built by the OKB-1 lab, a competitor of SL-11 and under the direction of the GKRE, (State Committee for Radio Electronics) which reported to Ustinov.

TWENTY-ONE

"...Considering her announced purpose of Communizing the world, it is easy to understand Russia's hope of dominating the Middle East...The Soviet rulers continue to show that they do not scruple to use any means to gain their ends. The free nations of the Middle East need, and for the most part want, added strength to assure their independence."
–from the Eisenhower Doctrine

ON JANUARY 31 1958, THE UNITED STATES, HAVING intended to be the first in space, began its attempt to catch up by launching the first successful American satellite, Explorer 1. Two days later the word Aerospace was introduced, joining Earth's atmosphere and outer space in one concept.

On February 26, Staros and Berg were awarded the Order of the Red Banner, a rare high honor in a country where neither the media nor the government created celebrities or heroes, but it was an honor that puzzled many of those who knew Joe and Phil only as hard working Czech engineers. The two Americans knew it was due to their wartime help. With this honor came much added prestige and a comfort zone of practical living. As weeks passed, they began taking an hour or two off at mid-day to go home to their wives for lunch, conjugal visits and a short nap. They also began spending Tuesdays in the Academy of Sciences Library to take notes on new developments as published in Western scientific journals. Also on Tuesdays they had dinner together with their wives at the foreigners only Evropeyskaya Hotel restaurant.

On March 11, a second B-47 bomber accidentally dropped an atomic bomb on Mars Bluff, South Carolina. Its conventional explosive trigger detonated and destroyed a house, injuring several people, but no nuclear explosion followed. At about the same time, yet another B-47 loaded with a Mark 36 hydrogen bomb, caught fire at an airbase in Morocco. The base was evacuated. The fire burned for hours, but there was no nuclear explosion. To some observers, such accidents seemed to present far greater dangers from nuclear weapons than the intense political threats.

In mid March, the US launched the Vanguard 1 satellite, followed in late March by the Explorer 3. On March 27 1958, Nikita Khrushchev became Premier of the Soviet Union. On April 3, Castro's revolutionary army began its attacks on Havana. From April 4 to April 7, demonstrators in Britain demanded the banning of nuclear weapons.

On April 14, as Sputnik 2 disintegrated during re-entry, young American pianist Van Cliburn won the Tchaikovsky International Competition for pianists in Moscow, an event which broke Cold War tensions and created one small area of common ground that would last for decades.

On May 9, Paul Robeson, with US passport reinstated, sang in a sold-out one-man recital at Carnegie Hall. His performance merited an encore a few days later.

It was about this time that Joe and Vera's second child, Robert Iosevich Berg, was born. Svetlana, tired of being the other woman, no longer a young twenty-something, left clear evidence of her presence in Phil's life. Anna could no longer ignore her suspicions. Though Phil's claims that Svetlana was only a way to keep his creative juices flowing somewhat appeased Anna, Svetlana's attempt to seize the upper hand resulted at last in her loss of contact with Phil who was far more interested in his work than in either woman.

Joe, on the other hand, became a doubly devoted husband and father, doting on his son, playing the viola and piano for Robert and Vivian. As Robert grew, he invented toys for him. One if the first toys that amused the little boy was a jumping jack, a loosely jointed stick figure attached to two thick wooden slats by heavy thread with a supporting brace halfway to the top so that when one end of the slats were squeezed the stick figure jumped wildly and surprisingly. Vera, seeing Joe's devotion to her and their children and his growing success in his job, did her best to overcome her objections to their cramped living quarters and the cold northern Russia weather. Vera and Joe would have two more children in quick succession, another girl, Alena, and another son, Anton, named by Vera after her father.

On May 15, the Soviet Union launched Sputnik 3.

On June 16, Imre Nagy, a leader of the 1956 Hungarian revolt, was hanged for treason in Hungary.

On July 26, Explorer 4 was launched and three days later, the US Congress created the National Aeronautics and Space Administration (NASA).

Admiral Aksel Berg's Moscow air defense 'system 'A', went on alert on July 30 1958, the world's first anti-ballistic missile defense set up. It would use the V-1000 missile to intercept enemy missiles which it was designed to track from a distance of about 430 miles, using a vacuum tube computer which could perform 40,000 operations per second.

On September 12, Jack St. Clair Kilby invented the first integrated circuit.

In early October 1958, Pioneer 1 was NASA's first satellite launch. On October 16, the first missile was launched from the USSR's Kazakhstan experimental missile defense facility, a V-1000.

Staros and Berg were now absolutely sure the future of computing was in semiconductors. They knew they needed major support to advance their idea against the wall of established Soviet belief in vacuum tubes. When Aksel Berg offered to introduce them to Andrei Tupolev, the famous aircraft designer, Phil quickly accepted. Tupolev, as it happened, had just witnessed the complete failure of a vacuum-tube-based would-be aircraft computer. He invited them for a visit and was impressed with their ideas. He shared with them his own history. "You know," he said, "you are dealing here always with an unpredictable Russian bear and I'm not talking only about Khrushchev or that scoundrel Stalin."

Joe practically jumped from his chair as though hit by high voltage. Tupolev nodded, "You seem surprised. But let me tell you I spent the war in Stalin's *sharashkas*, his prison design bureaus, designing bombers. That man was insane with mad paranoia and envy, a beast who nearly killed my friend Sergei Korolev."

Sergei Korolev was the father of Soviet space flight, and some would say mankind's father of space flight. At this time his leadership of the Soviet space program was a guarded secret, for fear of US sabotage or assassination.

Joe and Phil sat wide-eyed and dumb before Tupolev until Joe managed to say, "But surely Stalin did not know everything that was done in his—"

"—No," Tupolev interrupted firmly but gently, "Stalin knew everything and was personally and directly responsible for all of it."

"Well," Joe said, "even in Communism serious mistakes can be made."

"Communism! It's a rotten idea that has never worked and never will. And the Soviet state is the worst possible example, or the best example of what a failure it is. Communism! I begged them to rescue Korolev from Kolyma, and they did, almost too late; he was nearly dead, every bone showing, coughing, missing all his teeth. And who do you think designed the Sputniks?"

"But—"

"—Do you think for a minute that the work Aksel and I have done on cybernetics was possible without keeping it secret from the organs? (secret police) My friends, you are in a rotten spot and had better learn how to make the best of it, sooner rather than later."

Joe sat, more stunned than Phil.

"Well," Tupolev said "let's assume you are right about the future of operational control of aircraft and our future spacecraft. Let's assume that both will depend on transistors. Therefore, I'd like to introduce you to Aleksandr Shokin, the man in charge of the industrial use of transistors."

"Fine," Phil said, eager to make further contacts at upper levels.

"I'll make arrangements and get in touch when the time is

right," Tupolev offered his hand in farewell.

Once Aksel Berg's driver had dropped them off at SL-11, Joe was still struggling to absorb the shocking accusations Tupolev had leveled at Stalin, at Communism and the Soviet state. "His criticisms were extreme and irresponsible," Joe said to Phil.

"Perhaps his time in prison," Phil answered, "did some permanent damage to his opinions of the great helmsman."

"But he can say such things with apparent impunity!"

"Yes, that's because he's reached the point, through his vast abilities, of being untouchable. And Stalin is long gone."

"Yes, untouchable, precisely," Joe said. More than ever, seeing a living example before him, Joe vowed to achieve that same elevated status through his own abilities and contributions.

"More important," Phil said, "we should appreciate what trust he places in us to say those things."

"Yes," Joe said, "he apparently does not take us as complete fools."

The next day, Staros was invited to make a presentation before GKAT and GKRE in November, the two important ministries controlling the electronics industry. In November, as a result, of that presentation, SL-11 was authorized to start work on a prototype transistorized computer, even before finishing the improved helipot design for mass production.

CALLING WEST BERLIN A 'MALIGNANT TUMOR', Khrushchev gave the Western allies six months to conclude a peace treaty with both East and West Germany and the Soviet Union. Otherwise the USSR would conclude a peace treaty with East Germany, which would leave East Germany, having no treaties with the Western allies, to provide access to Berlin, and to control of the routes to Berlin.

On December 6, the 3rd launch of a US Thor space craft, carrying Pioneer 2, failed to ignite. On December 21, Charles de Gaulle, forced out of retirement, was elected president of France with a 78.5% mandate. On December 29, troops under Che Guevara begin t o invade Santa Clara, Cuba.

TWENTY-TWO

"When it comes to combating imperialism we are all Stalinists."   *--Nikita Khrushchev*

ON JANUARY 1 1959, CUBAN DICTATOR BATISTA FLED Havana as the forces of Fidel Castro advanced. The next day, as Castro's troops approached Havana, the USSR successfully launched the Luna 1 spacecraft from Kazakhstan's Baikonur Kosmodrome. On January 4, Cuban troops led by Che Guevara and Camilo Cienfuegos entered Havana. Many people in Havana welcomed the rebels and welcomed Fidel Castro himself the next day, even as his army began executing the worst of Batista's minions. The United States recognized the new Cuban government of Fidel Castro the next day.

Joe turned forty-three on January 1, though his Soviet passport showed him to be forty-one. With the new year, Joe and Phil were already working hard on the transistorized computer they had decided to call the UM-1. Having challenged orthodoxy, they were determined to prove it wrong. Um, in Russian, means intelligence; UM was also the initials of the long Soviet name for a computer, a machine that calculates.

The new resistance winding alloy Joe had devised for the helipots had proved itself so far, but specific values and smaller sizes were now demanded. "You give them something they like," Joe said, "they want more and better."

"Yankee ingenuity," Phil joked.

On February 6, at Cape Canaveral, the first successful test firing of a Titan intercontinental ballistic missile was made and, on February 17, the US launched the Vanguard II weather satellite. Useful science began to compete with stunning feats and military preparations.

By the end of 1958, Moscow had the first anti-missile

defense of any city in the world and fear of a US nuclear attack was high. The Soviet military began work on system A-35, designed at the Soviet Experimental Design Bureau OKB-30. A new missile, the A-350, was being designed at OKB-2. Unlike the V-1000, the A-350 was to have a nuclear warhead and be capable of intercepting several hostile incoming missiles outside the atmosphere simultaneously by using eight early warning stations and a central command center.

On March 16, Staros and Joe interviewed a young Polytechnic Institute graduate, Genrikh Romanovich Firdman (Later known as Henry Eric Firdman). They hired him as a junior engineer. Destined to become a major player in their lives and their work, Eric later described his first impression of the two men in his autobiography, *Maverick For Life*:

"Staros was shaved and cut his black curly hair short. I noticed that he had a strange habit of scratching it with his ring finger... His ears were clasped close to his skull. His nose was rather long, thickening on the way down, with wide nostrils looking at his neatly trimmed black mustache a la Clark Gable. However, the most remarkable part of his face was his eyes, large, dark brown, wide open and sparkling with humor. They seemed to live their own life, constantly changing their expression, sometimes to support and reinforce what he was saying, but sometimes doing something absolutely unrelated. It was like Staros was sending you a message that even though he was listening or talking to you, it was not as important as his thoughts that were far away from the conversation.

The taller man introduced himself as Josif Veniaminovich Berg, the SL-11 Scientific Director. He looked as disorderly as Staros was neat. His shirt was rumpled with one collar turned vertically up. His unimaginable multi-colored tie had a big asymmetric knot, and the shorter front part of the tie could not hide the longer back one. His trousers were too short for his

*long legs and exposed the long checked socks matching
neither his tie nor anything else he wore. Berg had a
long horse-like skull that was balding in spite of his
early forties and I couldn't help thinking that in a few
years his skull would look like the egg of a giant bird.
He was short-sighted and bespectacled. His glasses
magnified his sad, brown unmistakably Jewish eyes.
Berg's most remarkable feature was his looseness. He
was extremely flexible as if he consisted of joints only.
When he walked, it looked like his limbs were all on
their own, and neither they nor Berg himself cared
about their coordination."*

On April 9, NASA announced its selection of seven
military pilots, the Mercury Seven, to become the first US
astronauts, and on June 9, the US Navy launched the USS
George Washington, the first nuclear missile submarine. The
money being spent by the US and the USSR on space, bombs,
missiles and counter-missiles was comparable to World War II
budgets.

On June 23, Klaus Fuchs was released after only nine
years in a British prison, well before the end of his sentence.
Klaus was only forty-eight and was not a welcome visitor in the
United States. The British government considered offering him a
teaching position, but as London streets flashed by from the taxi
that took him to the airport, he felt no affinity for the new
London. As Herr Strauss, he landed in East Berlin to an official
welcoming committee to resume his scientific career in Dresden.

The first Soviet transistorized computer, SL-11's UM-1
prototype, was ready to perform in mid-July 1959. Among many
innovations created during the eight month development stage,
the two Americans had invented a much more efficient and
capacious memory unit. The UM-1 was tiny by Soviet computer
standards and could be lifted by one man to rest on a desk-top.
The little computer needed only the power of a 100 watt
lightbulb. While Nixon and Khrushchev, surrounded by shiny
home appliances in a model kitchen at the American National
Exhibition in Moscow—each arguing heatedly that his side's

economy worked better—discerning Soviet scientists were first hearing about SL-11's 'control computer'.

Shortly after US satellite Explorer 6 sent back the first picture of Earth from space in mid-August, Dmitry Ustinov dragged the top Soviet air force generals and other military brass up the stairs to the attic on Volkovskaya Street to meet Phil Staros and Josif Berg. When Joe and Phil began a UM-1 demonstration for these higher-ups, after it had run faultlessly for 200 hours, their revolutionary little computer crashed. Before Phil could become aware that the subject of his talk was dead, young Henry Eric Firdman connected a device which kept the UM-1's indicator lights flashing so that it looked alive. Partly on the strong testimony of previous witnesses, the demonstration was accepted in good faith. Not long after this successful event, Joe and Phil were both granted permission to purchase automobiles. They each decided on Grey Volgas, large sedans used mostly by government officials and the same model infamous as the Black Volgas, the KGB's midnight abduction vehicle of legend, the GAZ-21

ON SEPTEMBER 14 1959, THE SOVIET UNION

smacked Luna 2 into the Moon, the first man-made object to hit another solar body. Khrushchev arrived in Washington the next day to present Eisenhower with a souvenir memento of this triumph. Ike could not help thinking that any nation shooting the Moon could easily land an ICBM on Washington or New York. Two days later, on September 17, the first US Navy Navigation Satellite System was launched but didn't make orbit. On October 7, the USSR probe Luna 3 sent back the first photos of the far side of the Moon. On October 13, the successful launch of Explorer 7, which was designed to measure solar x-ray flux, trapped energetic particles and heavy primary cosmic rays. This did little to balance the striking propaganda and prestige advantage of the Soviets as seen by the world's emerging peoples.

On October 29, J. Edgar Hoover wrote to Special Agent in Charge (SAC) of the FBI's New York office suggesting that he "bring Communist Party leaders under suspicion of being FBI informants." The New York SAC immediately began reviewing

Party leaders with an eye to thus framing at least one of them. In a later memo, Hoover wrote, "definite plans can be made if the New York office first obtains a great deal of information concerning an individual, such as whether or not he uses a typewriter on a regular basis or uses longhand in his correspondence. The forgery of handwriting is preferrable." Hoover all the while turned over FBI reports to Meyer Lansky and would continue to do so, well into the 1960s.

In November, Dmitry Ustinov rearranged the USSR's electronics industry. SL-11 became Special Design Bureau 2, SKB-2 independent of OKB-998 and was moved from the attic on Volkovskaya street into the House of Soviets, the largest office building in Leningrad, a Stalinist edifice completed in early 1941 south of the downtown area and away from its frequent floods. *Dom Sovetov* had been used as the Leningrad Red Army command center during the Nazi siege. Empty concrete defense bunkers still guarded its street corners. When SKB-2 moved into their suite of offices on the third floor *Dom Sovetov* had become the home of the Soviet military electronics industries. Joe and Phil were able to drive their newly purchased Volga sedans less than three kilometers from Kutuzovskaya street down Moscovkii Prospect to park in the vast Moscovskii Square in front of *Dom Sovetov*. After passing through a voluminous marble 'interior vestibule' they were faced with shamefully feeble Soviet elevators, another result of the Soviet Union's primary funding of a fierce nuclear weapon and space competition against the much larger economy of the United States.

Staros took the big corner office with a balcony, secretarial outer office, sound-proof double doors and a personal phone line. He shared another phone line with Joe, whose large office was next door.

Their staff had grown to fifty people, but with the success and excitement generated by the UM-1, Joe and Phil were now in the center of a Soviet defense industry power struggle between two ambitious men: Valentin Smirnov, Phil's immediate boss, and Aleksandr Shokin, Smirnov's boss, who was the first deputy minister of GKRE and was in charge of industrial transistor development. Shokin, whose vision of microelectronics was much closer to their own than Smirnov's, had been recommended to them by Tupolev, the now untouchable aircraft designer. Staros, confident of the support of Tupolev, Ustinov and Aksel Berg, openly defied Smirnov in favor of Shokin, who needed the 'Czech' scientists as a stepping stone toward becoming a full Minister of the USSR, in a new ministry, created just for him.

TWENTY-THREE

"For the problems are not all solved and the battles are not all won—and we stand today on the edge of a New Frontier.... But the New Frontier of which I speak is not a set of promises—it is a set of challenges. It sums up not what I intend to offer the American people, but what I intend to ask of them."   *---John F. Kennedy*

JANUARY 2 1960, US SENATOR JOHN F. KENNEDY announced his candidacy for the Democratic presidential nomination. A week later, construction began in Egypt on the Aswan High Dam, a project long sought by Egypt and financed, after US Secretary of State John Foster Dulles reneged, by the USSR, which also supplied most of the engineering expertise.

On February 1, in Greensboro, North Carolina, four African-American students began a sit-in at a segregated Woolworth's lunch counter. Two days later, British Prime Minister Harold Macmillan delivered the *Wind of Change* speech to the South African Parliament in Cape Town signaling the opportunity for British colonies to become independent, a policy advocated by the US as a way of removing the temptation of Communism from subject peoples under imperialist rule. Ten days later, France tested its first atomic bomb in Algeria's Saharan desert.

In mid-March, Staros hired Mark Galperin to work in computer design with Eric Firdman, creating a life long competition and a long, but somewhat shorter, friendship.

On March 22, Arthur Leonard Schawlow & Charles Hard Townes received the first patent for a laser, using in-phase light waves, something Joel Barr had once dreamed of as a way to send information. He read the patent application closely, fascinated and confirmed in his theories.

On April 1, the US launched the first weather satellite, TIROS-1 and later Transit 1-b, the first step in a US Navy navigational system that would guide Polaris ballistic missile submarines. The United States was beginning to catch up with the USSR; the Soviet Union's achievements scored propaganda victories while the US concentrated more on science. About this time, the British cancelled their independent missile program to rely on US Polaris missiles for nuclear deterrents.

On May 1, Joe and his family marched in the May Day parade in Leningrad, something he'd always enjoyed from his days as a teenager in Brooklyn. He strode through the cool day amongst the banners of Marx and Lenin and the patriotic signs declaiming Communist mottos and victories.

As Joe enjoyed his favorite holiday, holding little Vivian's hand or carrying Robert, with often an arm around Vera, Soviet military intelligence was tracking a high altitude intruder in Soviet airspace fromt the USSR-Afghanistan border. MiG-19 fighter jets were sent to intercept and destroy it, but it was flying too high, some 20 kilometers above the earth's surface. Soviet radar tracked the spy plane first to the Baikonur and Plesetsk ICBM sites then to the Chelyabinsk-65 plutonium plant. Shortly thereafter, the Red Army fired three Soviet S-75 Dvina surface-to-air missiles. Only one S-75 performed, but guided by an improved version of the radar tracking system Joe and Phil had designed in Prague, the missile closed on its target. Armed with the Soviet version of the proximity fuse supplied to Aleksandr Feklisov in 1944 by Julius Rosenberg, the missile warhead exploded in its closest proximity to the Lockheed U-2 CIA spy plane. The explosion blew off the U-2's fragile wings and sent it into a nose dive. The pilot, Francis Gary Powers, on a routine espionage run over Sverdlovsk, deep in Soviet airspace, bailed out and was captured.

Khrushchev allowed Washington to believe pilot and plane had been destroyed. CIA director Allen Dulles fabricated and published the false story that the US plane downed in Russia was a NASA atmospheric research plane. He painted a U-2 spy plane with NASA colors and insignia and released photos to the world press. Only then did Khrushchev reveal that he had the spy pilot and his spy plane and that the Francis Gary Powers had explained his spy mission. When Khrushchev sprang this surprise, Eisenhower muttered to his secretary, "I wish I could resign." Then Nikita—often rude, never shy—accused the CIA of sending the U-2 deep into the Soviet Union solely to create an incident that would ruin the up-and-coming Paris peace talks.

Joe and Phil knew they were now part of the Soviet struggle for national survival and world leadership.

ON MAY 15 1960, SPUTNIK 4, AN UNCREWED prototype performed 64 orbits of the Earth, but the reentry maneuver failed, which didn't stop Khrushchev from demanding that Eisenhower apologize for the U-2 spy missions. He made a public apology a condition for his participation in the Paris summit.

Eisenhower refused to apologize.

On May 23, Israel's David Ben-Gurion announced that Adolf Eichmann had been captured and would be tried for the mass murders of Jews.

In June, Eric Firdman left SKB-2, afraid he'd never make enough money there to support a family. On July 1, a Soviet MiG-19 shot down a 6-man US RB-47 reconnaissance plane north of Murmansk in the Barents Sea. Two US Air Force officers were captured and placed in the Lubyanka's subterranean cells.

As Lyndon Baines Johnson traveled to Los Angeles for the Democratic Party's national convention in early July, he expected to receive the nomination for US President. He was the party favorite and J. Edgar Hoover was backing him with plenty of information on his sexually promiscuous rival, Senator John F. Kennedy. Hoover had snooped on Kennedy since before he came to Washington as a Senator. The facts that Kennedy suffered from Addison's disease and that his father had been pro-Nazi were spread around in the press. Hoover held in reserve Kennedy's flagrant womanizing, his support from organized crime and his sexual liaison during the war with one of Hitler's girlfriends. But on July 13, neither J. Edgar nor Johnson expected

Kennedy to win the nomination on the first ballot. It was over before Johnson could twist arms or use Hoover's heaviest dirt. When Johnson discovered he was not even being considered for Vice-President, he threatened to destroy Kennedy's family values image. Anguished and angry, but figuring it wouldn't mean much, Kennedy at last yielded. Johnson, knowing one out of four presidents died in office, accepted the odds. Edgar, like any competent KGB master under Stalin, had successfully subverted his government.

On July 28, two dogs by the names of Chaika and Lishichka were launched into space by the USSR, but an explosion killed the dogs.

On August 19, spy pilot Francis Gary Powers was sentenced to ten years imprisonment and hard labor. On the same day, the Soviet Union launched Sputnik 5 on a Vostok spacecraft which completed eighteen orbits with dogs Belka and Strelka, 40 mice, 2 rats and a variety of plants. The spacecraft returned to earth the following day with all animals alive and healthy The USSR was the first to recover living creatures from outer space. To follow up this feat, the Soviet Union sent a total of six dogs into space, but not all the missions were successful.

In September, Joe and Phil began work on the UM-1NKh, an advanced version of the prototype UM-1 aimed at mass production and meant to operate on airplanes and ships as fire control, and to operate radar stations, food processing plants and power plants.

On October 12, at a meeting of the United Nations General Assembly, the Philippine representative accused Nikita Khrushchev of hypocrisy for berating Western colonialists while he made colonies out of Eastern Europe. Khrushchev, forbidden to interrupt the Philippine representative, pounded on the table with his shoe, scandalizing all delegations including his own. Less than two weeks later, a rocket exploded at the USSR's Baikonur Space Center killing 91 people.

As Staros and Berg's upward movement brought them into conflict with their boss Smirnov and his struggle with Shokin, it was clear that these Soviet bosses considered it much easier and safer to copy western technology or to follow stolen advanced development plans than to invest in original research and pioneering efforts. Joe and Phil knew they had now both proved themselves far advanced beyond anything they'd done for the US military or any technology they'd stolen.

"We are nearly in a position to put Socialism and Communism ahead of the imperialists, Joe," Phil said. "Socialism could lead the way. Did you ever think?"

"Yes, we know the way and how to do it, among the few in the world. It would be our dream come true."

"This country has the possibility for a tremendous focus of resources and support," Phil said in hopeful awe.

On November 8 1960, John Kennedy defeated Nixon by the votes from a Chicago ward, bought by his father, Joseph Kennedy with help from the mob. In the popular vote, Kennedy led Nixon by only 49.7% to 49.5%, In Electoral votes, he won 303 votes to Nixon's 219 but fourteen electors from Mississippi and Alabama refused to support him because of his support for the civil rights movement. They voted for Senator Harry F. Byrd of Virginia, as did an elector from Oklahoma. Kennedy became the youngest elected president at 43.

There was as an immediate swelling of excitement and support as a major generational change seemed about to unfold. What did unfold would change the world and the lives of Phil and Joe indelibly.

On December 1, a massive 5-ton Soviet spacecraft containing animals, insects and plants was launched into orbit. Days later, Staros was invited to make a presentation to a colloquium of high-ranking military engineers about the future of computer technology. When he explained that within ten years there would be millions of computers in the world and that the time to leap ahead of the West was now, his discourse was almost entirely ignored. But even before the UM-1NKh prototype was complete, SKB-2 began work on the UM-2, radically designed to use the latest solid-state components with SKB's two bright young engineers, Galperin and Firdman, competing to make it better, faster, lighter and sexier.

TWENTY-FOUR

"I looked and looked but I didn't see God."
---Yuri Gagarin

ON JANUARY 3 1961, PRESIDENT EISENHOWER announced that the United States had severed diplomatic and consular relations with Cuba. At the US National Reactor Testing Station near Idaho Falls, Idaho, atomic reactor SL-1 exploded, killing three military technicians. On January 9, Britain revealed the discovery of a large Soviet spy ring in London. January 17, Eisenhower, in his Farewell Address warned of the increasing power of a 'military-industrial complex'.

On January 24, a B-52 Stratofortress, armed with two nuclear bombs, crashed near Goldsboro, North Carolina. The following day, Khrushchev freed the two American RB-47 pilots, an inaugural gesture to incoming President Kennedy who, in the first live presidential news conference, announced their release.

On January 31, Ham the Chimp, a 37-pound (17-kg) male, was launched into space aboard a Mercury-Redstone 2 rocket to test the capsule, designed to carry US astronauts into space. The next day, the US tested its first Minuteman 1 ICBM.

By February 4, two weeks into the Kennedy's presidency, there were already reports of strife between Attorney General Robert Kennedy and J. Edgar Hoover over RFK's declaration of war against organized crime. Hoover claimed that a special new task force to fight the mob would make the FBI look bad. When Hoover greeted Kennedy as incoming Attorney General with a memorandum that described Communism as America's greatest danger, Robert answered, "Why waste time prosecuting the Communist Party? It couldn't be more feeble and less of a threat, and besides, its membership consists largely of FBI agents." Joseph Kennedy urged both his sons to get along with Edgar but between Jack's being blackmailed into accepting Johnson as vice-president, and Robert being bluntly stonewalled on organized crime, they decided to get rid of Hoover altogether.

On March 1, another B-52 crashed near Yuba City, California after cabin pressure was lost and fuel ran out. Two nuclear weapons were recovered.

In early March, the Kremlin created the State Committee on electronic technology, GKET, the equivalent of a new ministry with Aleksandr Shokin as minister. Shokin's dream had come true. He knew Phil Staros and Joe Berg had helped make that happen and he made SKB-2 independent of Valentin Smirnov, the Leningrad region (Oblast) Party chief. But Smirnov and the Leningrad Obkom (Oblast Kommittee) were not done with them yet, though Phil and Joe were winning the early rounds. They were going to collide with Grigory Romanov, the man behind Smirnov.

"You played that just right, Joe told Staros in private.

"*We* did," Phil said. "I'm always listening to you, even when you're not speaking."

"So far, so good," Joe said. "What do we do next?"

"We need to create a whole system, not just one lab," Phil said.

"An R&D enterprise like Bell Labs, is sorely needed," Joe agreed. "What are our chances of doing that?"

"It will be *The Soviet Center for Microelectronics*," Phil said.

"With you as the big boss," Joe said jovially. "With a manufacturing arm like Western Electric." *For some interesting new inventions,* Joe thought.

"There will be a University of Microelectronics," Phil declared. "We will be the teaching fellows. It needs to be an entire new city."

"From your mouth to God's ears," Joe said. "Let's get back to work. I need to invent a way to develop bigger memories."

In April, reading about the trial of Nazi Adolf Eichmann in Jerusalem, Joe allowed himself a moment of lament: *What would Julie think? So little, so late? Sad retribution? You loved freedom, believed in it with all your heart, you were always yourself, never afraid, leading the way. They killed you for it. Symbolic union with the Nazi murders in the heart of America.*

Khrushchev was on a roll. On April 12, Yuri Gagarin became the first human in space, orbiting the Earth. Out of three candidates he was not picked as the strongest physical specimen nor as the most intelligent, nor as the best pilot, but as the most fearless. After gaining approval from the Politburo, a modified version of secret Chief Designer Sergei Korolev's R-7 rocket was used to launch Gagarin into orbit. Korolev served as capsule coordinator, and was able to speak to Gagarin inside the space craft. The first human in space and the first in Earth orbit returned to Earth via a parachute after ejecting at an altitude 23,000 ft.

SKB-2'S POTENTIAL MILITARY CLIENTS HEARD about the UM-2 and were reluctant to buy the UM-1.

"They're stalling," Phil said, "really because they're afraid of it, but they say it's because they'd rather have the UM-2. Whatever it is, the people who should have them, aren't buying."

"The UM-1 is already vastly better than anything they've got," Joe said, "better than anybody has right now, anywhere."

"They're stubborn,' Phil said.

"So put the UM-1 on the the commercial market, to automate canning production, wherever process control is needed in the economy. It would pay for itself almost anywhere complex work needs to be done. If the bosses don't want it, give it to the workers."

"You're brilliant you know that?" Phil said half-seriously. "You do, don't you?"

On April 17, an invasion attempt took place at the Bay of Pigs in Cuba by CIA supported Cubans seeking to overthrow Fidel Castro. Three days later, Castro announced that the invasion had been defeated and the invaders captured. The whole situation angered a lot of mean, nasty people.

On May 5, Alan Shepard became the first American in space aboard a Mercury-Redstone 3 in a sub-orbital flight. On May 8, British Soviet spy George Blake was sentenced to a record 42 years imprisonment.

When Joe heard that a US FCC chairman had described US commercial television as a 'vast wasteland', he commented, "Maybe we're not missing much…"

"Capitalism, what else can you expect?" Phil said.

"People fire-bombing a freedom riders bus? Beating to death any one who protests?"

On May 19, the Soviet Venera 1 became the first man-made object to fly-by another planet: Venus. It did not send back any data. On May 25 1961, President Kennedy spoke before a joint session of congress:

"…if we are to win the battle that is now going on around the world between freedom and tyranny, the dramatic achievements in space which occurred in recent weeks should have made clear to us all, as did the Sputnik in 1957, the impact of this adventure on the minds of men everywhere, who are attempting to make a determination of which road they should take. …it is time to take longer strides--time for a great new American enterprise--time for this nation to take a clearly leading role in space achievement, which in many ways may hold the key to our future on Earth.

…Recognizing the head start obtained by the Soviets … we …are required to make new efforts on our own. For while we cannot guarantee that we shall one day be first, we can guarantee that any failure to make this effort will make us last. … But this is not merely a race. Space is open to us now; and our eagerness to share its meaning is not governed by the efforts of others…

I therefore ask the Congress, above and beyond the increases I have earlier requested…to provide the funds which are needed to meet the following national goals:

First, I believe that this nation should commit itself to achieving the goal, before this decade is out, of landing a man on the Moon and returning him safely to the Earth. No single space project in this period will be more impressive to mankind, or more important for the long-

range exploration of space; and none will be so difficult or expensive to accomplish. ...But in a very real sense, it will not be one man going to the Moon...it will be an entire nation...

On June 3-4 1961, in Vienna, Kennedy and Khrushchev met for the first and only time. They were able to find a common language with regard to Laos, but their positions on West Berlin were diametrically opposed. Khrushchev demanded that the American, British, and French sectors be demilitarized. Kennedy replied that if Western troops left, the Western sector of the city would be completely surrounded and defenseless inside East Germany, and therefore he rejected the idea. Having used all means at his disposal, Khrushchev threatened to sign a separate peace treaty with the GDR and cease to recognize the West's rights over West Berlin. Kennedy, who viewed the Vienna summit as a way of getting to know the Soviet leader personally, didn't give an inch. As he left Vienna he commented, "Yes, it's going to be a cold winter!"

On July 21, Gus Grissom, piloting the Mercury-Redstone 4 capsule Liberty Bell 7, became the second American to go into sub-orbital space. Upon splashdown, the hatch prematurely opened and the capsule sank.

ON JULY 25 1961, KENNEDY SPOKE IN A WIDELY watched TV speech responding to Khrushchev's threat to West Berlin, promising support, open diplomacy, and force if necessary, reminding the world that West Berlin was under NATO protection.

"He's ordered triple the draft into the military," Joe said.

"He's calling up 250,000 reserves," Phil agreed. "And wants another $6 billion for guns, rockets and bombs."

"He's telling US citizens near the big cities to build fallout shelters below their basements or in their back yards."

"The cold war is getting colder," Phil said, "and hotter. They're going to defend Berlin to the death"

TWENTY-FIVE

"Under the leadership of the Party, under the banner of Marxism-Leninism, the Soviet people will build Communist society. The Party solemnly proclaims: the present generation of Soviet people shall live in Communism."   *--Nikita Khrushchev*

AUGUST 6, SOVIET KOSMONAUT GHERMAN TITOV became the second human to orbit the Earth after Yuri Gagarin and the first to be in outer space for more than one day. Moscow's answer to Kennedy's West Berlin speech came a week later: Berlin was to be cut in half by a wall. The underground trains that allowed free passage without identity checks between the two parts of the city, but also between the two enemy camps, were also shut down. Construction of the Berlin Wall began forming a clear boundary between Western Europe and Eastern Europe.

On September 1 1961, shortly after building the wall, and after a three-year moratorium, the USSR resumed its nuclear tests in the Novaya Zemlya archipelago with a series of 50 megaton plus thermonuclear explosions. Around the world, people feared the Berlin crisis could lead to nuclear war. The bombs were getting bigger and proliferating.

Dmitry Ustinov was awarded the Hero of Socialist labor for a second time from Nikita Khrushchev for his work in ensuring that the first man to orbit the earth was a Soviet kosmonaut, Yuri Gagarin.

The 22nd Congress of the Communist Party of the Soviet Union was held October 17-31 1961. It made the Sino-Soviet split official, the last to be attended by the Chinese Communist Party.

On October 27 1961 NASA began the Apollo program with a test of a Saturn rocket that would eventually launch the Apollo missions. It was a major escalation of the space race. Joe and Phil listened carefully. They knew their work was now connected to Soviet space programs.

On October 27, a standoff between Soviet and American tanks in Berlin heightened Cold War tensions. On October 30, the USSR detonated a 58-megaton hydrogen bomb known as Tsar Bomba, the largest ever man-made explosion. On October 31, Joseph Stalin's body was removed from the Lenin Mausoleum and days later Stalingrad was renamed Volgograd.

On December 2, in a nationally broadcast speech, Fidel Castro announced that he was a Marxist-Leninist and that Cuba would adopt socialism as its form of government. A little over a month later, Cuba and the Soviet Union signed a trade pact. Communism had spread to within ninety miles of US shores.

US RANGER 3 WAS LAUNCHED JANUARY 26 1962 to study the Moon, but then missed the Moon by 22,000 miles. On January 27, the Soviet government changed all place names honoring Stalin's henchmen: Molotov, Kaganovich and Malenkov.

On February 1 1962, the FBI sent agents to Rio de Janeiro to capture Joel Barr, ignoring reports from Morton Nadler that Sarant and Barr must be in Russia. February 3, the US embargo against Cuba was announced and four days later, all Cuban imports and exports were banned.

On February 10, captured CIA U-2 spy pilot Francis Gary Powers and American student, Frederic Pryor, were exchanged for the Soviet hollow nickel spy Rudolf Abel at the Glienicke Bridge in Berlin. After his return to Moscow Abel was rewarded with the Order of Lenin.

The lines between peace activists and spies were blurred on February 12 when six leading members of the Campaign for Nuclear Disarmament were found guilty of violating the Official Secrets Act. Three days later, Joe and Phil completed the prototype of UM-1NKh, a new milestone in Soviet technology though not ahead of US developments. The two were riding successes and didn't remember or heed the warnings: *Hire fewer Jews.*

On February 20, John Glenn became the first American to orbit the Earth, three times in 4 hours, 55 minutes. On February 22, Joe and Phil received their first of dozens of Soviet patents for the ferrite memory cube they had invented for the UM-1 in 1958.

ON MARCH 4 1961, PHIL AND JOE HEADED for Moscow in Joe's Volga. Though Joe preferred traveling by plane, he enjoyed driving and Phil didn't mind taking turns. They'd agreed the long road trip would give them a chance to discuss Phil's presentation of their plans to government officials in the Kremlin, for an entire city to be called The Center for Microelectronics. In addition to such important business, Phil, especially, had in mind the fabulous March 8th parties always given to celebrate International Women's Day, which seemed to loosen women's inhibitions and which provided working women a feast of opportunities and left housewives to suffer shortages.

Nearing Moscow, when Joe had had plenty of time to repeat the question, full of skepticism, but he asked again, "Are you sure it's wise to ask top leadership for a whole new city?"

"Don't forget what we are offering them; the future we all dream of. World leadership."

"Built from scratch? A city? When's the last time they build one."

"They do it all the time."

Secretly Joe admired Phil's *khutzpah* and listened with admiration as Phil concluded, "I'll see how it goes, play it by ear. Stop somewhere quick, will you? I've got to pee. We could both use a good stretch before hitting town."

The sun was already heading for the southwestern horizon when Joe pulled over at an extensive construction site only twenty kilometers from Moscow, near the village of Kryukovo. Stepping well away from the road, Phil commented, "They're already building a new city right here. How can whatever this is be more important than the vital future of microelectronics? Is this place going to be key to competing with the West and defending socialism from military attack? I don't think so!" Phil's mustache moved decisively from side to side as he shook his last drops to the ground. Just then a man approached them, clearly curious as to who these intruders were and what they were doing. Seeing steam arising from excavated earth, he seemed to relax, "You just stopped for relief, did you?"

"What is this place?" Phil asked. "What are they building here?"

"Who are you that I should inform you? I'm the foreman and supervisor here."

"I'm Director of The Center for Micro Electronics, on my way to the Kremlin for meetings with the leadership. So tell me, even for a Sunday, it looks pretty dead here. Where's your machinery, your cranes, your bulldozers?"

"We're building a city here for the manufacture of ball bearings and timing devices."

"Timing devices?"

"Well, clocks."

"Clocks? They're building clocks here?" Phil was beside himself yet nearly laughing, "You'd better get cracking. Clocks are vital; you can't sit around."

"We've been halted, for lack of funding, I've been told."

"This is it!" Phil's eyes beamed bright at Joe, "What can they say? If they've started a city for clocks, they can build a city for what is far more important, right here. The Center for Microelectronics. Vast manufacturing; state-of-the-art R and D."

The caretaker was taken aback by Phil and even suspicious, but Phil reassured him with a friendly clap on the shoulder, "Today is your lucky day; you'll get your city; only it won't be for clocks. At least not the kind you hang on the wall."

Back at the car, Phil took the wheel and, knowing Joe was waiting for some indication that he hadn't lost his mind, he said, "They've cleared a huge track of land, they've made already a large investment, but they've realized there's a problem with priorities. All it will take is the right nudge."

Content to admire Phil's daring while firmly retaining his doubts, Joe said, "That will need to be some nudge."

MARCH 22, J. EDGAR HOOVER WAS SUMMONED to the White House. President Kennedy intended to force his resignation. But Hoover brought proof not only of Kennedy's womanizing but of his close relationship with Chicago mob boss Sam Giancana, who Edgar knew had been involved in the CIA plot to kill Fidel Castro. Edgar had wiretaps that proved Judith Cambell, a Giancana girlfriend, was one of John Kennedy's lovers, often at the White House. Edgar left the White House, still FBI director.

TWENTY-SIX

"Orbiting Earth in the spaceship, I saw how beautiful our planet is. People, let us preserve and increase this beauty, not destroy it!" — *Yuri Gagarin*

BY APRIL 1 1961, THE UM-1NKH WAS SET FOR MASS production. Two weeks later, with SKB-2 now designing components for Soviet Intercontinental Ballistic Missiles, Sergei Khrushchev, Nikita Khrushchev's son and the engineer in charge of ICBM production, came to visit the SKB-2. Phil had a chance to speak to him and outlined the course of the future should microelectronics be taken seriously. Sergei Khrushchev was one of the few in Russia who knew who Joe and Phil really were. Impressed, he spoke to his father about his interesting visit to their lab. Nikita Khrushchev decided to visit SKB-2 and to meet the two American scientists. Phil and Joe were informed of the great honor and opportunity. Days later, Joe appeared in Phil's office, saying, "See what I've made for Comrade Khrushchev." He held out what looked like a hearing aid.

"Stop joking. We need him to like the UM-2."

"He needs to like us," Joe said. "This will be his new personal radio. Try it."

Phil tried turning the miniature volume control. He seemed pleasantly surprised, but said, "We can't show him that; he'll think we're wasting precious time and materials making toys to pander him."

"The point you want to make here," Joe said, "is not so much that the UM-2 can control a spacecraft. The first point to make is miniaturization itself. We'll set up a comparison between the standard home radio set, which weighs thirteen kilos, and this, weighing a few grams. We'll tune in the Moscow radio station. He'll be able to see that it's a real broadcast. That'd be far more dramatic than telling him the UM-2 can out-do a current computer that weighs ten tons and takes up a whole room—even if he believed us, which he wouldn't."

"You used four engineers for weeks making this? While their assignments languished?"

"Five engineers, but they worked off the clock, after their assignments."

"Let's hope your extensive investment works."

Joe retrieved the world's first miniature radio from Phil, saying. "Yes, let's hope so. I'll set it up."

MAY 4 1962, WELL-PREPARED, JOE AND PHIL watched from their third floor windows at *Dom Sovetov* as Nikita Khrushchev arrived in the square below with a large, high-level entourage.

After greeting Khrushchev, Marshal Dmitry Ustinov, GKET Minister Aleksandr Shokin, two dozen military higher-ups and most significant for their future, Admiral Sergei Gorshkov, Commander-in-Chief of the Soviet Navy, Phil led them into the room adjoining his office which Phil and Joe used as their private lab. There, set on a table were the standard Soviet *Motherland* radio and Joe's micro receiver. Khrushchev took a liking to the miniature radio as soon as Staros helped him put it in his ear, smiling as he adjusted the volume himself.

When it came time to demonstrate the UM-2, an hermetically sealed steel box with wires crossing the desktop in various directions, Khrushchev asked, "Since I am not the scientist you are, tell me what this box will do for the Soviet Union, in your opinion." The supreme commander's voice was not unfriendly and Phil took heart:

"This computer will control missile firing on a submarine, aircraft navigation or guide a spacecraft in flight. Or, it can automate a large factory, for example."

Khrushchev smiled as he adjusted the radio volume in his ear. "It seems hard to believe, but I find it easier to believe, knowing you have made a radio this small, with such clear sound. What is the key to these new products would you say?"

"It is *mikroelektronika*. But what is most important, Nikita Sergeyevich, microelectronics will be an international race for leadership that will make the arms race and the space race quite secondary." Phil's passionate belief combined with his warm Greek charm held every one in the room nearly spellbound. Joe was proud of his friend, silently cheering him on. They had talked about this so often.

"The race to develop miniature electronics and the most powerful and versatile computers," Phil continued, his open face and direct eyes meeting Khrushchev's, "will be the key to all other economic and military competition. The computer calculations needed to guide vehicles in space and control living conditions for pilots are on such a large scale that vacuum tube technology cannot cope with it."

"Certain of my aids," Khrushchev said "who are more knowledgeable about these things than I am, tell me that you are as sincere and worthy as you seem. They tell me neither your ideas nor inventions are to be dismissed. I must say that today confirms your record of achievement on behalf of the Soviet Union and confirms what has been said in your favor."

"Thank you for your confidence, Nikita Sergeyevich." Phil understood that Khrushchev was fully aware of what Al, Joel, and Julius had done during the war and afterwards. With a magnetic smile and the slightest movement of his mustache, Phil asked, "May I elaborate on my ideas for a Center for Microelectronics?"

"I'd be glad to listen," Khrushchev said.

"Come let me show you," Phil offered. With that, the entourage followed Staros into another room empty except for a large poster easel. In less than five minutes with deft use of a pointer and dramatic page turning flourishes, Phil explained: "To compete successfully in microelectronics, there would need to be research institutes attached to design bureaus working directly with a manufacturing plant. There would be an engineering university and technical training schools. Housing for workers and directors would be situated near their work."

Khrushchev asked, "In your view, this is the way to win the *mikroelektronik* race you are talking about?" The new word was still being tasted on Nikita's lips.

"I believe it is the way to protect the Soviet Union from losing world leadership to our adversaries."

"My instincts have not always been wrong," Khrushchev said, "and now they tell me that your devotion to our cause, which has been unerring, would make it no mistake to trust that your knowledge is superior, and Comrade Ustinov reminds me of other contributions you have already made to our defenses. But tell me, where such a city as you envision might be located, where the necessary resources could be supplied close at hand. Are you thinking of Novosibirsk or Irkutsk?"

"As it so happens," Phil's eyes twinkled in his warm, smile, "I know of a perfect place, a few kilometers from Moscow, near the village of Kryukovo."

Joe smiled, thinking, *Where he marked his territory with a long, leisurely piss.*

"Comrade Staros, why this particular place?" Khrushchev asked.

"The construction of a city there has already begun, but has, apparently, been abandoned." Staros knew that most in the entourage were aware of the USSR's severe shortage of funds, and would suspect that economic difficulties had halted the project.

"Do you happen to know," Khrushchev asked, "what this new city was originally designed to do, before construction was halted?"

"I was told it would be a manufacturing center for clocks."

"And you believe a center for microelectronics is much more important than our country's need for keeping time?" There was teasing irony in Khrushchev's tone.

"I must say that I do. Microelectronics and the devices it makes possible will soon be integral to almost every aspect of human life, especially in weapons, counter-weapons and in space."

"Well, it may surprise you, but I am going to give my full support to converting this clock factory into advancing our nation's new electronic technology."

This caught Joe and Phil by complete surprise and no less so the Chairman's own entourage. Was it simply a gesture of approval? But the pleasure Khrushchev took in his next statement made everyone wonder if he might be serious:

"As you no doubt are aware, I have been a strong supporter of our efforts in space and in a strong missile defense system, and generally in ways to reduce a massive and expensive army in favor of modern technology. But perhaps you are not aware," Nikita turned to look around the room at Phil and Joe and at each of his own ministers and military leaders, "not aware of my thoughts on what we must do to catch and surpass capitalist societies, thoughts about the best steps to achieve such goals and I can find no contradiction to my instinct that your vision is one of the best choices we can make in this direction. Your past history of devotion to our cause, your consistent successes in advancing our technical science, all leave me with no better or similar prospects. I am convinced that *mikroelektronika* science is the key to our future. Therefore I will shortly issue a decree that initiates work on your city."

For a moment there was only a stunned silence in the room. Joe's heart beat fast as he watched Phil recover and say, "Yes, I'm quite surprised, but I have to agree that implementation is urgent, that not a moment should be lost. I had no idea it could happen so quickly."

"I would not have come if I had not had strong hopes that meeting you would confirm my suspicions."

"Your faith and confidence are among the greatest honors of my life," Phil said.

"Well then," the sly, rotund, uneducated peasant said, "we both have work to do. Before I go, I must warn you that my decision will not make everyone happy. There will be detractors and foot draggers. Not so much enemies of the people I would say, but enemies of your success. I'd like to know that my Party is supporting you any way they can, that our bureaucracies are not causing delays. Let me ask you, are you currently receiving the full support of your Leningrad Party leadership?"

Before Phil could answer, the Leningrad Party chairman, Vassily Tolstikov stepped forward: "Of course we have fully supported KB-2, and we stay in close contact in order to respond to the needs of this important design bureau."

Aleksandr Shokin, among others in the room, but especially Joe and Phil, knew this was a boldfaced lie. Khrushchev turned to the two Americans to look at them through his rimless glasses and say, "The bureaucrats will try to stall you and highjack you. If you have any problems with them, contact me directly through my assistant, Grigory Shuisky."

As Shuisky acknowledged this with a formal smile, handing them each his official contact card, Phil and Joe nodded, unable to speak. Khrushchev had warned the Leningrad party not to interfere.

"I can see you are surprised," Khrushchev said, "but have no doubt, you will meet opposition and you will need my help."

Almost as if in a trance, they said goodbye and the powerful crowd departed. They watched still quiet from the windows on the third floor as Khrushchev and his high echelons of military science rejoined the large dark sedans that had waited, engines running, in the vast square below. Only as the caravan swung around and drove away, did their stunned silence explode into whoops of joy. Soon the the entire staff had heard the news. But there was one celebration that only two people in the USSR could share. Once order had been restored, when Joe and Phil were alone, they looked into each other's eyes as tears came and Joe said in English, "This is not just good news; this is even beyond our wildest dreams."

Smiling with all the fond magnetism familiar from their earliest friendship, Phil asked, "Could I be hearing things or did he say he would issue a decree within weeks?"

"'Construction to start this summer.'"

"How about Tolstikov's face, right after making him lie," Phil said, "when Nikita Sergeievich told us to report him if he tried to stop us."

"It's Romanov who scares me," Joe said. "He was unmoved. He hates us as foreign Jew spies. He has no respect for Khrushchev either."

"He could become a major figure in Soviet affairs," Phil said. "He'd make a staunch enemy.

Only the next day would Khrushchev's visit and all it promised seem real, when the feeling of a supreme victory would overcome their doubts and shock and they were capable of thinking clearly: *nothing can stop us now. We are going to be untouchable.*

TWENTY-SEVEN

"...our leadership in science and in industry...require us to make this effort, to solve these mysteries, become the world's leading space-faring nation."
--John F. Kennedy

AS WEEKS WENT BY, THEIR RELATIONSHIP TO Khrushchev's aides reassured them that their dream would come true. Joe and Phil were consulted constantly on what departments of research there should be, what sort of manufacturing facilities were needed? So elated that they were almost beyond the considerations of daily routines and responsibilities, they made trips to and from Moscow to consult and inform on plans for labs and housing in the new city construction site. But then:

On May 30, Joe boarded an Aeroflot flight from Leningrad to Moscow, headed for meetings with manufacturers interested in using the UM-1NKh for process control automation. Sitting next to him in one of Aeroflot's comfortable Ilyushin Il-18s was a stunningly attractive blue-eyed blonde Siberian woman, Elvira Valueva, a 22-year-old engineer also traveling to Moscow for professional meetings at an outlying factory. By the time the plane was in the air, Joe had learned her name, age and occupation. When they landed in Moscow, he insisted on conducting her to her hotel. By this time, Joe kept his car in Moscow while they used Phil's Volga in Leningrad. On the way to her hotel, he invited Elvira to a concert in town and, upon parting with her, he presented his business card with their Metropole hotel telephone number jotted in on the back. "Call me if you'd like to attend a concert."

Elvira did call and Phil answered. As Phil handed Joe the phone, he noticed how Joe blushed as Elvira asked where to meet him near the theatre.

"No," Joe said, "I'll be there at your hotel to pick you up at seven."

"Who is this person?" Phil asked when Joe put down the phone. "Is the devoted and faithful Czech paterfamilias tempted to stray?"

"You'll see who she is, soon enough," Joe said. He was elated; he'd managed to get tickets from a Metropole hotel colleague for that evening's Benny Goodman concert, the warmest spot in the brief 'Khrushchev thaw' and a major cultural event, to be attended by Nikita himself.

The concert was stunning. There were lines of people outside without tickets. Some pressed their ears to the building's wall, hoping to hear the high notes from inside. The crowd inside went wild. Nikita Khrushchev led the applause.

Joe was in love. Who of us can deny that such things happen? Suddenly life changes; there is very little considered choice involved. The next few days were a whirlwind of love and romance. Joe drove Elvira 200 kilometers to her factory, they camped in the woods on the way, cooking over an open fire. He introduced her to the American custom of roasting marshmallows and she was amused by the carefree indulgence and vicarious gluttony of it. Pink Russian marshmallows. Later they camped in a tent on the site of the future Center for Microelectronics. Joe told her, "I love you very much but you should know that I'm married, have children and will never leave my wife."

"I, too, am married, to an Aeroflot engineer. But I should also tell you that I married him after only knowing him a few days. I was desperate to get out of my father's house."

"Do you have children then?"

"No…He seems not very interested in children."

"But you are?"

"…Yes, I think so."

THE DAY AFTER MEETING ELVIRA VALUEVA on the plane to Moscow, a meeting that was going to change his life forever, Joe saw an article, *Escape From Alcatraz* about three men disappearing from the island prison. He thought sadly, *That's where they're keeping Morty.* Joel had not been as close to Sobell as he was to Julius, but the executions had brought him closer to Morty, in heart and mind.

On June 15, Eric Firdman met Staros in Moscow hoping to be re-hired into what was now KB-2, an independent firm within the State Committee on Electronic Technology (GKET). In discussing and describing the meeting with Khrushchev six weeks earlier, Phil took full credit for the idea of charming the powerful Party Chairman with the micro receiver. It was not the first nor would it be the last time he took credit for Joe's inventions. Anxious to re-hire Firdman, Phil divulged that Khrushchev had promised to build their dream city. Firdman gladly agreed to rejoin Staros.

As the summer warmed and the white nights illuminated Leningrad, Elvira invited Joe and Phil to bohemian parties and musical gatherings frequented by her young crowd. As the romance bloomed between Joe and Elvira, the two American engineers joined the young people, Phil playing his guitar and Joe the viola. Joe's love for Elvira opened his heart to the youth of Leningrad and Moscow and their unruly musical tastes. Little did they suspect that they were meeting the underground musical artists who would soon become tomorrow's sensational musical stars.

JULY 10 1962, AT&T'S TELSTAR, THE WORLD'S first commercial communications satellite, was launched into orbit and began operating the next day. Less than two weeks later, Telstar relayed the first trans-Atlantic television signals.

On July 30, KB-2 moved to Radishchev Street, a move which solidified its independence from other design bureaus. The security by the KGB was, if anything, even more careful. KB-2 was a top secret laboratory. As usual, this security level did not bother those who worked there; they were glad to go through the formal nods and occasional document presentations required to maintain the dignity of their comrades at the entrance desk.

On August 8, Khrushchev initiated the Center for Microelectronics by decree. It was to be as Staros had imagined when they stopped to urinate at the site near Kryukovo. Staros drove the first stake in the ground to begin new construction. The caretaker who'd caught them urinating was there, a stunned smile on his face. With another Khrushchev decree, Staros was made a member of the CPUSSR. But, in bypassing many of the ordinary initiation processes for Communist Party membership and by awarding Staros a remarkably low membership number, a number lower than some members of the Politburo and Central Committee. Thus, this decree angered some hard fought Soviet Communists and set them against the two Czech scientists.

On August 27, NASA launched the Mariner 2 space probe and on September 12 1962, at Rice University in Houston Texas President Kennedy gave a speech entitled, *We Choose to go to the Moon.* A day later, behind the sound lock closed doors of Phil's office, Joel read portions of Kennedy's speech aloud:

...Those who came before us made certain that this country rode the first waves of the industrial revolutions, the first waves of modern invention, and the first wave of nuclear power, and this generation does not intend to founder in the backwash of the coming age of space. -we mean to lead it. For the eyes of the world now look into space, to the Moon and to the planets beyond...

We set sail on this new sea because there is new knowledge to be gained, and new rights to be won...and only if the United States occupies a position of pre-eminence can we help decide whether this new ocean will be a sea of peace or a new terrifying theater of war. ... Its hazards are hostile to us all. Its conquest deserves the best of all mankind... Some say, why choose the Moon? Why choose this as our goal? And they may well ask, why climb the highest mountain?

...We choose to go to the Moon in this decade...because it is hard, because that goal will serve to organize and measure the best of our energies and skills, because that challenge is one ...we are unwilling to postpone...

"...to be sure, we are behind, and will be behind for some time in manned flight. But we do not intend to stay behind...

...This year's space budget is three times what it was in January 1961, greater than that of the previous eight years combined, $5.4 billion per year, a staggering sum, though somewhat less than we pay for cigarettes and cigars...

"He sounds deadly serious despite his crack about the expenditures on tobacco," Phil said.

"They're taking up the challenge of the Sputniks," Joe said, "and he's saying they have the money to do it."

"Capitalism sees profits ahead," Phil said.

"But you know what this means, for us don't you?" Joe said. "We're going to be in the middle of a space race; we're going to be vital to the Soviet race to the Moon."

"It means we're going to work very hard and our laboratories will get much larger," Phil said. "Our Center for Microelectronics will be the essential instrument of victory in this struggle, a city devoted to developing the science and technology to achieve it supremacy in space and in microelectronics."

"It's the challenge we've been looking for..." Joe said.

"I feel myself ready," Phil said, don't you?" It was hardly a question.

On October 3, Walter Schirra orbited the Earth six times in the US Sigma 7 space capsule.

PICTURES OF SOVIET MISSILE SILOS IN CUBA, taken by a U-2 spy plane on October 14 1962, showed intercontinental ballistic missiles being installed. President Kennedy was immediately informed. Eight days later, on live television, he told the world. Two days after that, the US Navy confronted a Soviet freighter on its way to Cuba with more missiles. The vessel turned back. On October 28, Khrushchev announced that he had ordered the removal of the Cuban missile bases. Three days later, the Soviets began dismantling the silos. A week later, Richard Nixon conceded the California governor's race: "This is Richard

Nixon's last press conference," he said, "you won't have Nixon to kick around any more."

For Joe and Phil, the nearly deadly direct confrontation between their new homeland and their old was sobering. There could be no hesitation now in their determination to further Soviet interests. For Joe, killing Julie and Ethel had galvanized his loyalty to their cause.

In November the Soviet Central Committee expanded the electronics development budget, further supporting the Center for Microelectronics city near Moscow.

One Day in the Life of Ivan Denisovich was published in the Soviet literary magazine *Novy Mir*, a perfect literary gem which joined and sustained the wave of change under Khrushchev.

On December 14, the Mariner 2 flew by Venus and sent back data. The US science premise and purpose began to shorten the substantial Soviet lead in space and began to vie with them for propaganda advantages.

Despite the general suppression of religion by the ruling Soviet Communist Party, Vera Bergova was raised a devout Catholic and Christmas was the most important day of the year for her up to the time she met Joe. In love with her, Joe had no problem entering into the spirit of the season with her, making presents for his children, buying special treats, getting good tickets to good shows. That was the way it had been. But 1962 had been one helluva year: the supreme leader of half the world building them a city and a blonde angel falling in love with him. So it was time to celebrate with his loving wife and family. And, he couldn't very well neglect Elvira. So, as the Christmas days came he comforted himself that at least it wasn't Hannukah. *The new year is coming.* He was nearly 47 though listed as 45, but keeping up with Phil and Vera, Vivian, Robert Anton and Alena and consulting constantly on the construction of the new city, he arrived home for Christmas dinner figuratively out of breath, like a passenger who has held up the train, afraid he's forgotten his baggage.

Vera had the table set, candles lit. It was crowded in their little apartment, but they'd all grown used to it, even Vera. Joe came in pulling treats and gifts from his pockets and bags. The children screamed and laughed, delighted not only with his generosity but loving the whole production of his entrance and the show he put on for them.

"Not until after your dinner," Vera cried, "which will be ready soon. Robert was about to cross the line from admiring his favorite special chocolate holiday treat wrapped in cellophane, to sticking his finger under the cellophane corner and lifting it away.

"She knows what you are thinking," Vivian said to Robert even as she patted her own sample of the same traditional holiday baked fudge.

"Here," Vera said, "put all the candies and cakes on the counter here till after dinner."

No one moved. Anton and Alena watched open mouthed to follow the example of their older brother and sister. Joe busied himself with hanging up his overcoat, emptying his satchel of bread and wine, tucking away several small items for later.

Vera noticed that the wine he had brought was not their traditional Georgian wine, one that Stalin drank and Vera liked in spite of her dislike for the fallen helmsman. She retrieved the treats and put them up on the counter while suffering complaints from her children. "It doesn't matter if you get the same one," she told them. "You are lucky to have any. On this rare occasion she insisted on at least a sort of prayer of gratitude for the health of the family and the good dinner she had prepared."

Dinner was served and, traditional as usual, it was plentiful, creative and delicious. The children at last reached the time for enjoying their treats and trying out new games and puzzles, but Vera stopped them:

"Now it is time for the special Christmas cheesecake." But suddenly a thought struck her and she looked at Joe. "Where's the apricot cheesecake?" She'd realized he didn't have it when he came in.

At first mention of Christmas Cheese Cake, Joe had gone pale and suddenly crestfallen. This special cheese cake was part Vera's Christmas celebration not only from her earliest memories as a child, but all the years of her marriage to Joe, Joe had honored it by always bringing home her special treat.

"I can't believe you forgot?" Vera said incredulously.

"Well no," he fairly stammered, "I've been so busy lately, and—"

"First it's a different wine, not the one we always liked, but you forget to get the cheesecake?" There was more wonder than rebuke in her voice.

"And the first place," he said feebly, "the regular place... didn't have it—"

She stopped him with her hurt but stern look and he said, "I can't believe it. I forgot all about it. I'll get it tomorrow and we'll have it tomorrow night." But his voice trailed off to nothing as he realized he was only making things worse.

TWENTY-EIGHT

"Could anyone in his right mind speak seriously of limited nuclear war? It should be quite clear that the aggressor's actions will instantly and inevitably trigger a devastating counterstroke by the other side. None but completely irresponsible people could maintain that a nuclear war may be made to follow rules adopted beforehand, with nuclear missiles exploding in a "gentlemanly manner" over strictly designated targets and sparing the population."
--Marshal Dmitry Ustinov

THIS WAS A TIME, EARLY 1963, WHEN JOE AND PHIL moved back and forth from Leningrad to Moscow, between KB-2 and their satellite dream city, semi-delirious with happiness and pride. But, with Khrushchev's sponsorship, came growing opposition to the two high-flying, *weird* Czechs. Leningrad Party bureaucrats and KB-2 competitors increased their scrutiny and amplified their criticism. But all the while, the two American engineers worked with Firdman and Galperin on perfecting the design of the UM-2. They all knew that it was a startling advance in computing power. Not only had they designed a versatile and powerful computer, Staros and Berg solved the problem of unreliable transistors by designing circuits that contained enough redundancy, by asking the same questions twice, so to speak, or three times, enough to assure reliable system results. Furthermore, they had hermetically sealed the electronics and controlled the temperature and humidity, what they called the 'micro-climate', inside this sealed shell. 'Micro-climate' electronics was a new term for everybody.

Eric Firdman and Mark Galperin, as they consulted and

helped complete UM-2 hardware and software, became its salesmen. With 'first form' top military clearance they visited hundreds of the top secret firms and installations which were developing and manufacturing electronically controlled weapons.

JANUARY 15, 1963, THE MOSCOW EXECUTIVE

Committee named the new microelectronics satellite city, *Zelenograd*, Green City, to be a home to 65,000 people. Zelenograd began to grow like a mushroom. Phil assumed he would be named general director with Joe as chief scientist and he enjoyed an expanding ego: their dreams were about to all come true. The name of its scientific institute was not to be The Center for Microelectronics but The Science Center. Why tip off sneaky American spies? It was all entirely glorious.

JOE'S MARRIAGE HAD PROBLEMS BEFORE

he met Elvira. His wife, Vera, had never been happy in cold, damp, cramped Leningrad. She never became entirely comfortable amidst the hungry, crowded Russian people. Missing life in Prague, she retained and resurfaced her father's dislike of Communism. With more kids and less help than she'd had in Prague, she had little time to think, or enjoy life. Joe was more and more absent; sparse conjugal time seemed hurried or cold. Then, when Joe took up with Elvira, Vera had to depend for her satisfaction on the knowledge that she was married to a successful man who provided well for her family. But this solid bedrock sprouted no happiness, no joy, though it supported all her material needs.

When the UM-1NKh went into mass production, Joe was happy to travel throughout the Soviet Union to oversee and consult on its installation in nuclear power plants, steel mills and paper plants. These projects provided time with Elvira: camping, staying in quiet hotels and enjoying top entertainments in Russia's two great cultural cities. Joe felt lucky to be doing the people's work for Communism with a beautiful, loving companion, aged less than half his forty-seven years. What Vera didn't know and even Phil did not yet know, was that by April, Elvira was quite noticeably pregnant. The two lovers seemed sure it was Joe's child, not Elvira's husband, Anton's. Was that maybe just wishful love talking?

In February 1963, Phil Staros was shocked out of his inflated dreams when another man, Fyodor Lukin, was appointed general director of Zelenograd. Staros was angry and felt betrayed by GKET minister Aleksandr Shokin who told him, "Be grateful you're not burdened with administrative duties. You'll be free to pursue science. As deputy director, you'll have twenty-thousand people working under you. Fyodor Lukin is a good man who will give you full support. He was the chief at KB-1 you know—"

"—I know who he is." *You patronizing ass,* Phil thought.

Phil refused to get along with Lukin even though Lukin bent over backwards with peaceful overtures. Staros was counting on Nikita Khrushchev and Marshal Dmitry Ustinov to put him back on top. Joe tried to console Phil by reiterating that they were still in charge of KB-2 and could use it to forge an important role in Zelenograd.

"Only if we get the UM-2 airborne," Phil said. "Once it's in use, it will speak for us loud and clear. That has to be our best play."

In April 1963, the CIA issued a secret report: "the Soviet microelectronics industry is expanding rapidly." The CIA had no idea who was behind it; they thought Joel Barr was in South America like the Nazis that only the Israelis could find.

On May 23, Fidel Castro became Khrushchev's guest of honor in Moscow.

IN JUNE, STAROS'S AND BERG'S OPPONENTS in the Leningrad Party central committee, Vasily Tolstikov and Grigory Romanov, made an outright demand that the UM-2 be proved in two or three airborne applications before certification for general mass production. The two American engineers and their teams were thinking about a family of UM-2s, specialized for aircraft, submarines and space vehicles, each with programmable software. They bragged about its versatility and usefulness in all defense applications, not realizing that this universal quality would pit competitors against them from all sides.

On June 16, Vostok 6, weighing nearly 2.5 metric tons was blasted into orbit in the morning light of the Kazakh desert by a Vostok-K rocket. It carried the first woman in space, attractive young Soviet kosmonaut Valentina Tereshkova. Alone, she circled the earth at an altitude of between 110 and 144 miles sixteen times a day for three days. The flight received world-wide attention and popularity, another major propaganda victory for the USSR. Joe and Phil knew that Vostok 6 was designed and built by OKB-1, headed by space pioneering giant Sergei Pavlovich Korolev, the 'father of space flight, facts the Soviet government kept secret, Joe and Phil now shared the secret that Korolev was the chief designer of the Soviet space program. "What are our chances," Phil asked, "of a UM-2 flying one of Sergei Pavlovich's deluxe models?"

"If not Vostok 7 maybe Vostok 8," Joe kidded back.

"Operating the first space station," Phil countered.

"From your mouth to Nikita's ears," Joe offered.

"Lately," Phil said, "you do nothing but make our UM-1NKh clients happy."

"But they *are happy*. By and large."

"How's Elvira?" Phil was not yet used to Joe and Elvira.

"…She's going to have a baby fairly soon."

"…You're the happy papa?"

"We think if the husband was going to score he'd have done it before now."

"What happens when Vera finds out? They always do."

"She'll cut my throat."

"Maybe that's not all she'll cut."

June 20 was not too early to establish the Moscow–Washington red telephones and teleprinters, what with the missiles in Cuba and other nuclear war brinksmanship.

DESPITE PHIL'S *DE FACTO* DEMOTION,

they tried to stay cheerful as they contemplated moving into new houses in Zelenograd—because Phil was convinced he could reverse the decision. *It was a mistake that will sooner or later be corrected* But the Leningrad Party committee had been deeply offended by Phil's high-flying ways and called KB-2, "with its 40 per cent Jewish staff, "a nest of Zionists." When Phil heard this, he thought of Viktor Taroikin's warning, seven years earlier, the two per cent quota that Joe had bragged to Viktor's face he'd use to their advantage. *Has Joe got me in the shit once again?* Phil wondered. He was reminded that Viktor Taroikin had left a casual message recently to get in touch. *I should call him; he's never hurt us. And maybe he can help with this, even some good advice.*

As time went by, angry and frustrated over losing control of Zelenograd, Phil, partly with Joe's urging, wanted to set up a separate team, to prove he could deliver the next generation computer, the UM-3. Phil reasoned somewhat illogically that he should control all technological development in the Soviet Union's microelectronics. "It's the only way we will get ahead of the West," he insisted. "What does Fyodor Lukin know about microelectronics or computers?"

On July 26, NASA launched Syncom 2, the world's first geostationary satellite, a stunning development in terrestrial communications. Days later, the Soviet newspaper Izvestia reported that British double agent Kim Philby had been given asylum in Moscow. Joe and Phil worried that such notoriety would draw attention to them, from both their Soviet colleagues and the CIA. Not to mention the hostile Leningrad Party committee.

ON AUGUST 8 JOE AND ELVIRA WERE IN KAZAN where Elvira was to meet with the faculty of an engineering institute. She was just over eight months pregnant when her water broke. They hurried to a local hospital. Joe, nervous, could not help being glad they were not in Moscow or Leningrad. Despite the potential social, political and domestic dangers the situation presented, Joe felt involuntarily thrills at the thought of having a child with the woman he loved, even as he thought ruefully, *I'm old enough to be her father.* He paced the maternity ward waiting room, more anxious than the two twenty-something husbands who shared the expectant wait. One of the young men asked, "Hey Pop, what? It's your first grandchild?"

"No," Joe said, "my wife is much younger." Atypically, Joe made no attempt to engage them in conversation, but took a seat, hoping to put an end to their attention to him. Waiting an hour, his biological elation cascaded into a spine wrenching fear of life spiraling out of control into domestic chaos.

A nurse came out. Cheerless, she told Joe, "The baby, a girl, has been born dead. There was nothing to be done."

"That's terrible. Is the mother alright?" Though anxious for Elvira, Joe wondered, *Will she think I'm glad it happened this way? That I'm glad to be off the hook?*

"Oh she's fine. Your wife is a very healthy woman. You can go in now if you like. I'm sorry about the baby."

When they beheld each other, with that first look into each other's eyes, Elvira knew Joe had not wanted 'their baby' to die. He knew she knew that, and they both knew they would go on. Their love had not changed. "I'm sorry," she said.

"Me too," Joe said.

Elvira was able to leave the hospital an hour later. They were together again.

On August 28, Martin Luther King, Jr. delivered his 'I Have a Dream' speech on the steps of the Lincoln Memorial to over 250,000 people. Upon reading about it, Joe thought of Julius and the Scottsboro boys and Julie's continued staunch interest in black civil rights, how he had made friends with black leaders in Harlem and had felt honored by those friendships. *And he understood its importance to the Communist Party. The beauty of its politics, the beautiful clarity.*

Less than three weeks later, on September 15, at Birmingham Alabama's 16th Street Baptist Church, four young black girls were ripped apart and twenty-two other people were injured by a cowardly Ku Klux Klan bomb.

ONE DAY THAT FALL OF 1963, ERIC FIRDMAN was summoned to a KGB office and handed the complete plans for the IBM 360 family of computers, a year before those systems made it to market, another victory it seemed for the old Russian belief that intel was the greatest and least expensive weapon, that espionage was the poor man's only way to compete against superior material strength. Eric later joked that those plans and the 360 itself were the CIA's most destructive weapon against the development of Soviet computers and microelectronics. "They tried to put us on the wrong track," he said. Fortunately, Staros, Berg and KB-2 did not get sucked into the rush to emulate the 360, which served to stunt Soviet innovation. The IBM plans were stamped Top Secret by the US government, likewise in Russian, a measure designed to prevent endangering the US sources who had blatantly ignored the original warning.

TWENTY-NINE

"The guns and bombs, the rockets and the warships, are all symbols of human failure."

--Lyndon B. Johnson

AS THE UM-2 BECAME A VIABLE PRODUCT, because of pressure from the Leningrad Party committee and especially Grigory Romanov, it needed to be approved by an Inter-Ministry State Commission headed by the Major General responsible for testing devices intended for military use. Membership of the State Commission included many KB-2 competitors for military funds and industrial contracts. Because the UM-2 was submitted as a computer for aircraft, submarine and spacecraft applications, necessarily small, lightweight and hardy where space was limited and extreme conditions existed, it threatened all Soviet firms who sought contracts from any of the military branches. So, for virtually everyone else in Soviet computing, it was open hunting season on Staros, Berg and KB-2. A year long, hard, tedious battle lay ahead for KB-2's top engineers Firdman and Galperin to prove that the UM-2 was matchless. Phil and Joe wanted to get to work on the next generation computer, the UM-3, but they knew they needed to stay with the U-2 a little longer. So behind Phil's sound lock doors they discussed it in the English language.

"Then besides every other computer firm in the USSR, we've got the Leningrad Obkom to deal with," Phil summed up. "The only way to get by those bastards, will be if we can put a UM-2 in a military aircraft or spacecraft."

"Or a submarine, even," Joe said.

"We need the support and confidence of one of the untouchables," Phil agreed.

"Well, we know who to ask, don't we? Joel said somewhat rhetorically.

Staros and Berg went back to Andrei Tupolev who had designed half the aircraft in Russia, many from inside a *sharashka,* the *gulag* for the talented creators of advanced technologies. Tupolev had also been instrumental, as he'd mentioned to them earlier, in rescuing Sergei Korolev from Kolima, one of the must brutal and lethal of Stalin's *gulags.* Kolima was nothing like a *sharashka,* nothing like being locked up in not uncomfortable quarters designing bombers. The secret father of space flight had barely survived. Though the two American engineers knew they needed the opportunity to prove the UM-2 in a Tupolev bomber, they dreamed of putting a UM-2 or a UM-3 in a Soviet Spacecraft. Such a victory and honor never slipped their minds.

At his design lab, the tough, outspoken Tupolev with the habitually skeptical eyes greeted them himself, "Come sit down, good to see you again." His smile was relaxed, enjoyable. "My friends tell me about your doings. I'm glad for your good news, but I must tell you to be careful. There are lots of rotten bastards looking to tear you down."

"We try to concentrate on inventing the future of microelectronics," Phil said half seriously, "and to avoid all the politics."

"That's where you are wrong; you have to fight back, you have to scare them. Only fear will stop them."

"We have plenty to do just producing the UM-2," Joe said.

"Yes I've heard about your UM-2. I've listened to first hand accounts of your demonstrations. I've talked to experts who have examined your plans, your elaborate documentation."

"You have?" Phil asked, not terribly surprised. "Our design documents? Production plans?"

"I certainly hope you don't think anything at your level now is entirely secret," Tupolev said.

"Yes," Phil agreed, "I suppose not."

"Well now," Joe said jovially, "since you had an unusually close look, what do you think?"

"I think you should install the UM-2 in my new long

range bombers."

"Really, no tests, no red tape?"

"Of course there will be red tape as you 'Czechs' say, but I have it from those who know what they are talking about; your UM-2 is the way to go."

"Well," Phil said without missing a beat, "we'll call it the UM-2T."

"You will have my contract within a few short weeks," Tupolev said. "You have done your job well."

Did Tupolev know they were Americans? Ex-spies? Maybe he did.

ON NOVEMBER 22: ALLEN DULLES'S ASSASSINS attacked President Kennedy's motorcade in Dallas. Kennedy was dead within the hour. Lyndon Johnson was sworn in as the 36th US President aboard Air Force One. At Walter Reed Bethesda Naval Medical Center, the evidence of multiple shooters was adulterated, forged away and destroyed. With the first news from Dallas, J. Edgar Hoover began interfering, hoarding evidence and was soon pushing the conclusion that it was the work of a lone assassin. Within four hours of the attack, Hoover claimed the FBI had arrested the culprit, Lee Harvey Oswald The day after the president's murder, on Saturday, November 23, Hoover went to the racetrack as usual to bet on horses. The next day there was the horse drawn casket procession to the Capitol rotunda. If that wasn't riveting enough, Jack Ruby murdered Lee Harvey Oswald before a world-wide television audience.

On November 29, President Johnson established the Warren Commission. By December 3, the cover-up was under full sail. When, against his wishes, Hoover was not chosen to chair the Warren Commission, he began a campaign of pressuring members, intimidating witnesses; distorting, concealing and destroying evidence. Lying, Hoover denied that Lee Harvey Oswald and Jack Ruby were both sometime undercover informants for the FBI.

The Commission did what they had all agreed *not* to do: rely on the FBI for the evidence. There were hundreds of leads and dozens of witnesses connected to Cuban exiles, to US intelligence operatives, to the mafia and to Edgar's own oil rich friends that Edgar failed to bring to the attention of the Warren Commission. The FBI had received credible warnings of threats to Kennedy's life in the days before Dallas. Edgar did not discuss these warnings with the commission, having broken the law by not reporting them to the Secret Service in the first place. For Hoover, Jack Kennedy's murder meant the end of Robert Kennedy's pressure to pursue organized crime. It meant the end of any threat to his fiefdom. He couldn't have been happier if he'd pulled the trigger himself.

Weeks later, while Soviet leaders and citizens were stunned by the murder of "our man in the White House," as Kennedy was fondly called in Moscow and Leningrad, Eric Firdman and Mark Galperin had worked their introduction of the UM-2 up the OKB-1 hierarchy and, as they approached the top to Sergei Korolev, Joe and Phil were invited to a meeting with OKB-1's secret director. Sergei Pavlovich Korolev entertained them on a late Sunday afternoon wearing a moth-eaten sweater that showed his hairy chest. He seemed tired, but his eyes shown with intelligence and wit. What the two Americans had heard about Korolev was that he was ailing in some mysterious way, that he was an intense worker and could be very sharp tongued. They were wary. After gruff pleasantries, the stocky, powerfully built man with the big head and short neck said to them:

"Your two youngsters seemed to have made quite an impression on some of mine."

Phil spoke in careful, precise Russian, "Both Mark Galperin and Eric Firdman have worked very hard on the UM-2 and they know its capabilities very well." Eyes sparkling and flashing, Phil saw no resistance, only interest, in Korolev's steady gaze. He went on, "We were hoping there might be some interest in using our UM-2 in your spacecraft."

"What would make you think that?" Korolev asked.

Phil felt the almost brutal bluntness of the challenge while Joe was interested to see the play between the two. Phil, with a single snap of his mustache to the left, taking a breath, said, "The Americans now are preparing to use an IBM computer on board in their Gemini spacecraft." He turned toward Joe, "We know the UM-2 is far superior. Perhaps you know about it from your team?"

"And you 'Czechs' would know all about what the Americans are doing?" Korolev asked, a subtle smile playing from his eyes. Did he know?

"We get the reports from the State Security Committee, (KGB) which have been reliable, as far as we know."

"Well, I can't disagree that an onboard computer could provide certain advantages. A useful tool for our kosmonauts."

"The timing necessary for delicate maneuvers is too slow from earth station computers," Phil stated the obvious in a genial, collegial fashion.

"I will also tell you," Korolev said in a more relaxed manner, "that I have no candidates for on-board computers beyond the UM-2." He added skeptically, "If only it were it possible to include any computer on board a Voshkod or Soyuz spacecraft..."

"So, if you are concerned that the UM-2 has not been proven in previous installations, we are working on that with a leading aircraft designer and—"

"—I care about a test in another vehicle like I care about last year's snow. The problem is not to magically produce some convincing demonstration or to pass some nuisance of a State Commission test. The problem is that the advantages of onboard computers are expected, but not known. How do I weigh those unknown advantages against 25 kilograms of additional payload?"

"Certainly with all that is being hurled up into space," Joe said, "even 25 kilograms can be incorporated. Besides, we are working constantly to reduce the weight."

Korolev looked at Joe, rolling a thought over in his mind, he scratched his chest and said, "Can you afford to begin work on the idea with me, if there is yet no signed contract from the State? You two are very controversial right now; perhaps you are aware?"

"We would be glad to do so," Phil said, turning slightly to Joe who nodded firmly. "To work with you on this is a risk well worth taking."

"Then let's do it this way," Korolev said, "I'll commit

right now to let's say a UM-2M to be used for testing, debugging and programming and a UM-2S to be used in a Soyuz space capsule once the UM-2M has done all the preliminary work."

"That would be perfect," Phil said, clearly pleased. Joe nodded and flashed a smile of warm affection for his partner.

"We'll set up an area and get to work on it right away," Joe said.

"I'll send a man to set up over at your shop," Korolev said, "to keep us in touch as work progresses. And to make sure you get a contract."

They all shook hands and Phil and Joe were somewhat surprised, but not disappointed, that they toasted their agreement with black tea and not alcohol. Korolev wasn't a drinker. The two Americans left the OKB-1 lab pleased and excited and now more confident that they would win out over the forces of green envy and lizard-brain darkness.

To Joe, after that meeting, Phil's apparently hopeless notion that leadership of Zelenograd was still within his reach did not seem so hopeless. *If all this works out,* Joe thought, *Soyuz! The future leading spacecraft. All the way to the Moon.* He marveled, remembering project Diana when mankind first reached out to the Moon, with a radar bounce, and now the race was on, to go there.

They did not yet know that the Politburo had decided to beat the Americans in putting the first man on the Moon. They didn't yet know Korolev had been designated the man to make it happen, putting a Soviet Kosmonaut first on the Moon. So they did not fully realize they'd been chosen to make the guidance system for Soviet manned Moon landings; and hadn't yet felt the weight of that. They fantasized, surmised, but there had been no decree.

IN MOSCOW AND LENINGRAD WERE MEN high up in State and Party hierarchies who hated Jews, who hated foreigners and who hated innovation—especially when Soviet innovation came from foreigner Jews. These were ruthless, men long practiced in manipulating the course of state decisions. In America there was J. Edgar Hoover. Toward year end, when *Time* named Martin Luther King, Jr. 'Man-of-the-Year', an honor Hoover had received, Hoover was furious. Having ducked rumors all his life that he himself had Negro ancestry, he had not only condemned homosexuals to cover up his own homosexuality, he had always demeaned blacks as servants. As the civil rights movement built momentum, Hoover directed his agents to spend their time investigating the activities of black leaders instead of the brutal crimes of the Ku Klux Klan and the Mafia. The smear of 'Communism' had worked on Marcus Garvey and Paul Robeson so Edgar tried it on Martin Luther King. Blackmailing Robert Kennedy, Edgar extracted permission for a wiretap on King and began a massive surveillance operation that included dozens of illegal wiretaps and hidden microphones. But the smear of Communism didn't work on King, so Hoover switched his attention to King's extra-marital affairs, using dozens of agents to gather dirt. He smeared King out of an honorary degree at Marquette University and used pictures of King going into a hotel with a white woman to kill the leader's support from certain church organizations.

On December 26 1963, the US military deployed the Semi-Automatic Ground Environment, a gigantic computer automated nuclear defense system which cost more than the atomic bomb itself. It could send attack signals directly to in-flight aircraft and missile silos.

In America, computer innovation was exploding, driven by people like Ivan Sutherland who wrote the revolutionary Sketchpad program at MIT. KB-2 engineers especially Eric Firdman took note and were the first in the USSR to realize that Sketchpad could be the basis of computer aided design, a program which could track all the iterations of a design and change them when the master drawing was changed. Firdman was a rare thing at the time, a Soviet innovator.

THIRTY

"...I understood the Soviet system much better than my bosses. [Joe and Phil] *After all, they were genuine Communists and thus believed in the system's goodness. Joe believed it more than Phil. I did not at all. If you were born in the Soviet Union, you sucked in the knowledge of the system's evil with your mother's milk."*   **--Henry Eric Firdman**

AS AFRICAN COLONIES DECLARED THEIR independence, amidst ousters, coups, assassinations and even rare elections, headlines about nuclear bomb-tests subsided and the feats in space replaced them. As the year 1964 began, certification requirements for the UM-2 before the State Commission were still absorbing KB-2 engineering time, especially for Firdman and Galperin. Joe and Phil clearly understood that final commission approval would not stop their enemies, even once those enemies had been reduced to saying the UM-2 was not as good as the computers they could produce in the future. The two American engineers also knew that only when the UM-2 had been successfully installed in aircraft, submarines or spacecraft, making those vehicles more controllable, efficient and reliable, could they hope to celebrate. At least one of the Soviet Union's genius Chief Designers, those inspirational leaders of military, space or aircraft development like Tupolev or Korolev or Kurchatov, would need to risk his career on their unproven device, built by strange foreigners using a queasy, suspect technology.

On January 28 1964, Soviet MiGs shot down a US Air Force jet training plane over East Germany, killing the three crewmen. The next day, the Soviet Union launched two scientific satellites, Elektron I and Elektron II, from a single rocket. Almost simultaneously, NASA launched Ranger 6, to televise the Moon.

On February 7, the Beatles were greeted at JFK in New York by screaming fans. Two days later during the course of the *The Ed Sullivan Show*, they performed live for 73 million viewers, *All My Loving, Till There Was You, She Loves You, I Saw Her Standing There*, and *I Want to Hold Your Hand*. Joe and Phil read about such a popular musical sensation with interest and soon were able to listen to bootleg tapes given to them by young friends of Elvira's.

When the military commission finally approved the UM-2 in February, Firdman and Galperin were already preparing to design and build the UM-3, an advanced machine to use photo-printed integrated circuits.

But the UM-2 had not won universal appeal. Tupolev's watchdog, Isaac Schtern, stationed at KB-2 in Leningrad, hated them and did everything he could to sabotage the UM-2T. Korolev's man, Ivan Pertzovsky, also installed at their elbows, was equally harsh though not specifically bent on making them fail the benchmark tests.

"Maybe we're spread too thin," Joe suggested. "Perhaps it's time to retreat from Zelenograd while we can, stay in Leningrad and make KB-2 the undisputed leader, like OKB-1."

"These bureaucrats have made a mistake that can be corrected," Phil replied. "They will not put us ahead of the West. We could make that happen. They must realize that."

"They may never admit it," Firdman said quietly.

"If we make UM-3 a success," Joe said, "whether we're here in Zelenograd or back at KB-2, won't matter. They'll have to admit we've made a computer superior to the US efforts."

"Excuse me," Eric said, "but as a native Soviet citizen, I suggest you can't be certain that even a stunning UM-3 success would lead to the Party handing over control of a major defense industry to—"

"—To a foreigner! Let me tell you, I was a Communist where they hated Communists—" Phil stopped abruptly, flashing a charged glance at Joe.

"Do you know the story," Eric asked, "of the Russian

muzhik who was traveling along in his cart and found God stuck in the mud up to his belt buckle? No? Well of course this Russian *muzhik* helped God out of the mire and gave him a ride in his cart. So God granted him a wish on the condition that whatever he wished for, his neighbor would gain the same twice over, so that his neighbor would suffer no envy or enmity. The *muzhik* thought long and hard before answering: 'Take out one of my eyes,' he said at last. That, is who you are dealing with here. Fat little *muzhiki*."

On April 7, IBM announced their System 360, plans for which KB-2 had seen months earlier. The next day, the USA's Gemini 1 was successfully launched, the first unmanned test of the 2-man spacecraft. Then too, *From Russia with Love* premiered in the US. A criminal empire, not the Russians, was the villain, personified by a lovely woman who saved Bond's life and joined him in bed.

On April 14 1964, a Delta rocket's third-stage motor ignited in an assembly room at Cape Canaveral, killing 3 people.

On April 20, Lyndon Johnson in New York and Nikita Khrushchev in Moscow, simultaneously announced plans to cut back production of nuclear warhead materials.

Facing fierce and hostile opposition, Joe suggested that Phil meet with Captain Taroikin, which Viktor quickly arranged. After greetings, sensing each other's mood, Joe said, "I feel like we're being threatened, that certain people wish we were dead. Or I wake up certain I'll be shipped to a *gulag*. You know? I'm just saying how I—"

"I know! I know" Viktor studied Joe with a pleasant expression on his face. "I understand your concerns, but remember our (KGB's) support over the past decades which I think you will agree has never flagged? That will not change. We understand what you have done for our country and what you are capable of doing. You will always have our support and protection, regardless of brief political winds."

"Your reassurance is greatly appreciated," Phil said.

"I can't help worrying," Joe said, "that we will be unmasked as Americans and with the current climate that could be—"

"—Joe, my advice is to make sure you are familiar with current events back home in South Africa where change is happening. Familiarize yourself with the speech of this black anti-apartheid leader, Nelson Mandela. He faces life in prison, saying he's glad to die for his beliefs. Don't let some stooge trip you up; every emigré watches his homeland." This admonition added just the right hint of danger and caution, Viktor thought. "It wouldn't hurt to refer to your life and work in Prague, either, from time to time," he added.

On May 19 1964, the US State Department declared they'd found more than forty hidden microphones embedded in the walls of the US Embassy in Moscow. They shouldn't have let the Russians built it, they decided.

LATE JULY, THE MAGAZINE *SOVIET UNION* published an interview with purported UM-1NKh designer Fillipov (Philip Staros). The CIA studied the specs and statements about the computer and admitted that the UM-1NKh, though behind Honeywell and IBM, was not behind by much. They knew nothing of the even more advanced UM-2 or the projected far more powerful UM-3.

A frustrated, anxious Staros decided he must appeal to Khrushchev for control of Zelenograd. He called Grigory Shuisky, Khrushchev's adjutant, to ask for a meeting with the leader. Shuisky replied that Khrushchev was just leaving for a vacation on the Black Sea. Without thinking, Staros asked for a meeting with whoever was in charge in the interim.

On July 31 1964, Ranger 7 sent back the first close-up photographs of the Moon, far clearer than anything ever seen from Earth. On August 4, the bodies of murdered civil rights activists Michael Schwerner, Andrew Goodman and James Chaney were found. They had been registering black people to vote.

As delegates poured into Atlantic City for the Democratic Convention, under a cover story of crowd and riot control, FBI wiretaps and bugs were used by three dozen FBI agents, technicians, and stenographers to spy on senators, congressmen, delegates, civil rights activists and especially on Robert Kennedy.

Secure phone lines linked Atlantic City operations to FBI headquarters. Though Johnson worried that Robert Kennedy might get nominated for Vice president, the FBI listened to the most important private political conversations and all went well for Johnson until weeks later when his top aide, Walter Jenkins, was arrested in a YMCA toilet for having sex with a male soldier. Edgar hadn't warned Lyndon that his right-hand-man, Jenkins, had had vice arrests years earlier, *in the very same toilet.*

BY MID-AUGUST 1964, FYODOR LUKIN TOOK over Zelenograd. He clearly intended to be the big boss. Then Leonid Brezhnev was the one who answered Phil's insistent request for a meeting. Brezhnev had taken over in Khrushchev's absence. Leonid Brezhnev arrived with an elaborate entourage at KB-2, clearly having been briefed about who these Americans were and what they'd done during the war, in Prague, and while in Leningrad. Yet, unlike country bumpkin Khrushchev, there was no warmth, no avowal of recognition from Brezhnev. But it was Brezhnev's diamond cuff links and a large diamond tie pin which offended Joe much more than his lack of warm support. *The pure vanity! He's a phony. No true socialist leader flaunts wealth like a capitalist lackey, abusing collective resources...not like Stalin's simple tunics and basic military clothes.* Joe admired both the humility that Stalin's dress represented, and Stalin's cunning in displaying it.

Brezhnev barely listened to Phil's pleas for reconsideration of Shokin's and Romanov's decisions to make Staros merely Deputy Director of the Center for *Mikroelektronika*. Then Brezhnev said, "Our country deeply appreciates your help, but you don't quite know how our Soviet system works yet. You should understand that no action is going to be taken as a result of your complaints. But perhaps things will turn out well, anyway." He smiled showing his large beaver-like teeth.

Firdman was shocked to hear Joe say just after Brezhnev departed, "I haven't seen a man like that since I...except in...a movie about New York." To Eric, it sounded as though Joe had almost said, *I haven't seen a man like that since I left New York.*

"Like a fat German Jew with polished fingernails," Joe added as he remembered rich *yekhes* he'd seen entering the fancy furnishings stores on Fifth Avenue when he was a kid. "We'll have to wait until Khrushchev returns."

Phil nodded in glum, deep disappointment. "Yes, Brezhnev can't be the final answer."

"No, not coming from that guy," Joe agreed. He's a fake."

Firdman was disturbed and thought, *They don't know what they're up against!* But he didn't want to pop their bubble. *I won't say anything unless they get into really deep shit.*

On September 24 1964, the Warren Commission Report's betrayal of the truth, that Hoover had orchestrated, fueled confusion, popular distrust, extended controversy and constant suspicion. When Hoover heard that Martin Luther King, Jr. was to receive the Nobel Peace Prize, something Hoover had long coveted, he called King, "the most notorious liar in the country." Hoover's rants made front page news which Edgar followed-up by offering tapes and transcripts to prove King's debauchery. King, aware of all this, requested a meeting only to encounter Hoover's threatening diatribe.

THIRTY-ONE

"Well, I don't know, but I've been told
The streets in heaven are lined with gold
I ask you how things could get much worse
If the Russians happen to get up there first.
Wowee! Pretty scary!
Now, I'm liberal, but to a degree
I want ev'rybody to be free
But if you think that I'll let Barry Goldwater
Move in next door and marry my daughter
You must think I'm crazy!
I wouldn't let him do it for all the farms in Cuba."
---Bob Dylan

JOE, HIDING HIS EXCITEMENT, SLIPPED OUT OF
his family's Leningrad apartment, saying, "I'll be in the garage,
fixing the Volga's tail lights." It was not an odd thing to say; he
often modified or repaired his prized automobile. Outside this
time, he joined Elvira who he hadn't seen in weeks. She had
signaled him with a note delivered by a messenger. They made
their way to Joe's garage, some forty meters from the apartment
building entrance, which, like many in the USSR, was a steel box
built roughly to the dimensions of the automobile. Some were
actually shaped to the specific model of car which had to be
pushed by hand into the enclosure. Joe's garage was large enough
to squeeze oneself into the Volga.

In the backseat they "did the business" as Joe still thought
of it. It wasn't their first time in the Volga nor even the first time
in the garage. It wasn't just the sex; Joe told her his troubles. She
responded intelligently as she always did. He reassured her of his

love and support then returned to his family and played happily with his children until bed time. Vera seemed satisfied that his mood was generous.

OCTOBER 2 1964, IMPATIENT AND DESPERATE, Joe and Phil huddled with Eric to plan an approach to Khrushchev. They brought up the idea of writing him a letter. Eric, disturbed by their naivete, told them, "What you suggest is very dangerous, especially right after the Brezhnev meeting. The big boss told you to drop it. I suggest you wait at least until Khrushchev returns, maybe longer."

"Eric," Phil said, "you weren't at our meeting when Nikita Sergeyevich visited us in May of 1962, so you have no idea how much he likes us."

"You have complained about some very powerful people to Brezhnev," Eric said, "who clearly does not like you. Such political folly brings your judgment into question. They will not just be annoyed; they will assume you are crazy, or stupid. There is no way to know how this will backfire. You must wait."

"What do we gain by waiting, besides being pushed farther aside?" Joe asked.

"Well, whatever you do, don't put anything in writing. If you must pursue Khrushchev over Brezhnev's head, at least wait to see him. Leave no paper trail."

"No, we should write him," Joe insisted. "Shuisky will be sure he gets it."

"I'm telling you that's a bad idea. Ask anyone you trust who was born in this country. They will tell you the same thing. Anyone at all."

When Eric had been excused, Joe prevailed upon Phil to write Nikita Khrushchev. Their letter began thus:

"Dear Nikita Sergeyevich!
You were absolutely right when you told us that your bureaucrats in both the Central Committee and State Committee of Electronic Industry would try to impede our progress. In fact, they have been preventing us from accomplishing what we promised you more than

two years ago."

They detailed the hostile acts of both Minister of Electronic Industry, Aleksandr Shokin and Leningrad Party Chairman, Grigory Romanov, who they didn't know was soon to be made a candidate member of the Soviet Politburo, that small group of men next to the man at the very top. They delivered their letter to Grigory Shuisky who placed it in Khrushchev's personal office safe to await his return.

On October 12, the Soviet Union launched Voskhod 1 into Earth orbit. It was the first spacecraft with a multi-person crew and the first spaceflight without space suits, further clear propaganda victories for the USSR.

ALSO THAT DAY, MARSHAL DMITRY USTINOV, Chairman of the Supreme Council of the National Economy, was ordered by the Politburo to fly down to the Black Sea and bring Nikita Khrushchev back to Moscow. Ustinov arrived there the next morning as Khrushchev was talking with French Atomic Science Minister Gaston Palewski. Ustinov insisted that Khrushchev return immediately to Moscow for a special meeting of the Presidium. At sunset, Khrushchev and Ustinov landed at Moscow's Vnukovo Airport where a ZIL limousine waited to take them to the Kremlin. There, behind the high, red brick walls, Nikita Khrushchev was deposed as leader of the Soviet Union. Leonid Brezhnev assumed power and made it clear there would be no going back.

Four days later, on October 16, Joe and Phil were having breakfast at the Metropol Hotel when they saw a copy of *Pravda* on the next table. It announced Khrushchev's 'retirement'. Kosygin and Brezhnev had taken over.

"Damn, this is not good," Phil's fist descended violently but, seeing Joe's stricken face, he set his hand down without smacking the table.

"Everything has changed," Joe said; his face was ashen.

"For the much worse!" Phil said, nearly accusingly.

"Where is that letter we sent?"

"We shouldn't have sent it. We should have listened to

Firdman and we should have waited."

"Let's hope Shuisky has enough sense to hide it from Brezhnev."

"Don't kid yourself; he's a loyal party man. He'd never dare do that."

KHRUSHCHEV'S SAFE WAS DULY OPENED and Brezhnev read their letter then passed along copies to Aleksandr Shokin and Grigory Romanov. Joe and Phil heard nothing and were terrified. Phil, though, could not bear waiting for doom without knowing what it was or when it would come. He called Viktor Taroikin and was overheard by Eric, in whose mind another piece of the puzzle of 'the two Czechs' fell into place: *The KGB is their last refuge; the connection must go way back. Which means...*

When Phil met Taroikin the following day he told Viktor what had happened. The KGB man listened patiently, appreciating nuances to what he already knew. "We of the first directorate would be counted as useless if I was not already acquainted with your situation. But what you've told me answers some questions."

"Viktor, do you know what will happen to us? Is it the end of everything? They regard us as traitors. Will we be arrested?"

"May I answer your questions one at time? No, I do not yet know what will happen to you as a result of your mistake. I don't think it will be the end of everything. You are too valuable. But, you must be very careful right now. Both of you! How is Joe? What a gentleman he is, always joking. BUT now be very careful! Treat them like dumbasses who don't understand how smart you are at your great peril. I do hope there will be nothing so old fashioned as arrests. Or anything worse."

On November 3, Lyndon B. Johnson defeated Barry Goldwater with over 60% of the popular vote. On December 10, Dr. Martin Luther King, Jr. was awarded the Nobel Peace Prize in Oslo, Norway.

Phil and Joe did not have to wait long to discover their fate. In early December 1964, they were ordered abruptly to appear before a board meeting of the GKET, the State Committee of Electronic Technology, a meeting called a *kollegiya,* a large gathering of their powerful enemies and various hostile authorities. They could be accompanied only by Mark Galperin and Eric Firdman. Eric explained to them, "It's a show trial, a public trial of you and all your errors and crimes. It is meant to shame and condemn you. They have all the proof of your treachery they need in your letter, that you have attacked very powerful people. Your only choice is to bear it and await their decisions."

"If I have a chance," Mark Galperin said, "I will speak on your behalf, to say that you have steadfastly pursued the goals of the Communist state."

"No," Eric said sharply, "the last thing you need is the words of young Jews like us. It is time to keep quiet and take the beating they give you."

Mark's Galperin's face was tense with the friction that was growing between himself and Eric Firdman.

Inside the meeting hall, which was full to capacity with, it seemed, the faces of everyone who had ever felt suspicious of, or slighted by the high flying Czech engineers. The four of them were seated at a separate table near the podium. , Eric noticed that Joe was shaking as he tried to ease into his chair.

Aleksandr Shokin, after announcing that they were all there to consider the treachery of the two Czech engineers, read aloud phrases from their letter to Khrushchev. "Here's what these two had to say:"

"...Grigory Romanov using Soviet power, while ignorant of the issues, to make overbearing blockades to progress...

...Aleksandr Shokin, who though often supportive makes unilateral decisions he is not competent to make alone."

The humiliating public attack, hearing their words read back to all present in anger, shattered Joe's heretofore reliable confidence. He sat frozen, listening to a diatribe against the clean rooms necessary in producing integrated circuits, Shokin's voice full of scorn, "rooms inside of rooms, a pretense of capitalist imperialism." Fearing the gulag of Solzhenitsyn's *One Day in the Life of Ivan Denisovich,* Joe imagined handcuffs awaiting him just outside the chamber doors. *I'll never see my kids; they'll be ashamed of me for the rest of their lives. Even Elvira will desert me.*

Phil, after his talk with Taroikin, was not so panicked as his old friend, but he knew their dreams of glory and re-elevation to head Zelenograd were dead. Speaker after speaker described their various failings, both real and fictitious, all in the most damning terms. The two strange Czechs had flaunted Soviet rules and traditions in the most arrogant fashion.

After more than five hours of punishment, and further suggestions for more punishment, the GKET board meeting ended with a prepared and rehearsed motion for forgiveness, to be accompanied by unlimited and indefinite probation. Their connection to Zelenograd was severed entirely. Phil retained the title of Deputy Director in name only, without an office or secretary in the new city. Joe would have no title or connection to the city that they had started with a quiet roadside piss. They left the gathering shaken and disoriented, to feel terribly lonely and afraid.

TWO DAYS AFTER THE DEBACLE IN MOSCOW, GKET minister Aleksandr Shokin sent his deputy, Vladislav Mikhailov, to KB-2 in Leningrad with a twenty page summary of the GKET indictments against Staros and Berg. Mikhailov was there to read it aloud to KB-2's full staff, so everyone working with the two foreigners would know all the dirt. Again, it included quotations from their letter to Khrushchev. As if these cruel humiliations were not enough, Mikhailov was there not only to make known to their workers what sort of shirkers, criminals and fools they were working for, what sort of traitorous Zionists, but to urge, to provoke and to elicit from KB-2 staff further criticisms and humiliations.

When Mikhailov finished reading the accusations, he called upon several blue collar workers to confirm and expand the indictments. Their answers were meekly non-committal until Mikhailov called upon Ivan Prokherov, who was one of SL-11's first employees, now at KB-2, still operating lathes, producing initial hardware. Ivan remembered seeing Dr. Berg operate his lathe.

"Ivan Pavlovich, do you not believe that a disorganized and frivolous atmosphere at the KB-2 laboratories contributed to immense wastes of resources and manpower as the GKET board has laid forth here to you?"

"No, I do not," Ivan gasped for a deeper breath, "In order to discover completely new solutions to technical challenges, a process of trial and error is needed to discover what will work. I don't think any failures or delays were the fault of General Director Philip Georgievich or Chief Scientist Dr. Dzhosef Veniaminovich. Both men worked tirelessly and attentively on each project and I believe made sure our projects were successful. Something that cannot be said for a number of *our* suppliers. If there was any fault at KB-2, it was the fault of all of us, every man and woman; we're a team. More likely whatever faults can be found were not the fault so much of KB-2, but of the ministry, for providing only token support."

"Silence!" Beet red and nearly breathless, Mikhailov tried to move on, but Ivan Prokherov had opened the gates. Other KB-2 employees spoke up, most less bluntly, but clearly refuting Shokin's accusations. These blue-collar workers had no party membership to lose, no position in a hierarchy to defend. They were devoted to Phil and Joe, and to the truth.

Though there was reason to believe that such strong support from one's employees might be seriously detrimental, Phil and Joe took great heart from this highly unusual expression of loyalty, regardless of the consequences. Certainly Mikhailov now hated them with a passion. He would tell his superiors that Staros had orchestrated a counter-revolutionary demonstration. Party bosses would renew their attacks and privately accuse 'the two Czechs' of everything from child molesting to counterfeiting Soviet currency, embezzlement of state funds and treason. And of course, unbeknown to most of their tormenters, they lived in constant fear of being unmasked as Americans, the principal adversary.

ON THE DAY FOLLOWING MIKHAILOV'S
angry, sudden departure, Eric was called in to see Phil. "You were right," Staros said, it was pure foolishness to write that letter. I should have listened to you rather than let Joe ruin my life a second time."

"A second time…Meaning?" Eric asked, again sensing the secret past he had often wondered about.

"Nothing. Forget it; what's done is done, I suppose."

Another piece fell into place for Eric: *They worked together before! In the USA maybe, not only in Prague. Phil must think Joe is the reason he had to flee. If so, they were sponsored by the KGB, which even now protects them…*

"Well," Eric said, "I understand I am to accompany you back to Moscow, to meet with Comrade Shokin?"

"Yes, I must appear at Shokin's office next Monday. We must prepare carefully and well. I expect to receive further abuse, but perhaps I will be allowed to defend myself, and beg for another chance."

"I think Comrade Shokin understands how valuable you are and will give us the opportunity to achieve further success for his ministry."

Just then Joe came in and said to Phil. "Lend me ten rubles. Man here came in with some fine lamb chops."

"Here's five. There'd be more if you ever paid me back."

Eric saw the quickly veiled hurt on Joe's face. He'd never heard such a rebuke between the two before.

"Eric is coming with us to Moscow," Phil said to Joe who merely nodded and stepped back out of the office.

"YOUR LOYALTY IS NOT UNDER QUESTION
as far as I'm concerned," Shokin told them on Monday, "but your judgment was proven wrong. I hope you have digested that clearly. You have much to learn about how we do things here in the Soviet Union."

Phil cleared his throat and moved his mustache somewhat carefully from side to side before saying, "My goal is confined to moving Soviet advanced electronics ahead of all competition from the West. I never intended anything el—"

Shokin waved away Phil's speech, so carefully prepared with Eric, "Let's say what's past is past and what matters is what happens now. I'll leave all that behind us if you will."

Eric was sure he noticed an unhappy brusqueness in Shokin's manner as he spoke these apparently generous words. *He's still boiling over what Phil had the nerve to say of him in that letter... It's as if something or someone constrains him. If so, it certainly isn't Brezhnev...or even Ustinov, who's stopped answering Phil's calls. There is only one directorate with the power to wield that influence. If in fact the KGB squashed Shokin's anger, it means they were both Soviet spies in America... Or is Shokin only curbing his fury because KB-2 has such value to his ministry? That's possible, but there seems to be more to it... a strong support from the internal organs...*

THIRTY-TWO

"It's been a hard day's night,
And I've been working like a dog.
It's been a hard day's night,
I should be sleeping like a log.
But when I get home to you,
I find the things that you do
Will make me feel alright."
--The Beatles

LEONID BREZHNEV WAS FRIGHTENING, LIKE the figure at the prow of a war vessel He was riding a rising wave of Soviet mediocracy and decay. *Zastoia.* KB-2 had been considerably demoted and. Phil's reaction to these crushing blows was scattered and inconsistent. He played contraband Beatles tapes, and predicted their immense popularity in the Soviet Union: "They're saying what people want to hear and it's beautiful," he said. "Their popularity will mean changes everywhere."

Joe could not forget the Brezhnev he had seen wearing diamonds, the one so often bedecked with military ribbons. Joe could no more put aside the truth of Brezhnev's corruption and vanity than he could simply forget about Vivian Glassman. Brezhnev eroded from Joe's mind some of the glory of Socialism and Communism that Stalin had always inspired no matter what. This entity of Brezhnev introduced in Joe a new wariness regarding the nation he longed to love unconditionally. But scary Brezhnev did not change Joe's own loyalty to his ideals or his determination to be a true Communist.

Music's motivations and inspirations were part of Joe's being, a language more basic than Swedish, French, Czech,

Russian or English. As he listened to the Beatles with Phil's extolling predictions, he saw more clearly than ever Phil's love of folk music. *He needs to hear it said in so many words. To hear the hope of it, the hope he needs now.* Joe was glad for his old friend's resilience however fragile. It was good Phil was not talking about how to get back on top or even about computers. It gave Joe a new more general form of hope for both of them and their deep friendship.

In the special restricted library, which they still had access to, Joe discovered the review of a book, '*Invitation to an Inquest, Reopening the Rosenberg 'Atom Spy Case'.* According to the reviewer, the book argued that the Rosenbergs were 100% innocent, and had been framed by the US government to take the blame for the nuclear weapons proliferation nightmare. Then they were convicted and murdered to wring Communism out of American society forever. The author claimed the evidence for their conviction was all forgeries, perjuries and misconstructions.

The sadness Joe felt as he re-read parts of the review was for Julie. *The truth, the real truth of what you did, who you were, will never be known. You were guilty of a great innocence, a great idealism. Maybe a foolish purity…but if ever there was a heart in the right place…*

When Martin Luther King returned from Oslo with the Nobel Peace prize, he was greeted with a massive, joyous welcome by large crowds. Hoover's costly criminal smear efforts had failed. Hoping to drive King crazy and destroy his family, Edgar sent Coretta King a compilation tape of her husband's hotel bedroom sexual activities with a nasty anonymous note. King, though tortured and depressed by all this, did not break.

BACK IN LENINGRAD AND AT KB-2, NOT LONG after their meeting with Shokin in Moscow, Phil Staros suffered a nervous breakdown. Disoriented, depressed and somewhat delusional, he was placed in a rest hospital, due officially to severe weight loss. To Joe's surprise, in the midst of his anxiety over Phil and the increasing attacks from all sides, Shokin defended them against the Leningrad Party leaders who wanted them guarded as Tupolev, Korolev and Kurchatov, the nuclear physicist who had headed the Soviet atomic bomb program, had all been kept and made to work as virtual prisoners.

Eric Firdman visited Phil in the hospital alone, at Phil's request. They talked about Joe. Eric was able to further consider their origins and history together. Later he would write:

"Here they were, two lonely foreigners in a large country populated by strange people, fawning and hostile at the same time. They distrusted these people and thus could rely only on each other, which shackled them together for the rest of their lives. ...it looked like Joe was unconditionally devoted to Phil, often ignoring mockery that sometimes turned into humiliation."

Firdman suggested to Phil that he should make greater efforts to protect himself from the Leningrad Obkom, the Party Oblast Committee. "Grigory Romanov regards you as evil incarnate. They will not desist on their own."

"What can I do that we're not already doing?" Phil asked.

"Get yourself a serious academic degree, accumulate credentials as a scientist. The Soviet Academy of Science is not nothing. After all, Soviet Academicians have finally repudiated Stalin's Rasputin, Trofim Denisovich Lysenko! He's been disgraced and banished. Physicists Yakov Borisovich Zel'dovich, Vitaly Ginzburg, and Pyotr Kapitsa boldly denounced Lysenko. Your Khrushchev liked him. Even here in the Soviet Union real talent and ability can be formally recognized. It is the only way a reputation does not depend solely on the likes of ignorant, incompetent Party thugs. Not entirely."

As Eric's speech verged on treason, Phil listened closely and recognized the trust they shared. "I believe I've met those physicists you mentioned, here and there," Phil said. "I consider Pyotr Kapitsa, a friend."

"Of course. They are making bombs and missiles like the rest of us. But Pyotr Kapitsa is an interesting guy. A man of integrity. You may find a sympathetic ear with Kapitsa regarding your academic aspirations."

ABOUT THE SAME TIME, JUST AFTER THE US unmanned Gemini 2 was launched into a suborbital flight to test its re-entry shield on January 19 1965, Joe met with Aleksandr

Shokin in Phil's absence, ostensibly to consider KB-2's needs.

"He'll be alright," Shokin said of Phil; "he'll be back after a rest. What about the Gemini program? It looks like they're still following Kennedy's orders." Both men understood from classified bulletins that Gemini was the US preparation for human spaceflight to the Moon.

"If they're going to the Moon," Joe said, "they'll have to have on-board computers."

"You may well be right. But they're not wasting any time."

"Which means we have no time to waste?" Joe said.

Joe hoped for confirmation, but Shokin gave him a look: *Careful, what you assume and talk about!* Then with a sort of facial nod and shrug, he said, "You better make your UM-2T and UM-2S work like a Switzerland's watch."

So, Joe thought, *we're still being counted on, still in the running.* There was relief but with added weight. It meant that at least for now Shokin was not going to crush them. Joe redoubled his efforts and he told Vera, "I'm going to apply for Soviet Citizenship." *If she doesn't yet know we're not going back to Prague, it's time she did.*

"Why do such a thing?" She asked. "And why now? What's changed?"

"As you know I have to travel often to these factories to install our computer equipment..."

Vera did not look particularly convinced or interested; ;she nodd, *Okay, that's nothing new!*

"Whenever I travel I'm forced to stay in InTourist hotels because really I'm a foreigner with only a Czech passport to show."

"But you'll keep your Czech passport so that—"

"Vera, face it, we're not going back to Prague."

"Well, do what you want, you always do! But I'm not going to join you or these barbarians you call comrades."

"What are you doing, Papa," Robert asked. "Why is Mom unhappy?"

"I'm not unhappy," Vera said.

"She was just talking out loud," Vivian said.

"Look," Joe use Russian, "I'm only changing overdue

paperwork. I'm not gong where I haven't been going already."

"Let's go for a ride by the river park," Vera suggested.

"Very good, Mom," Vivian said in Czech, "Here in Russia where we live," she added in Russian.

Joe applied for Soviet citizenship. It was an action of commitment to the Soviet Union. Through all the heights and depths of Joe's Soviet career with Phil, the recent catastrophes had somehow made him feel more at home in Russia. *'Cleansed'* would be the wrong word. He felt he'd bled his own blood into Soviet soil. And he wanted to melt into the population, to be less conspicuous. When he spoke to Viktor Taroikin about Soviet citizenship and a Soviet passport, Viktor kidded, "So, you're thinking of staying are you, Dr. Berg? Had a look around and want to settle down, eh? You're sure ten years was sufficient introduction?"

Joe colored, for it was something like that. "Yes, I guess that's it," he said agreeably.

"Next, you'll be wanting Party membership, no doubt?"

Joe looked Taroikn dead on and stammered, "It's—that has been a life-long dream."

"Sure, now that you're planning to stick around, it might be a good time to press your application with the local KB-2 Party committee."

On February 20 1965, the US Ranger 8 mission sent back hi-res close-ups of Moon landing sites for Apollo astronauts. On March 18 Cosmonaut Alexey Leonov left Voskhod 2 for 12 minutes, the first human to walk in space. On March 23, NASA launched Gemini 3 into orbit, the first US 2-person crew.

With what sort of onboard computer for Gemini? Joe wondered.

On April 3rd, the world's first space nuclear reactor, SNAP-10A, was launched from Vandenberg AFB, California. The reactor operated for 43 days but remained in Low Earth orbit.

In mid-May when Joe read about pianist Vladimir Horowitz's triumphant Carnegie Hall return to the New York stage, after a twelve-year absence, he reflected, *Horowitz left here to go there and I left there to come here...* It was not about what might've happened to him had he himself pursued a career in music, but about how, if things had been different, he'd have gone to that concert with Vivian Glassman. He still missed Vivian intensely at times and couldn't help thinking he would never see her again.

On June 3, US Gemini 4 was launched and astronaut Edward White made the first US space walk, twelve minutes tethered to the capsule, floating in space. For Joe, Shokin, Firdman and Staros, not to mention Ustinov and Brezhnev, it was a sign that the US was catching up.

Weeks after Gemini 4 had successfully landed its two crew, Joe visited Taroikin's Lubyanka cubbyhole, as he had been asked.

"Happy fourth of July," Viktor handed Joe a large folder, and added, "You keep harping that for Americans to send a manned Moon lander, an on-board computer is essential."

With nervous hands, Joe opened the folder and turned several pages. "Damn, this is the Gemini spacecraft's on-board IBM computer! This is fantastic! I won't ask where you got it, though I can easily imagine." He'd noticed that the documents were not copied, but were the original printed multicolored documentation. No where were they stamped Top Secret. "Give me a few minutes to look this over," he pleaded, "If it shows that the UM-2S is way ahead of this, it could make a point."

"It's yours. Keep it, Taroilkin said. "Our meeting today is not official. You found the folder on your desk, if asked."

Joe looked up surprised, more impressed. "Can I tell anyone I have it? Shokin for instance?"

"But of course you can!" A mischievous glint flashed in Taroikin's eyes. *Why do you think I gave it to you?*

Joe smiled a friendly sheepish smile of appreciation for Viktor's trust and skillful support.

AFTER STUDYING THE GEMINI PLANS, JOE went to visit Aleksandr Shokin again.

"What's come up?" Shokin asked, hinting impatience.

"I have here the proof that the computer being used in the US Gemini missions is little more than a navigation calculator. The UM-2 is capable of much more and it weighs less." Joe offered the stolen folder to the GKET minister.

Shokin waved it aside and said, "Did I ever once say that I doubted you?"

When Joe brought the same Gemini folder to Sergei Korolev, he growled at Joe, "I've never disputed that on-board computers are a piece of the big picture, nor that I need that piece. But your machine still weighs 25 kilograms, which means burning 1000 kilograms of fuel."

"We're shrinking the UM-2S by fifty per cent," Joe said.

"You'll never do fifty per cent," Korolov growled, "but every lost kilo helps. We're up against overzealous bureaucrats here."

"We're working on it."

"Why are you sill here then?" Korolev smiled. "You want it launched into space, don't you?"

Joe liked Korolev, but he didn't like OKB-1's KB-2 baby sitter, 'Korolev's devil', Ivan Pertzovsky.

ON JULY 10 1965, DZHOSIF VENIAMINOVICH Berg became a Soviet citizen. Vera again made it clear she had no intention of doing likewise, militantly retaining her Czech passport and those of all four children.

Four days later, US Mariner 4 flew by Mars, the first to return images from the Red Planet. On July 24, while the CIA and FBI were still wondering where Joel Barr had gone, four US F-4 Phantom Jets escorting a bombing raid at Kang Chi, Vietnam, were hit by Soviet anti-aircraft missiles, the first such attack. One F-4 was shot down, three were damaged.

Two days later, Elvira called Joe at home, against their protocols, "I have a daughter; I'm calling her Valeria; she looks like you." Elvira's husband Anton believed Valeria was his.

The next day, July 27, Philip Staros returned from the rural sanitorium. Though he projected a renewed determination to make the best of the situation, he seemed weak, not rested, still stressed and lethargic. Joe sat with him in his office and tried to bring him up to date. Phil's mind seemed elsewhere; he scowled and moved his mustache scornfully, as if thinking of something distasteful. He didn't want to hear about the successful UM-1NKh installations which were well on the way to becoming universal in the USSR. "Only the UM-2T and the UM-2S matter now," he said. "In Tupolev's bombers or Korolev's Soyuz, we'd have a chance to recover. Then we will still have a shot at the top." There was a frail but dogged persistence to Phil's tone that worried Joe.

On August 15, when the Beatles packed New York's Shea Stadium with 55,600 fans, Joe knew things were changing in the USSR, because all the younger people he, Elvira and Phil knew in Moscow and Leningrad would have given anything to be at that concert performance.

Three weeks after his return from the sanitorium, Phil was still in a gray mood. Joe said to him, "Let's call ourselves lucky; we're free to pursue our work; they aren't touching our salaries or imposing any travel restrictions."

"You did it to me twice. What a fool I've been to listen."

"What? I was just saying, *Cheer Up*."

"You in*si*sted on writing that *letter!* Calling them 'ignorant'! 'not competent'! Whose bright ideas were those?"

Joe hung his head. "Why harp on that now? We both agreed; you wanted to sign it. Be happy Viktor is still with us."

"That's your answer?"

Though Eric Firdman overheard some of this, he did not understand English well enough yet or hear it clearly enough to connect it with what Phil had told him earlier, at the sanatorium.

In the next few days, as the Auschwitz trial in Frankfurt convicted 66 ex-SS personnel to life in prison and others to shorter stays, Joe thought of how paltry such justice would seem to Julius. *He'd be doubly proud of what we did, that we did not hesitate too long. We didn't think of that way then, but the balance of power has been maintained....*

About the time the US launched Gemini 5 with Gordon Cooper and Pete Conrad, "You'd think," Joe said to the still brooding Staros, "that there'd be some concern over the danger of depending on fuel cells for electricity during their first one-week flight."

"They'd be lighter than the batteries," Phil said, "maybe share your thoughts with Korolev. Save thrust for the UM-2S."

"NASA will tell us how they liked fuel cells, but I doubt

they'll disclose much we don't already know about the on-board computer."

"So Viktor gave you the complete plans?"

"On the Q-T."

"So ask him for the data on the flight."

"Maybe."

"What was the weight?"

"Fifty-nine pounds. One point three-five cubic feet."

"Tell that to Korolev's devil."

"Phil, Viktor told me something else. He's been promoted, by the way; he's now Major Taroikin."

"What else did he tell you?"

"Not in so many words, you understand, but he more or less confirmed that Korolev is directly in charge of a program to beat the Apollo missions to the Moon."

"What were his *exact* words?"

"No, I'm not kidding. He said, 'You don't think the leaders in space will let the Americans get up there first, do you?' Something like that. We'd been talking about Sergei Pavlovich. He says there's talk of a Moon colony, mineral mining and staffed research operations."

"Do you suppose once a UM-3M runs the Moon colony, they'll take my advice on Zelenograd And make me the General Director?" Phil asked.

Joe didn't answer. He didn't want to say what he thought, that Phil's obsession was delusional.

THIRTY-THREE

"All structures on Gorodomlya island were renovated and living conditions were quite decent for those times. At least married specialists received separate two- or three-room apartments. Visiting the island, I could only envy them, because I and my family lived in Moscow in a shared four-room apartment, where we had two rooms of 24 square metres (260 sq ft) combined. Many of our specialists and workers lived in barracks without the most elementary necessities. This is why life on the island behind barbed wire could not compare at all to prisoner of war conditions." ---Boris Chertok, USSR Space Control Systems Designer

SOON, BUT ONLY AFTER ERIC FIRDMAN AND Mark Galperin had designed the UM-3 with Phil and Joe's oversight, they were faced with the fact that the USSR did not have the technology to make the hybrid thin-film integrated circuits planned in their design. From their current political position in the political toilet, there'd be no help in acquiring that technology. The UM-3 was thus stalled while their adversaries continued to threaten the UM-2.

In October, Brezhnev 'reorganized' Soviet industry. KB-2 was demoted to the Leningrad Design Bureau, LKB, subservient to the Science Center in Zelenograd. Dmitry Ustinov became a candidate member of the Politburo and secretary of the Central Committee with oversight of the military, the defense industry and security organs. He was now directly in charge of developing the Soviet Union's intercontinental ballistic missile systems. He wasn't answering their calls.

Junior engineers were put in charge of the UM-1NKh installations in plants throughout the USSR while Phil, Joe, Eric and Mark were busy preparing the UM-2M and the UM-2S for the Soyuz spacecraft to guide a manned Moon landing. Or so they often thought.

On October 16, anti-Vietnam war protests drew 100,000 in eighty US cities. The USSR increased its military aid to North Vietnam. When, on November 9, Vermont, New Hampshire, Massachusetts, Connecticut, Rhode Island, New York, New Jersey and parts of Canada were hit by a series of electricity blackouts lasting over thirteen hours, Viktor Taroikin said affably to Joe, "We've had our share of electrical shutdowns, but nothing quite like that."

"A modern system, controlled by even the UM-1NKh, would scale down usage by lowering voltage or shutting down prepared sections," Joe offered. "No simple mistake could trigger such a cascade of failures."

SERGEI G. GORSHKOV, ONE OF THE USSR'S

most powerful military men—Admiral of the Fleet of the Soviet Union, equal in rank to a Marshal in the Army—was already familiar with Staros and Berg; he'd heard about them from Admiral Aksel Berg soon after their arrival in Leningrad in 1956. He'd visited them in 1959 along with Dmitry Ustinov and many other military leaders. And Gorshkov had been one of the first to be included in Khrushchev's entourage for the May 4 1962 visit to their lab at the Palace of Soviets, a visit which whetted Gorshkov's interest in them even further and secured his close ongoing attention. As Khrushchev's appointed Commander-in-Chief of the Soviet Navy, further promoted and awarded by Brezhnev, Gorshkov was on his way to expand the Soviet Navy into a global force, over several decades if necessary. He would succeed; the USSR would come to have the mightiest submarine force in history. Relatively numb to politics, Gorshkov's firm grip on reality made it clear to him that these strange Czechs were a key to making the USSR a powerful seafaring nation. If he knew they were former American spies, he wasn't telling anyone. In early November 1965, he was happy to receive an invited visit from Joe and Phil along with Eric Firdman and Mark Galperin. Several of Gorshkov's top admirals and brilliant naval engineers were there. When they were all seated and had exchanged greetings, Gorshkov addressed the two American engineers:

"What I know that perhaps I should not, is that you have recently delivered a small but powerful airborne computer you call UM-2M to OKB-1 for testing its possible use on Soyuz spacecraft. You should not tell me and I should not ask you to tell me, but anyway, is it true, the claims that have been made?"

When Joe smiled, Eric cringed, afraid Joe would make some sort of joke in a happy effort to join Gorshkov's sense of humor. Phil, too, was amused by Gorshkov's mockery of subterfuge and he said quickly, but comfortably, "The UM-2 can do whatever is needed for the Soyuz craft. So yes, it's true, all the good things you may have heard." He winked good naturedly.

Gorshkov nodded, studying Staros. "No doubt you have high hopes."

"Reasonable ones, I believe."

"If you are not too busy with outer space, perhaps you might consider modifying your computer to operate fire control and navigation on our submarines? In fact, what we need is a revolutionary Combat Information and Control System." (CICS)

Phil and Joe were well aware that the go-ahead for the use of the UM-2S on the Soyuz spacecraft was caught in a controversy at OKB-1 over what must be removed from the Soyuz craft to make room in compensation for the added weight of the UM-2S. They were at a virtual standstill there.

"...Certainly, well worth considering," Phil said. "This should not be such a large problem, to be accomplished in a fairly short time, and at no great cost."

"I'm afraid," Gorshkov said, "I cannot agree with you about any of that. I think you'll find converting a space craft computer to a submarine is a bigger job than you imagine. Your machine will need to coordinate enemy movement information from sonar and radar inputs, compute navigation, operate propulsion and torpedo firing plus a number of other combat functions as well as controlling the habitat atmosphere and the lighting of the combat vessel."

As Phil recovered from his surprise at Gorshkov's offer and this admonition, he began to give a solid presentation of the UM-2's distinct advantages. Watching Gorshkov listening, Joe realized that missing from Gorshkov's manner were any signs that he regarded them as tainted or damaged goods. *It's as if he didn't know we were put to shame at the GKET kollegiya. But he does know…and he's ignoring the accusations of Romanov and the Leningrad Obkom. Is this how he goes? No one fucks with Gorshkov? Is that his shtick?*

"I feel certain the UM-2 can handle everything you require, and more," Phil concluded.

"Let's begin our work immediately then," Gorshkov said. "You can begin by testing your computer's ability to calculate navigation on a fishing trawler and after that on a Navy minesweeper, and then begin work with the 24th Naval Research Institute at Kronstadt."

"That's immediately doable and I promise a positive outcome," Phil said.

Gorshkov replied, "If further disclosure proves what I suspect, we'll get you an order for a prototype. There are, of course, quite a number of submarines in our navy, and we may be selling them to other friendly nations, as well."

At this time, Russia was becoming a major supplier to the world market of combat submarines, to India and China, for example.

He's the real thing, Joe thought, *he uses the scientific method to sort the gems from the gravel. He and Phil will get along well—Maybe he'll keep Phil focused, and off his sorrows.*

"I'm grateful for your confidence," Phil was saying, "we will work hard and we will do well."

"Eventually you'll be working with the 81st Design Bureau and Reserve Command Center of the Baltic Fleet in Liepāja, Latvia. I'm planning to close that port to commercial traffic. I expect that by next year you'll be working on early tests with our 14th submarine regiment. You'll be in Liepāja in 1968, by year end, at least."

"We'll do the early tests at LKB here in Leningrad," Phil said.

"First proof of performance on our trawler and mine sweeper."

"I'm sure the UM-2 will be up to the task," Phil said.

"Let's have our own name for our computer," Gorshkov said, "not so much *Um* (the Russian word for intelligence) as *Uzel* (node or knot). I'm not suggesting this as a code name, just a pet name among us. *Our* computer: Uzel!"

"Uzel," they all said softly. *Eto Nasha.* It is ours.

Joe, Eric, Mark and Phil returned to LKB not yet fully valuing Gorshkov's comment that conversion of the UM-2S to combat submarines would be anything but straight forward. Phil was still focused on his hopes for guiding the the Soyuz craft to reinstatement as leader of mikroelektronika in the USSR. Working underwater seemed far less glorious than flying jet bombers or landing men on the Moon, but it was far better than the basic nothing they'd been having—except for the growing success of the UM-1Nkh, under Joe's guidance, in controlling the processes of the national economy. Joe loved doing it; it matched his dream of using technology to make more of what people needed for the good life of a successful communist society.

Phil assigned Mark Galperin to take the lead in designing and preparing the Uzel, in effect making him the Chief Designer of the *Uzel*. On a daily basis, Mark would oversee everything and everybody from design engineers to relations with the Soviet Navy's engineering hierarchy. Phil Staros would be ultimately responsible, and would be so recognized by both the GKET and the Soviet Navy. As they prepared for testing the UM-2S on available surface vessels, Phil seemed half-hearted and distracted while Joe was happy they had a challenge to work on, and Mark felt greatly honored, ready to devote heart, mind, body, life time and soul.

TWO OFFICERS FROM THE NAVY'S COMPUTER science group at the 24th Naval Research Institute came to LKB to tell Staros and Galperin that Gorshkov would be satisfied if the UM-2S was capable of 'double accuracy'. Once there was a successful test for navigational accuracy in real 'warship conditions' they would go ahead. So, late in 1965, they set up aboard an old trawler, with a recent iteration of the UM-2S. When tested, this would-be Uzel supplied rapid, highly accurate measurements at sea. The process was then repeated on a Navy minesweeper moving rapidly on an erratic course. Whereupon, the much impressed commander of the minesweeper signed off on both trials.

Two days later, Vice-Admiral Abram L. Genkin came to the LKB in Leningrad and, in conference with Phil Staros, agreed that he was ready to trust LKB to create a system superior to all prior CICS for strategic submarines. "But a system," he said, "which would be ten times smaller than the smallest existing CICS, otherwise it would not gain a place in the tightly packed boats."

"Otherwise no deal, I agree," Phil said. Joe and Galperin nodded solemnly. *It was not unreasonable if our thinking has been correct...* They all shook hands. Genkin joked, "All we need now is 'Rothchild's signature.'"

"How difficult will it be, the funding?" Phil asked sternly.

"Don't worry," Genkin said, "I will take care of it."

Years later, Mark Galperin would realize that Admiral A.L. Genkin and Minister A.I. Shokin had been in close cooperation for decades in testing and producing ship radar systems during the war and postwar years. Thus it was not strange that Genkin had made such short work of their early vetting process.

In late 1965, just before the new year, the Central Committee of the CPSU issued a decree and the Council of Ministers approved it: a new extensive Naval shipbuilding plan wherein was spelled out the development of the Uzel.

Almost immediately, individual submarines of different types, including some still in the design stage were designated to be one of the first three boats to test the new system under different avionic conditions and torpedo accommodations. This meant Staros and LKB would be dealing with many different chief designers and equipment manufacturers, a prospect that worried Staros more than it worried Joe.

NOVEMBER 16, THE SOVIET UNION LAUNCHED
the Venera 3 for Venus, infusing her citizenry with successive

surges of sometimes reluctant patriotic feelings. *Eto Nasha.* Joe thought, *If we can stay ahead of the US in space, there's no reason we can't develop whatever technology is needed to create a worker's paradise.*

On December 5, the USSR's constitution day, some fifty people met in Pushkin Square in Moscow. This 'Glasnost Meeting' was about only one thing: an *open* trial for dissident writers Andrei Sinyavsky and Yuli Daniel, an *open* trial as specified in the Soviet Constitution. A handbill explained this 'people's request'. From a friend of Elvira's, Joe had seen this handbill and he read a *samizdat* (self-published) account of the arrest of the participants who included curious bystanders. It was the beginning of *glasnost* (openness). When Joe showed this 'contraband literature' to Phil, Staros said, "I suppose you think it's the beginning of a counter-revolution? You're right, not everybody loves this Communism as much as you do. But instead of bothering with these nuisances, what are we doing about UM-2S weight reduction for Sergei Pavlovich?"

"We've scrapped steel to use titanium, redesigned the cooling system and incorporated all circuit changes that have been tested. The weight of the spacecraft computer will be down to 18 kilograms."

"What about further circuit changes?"

"Retesting and de-bugging would take too long. We need to deliver a guidance system that can do the job, on time."

Days later the two men read in the *New York Times*, that US Gemini 6 and 7 had performed a controlled rendezvous in earth orbit.

"Bringing the two nose-to-nose, 120-feet apart, 185 miles over Hawaii could only happen with those IBM computers doing all the calculations on the spot," Joe said.

"With twenty-thousand byte memories, performing 7,000 calculations a second!" Phil's voice had some of his old energy.

"The UM-2S can run circles around those IBM 360's."

"Let's get it done and maybe we'll have a chance to prove it." Phil was trying to come back. He wanted to take charge again, to care again. And he was trying not to denigrate Joe's decisions made while he was gone, though his feelings of being stuck and trapped sometimes prompted him to blame Joe.

On December 21, the Soviet Union announced that it had shipped SAM missiles to North Vietnam, something American pilots already knew only too well. The S-75 Dvina, the missile that shot down Gary Powers, had brought down US war planes for some time in Vietnam. Soviet anti-aircraft defense was top notch.

When, on December 22, David Lean's film of Boris Pasternak's controversial novel, *Doctor Zhivago*, starring Omar Sharif and Julie Christie, was released, Joe could not help a strange feeling at the prospect of Americans, especially Vivian, seeing the Bolshevik revolution through that lens.

THIRTY-FOUR

"We're more popular than Jesus now..."
--John Lennon

ON A SUNDAY, JANUARY 2 1966, JOE WAS NOT surprised when a call came from Ivan Pertzovsky, Sergei Korolev's man at LKB, asking that he, Phil and Eric Firdman come promptly to meet Korolev at OKB-1. Joe called Pertzovsky back twenty minutes later to say that Phil was unreachable and Eric was out of town. Joe suspected that Phil had occupied himself with one of his girlfriends, an habitual solace.

"Yes, I know," Pertzovsky said, "I've checked."

"Perhaps later today or tomorrow Phil will be—"

"--You will come anyway. How soon can you be here?"

"Give me forty minutes."

"Make it thirty. I'll meet you at the main entrance."

"So much for a little stroll or a drive to the parks," Vera lamented when she saw that her husband's attention had been seized as if by the voice of God himself.

"I've been asked to go alone to an important meeting," Joe said, "But I'll be back in an hour or so."

"Then it will be too late, at least for the parks; besides, it won't be just an hour. It never is."

Twenty-eight minutes later, Joe was ushered into Sergei Korolev's office. Korolev was alone. He waved Pertzovsky to leave and for Joe to take a seat.

"Sorry to say," Joe offered, "I've had to come alone."

"*Nichivo,* (nonsense) you are the scientist, we understand one another. I'm going to be out of touch next week. Next Sunday I'm going into hospital for some minor surgery." In response to Joe's look of concern, Korolev confided, "These doctors think they can fix my hemorrhoids. After nearly killing me in their prisons, now they are worried about a few hemorrhoids. I'm not saying I'd mind losing them."

"Of course," Joe said. "Of course."

"So I thought I'd let you know of a decision I've made before you hear rumors during my absence."

Joe, numbed by fear that Korolev was about to cancel the UM-2S, spoke into the slight pause in Korolev's declaration, "I'll relay to Phil whatever you tell me, word for word."

"No. Tell him only what I'm about to tell you. My security detail insists that my whereabouts, the hospital visit and so on, be kept secret. They fear American sabotage; I told *you* only because we are alone and I'm tired of them. But here it is: you can tell Phil that the UM-2S is acceptable as the guidance system for Soyuz spacecraft. Next week I will draft and sign an order to place the 2S on board the first Soyuz. If Soyuz 1 is a success, it will control navigation and the docking of our capsules in space, including eventually a landing on the Moon."

"That's fantastic!" Joe cried. "I wish Phil could hear you say it."

"You will tell him. We can celebrate, if you like, later this month. The weight of your latest version is reasonable and I agree with you that any attempt to reduce it further will cause unacceptable delays."

"We'll be able to concentrate on application software development then," Joe affirmed.

"As I mentioned, we understand each other. But make sure you do not repeat Soyuz plans to anyone outside our circle, including people here, comrade Pertzovsky, for example."

"This is the best possible news for the new year." Joe was tempted to ask questions about the specific plans to put a Soviet Kosmonaut on the Moon. *If anyone knows the true details, it must be Korolev. Hey, don't get ahead of yourself. There'll be a better time...*

The following day, when Joe shared this encounter, Phil's frustration at missing it, at having no way even to confirm the truth and range of it, was obvious. Neither man said anything about why Phil had been unreachable, or about Phil's woman from the staff of another firm, Olga V. Joe emphasized the need to keep quiet about the Soyuz plans: "You'll hear it all from

Sergei Pavlovich, later this month."

Phil flared his left nostril and raised the left side of his mustache as though preparing his face and lips for the smile that followed at last. "Didn't I say this is great news and I'm glad you were around to see Sergei Pavlovich?"

"I think you did. I'm pretty sure." They exchanged the old conspiratorial smiles.

ON JANUARY 15 1966, PERTZOVSKY CAME TO LKB to inform them that Sergei Korolev had died on the operating table the day before. Not only were they dumbstruck with grief and horror at the thought that this central and important supporter was gone, but of course there was the question of whether Korolev had given the order to use the UM-2S to guide Soyuz spacecraft and, if he had, would his successor obey the order? Phil knew of only one person, Joe, who had heard Korolev say the 2S would guide Soyuz and he said to Joe when they were alone, "Tell me again exactly what he told you."

"I've told you. He called us there to tell us he'd decided to do it. Do you want a direct quote? Okay: *'next week I will draft and send the order.'* I was to tell you and whoever you decided to share it with. Why doesn't it bother you more that a guy going in for hemorrhoids comes out dead?"

"Do you suspect foul play?"

"Maybe, but how will we stay ahead of the Americans without him?"

"Yes, damnit," Phil swore, his nostrils flaring, "his death is going to ruin the Soviet space program! You're sure it wasn't just a maybe? Had he been drinking? Did he offer you a drink?"

"He was cold sober. And, if you haven't noticed, he doesn't drink. He wanted to tell you in person, but you were…off somewhere—making Anna very suspicious by the way whenever she finds out that I don't know where you are, either."

Phil said nothing but glared at Joe, resenting Joe's sympathy for Anna. *Is the pot calling the kettle black?*

"What worries me," Joe said, "and should worry you, is, if what Pertzovsky thinks is true, the next chief designer at OKB-1 will be Vasily Mishin, a so-called rocket engineer who based his career on examining and reporting on the Nazis' V-2 design facilities in 1945, twenty years ago. And unlike Sergei Pavlovich, he is a drinker."

"Mishin was Korolev's right hand man, so he's the logical choice I suppose." Phil was glum.

"He's not our best friend. And does the right hand still do what Korolev would have done?"

"You're right; Mishin was a yes man; we have no idea what he'll do now."

"The man likes his vodka," Joe said without emphasis, but which drew a nod from Phil who said:

"We need to get a meeting with Mishin as soon as—what about the UM-2T? What's your theory as to why there's no progress with Tupolev?"

"My theory? Is that Tupolev doesn't have a bomber to be navigated yet."

"They no doubt want it to be better than the B-52. Maybe the big bosses keep changing their minds?"

"Probably something like that," Joe conceded. "They have advanced the ICBM programs for sure. Maybe they think they don't need bombers…"

On January 17 1966, at a time when the two nations maintained fleets of bombers constantly aloft, laden with thermonuclear weapons, a B-52 collided with a KC-135 Stratotanker over Spain, dropping three 70-kiloton hydrogen bombs near the town of Palomares, and another one into the sea nearby. None detonated.

BY EARLY IN 1966, THE SINGLE, SIMPLE phrase of the Soviet Naval re-armament decree that referred to a classified, detailed technical sketch of the Uzel, meant that LKB received an order from the Central Committee of the CPSU as a part of the large naval shipbuilding plan; to develop the Combat Information and Control System, Uzel. Joining in the Uzel project with the Soviet Navy meant introductions to all the Navy experts and top brass of the submarine regiments. Some could and would be extremely helpful, others would be skeptical, at least at first. But almost immediately with that decree, came newly ever-present representatives of the Soviet Navy and a new security detail from the State Security Committee.

Because secrecy was paramount, Mark set up a separate room to meet and gather his team and isolated them from all other work at LKB. He began to collect the young and bold, great engineers, real scientists, great jokers, fine basketball players, and would-be musicians, to build the Uzel CICS from scratch, with only the UM-2S design to start with. They must create the algorithms and program scheduling computational process, incorporating stringent timing charts, making full use of system interrupt programs.

Because there were no trained programmers at LKB, Mark needed to select and train young LKB generalists. But from the 24th Naval Research Institute, Galina Fedorovna, joined the staff at LKB. She was an already established and highly respected programmer who would become a convivial colleague. It seemed she had the expertise to successfully coordinate all the algorithms of the system to deal with the distribution of resources, speed, RAM and non-volatile memory.

They needed system structures based on flexibility in the use and distribution of hardware and software techniques. They must not only implement computing tasks, but to display, simultaneously at several locations in the submarine any problems, sensor reception, info transmission, or communication. It must be a system defined by the science of choice and justification: the implementation of the main system solutions to given combat situations.

They began to receive from the Navy not only the goals that needed to be met, but often ready algorithms for calculating those solutions. They would be able to test and examine the two main competitors to the Uzel: Combat Information and Control Systems, Cloud and Accord.

Both Cloud and Accord. had passed initial state tests and were expected to be certified in 1967. They were being further developed for a new class of submarines with a newly designed nuclear power plant. Accord had set the direction for submarine automation, the first system designed to provide control of combat activity using a single remote control to manage all electronic equipment and weapons. But both Cloud and Accord were based on vacuum tubes, weighed hundreds of kilograms, took up vast spaces and drew thousands of kilowatts of power. But, because they had been created recently, they were considered modern and up-to-date. There seemed to be no urgent need for change; things worked and were stable. Their need for huge amounts of space, energy, heat dissipation and operating personnel had already been justified and funded. Cloud and Accord satisfied the main purpose of the combat submarine: *effective readiness for combat.*

One of the few advantages that the LKB Uzel team had against competitors and detractors in the constant propaganda wars and rumor battles, was that Phil Staros had been so thoroughly . discredited by the *Kollegiya* show trial and by being kicked out of Zelenograd. Their most dangerous enemies thought a tiny digital computer, based on transistors stood so little chance of survival in attempting to operate a modern submarine, that it was smart money to let the Uzel die of its own diseases rather than murder it.

Though the older experienced hands, the designers of previous torpedo and navigation systems, often had developed useful or even essential algorithms for dealing with aiming weapons from position, distance and direction data, and data about water conditions affecting underwater maneuvering, the LKB Uzel team needed to overcome other technical, financial and psychological obstacles as well as making sure all the algorithms were talking to each other at lightning speeds.

At first, Staros refused to accept any component equipment into the Uzel controlled system that was not manufactured by LKB. But the designers of the "Height" torpedo control system demonstrated how such interface problems were solved in the development of Height and could be solved for the Uzel in the same way. Staros, who never argued with the best technical solutions, soon accepted the proven methods of interfacing analog and digital sources.

For Mark Galperin and his deputy chief designers, Zhukov, Kuznetsov, Pankin and Nikitin, one of their first encounters with the Navy's introduction to their world of combat beneath the oceans was a demonstration aboard a submerged combat submarine by the Navy Academy of Torpedo Shooting, to show them the sequence of control steps. They were reminded that destruction of the enemy was not the only reason for accuracy in hitting the target. It was important to hit the target in order not to lose the torpedoes. Something for the mind of every Soviet patriot.

A schedule was set to complete bench tests of all component equipment within a year and a year later to install a system in a submarine at the Kronstadt Naval plant. The problem of dead reckoning, finding a target from known direction and speed to predict future position for an intersection by torpedoes, was inherited from the UM-2S calculations of space objects. And yet, the algorithmicalization of dead reckoning would remain one of the hardest calculations to install in the computer, and for its operators to perform.

AS COMPUTER NAVIGATION ULTIMATELY had so much to do with obtaining exact global positioning, it is interesting to note that the earliest Soviet attempts at navigation satellites, GPS, which they proposed in the early 1950s, were inspired by the hunger for fresh fish. As it happened, the Ministry of Fisheries used airplanes to spot schools of fish along coastal shoals. The pilots provided highly accurate coordinates, but the fishing boats could not use the information because they could not determine their own positions accurately enough. Knowing where you are within a kilometer or two is good in setting a course for home, but it doesn't put you atop a school of blue fin tuna.

On February 3, Soviet Luna 9 made the first soft landing on the Moon and on March 1, Soviet space probe Venera 3 became the first spacecraft to reach another planet's surface by crash-landing on Venus. So far, Korolev's death had not discernably affected Soviet Space policy or achievements. There was some excuse for reasonable optimism.

On March 16, US Gemini 8's David Scott and Neil Armstrong conducted the first docking in space, to an Agena Target Vehicle (ATV). It was a significant milestone: the Moon racers needed successful docking to go from Earth orbit to Moon orbit to the Moon's surface, and back. It required instantaneous computer control of capsule navigation and propulsion. The Gemini news was taken seriously by the Soviet Politburo. A harried and frustrated Minister Shokin told Joe, "How do we compete with people like that? They send up a spaceship just so it'll be there for the Gemini ships to practice docking."

"Not just one target vehicle, either," Joe said agreeably, "they sent up three at once. They have what we do not have, endless back-ups."

"You haven't met with Vasily Mishin yet?" Shokin asked.

"We're still waiting. We've heard nothing back from him."

"I'll see what I can do."

"I don't feel very optimistic."

"He hasn't called you."

I think if I were to be optimistic, I should have heard from him a few weeks after Sergei Pavlovich's passing."

MARCH 29 1966, THE 23RD COMMUNIST PARTY

Congress began in Moscow. It was Leonid Brezhnev's first Party Congress as boss. To further cement his power, the Politburo had urged then threatened Sergei Korolev to launch Soyuz 1 to celebrate this great occasion. Korolev had refused. The spacecraft could not be ready in time for their party. Two days into the Congress, Vasily Mishin, Korolev's hard drinking replacement, claimed responsibility for the successful launching of Luna 10 to the Moon and accepted praise for it. Four days later, a Sunday, Luna 10 became the first spacecraft to enter orbit around the Moon. It was another Soviet first, but Luna 10 was a stopgap measure, to prevent the far more advanced American Lunar Orbiter from getting there first. Luna 10 carried no cameras but merely broadcast the 'Internationale' to cheering Communist Party delegates in Moscow, whose excessive exuberance was clearly meant to celebrate Leonid Brezhnev's leadership.

Joe and Phil stirred each other with hope and dread about the race with Apollo. Maybe things wouldn't fall apart with Korolev gone. Maybe not.

To bring the 23rd Congress to a close on April 8, Brezhnev was re-elected General Secretary of the Communist Party of the Soviet Union, ignorant, unprincipled narcissist that he was.

APRIL 10, AFTER MONTHS OF POSTPONEMENTS

and second-hand reassurances, Joe, Phil and Eric Firdman were finally invited to meet with Vasily Mishin who, as feared, was now OKB-1's Chief Designer. After waiting well past their 11 AM appointment, they were ushered to Mishin's office. After shaking hands with a flush-faced, red-eyed Mishin, Phil congratulated him on the success of Luna 10.

"Thank you, Philip Georgievich," Mishin said. "So far we've been able to get by without the help of Sergei Pavlovich... Luna 10 is surveying both sides of the Moon as we speak." But he was slurring is words as he spoke to them.

Here is my chance to ask about the manned mission, Joe thought. But he waited then said nothing. Mishin's responses, when there were any, were sluggish. *Useless to ask, unless we can surprise him,* Joe decided.

"...Ah," Mishin continued after a pause, "you have waited patiently to consult with me. Tell me, what's on your minds?"

"As you may know," Phil said, "we had reassurances from Sergei Pavlovich that the UM-2S would be the guidance computer in the Soyuz-1. And—"

"—He told me days before he died," Joe said, "that he was signing an order to make it happen."

Mishin waved a hand before him as if to clear away fog, perhaps his own fog; he was clearly inebriated: "But as far as I know...as *I know*, Sergei Pavlovich never signed such an order. Besides, the outcome must follow established process of development. You must keep working to make your guidance system effective and practical."

After several more questions, the two Americans received no reassurance whatsoever. "What about a manned Moon landing?" Joe asked. "Will we make it before the Americans do?"

This elicited the surprise Joe had hoped for, but not the answer. "What? Are you under the impression there is to be a manned Soviet expedition to the Moon? And if so…where did you get that idea?" Mishin's words were no longer as slurred though cumbersome on his lips and tongue. His bloodshot eyes probed them as his brain seemed to struggle mechanically.

Phil looked at Joe: *You open your big mouth again, you're on your own!*

"When working with Sergei Pavlovich," Joe said, "the urgency and direction of development were clearly headed toward a manned Moon landing. It was discussed in a quiet—"

"—What would you say if I told you," Mishin leaned toward them across his desk with energetic imprecision, but clearly meaning to make a conciliatory gesture, "what if I told you the manned Moon mission was not only Sergei Pavlovich's idea and plan, but mostly Sergei Pavlovich's method of getting enough funding out of the Politburo to complete the basic Soyuz program itself? To his own satisfaction of course."

"You're saying there is no such mission, and never was?"

"No. No. But, if there was, it would depend on Sergei Pavlovich's N-1 rocket, to be tested next year. I can tell you all this of course only because you three have First Form clearance. My advice is to keep working. Do I understand that we expect shortly to take delivery from you of the completed UM-2S?"

"Yes," Phil said, "that is correct."

"Well then, matters will take their course…"

"May we look forward to working with your lab in further development?" Phil asked politely.

"Perhaps in good time." Mishin stood to end the conversation.

Afterwards, Joe asked Phil, "Do you see any hope?"

"Not much," Phil admitted, "but it could still happen."

"You're actually optimistic?"

"No, desperate is more like it."

"He's a drunken procrastinator who won't decide anything because he's waiting on details, what he calls 'the final facts'."

"He's who we must convince, nevertheless."

"What's the point of working on it any longer? We'd be better off working on Gorshkov's submarine Combat Control

System. Gorshkov is a sober and serious man who has followed us from our first days at SL-11."

"I'm not arguing with you."

TEN DAYS LATER, JOE WAS INFORMED BY the LKB Communist Party Committee that his long-standing application for CPUSSR membership was being considered. He should be ready to present himself. *I've always wanted this,* he thought, *now at last I'll be a real part of it, Communist Number One.*

With their villas in Zelenograd long gone, Joe applied for larger apartments for both families on the top floor of new buildings on Budapeshtskaya Street, southeast of their cramped quarters on Kuznetskoya, farther from the center of Leningrad, but not much farther from their LKB laboratories and offices.

Vera did not share Joe's enthusiasm and happiness at the prospect of her husband being inducted into the Communist Party of the Soviet Union, and this prospect did not explain his increasing distance and seeming indifference to her charms. He tried to explain it to her:

"Can't you understand, it's not that everything will be different. I'm not going to change that much. The only difference will be that something is happening that will make me happy. Maybe I'll smile even more... Don't you have dreams from your youth that make you happier when they come true? This is my dream come true, that's all?"

"What's your dream like that, Mom?" Vivian, a twelve year old teenager, asked.

"My dream has already come true," Vera said. "I dreamed of marrying a smart, sensible man and having a big family."

Both Joe and Vivian eyed Vera wondering what was coming next. "My dream," Vivian smiled at her father, "is to become a great musician, to play the Cello in exhibitions around the world."

Joe and Vera both smiled at her.

"I have my dream," Vera said. "I just don't want to wake up and find out it isn't real."

"Oh, Mom," Vivian cooed.

"Things can change, my girl," Vera said.

"And they usually do," Joe added cheerfully then met Vera's eyes but was unable to sustain the full gift of his charm in her pleading eyes.

"Come on, girl," Vera said, "let's go for a walk to the shop and back at least, maybe once around the park. Grab your jacket, come on."

"I'll go if Papa goes too," Vivian said. "I want to be with Papa, too."

"Of course," Joe said, "no way I can pass up that offer...my two favorite girls," he lied, "of course we'll go together."

THIRTY-FIVE

"If you're a sailor, best not know how to swim. Swimming only prolongs the inevitable—if the sea wants you and your time has come."
—*James Clavell, Tai-Pan*

THERE WAS AN UNDERCURRENT OF AMUSED and lively cheerfulness among the Leningrad Design Bureau Communist Party members when Joe joined their meeting one Monday evening in early May 1966. The party secretary brought the meeting to order then announced: "As you know a main item on today's schedule is our consideration of the application for party membership from Dzhosef Veniaminovich Berg. We've had almost a year to consider it, and it is time a decision was made." Stirs of interest accompanied unguarded smiles. Joe was introduced as though everyone did not already know him and like him. He was asked to inform them with his autobiography.

Joe stood before them, cleared his throat and said, "I grew up in modest means in Johannesburg, South Africa. As you may know, my homeland was and still is troubled by apartheid, the brutal separation of black people into crowded ghettos." He paused and looked around. The others waited, perhaps anticipating his normal joking style. "I must admit that as a child, I was not overwhelmed with how wrong apartheid was. I could not understand it, but I did not condemn it. Then as I got a little older, and became an avid reader, I was given a copy of Maxim Gorky's wonderful novel, *Mother*. That was when I began to understand the universal nature of the class struggle." *Who says I can't sling the bull?*

"And by the way," Joe said, "Pelagueya Nilovna, (title character) was not unlike my own mother." Joe thought of

Rebecca, her constant struggle for the family, the times she had pointed him toward the good things in life: music, people, how to live fully on close to nothing. The thought of how seldom he'd remembered her recently troubled him as he said, "But that book made me realize that at any time there are people squandering resources while depriving other people of those resources. At any given time, people are being compelled to make others rich while they are hungry. It is wrong. A human being won't tolerate it. Not for long."

"So what did you do?" someone prompted gently, amused. "How did you join the class struggle on the side of the working people?"

"No, I was slow to act, but I expressed my opinion, that apartheid was a state crime against the people...and of course this won me enemies among both neighbors and officials. But in reading the great Lenin and the works of Karl Marx, I began to understand that apartheid was only one example of class struggle, and that there were socialist forces pushing back against imperialism and brutal exploitation. By the time I was twenty I knew I wanted to be part of the world struggle for Communism."

"So," came a teasing question, "do you see yourself as Pavel Mikhailovich?" (the protagonist's son in *Mother*)

"Oh, no," Joe said smoothly, "far from it, but my mother believed in me, as his mother did; she accepted who I was, I'd say."

"He looks like Andrey," someone whispered, "the 'Little Russian'. (Pavel's tall, close friend in the novel)

"He's tall enough," someone agreed.

"Well things got hot for me in Johannesburg..." Joe thought of escaping Paris, being terrified on the train to Zurich. "so I got out of South Afrika and came first to Prague, then here to Leningrad, which I am happy to call my home. I have a family"—*almost two families*—"a good wife and four bright children. I work with fantastic people, great people."

They all laughed and when it came to a vote, it was unanimous. His performance had been a traditional ritual rather than a challenge. He'd laid it on thick, but the welcoming Party liked it thick.

"Congratulations, Dzhosef Veniaminovich, the chairman said, "you are now a probationary member of the Communist Party of the Soviet Union."

"A young man's dream fulfilled," Joe said politely.

"Well, Joe," the party cell chairman said, "I want to turn over the chair to you, as you may have things you'd like to say as a Party member, issues you'd like to bring up?"

"All joking aside, I want you all to know," Joe said, "that this is the fulfillment of *my* life-long dream. Today will always be one of my proudest days. I've been saying for years now, 'I'm Communist Number One;' it was my nickname in Prague at times. But today you have given me the chance to grow into the part. I promise to be a good and true comrade."

Generous smiles greeted him.

IN MAY, A REVIEW OF SOVIET COMPUTER technology in *The Journal of Control Engineering,* favorably compared the UM-1NKh with its Western competition. The review praised the computing power and 'remarkably small size and low power consumption' of the UN-1NKIh. Joe knew: *the UM-1NKh is nothing compared to the UM-2, still being blocked by the Leningrad Obkom. We must install it on an airplane or ship before they will certify it for mass production and broad use.* Though Phil Staros continued to hope that the UM-2S would guide Union (Soyuz) space craft, Joe tried gently to focus Phil on the Uzel and the job of satisfying the powerful and steadfast Admiral Gorshkov.

"Damnit Joe," Phil said often, "I want us to be the ones to land the first man on the Moon. The UM-2S is deliverable right now."

"But pouring our resources into applications specific to the Soyuz craft are almost certainly a waste of time, with Vasily Mishin in charge. Better to focus on the Uzel with Galperin. Wide use in submarines is our best shot at certification. Our best chance to recover our reputations."

"We're doing it, what more do you want?"

"I don't know," Joe said. "For you to cheer up and be like old times," I guess."

As Dr. Martin Luther King Jr. began to make public

comments against the Vietnam War, he spurred Ed Hoover to make new plans for destroying him, dire criminal plans which could not be openly discussed.

ANY COMPANY THAT DEVELOPED OR TESTED electronic systems in the Soviet Union required specially equipped facilities, trained specialists and allotted time for testing and re-testing of individual devices. Above all, they needed a space large enough to assemble an entire system in one place. This assemblage of such a proto system was called The Chief Designer's Stand. Working until now with relatively small systems, primarily the UM-2 itself, now LKB needed to test not only thousands of software and programming fixes, but heat and humidity tolerances on all the individual devices connected to the central processor. The whole system soon included remote commander units, ancillary devices to simulate data from surface sensors, sonar and radar. And now, Joe's separate UM-2 for torpedo firing control. It all needed to be created into a viable military product in less than a year.

The only room at LKB with the capacity to house this Chief Designer's Stand was Phil's private office, a spacious chamber that had been visited by an endless stream of generals, admirals, industrial ministers, factory chieftains and Khrushchev himself. Still clinging to hopes for the UM-2S to reach the Moon, Phil reluctantly but cheerfully moved himself into a much smaller room. The Chief Designer's Stand for the Uzel was supposed to give birth to systems for three submarines, diesel-electric boats. In addition to the Chief Designer's Stand in heavily secured Phil's former office, there was need of a separate cubicle for the remote commander unit which soon took over the room next to Phil's office, his personal laboratory where he and Joe had devised the unique capabilities of the UM-2S for its trip to the Moon. Quietly, Phil watched the submarine project take over his arena of hope for that ultimate achievement. He was not happy to be swept from his professional turf.

ON JUNE 2 1966, US SURVEYOR 1 LANDED IN *oceanus procellarum* on the Moon, the first US spacecraft to soft-land on another world, only four months behind the Soviet Luna 9, the first controlled Moon landing. On July 18, John Young and Michael Collins blasted into orbit and docked their Gemini 10 with an Agena Target Vehicle. Joe found himself thinking, *They made it look easy. The IBM on-board computer made that possible.*

Two weeks later, LKB delivered the complete and thoroughly tested UM-2S to Vasily Mishin at OKB-1, an event which created an atmosphere of hopeful apprehension at LKB. Phil assured OKB-1's babysitter Ivan Pertzovsky that they would be standing-by to begin developing applications.

Even Phil did not really expect to hear from OKB-1. Pessimistic but feeling some sense of accomplishment, Joe decided to get away and spend time with Elvira. He proposed to her that they drive south, maybe as far as Tbilisi. "Those Gruzian melons you like will be ripe by the time we get there," he said.

"But Joe," she said, "my husband is away for a long trip to South America with Aeroflot. You can stay with me, here in Leningrad. We will be quite cozy."

"What about Valeria?"

"No, she will stay with my mother at the *dacha*."

Joe told Vera it was "another trip to a factory in the Kavkaz; I'll be a few days." She asked that he call every evening to say good night. "Your children need you. And so do I," she added. He smiled, happy that she seemed relatively content.

JOE AND ELVIRA SPENT DAYS 'DOING THE BUSINESS' and talking. Joe told her, "I want to get out of Leningrad and Moscow. I'm a new citizen; I want to visit other parts of my country. Not this minute of course." He pulled her closer.

"If it is not to long a trip, I would love to go with you, of course," she said. "I have not seen much of the southern part of the Union, and you are right those Gruzian melons are worth the trip by themselves." They were both referring to the long yellow melons with the sweet pale green flesh that put the so called honey dew melons to shame.

It was the evening of their third day together when the apartment door opened and Anton, Elvira's husband, found them in *his* bed. He roared; Elvira cried out. Pulling a sheet around her, she jumped up as if to confront her husband. He slugged her then slapped her down, but Joe had time to yank on his trousers and a shirt before Anton grabbed him by the neck. Shoeless, with bare chest Joe was marched down the sidewalk in the bright summer evening to the local police station where Anton enjoyed a friendly reception by several bored officers who were delighted by the welcome diversion of domestic strife.

The angry husband thrust Joe down on a bench, saying to the attending officers, "I found this nasty, dirty old fool in bed with my wife. Comrades, I ask you to inflict every punishment you can think of! Keep him locked up for as long as possible."

"Of course. Absolutely," the sergeant in charge said. "We'll charge him ten times. He won't see the light of day for months."

"I'll kill you if I see you anywhere near my wife again," Anton told Joe as he turned to leave.

"Lock him up," the sergeant told his underlings in a loud voice for the departing cuckhold's benefit.

In a holding cell, ten minutes later, Joe was just wondering how to call for help and to whom, and how soon Vera would be informed. Just then the sergeant came, now smiling jovially, unlocked his cell and beckoned Joe back to the front desk. He told his nervous, disconcerted prisoner:

"You're free to go. Try to be a little more careful next time. Get a private room maybe. ...If I were you, I wouldn't go back to get my shoes and socks. Do you need a few rubles to get home on? Get yourself a pair of sandals?"

"I'm alright; I've got my wallet and my car keys. Here, let me give you a tenner."

"No thanks, unnecessary. Just be more careful next time."

"Please," Joe proffered the ten ruble note."

"Well, if I must. Thank you."

Two days later, four and a half months after Soviet Luna 10, the first US spacecraft to orbit the Moon, US Lunar Orbiter 1, began sending back photographs. It was clear to many, but especially to Joe and Phil that the US was performing each step more thoroughly and competently than the Soviet Union. They were not surprised, but continued to hold some small measure of hope.

THE UZEL PROJECT ENCOUNTERED MANY

decorated scientists and engineers who had been involved in artillery control systems, or torpedo firing systems, and these experts were often strongly influenced by the last generation of mechanical computing machines which used cam mechanisms and conoid shapes to pursue entirely numerical methods of computation. They worked in ministries, plants and research institutes. They came to see what was going on and to offer advice and opinions. One such man, among the many who had been working in fire control systems for Navy ships during the Great Patriotic War was their GKET Minister, Aleksandr Ivanovich Shokin.

As the Uzel team struggled for its right to exist, it was as if they were entering a stream of technical tradition in Soviet methods of weapons control populated by scientists who either resisted the complete innovation of the Uzel or eagerly embraced it in early perceptions of its power and flexibility, recognition based on having tried and failed at what was claimed that the Uzel could do. They saw in the Uzel new tactical opportunities in the digital processing and storage of sonar and radar data. Shokin knew very well how advanced the Uzel was and he did his best to defend and support it, but could not entirely quell the many detractors as the Uzel project gained traction. Though it may well have been too late to stop it, their enemies continued to make their jobs harder.

Testing for heat and humidity of each piece of equipment in the Chief Designer's Stand became a major roadblock to continuing the bench tests, debugging all the docking protocols, and developing individual equipment software, so that all units could communicate at high speed. The removal physically or isolation electronically in order to test a single equipment unit in working conditions destroyed system continuity and system testing.

Joe was the one to come up with a solution. He suggested building a plastic tent around the entire Stand, over all the individual components and all the links between them. Under his supervision, when this tent was completed, were placed electric heaters with automatic temperature control. Regulated humidifiers were also installed in the tent. Phil watched as his large prestigious personal domain disappeared in a makeshift artificial jungle. Again the scientist in Phil ably recognized what a great deal of time would be saved. So that, even as these long climate tests were carried out, precision testing of each instrument and its individual paths continued, as did debugging and acceptance of software.

One day in early August 1966, there was a group of Navy brass, acceptance officers and top level Navy program developers, sitting around at the Stand table outside Joe's tent, ready to discuss test protocol, when suddenly an alarm rang and LKB's man on duty jumped up, went behind a screen, and emerged less than a minute later in swimming trunks. He then disappeared into the tent to take readings of each control device as Dr. Berg had instructed.

Developers and programmers alike changed into swimming gear to work around-the-clock shifts, seven days a week. Readers probably think, *Not in the Soviet Union, no one can do this ,so it could not actually happen quite this way,* but this was the true fashion of these Soviet Navy officers and LKB's dedicated developers. Several sub-groups worked simultaneously in tense rhythm and though there was friction, they stayed proud and happy knowing they would never forget these days so sparse of even the hardest won victories. It was about algorithms and their software implementation in algorithm controlled layers, over and over again then changing yet again.

Under the watchful eyes of the regime services, LKB's work on the Uzel in Leningrad went full speed ahead. KGB security measures included check points guarded by very sharp men; few visitors ever made it anywhere near the Stand. Since their first days in the attic at 12 Volkovskaya Street with SL-11, KGB security had been vigilant, always ostensibly to protect Phil and Joe from any CIA assassination or kidnapping attempts. The secret of the two 'Czechs' and their work had been carefully guarded. This security overlay had never particularly bothered them or hampered their work, but it had always been present.

Now security would ensure that any access by anyone to the central LKB lab where the Uzel was under development, not only involved three check points, but tedious searches. Because of such intense scrutiny, of anyone coming in or leaving, even for the leading lights, there was no stopping by the lab early then going out for a breakfast roll and coffee or tea, then dropping back in. Some lesser but key personnel were delayed in the process of carrying out their duties.

Part of what must be kept secret was the design of the computer system itself including the changing design of the central UM-2 processor. As development moved forward the design and actual substance of the Uzel was constantly changing. At this point, Eric Firdman's work on the early versions of computer aided design and manufacturing, CADCAM, were proving useful for following and storing the constant changes at each stage of Uzel development. Firdman's program allowed for the immediate updating of all versions.

The chairman of the Navy Commission in charge of the Uzel project, Rear Admiral and Hero of the Soviet Union, Vladimir Konstantinovich Konovalov, much loved by his sailors, was very helpful to them; constantly acquainting them with the nature of submarine navigation and the current parameters of control. He generously shared his and other commanders' real world experiences, drew their attention to how carefully they must refer to the habits of the commander and officers of the boat when creating and introducing a new system. "You need to know how commanders are used to communicating with the traditional torpedo firing system, what the commander thinks as he sees boat silhouettes on the screen. These Navy divers are used to reading target motion data and making decisions by sensing an adversary's intentions."

Not only could the old timers explain to the LKB team just what the ship commanders had been accustomed to doing and what they would need to keep doing, and even *how* the Uzel could do it, some of these voluntary advisers had hosted a delegation from the US Sperry Instrument company in the 1940s, where Joel Barr later worked. They had gathered information for the KGB from that Sperry delegation which had come to pick the brain of Professor Sergei Arturovich Izenbek, the father of all Soviet combat control systems. Izenbek and these colleagues of his who had dealt with Sperry, were willing to share what they knew with LKB.

Only later, when the news got out that the Navy brass was loving the Uzel, did the detractors and enemies bring out their most lowdown dirt campaign. By then it seemed it might be too late to stop them.

ON SEPTEMBER 12, GEMINI 11 ASTRONAUTS Richard F. Gordon, Jr. and Pete Conrad performed a docking rendezvous with an Agena Target Vehicle 1 hour 34 minutes after launch *during their first orbit*, a stunningly efficient performance. Then Gordon and Conrad used the ATV rocket engine to achieve a world-record high-apogee Earth orbit. They even enjoyed a small amount of artificial gravity by spinning the two spacecraft connected by a tether. Gordon also performed two extra-vehicular excursions for a total of 2 hours 41 minutes.

The news of the Gemini 11 feats left no doubt in the minds of the Soviet Politburo that NASA was well on the way to reaching for the Moon. "They are, preparing," Joe said, "for a manned Moon expedition. They've made computer controlled docking in space, the key to that goal, look like an effortless exercise."

Hearing nothing more from Vasily Mishin or of the UM-2S, Phil asked Eric Firdman, who was helping to write Phil's doctoral thesis, to investigate the fate of the UM-2T at Tupolev's design bureau. Later, Eric's answer was, "Nothing has been done; the prototype is collecting dust on an open shelf. Tupolev told me the order was premature, but would eventually happen."

"It means his bomber design has not been approved," Phil said. "So, we are a long way off."

"The ICBMs are less costly and can strike more rapidly," Eric agreed.

Phil and Joe were kept fully informed and participated whenever needed in developing the Uzel. The most important Uzel mainframe modification by the LKB team in Leningrad was the radical expansion of random access memory (RAM) and mods which increased computer speeds in dealing with the complex, rapidly changing data for dead reckoning. Submarine combat demanded short reaction times.

In September, the US government prepared to make LSD the most illegal drug of all illegal drugs—it seemed key to the cultural threat presented by a new generation of young people slipping their bonds to get high and live for the fun of it, to be born again and never die.

On October 22, Soviet spy George Blake escaped from Wormwood Scrubs prison in London with the help of fellow prisoners who thought his sentence of 42 years was harsh. After hiding in Britain, Blake escaped to Moscow through East Germany. He told the world, "To betray, you first must belong. I never belonged." Joe knew he had once belonged to America, but he knew he had long ago ceased to belong.

On November 6, 1966 US Lunar Orbiter 2 was launched. *They are incessant,* Admiral Sergei Gorshkov thought. *Redundant preparedness. Infinite funding. Contingency programs for the contingency programs.* Six days later Gorshkov saw the smiling photos of Jim Lovell and Buzz Aldrin, after splash-down in Gemini 12, 600 kilometers east of the Bahamian islands. *Our side will never stay ahead of them in space or with land based missiles. And the US Navy rules the ocean surfaces. We are going quietly beneath the oceans, beneath our adversary. In the depths of the seas they are weak.*

As the bench test deadline approached, the LKB Uzel team had solved most of the purely system, programming and software problems. They had successfully staved off the attacks of enemies who sought to discredit, undermine and derail them: vacuum tube people, competitors old and new.

One of the last and most serious challenges remaining prior to the navy bench tests was how better to calculate dead reckoning, how to program the Uzel to calculate an enemy position from known direction, speed, and the elapsed time from last known position. Motion sensor data from accelerometers and rotation sensors, data from gyroscopes, all needed to be continuously integrated to calculate the position, orientation and velocity of any moving object without need for external references. How to improve the mathematical guess where only elapsed time was really known? With multiple instruments for measuring speed, several methods of determining direction, which were affected by wind and current—developing a system that not only integrated all instrument data, but judged the accuracy of each piece of data against the others? It was not easy. But by year end, Mark felt fairly confident that in developing the multiple algorithms needed for dead reckoning he and his team had performed well. They'd found that some of the work done for OKB-1 on maneuvering in space was useful. The problems and the controversies that arose had been dealt with sufficiently to be deemed acceptable progress by the navy engineers and high ranking officers in charge under Sergei Gorshkov. As the Navy commanders began to see that the Uzel opened a new vista of efficiency and facility, Navy brass took up their cause and used their muscle to defend them, to stun and quiet the destructive factions. Mark Galperin felt sure that by the eve of the new year, LKB and the Uzel would stand on their own merit.

The team of young naval engineers and LKB scientists led by the two American engineers had survived much of the controversy over whether the new system was worthwhile and, just barely in time for the 49th anniversary of the revolution on November 7, LKB met the previously agreed upon bench marks including testing the programs dealing with navigation, aiming and firing torpedoes, translating sonar data into navigational options as well as the controls for internal temperature and humidity. It would soon be time to run the program routines on the most powerful Soviet military computers. As this need to begin testing and debugging the Uzel's routines, Mark Galperin sought Phil's still mildly distracted advice on using scraps of available time at night on existing larger computers. Mark would later remark that he was stunned by how Staros made each ruble demonstrate its worth. Each kopek.

On December 25 1966 the LKB Communist Party Secretary informed Joe that he had been accepted as a full member in good standing of the CPSU. He gave Joe his red Communist Party membership book with the gold embossed hammer and cycle on the cover. Joe looked forward to paying dues every month and having the party secretary sign his book each time. He thought about showing it to Vera and decided he would show it to the whole family, gently. Of course he would show it to Elvira, he reflected, as he hurried home to his Polish Catholic wife and their large family to enjoy the last of the old year and look forward with hope to the new one.

THIRTY-SIX

"As a result of half a century of Soviet rule people have been weaned from a belief in human kindness." ---Svetlana Alliluyeva, Stalin's daughter

ON JANUARY 27 1967, AFTER MANY DESIGN FLAWS had been cited by US mission commander Gus Grissom, and had been remedied, Gus was joined by Ed White, and Roger Chaffee in a count-down launch pad test in the Apollo 1 spacecraft command module. Apollo One was presented as the historic and symbolic beginning of the program that would take humans to the Moon. Shortly after the cabin was filled with pure oxygen, as per launch procedure protocol, a voltage transient sparked a fire which burned explosively in the pure oxygen. All three astronauts were dead within four minutes. The disaster cancelled the February 21 launch date and set the Apollo program back twenty months. This humiliating catastrophe encouraged the Soviet Politburo to push the Soyuz program toward placing a Soviet kosmonaut on the Moon, ahead of the Americans. Joe and Phil though they disliked seeing the failure of any scientific endeavor and could only sympathize with the violent loss of human life, couldn't help wonder what difference the tragedy might make in the Moon race. They continued to work on the Uzel, to put out feelers about the UM-2S and the Soyuz program. They also tried to gauge the status of their recognition and reputations as it might influence a decision in favor of the UM-2S.

On March 12, when Joe mentioned to Phil that he'd heard over the BBC that Stalin's daughter had defected to the United States through the US Embassy in India, Phil replied, "She's been shunned since Khrushchev trashed Stalin and she's sick of it. Who wants to live in shame?"

"Apparently she doesn't speak well of her father."

"As of now," Phil said. "who does? Are we talking about this because you are angry with her for deserting the land of Socialism, or because we can't talk about the fucking mess we are still in?"

"What do you want to talk about?"

"...Let's talk about Marshal Dmitry Ustinov."

"He's more influential than ever. You want his help with the UM-2T? With Tupolev? Or with Soyuz?"

"He hasn't spoken to us since the *kollegiya,* has he?"

"You mentioned Ustinov to remind me that our letter, read aloud at the *kollegiya,* has alienated yet another friend?"

"I was merely wondering if it had," Phil said.

"Well," Joe said, "we hardly need his help with the UM-2T; Tupolev loves us and doesn't give a damn about the scandal. We'll eventually get his contract."

"No, Tupolev has other problems," Phil said, "and Ustinov seems hardly interested in the Uzel, which has become another mountain of obstacles."

"The problems of the Uzel can be solved. Mark Galperin is very steady, constantly determined to... I think the technology and the engineering are in good hands. But Mark is not so good at getting the best from his people."

"Gorshkov is thorough and patient," Phil was suddenly more upbeat, feeling a whisper of his old creative elan, "Gorshkov is determined to do things right."

"I'd say our relations with the Navy are pretty good." Joe agreed.

Joe, though a boss second only to Phil, had become a human relations counselor with a brilliant grasp of what was practical. His unassuming, friendly personality nurtured the human responses needed to propel innovative implementation and these talents of his were about to become even more vital. A hint here, a word there were often enough to keep things on course. "Give Dmitry Fyodorovich a call," Joe suggested, "see what happens. I wouldn't mention the 2S or Soyuz if I were you."

Upon reflection, Phil said, "I'd like to know if Ustinov still backs us. Though I agree not to ask for his help on finally certifying the UM-2 for military use in aircraft, spaceship or submarine. All that should have been done, long ago."

"If the 2S was going aboard the Soyuz, we'd have been working on application software with OKB-1. Ustinov won't change Mishin. Not for our sakes."

"I don't disagree. But Mishin is a worthless lush. Sooner or later that turkey has to come down to roost."

"For us," Joe said, "very likely everything will depend on the Uzel." *There's only one choice let's do it!*

Indeed, Dmitry Ustinov had gained power in the ruling bureaucracy due to his successes in the defense industry. After calling Ustinov's office, Phil was informed that his request for an appointment would be considered. A week later, on March 31, veteran Defense Minister Marshal Rodion Malinovsky died and it widely expected that Ustinov would succeed him as USSR Defense Minister. But no, the Politburo chose Marshal of the Soviet Union Andrei Grechko instead. Time passed with no word from Ustinov. "Perhaps he needs a period of adjustment," Joe said, as if on behalf of Ustinov himself.

LIEPĀJA, IN LATVIA, WAS A CLOSED CITY under the Soviets; even local farmers and villagers needed a permit to enter Liepāja. The Soviet Navy set up its Baltic naval base there. The nearby Beberliņš sandpit was emptied for the vast concrete construction of the naval base, which soon included underground nuclear weapon warehouses built in the emptied sandpit. As Admiral Gorshkov followed the progress of Uzel development, he made bold plans for the Baltic Fleet, including new submarines made from titanium. Toward the end of March 1967, Gorshkov completely closed Liepāja to all commercial sea traffic. Soon, one third of the city and naval base would be occupied by a military staff of 26,000. The fleet's 14th Submarine Squadron was stationed there with 16 submarines of various types, as was the 6th group of Rear Supply, the 81st Naval Design Bureau and the fleet's Reserve Command Center.

On April 4 1967, Martin Luther King, Jr. denounced the Vietnam War during a religious service in New York City. Ed

Hoover had FBI agents in the church. What King said, as reported to Hoover, sealed King's fate.

On April 20, the US Surveyor 3 probe soft-landed on the Moon and began sending back thousands of pictures. The Soviet leaders feared the sheer power of NASA spending. *Using such vast resources to create a learning process. NASA has constant new data to drive an implacable advance despite the Apollo 1 disaster.*

The Politburo wanted a series of space successes to stay ahead of the US in landing men on the Moon. They had wanted to have it in time for Lenin's birthday celebration in early April. They were sure it was time to take advantage of the Apollo 1 disaster. They rushed Vasily Mishin into agreeing to what Korolov had refused to do: to launch Soyuz 1 carrying Colonel Vladimir Komarov. Even though Soviet engineers reported over 200 design faults in the Soyuz spacecraft, launch it anyway. Yuri Gagarin, the backup pilot for Soyuz 1, was aware of the technical defects and political pressures. He tried to replace Komarov, believing that the Politburo would not risk a national hero like himself on a dubious and fault-riddled mission. Komarov refused to be replaced because he believed the flight would kill Gagarin.

Soyuz 1 was successfully launched on April 23 1967 from the Baikonur Kosmodrome. Mission planners intended to launch Soyuz 2, a day later, carrying Valery Bykovsky, Yevgeny Khrunov, and Aleksei Yeliseyev. Khrunov and Yeliseyev would walk through space over to Soyuz 1 to keep Komarov company. It would look easy and be stunningly impressive.

But one of the solar panels wouldn't unfold on Soyuz 1, which underpowered the orientation detectors and caused difficulty maneuvering the craft. By orbit 13, the automatic stabilization system was dead and the manual system barely worked. The crew of Soyuz-2 prepared for a launch that would include fixing the solar panel of Soyuz 1. Just before launch, a thunderstorm zapped the rocket's electrical system, cancelling the mission. The flight director scrapped the Soyuz 1 mission after 18 orbits. Komarov fired Soyuz 1's retro-rockets to re-enter the atmosphere, but the series of braking parachutes did not open properly. The capsule smacked into the Kazakh desert at 600 kph. Komarov was crushed to death still strapped in his flight couch.

This tragedy was a major blow to Phil and Joe. That such an heroic effort should be so shoddily aided. Mishin's name came up immediately in their reaction. Their hopes for the UM-2S Moon landing were also dulled. They'd always feared that Korolev's death had doomed that hope. But here was the further proof.

Immediately, on April 26, Elvira informed Joe that she had given birth to a baby girl, Angela, who she said, looked just like Joe. He now had six children with two different women. His imagination wove a net of daunting consequences. But this was just one more notch in the stick of possible trouble and destructive scandal.

On May 4 the US Lunar Orbiter 4 was launched. The US seemed determined to move ahead in the race to the Moon.

AS ARRANGED WELL IN ADVANCE, JOE TOOK a break from work on the Uzel in early May to visit Major Viktor Taroikin in Moscow. Once they were seated in his small office, Taroikin said, "You are involved in a vital top secret military project so I think you wouldn't be here unless you had a question only I might be able to answer?"

"Well, of course we had our appointment—

"—But you had every reason to postpone or cancel."

"Of course," Joe said. "I want to establish that LKB and the UM-2S are blameless for the Soyuz 1 disaster and Comrade Komarov's tragic death."

"The 2-S wasn't on Soyuz 1, so how could it be blamed? Has someone been bold enough to make such a claim?"

"Maybe they will say it failed a test; so they had to use something else."

Major Taroikin laughed. "I don't believe there was *any* onboard computer on Soyuz 1. I would bet the 2S was gone over right after you delivered it and is still being picked at. Or, it was discarded entirely with Korolev's burial. Your team wasn't the only victim. You and the UM-2S are blameless. But don't start saying that out loud."

"So, what happened? What went wrong? The ground

based computer system failed?"

"No. I'll tell you why comrade Komarov died. Which you will also not repeat."

"Ultimately it was parachute failure, wasn't it?"

"Yes. The drogue chute worked all right, beginning the process of slowing the capsule. But, when preparing the spacecraft, due to increased weight, the heat shield was made thicker and therefore heavier and the main parachute was made correspondingly larger. But the container for the main chute was not enlarged and the main parachute was pounded into the too-small container using wooden hammers. So of course it could not be released by a yank from the drogue chute!"

"*Pizdetz!*" Joe breathed then quickly added, "But there was a reserve chute, wasn't there?"

"Which became tangled in the unreleased drogue and also didn't open."

"How horrible. How terrible. For everyone." *Including us.*

"So no, you have no reason to worry that your computer might be blamed, not when you have a chain of incompetence like that. Does this answer your concerns?"

"…Unfortunately, yes." The trust Viktor placed in Joe's discretion after the revelations of their show trial were humbling.

"How's work for the Navy?" Viktor asked after a moment, "The Uzel?"

Of course he already knows. "It's going well, I think. Admiral Gorshkov is…"

"…A very serious man?"

"Yes."

"Well, good luck. Give my regards to Elvira. And your wife."

Taroikin's knowledge of Joe's personal life always bobbled him little. *Does he know I'm a father again already? Vera doesn't like him, but Elvira understands that he's a friend.* "So far all is relatively peaceful," Joe said.

"You've managed to keep it peaceful," Taroikin replied evenly.

"May I ask you," Joe said, "your opinion of what the present situation might indicate about a Soviet manned Moon mission?"

Taroikin's eyes narrowed and his head came forward led by the crest of hair combed high above his forehead. He studied Joe with eyes hinting admonishment. "What makes you think there is or ever was such a program?" he asked, with genuine curiosity, it seemed.

"From Korolev himself, from the Politburo's determination to compete with the Americans," Joe said.

What did Sergei Pavlovich tell you?" Viktor asked.

"No," Joe said, "when he told me he was going to put the successfully tested UM-2S in the Soyuz craft, I got the impression it wasn't just for an orbital launch. His enthusiasm for our work together had a *We're going to take it all the way* sort of feel to it." Joe did not betray Korolev's confidence entirely.

"*Feelings* you say?" Taroikin added customary skepticism to a source of unsubstantiated information.

"Look," Joe said apologetically, "call it my own idle curiosity and absent minded speculation."

"There *is* a manned Moon program,' Taroikin's eyes were weighted with what he was about to say, "it was begun under Nikita Sergeievich in 1962. It was in many ways more clever than the proud march of capitalism approach used for Apollo, more economical. But as we have seen, such clever, economical ideas are susceptible to human error."

"Of course," Joe said, wanting to hear more, "of course, so the program is still alive, still on course.? Or not?"

"That is a delicate matter of opinion that we are better avoiding."

"Of course," Joe said, disappointed.

"This leaves your mind when you leave here, but Korolev pleaded with Khrushchev to completely reorganize the space program and put it under one central leadership, presumably his own."

"But Khrushchev..." Joe muttered.

"But Khrushchev ignored him. Of course there were advantages to having competing design bureaus all working in parallel. It worked well with his collective power politics. Competition is not a bad way to seek solutions. But perhaps

Korolev saw that in a race to the specific goal of putting cosmonauts on the Moon, repeating and doubling efforts would be detrimental."

The level of confidence Taroikin was showing Joe made him feel he might soon know too much, but he said, "Of course, I can see what you mean. A central regulatory organization, like NASA."

"Yes, Korolev was painted as an empire builder and Khrushchev never acceded to a central organization."

"Of course," Joe said.

"Now there's this," Taroikin again leaned closer and lowered his voice, "the man that testified against Korolev and put him in the gulag, which nearly killed him, is still his nemesis, Vladimir Nikolayevich Chelomei."

"The long range ballistic missile guy..." Joe said.

"He too is making and launching rockets into space. Chelomei has suggested a space station armed with nuclear weapons weighing up to 75 tons."

Joe sat, not moving a muscle. The bleak reality of their chances in this sea of intrigue was overwhelming.

"So to answer your delicate question, yes there is an ongoing manned Moon mission, but just between us, only my strongest patriotic instincts prompt me to say it will succeed."

"Thank you for your confidence."

"Be careful what you share, even with your partner Staros. He has been in a volatile frame of mind lately, I believe."

Joe met Viktor's serious blue eyes, but said nothing and stood to depart. Taroikin took his hand in a reassuring clasp.

WHEN JOE RELATED TAROIKIN'S ACCOUNT of the Soyuz disaster, to Phil, Staros was furious: "Mishin is a worthless drunk who should have been shot. This is the end of any hope for a Soviet manned Moon mission and it is the end of Soviet leadership. Komarov was doomed by the death of Sergei Pavlovich. The Uzel is our only hope for recovery." But there was no note of hope in Phil's declaration, not even for the Uzel.

"Maybe Mishin was right," Joe said, "that Korolev was only going after funding. By planning a manned Moon landing?

So that a manned Moon landing never had a chance?"

"Do you believe that?"

"No," and Joe proceeded to tell Phil some of what Taroikin had said about the dangers of having secret design bureaus competing without knowledge of each other. Joe did not tell Phil all the sordid details, perhaps sharing Taroikin's view that it was unwise to exacerbate Staros's currently frustrated and impulsive nature. "So," Joe concluded, "we don't know what will happen with the Soyuz UM-2S and OKB-1?"

"I don't know," Phil said. "We've heard nothing. It's dead."

"The Uzel will keep us busy," Joe said.

"It's turning into, an immense effort."

The tragic death of Soviet hero Vladimir Mikhailovich Komarov reverberated back against Vasily Mishin. In mid May, leading cosmonauts Yuri Gagarin and Alexey Leonov criticized Mishin's "poor knowledge of the Soyuz spacecraft and his lack of cooperation in working with the kosmonauts." Fearless Gagarin asked that Mishin be thus cited in the official report of the Soyuz-1 crash.

Though the Apollo 1 disaster had set the program back nearly two years, US preparations continued relentlessly, like the proud march of capitalism KGB Major Taroikin had mentioned, and on May 18, NASA announced the crew for the first manned Apollo flight, Apollo 7: Walter M. Schirra, Jr., Donn F. Eisele, and Walter Cunningham, tentatively scheduled for a year and several months later.

THIRTY-SEVEN

Love, love, love
Love, love, love
Love, love, love
There's nothing you can do that can't be done
Nothing you can sing that can't be sung
Nothing you can say but you can learn how to play the game
It's easy
Nothing you can make that can't be made
No one you can save that can't be saved
Nothing you can do but you can learn how to be you in time
It's easy
All you need is love
All you need is love
All you need is love, love
Love is all you need
---The Beatles

MAY 19 1967, YURI ANDROPOV BECAME KGB CHIEF and Viktor Taroikin's ultimate boss. On June 1 1967, when Berg and Staros were moving their families into six room apartments on Budapeshtskaya Street, Anna's daughter, Kristina Staros, found Anna's unsent letters to Bruce Dayton and thus discovered that her mother had another family. Kristina also gained some inkling of who her parents were when her father, Phil, was invited as an important figure to speak at her Pioneer camp. The fake stories were beginning to unravel.

On June 25, 400 million viewers watched *Our World*, the first live, international, satellite television production. It featured the live debut of *All You Need Is Love*.

On June 27, Eric Firdman traveled to Novosibirsk to solicit Academician Sobolev's support for Phil's doctoral thesis which turned out to be a delicate negotiation finally concluding with a letter of support from world class mathematician, Sergey Sobolev.

On July 12, the Newark New Jersey police arrested an African-American cab driver for impatiently passing a police car and speeding on down the road. Tired of police brutality, tired of having no political representation, educational opportunities or jobs, the black populace began five days of violence that left 26 people dead and hundreds injured. The riots spread to Plainfield, New Jersey then to cities across the country including Detroit and Washington DC. Hearing news of the US riots, Joe began monitoring BBC broadcasts for American news. He passed on to Russian friends, who were hesitant to listen illegally to BBC broadcasts, what sort of capitalist, racist violence was going on.

On August 12, Tupolev's order for the UM-2T was officially canceled. Though disappointing this had not been unexpected. Joe took the opportunity to urge even greater dedication to the Uzel.

Next weekend, taking one of the last times before Vera and his children returned to Leningrad from Prague, Joe built a high fidelity music room in their new large apartment and began a record collection which in turn would attract Leningrad music students who heard that there was a rare recording in the home of a local scientist. All four of Joe's children, including young Alena and Anton were being educated in music, but Vivian and Robert were now 13 and 12 years old and the Hi-Fi room was meant to further their education by providing a place for them to listen to great classical music with their friends and other students. Then too, Joe, like his father Benjamin, wanted to experience advancing technology through its latest successful products. When electric organs and color TV's appeared in the USSR, he stood in line to purchase them.

ON AUGUST 28 1967, ERIC V. GOLOVANOV, commander of the Soviet Navy's Project 641 submarine number B-103, was on a mission under the Arctic ice when unexpectedly he was ordered to return 'for repairs' to the Soviet Navy base at Kronstadt on Kotlin island near Leningrad.

Project 641 submarines were nearly 100 meters in length, powered by three Kolomna 2000 horse power diesel engines which drove three electric motors and charged two decks of batteries to power the motors when the boat was submerged. Three drive shafts with six-bladed propellors drove the 641s to a top speed on the surface of 16 knots and 15 knots submerged. First commissioned in 1958, with a range of 20,000 miles, the subs could stay submerged for up to five days. They were equipped with 22 torpedoes, fired from 6 tubes forward and 4 aft.

Commander Golovanov expected orders to return with B-103 to the Arctic. He waited patiently, as repairs got underway, but within a month the 'repairs' became a full scale renovation to modernize submarine B-103. Golovanov, ready to complete a mission under the Arctic ice to Vladivostok in the far east, sought the advice of no less than Rear Admiral Oscar Solomonovich Zhukovsky.

Zhukovsky's further inquiries on behalf of Commander Golovanov revealed that Golovanov was to stay in a long training program and forego his dream assignment of an around the world tour; from Vladivostok around Afrika with stops in 12 ports along the way. He was therefore even less inclined to embrace replacing a fully workable torpedo firing system called TAS with a Combat Information and Control System, a transistorized semi-conductor based computer called *Node* (Uzel) *Node* was supposed to handle navigation, communication, air quality, and not only the firing of the torpedoes but would incorporate the inputs from sonar and radar as to the position, speed and direction of enemy targets. He was told he would be able to type in a set of coordinates and the computer would take him there. All, while acquiring 3 enemy targets aiming and firing up to 5 torpedoes simultaneously. It sounded like someone's pipe dream.

Once the decision was made, changes began happening quickly. Not only were there more top brass around and in-charge, but new top staff positions were created for the crew. Two new high level officers arrived from the 24th Naval Research Institute, computer trained engineers, to liaison and study with

LKB Chief Designer, Philip Georgievich Staros, Chief Engineer Josef Veniaminovich Berg, Chief system designer, Mark Galperin and a large team of LKB developers.

Commander Golovanov and the captains of two other submarines were being prepared for the new Uzel system and would spend weeks with the new officers and the LKB team.

It was just then, during those first weeks, that Eric Golovanov's orders to take command of another boat and begin his world tour arrived. But Rear Admiral Zhukovsky explained that this was old news. The order was soon withdrawn and Golovanov's dream of a fabulous voyage was killed a second time.

Though Golovanov found the training tedious, he was impressed by the number of important representatives of many scientific institutes, design bureaus and high tech factories who shared his training experience. He was also impressed by the measures taken to keep the meetings secret under the constant supervision of top KGB staff. Those attending Uzel development were not allowed to mingle with the public and were required to dress in civilian clothes. To reach the room with the prototype Combat Information and Control System Uzel, the Chief Designer's Stand, it was necessary to pass three points of inspection.

But Oscar Zhukovsky was the perfect man for developing a clear understanding between the Soviet Navy command and the LKB team. He was energetic, proactive and he had full entrée into all departments of the Soviet Navy, including direct access to Admiral of the Fleet of the Soviet Union, Sergei G. Gorshkov who had been commander of the Black Sea fleet during the Great Patriotic War, while Zhukovsky was his Fleet Operations Chief.

Zhukovsky organized the invitations of top Soviet Navy Commanders to visit Joe and Phil, their first high-level military contacts after Staros's dismissal from Zelenograd. Staros was fully aware of the importance of the meetings. He and Joe prepared carefully knowing that these first impressions of the top people were vital to the success of the Uzel CICS. The 24th Naval Research institute was not only the center of Naval computer expertise but the center of Naval Combat tactics. The trend to combine the two directions was led by Zhukovsky whose deep respect and trust of Philip Staros, shared with Sergei Gorshkov, did not depend on changes in the political situation, but was entirely based on the best interests of the Soviet Navy.

At the end of the third month of training, the group was visited by Chief of Naval Staff Admiral Sergeev and other full admirals and top experts. After a report on development progress with explanations and demonstrations by Staros, Admiral Sergeev ordered accelerated work and in the evening of the same day, he and the other top echelon visitors departed for Moscow to meet with the Central Committee and the Politburo.

JOE'S FIRM BELIEF IN THE BENEFITS OF technology, partially inherited from Benjamin, led Joe to another practical hobby: printing. It was a hobby he would use to thwart the Soviet traffic police. On a sunny, end-of-summer August day in the space age when Joel's native land threatened his adopted land, Joe was driving his Volga with the whole family inside. They had just returned from Prague and Joe was overjoyed to see them, leading them in song as he sped down the highway, a strange sight: a large family—when nearly all Soviet families were necessarily small. A private citizen driving a Volga was also quite unusual when most Volgas, model GAZ-21, were driven by government drivers for apparatchik bosses. Because the active conversations and youthful activity inside the rapidly moving Volga caused erratic movements of the vehicle, a policeman flagged Joe down. At the driver's window the officer demanded car registration and driver's license.

"Good afternoon, Comrade," Joe's strong Brooklyn accent made him clearly a foreigner as he opened a large folder of documents to find his license and car title, revealing his membership in the Communist Party, his important professional title and his various awards. Unlike most others before him, this traffic cop was unimpressed: "You were speeding and weaving all over the road. You put your family in danger as well as everybody else. Let me have your license. I'm going to punch you for a violation."

Joe handed his license over with apparent hangdog

reluctance, the moment when a guilty motorist would offer a gesture of respect in the form of a monetary contribution. Typically, the officer would then abandon his hasty intention of registering a serious violation by punching a special hole in the driver's license. But in this case, Joe said nothing, and made no move to bribe the police officer.

"I see you've already got quite a number of holes," the cop said. "Keep it up. There are heavy fines, and you'll lose your license altogether."

Joe nodded, as if not daring to make a customary gesture.

"Any suggestions as to how we might avoid all that?" The officer was thinking: *This bigshot can afford a decent gesture!* "I don't really want to punch you when you're so close to the edge…"

"No," Joe said, "if I've violated the law, isn't it your duty to record it on my license? No sense both of us breaking the law."

"Well, of course—"

"You have no choice. As a good Communist, I accept that."

As dark scowls go, the officer's expression was no record setter and he showed some pleasure as be brought the jaws of his metal tool to the license and punched out another violation against Joe's already riddled permit. "One more and you'll lose it."

As Joe pulled away from the roadside, the usual combination of chatter and strong expression was replaced by human silence. Vera and her children had all felt the antagonism, tension and awkwardness, but they were soon cheered by Joe's happy mood as he led them again in song, cheerfully commenting on roadside distractions as they traveled along. "Papa is a good driver," Vivian declared once she was sure her father felt no great guilt or fault.

It was time once again to print a new driver's license, one without all the punched violations. Joe drove, wondering what the policeman might think: *A Communist so dedicated he would not part with a few rubles?*

In fact, Joe felt no fault for being a good Communist who liked being well-off. Unlike nearly all of his fellow CPUSSR members and Soviet citizens, Joe was working for true Communism, which would make everyone rich.

On October 18, the Soviet Venera 4 descended through the Venusian atmosphere to send back astounding data: Venus was nothing like what had been believed. Its atmosphere was mostly carbon dioxide with intense heat and crushing pressure near the planet's surface. The next day, without learning anything new, the US Mariner 5 could merely fly by the inhospitable planet, apparently so misnamed after the Goddess of Love and Beauty.

AFTER STUDYING THE THEORY & PRACTICE

of mastering the devices on the remote Uzel CICS, selected Navy personnel including commander Eric Golovanov were passed into stressful independent study of the system including bench tests, at the Kronstadt factory. It soon became apparent to Golovanov that there was a continuous customization of the computer in its extremely limited, production and manufacture, so that documentation had to be adjusted directly in the workplace. However, the timetable for the installation of equipment in submarines could not be postponed by a single day. Preparation and testing were in parallel with the target debugging and system software. Day and night work went into rebuilding modules of permanent memory. Equipment problems appeared at every step. Not once was there an easy solution in the control unit of the digital servo system to provide the required speed and accuracy of data for torpedo fire control. Immense time was spent on the achievement of specified accuracy from related systems. But gradually the problems were solved, and the system came into compliance with operating conditions. There was a final strong push to achieve demonstrable operations in time for the 50th anniversary of the October Revolution in early November 1967, by demonstrating successful bench tests.

As bench testing and programming proceeded, the changes constantly being made were immediately reflected in the simultaneous manufacture of a second system for the second boat to be Uzel equipped, a Project 641B submarine. The initial order was for three Uzel installations to be followed by a possible second three to be industrially manufactured units which might progress to a full factory mass production schedule. It seemed an absurd dream to almost all those involved. Any prediction that there would be nearly 70 Uzel operated Russian military submarines beneath the oceans' waters, into the 21st century, would have been viewed as delusional. There were years of precarious struggle yet to come.

Driving a tremendous effort at debugging during nights, weekends and holidays, and equally intense work on the visual displays, and with all the problems of dead reckoning not entirely solved, the Uzel was able to meet scheduled bench testing in time for the 50th anniversary.

AS THE 50th ANNIVERSARY OF THE GREAT Socialist Revolution was celebrated in Moscow and Leningrad, with martial music, banner parades and long speeches, NASA's first Saturn V rocket lifted the unmanned Apollo 4 from Cape Kennedy into Earth orbit. In the USSR, those who had dreamed of Soviet cosmonauts on the Moon, the few who had also known that this was not an idle dream, saw more clearly now that the sudden tragic deaths of spaceflight's father, Sergei Pavlovich Korolev, and one of its favorite kosmonauts, Vladimir Komarov, severely threatened their hopes.

Precisely on the anniversary of the revolution, Phil Staros received a warm and informal letter from Admiral Aksel I. Berg, along with a gift, which touched Phil's heart and mind: a hand-made submarine commander ikon. The admiral's message was unmistakable and entirely trustworthy. It was nearly a promise of resurrection. From then on, Phil committed himself to work on CICS Uzel with true dedication. He understood that Admiral Berg and Aleksandr Shokin were old colleagues in developing naval radar and feedback controls. One would not act without the other. This was another sign of Shokin's support. Phil began pressing all his contacts for favors owed to secure computer time on the USSR's fastest computers to speed work on debugging the Uzel system routines.

Though by late 1967, the US showed signs of catching the USSR in space, the wild unrest in US domestic life was beginning to boil over: By early November, US Secretary of Defense Robert McNamara had recommended that President Johnson freeze troop levels in Vietnam, stop bombing North Vietnam and leave ground fighting to South Vietnam. LBJ refused and McNamara resigned. On November 30, Senator Eugene McCarthy announced his candidacy to challenge Johnson over the war. The Politburo saw their adversary bleeding and were determined to stay ahead of the US in the race to put men on the Moon.

BYPASSING THE INCREASINGLY HOSTILE Leningrad Obkom in late 1967, the UM-1Nkh control computer—already in use throughout the Union—was redesigned and improved. The new design, developed and debugged in-house at LKB, allowed for many new applications, and needed no tedious, contentious certification under the scrutiny of the Leningrad Party leaders. "This design will be much better at automating factories and power plants," Joe said to Phil. "It incorporates all the lessons learned and tracked by Firdman from dozens of our factory installations. We should submit it for the Stalin Prize."

"Need I remind you that that it's now called the Soviet State Prize? Haven't you noticed that Stalin has fallen into the pit of universal disfavor. But, even so, the State Prize? We are up to our eyes in shit and not on schedule with the Uzel. Even submitting an application will piss people off and make our situation worse. Which I for one am pretty sure we don't need." *What the hell are you thinking now?*

Joe replied in gentle earnest, "I have to believe serious Communists, who know the success of the earlier units, will not bow to pressure when so much is to be gained. 'Our situation' would improve, even if the new model was only accepted for consideration. And of course, I agree, the award itself would come under immense pressure and his highly unlikely."

"You're hoping that through some miracle, some mistake, we might win the State Prize and thus transform our plight?"

"It certainly wouldn't hurt. It's a long shot…one worth taking."

"Maybe."

THIRTY-EIGHT

"We shall have to remove everything that strangles artistic and scientific creativity."
--Alexander Dubček

ON JANUARY 5 1968, ALEKSANDR DUBČEK WAS chosen as the leader of the Communist Party in Czechoslovakia. Despite domination by the Soviet Union, he brought a period of political liberalization and democratization, a loosening of restrictions on the media, speech and travel, and decentralization of the economy. It was called the 'Prague Spring'. At the same time, Americans died in hellish Khe Sanh, Vietnam and a US B-52 Stratofortress released four nuclear bombs as it crashed in Greenland. On January 23, North Korea seized the USS Pueblo, a spy ship caught inside North Korea's territorial waters. On January 30, the Vietnamese Tet Offensive began with surprise attacks across the South, including an attack on the US Embassy in Saigon followed the next day by the execution of a Viet Cong officer by a South Vietnamese National Police Chief. A photograph of the bullet exploding the Viet Cong officer's head made the front pages of newspapers around the world. Americans realized, *This is what we are part of in this war!* It was becoming clear that sooner or later the US would lose the war. The US space program moved ahead with ever greater proficiency. Americans loved it, the adventure, its boldness, its danger and its relative innocence.

MID-FEBRUARY 1968, SOVIET NAVY COMMAND issued a official ID cards to Joe, Phil and Mark to enter and leave the closed city on the coast of the Baltic Sea, Liepāja, Latvia. They were invited to pay a visit. They needed to see the lab space set aside for the LKB development team in the submarine division buildings, near the submarine berth harbor. They were assured that their base passes would be waiting for them at the gates of the base. Though they would not be working on the submarine in Liepāja for nearly a year, Gorshkov's gesture was one of welcome, and said clearly: *Let's get to work!*

"He's telling us he is on board and we should be too," Phil said. "He long ago closed Liepāja to commercial shipping to make way for the new submarines, which should be operated by the Uzel."

"The 641B."

"Yes. a new line of patrol and attack submarines."

"When do you and Mark first visit Liepāja?" Joe asked.

"Gorshkov will expect at least the three of us there soon."

"Yes, he wants a finished prototype early next year.

"He knows the display hardware must be redesigned for submarines," Phil said. "We'll have to manufacture our own units. We don't have the factory connections to implement what we need. None of them could gear up in time."

"Even with Shokin and Gorshkov pushing," Joe agreed.

They took Phil's Volga; Joe driving.' Joe's car was in Moscow. Mark was in the back seat. They talked on the way, excited, especially Chief Designer Mark Galperin, expectant, edged with nervous anticipation. But no amount of individual certainty could chase away all their doubts of success. Was it going to work? Would submarine commanders embrace it?. Phil, hoping success would restore his power over the development of Soviet microelectronics, was quiet, not quite sullen in counting on the Uzel project to correct the past wrongs, to vindicate them above all competitors. Mark and Phil were both entirely occupied with what the Uzel could mean for them. But, while Joe discussed their prospects with them, his mind covered the practical considerations of his complicated domestic life: his children, the needs of their musical education, his wife, her moods and signals, the hints of engineering solutions to problems he was working on, thinking about the effect of heat and humidity on system performance inside a submarine. He liked the idea of working in a foreign city late this year or early next. *Sea trials in the Naval proving grounds under the Baltic Sea. It's like something out of Jules Verne.* But most of all, Joe was excited to be driving to Latvia, already thinking of good times with Elvira, away from Leningrad,

IT DID NOT TAKE THEM LONG TO REALIZE

that Liepāja was a very different sort of place from Leningrad or Moscow. Or anywhere else in Russia. There were small attractive shops, bakeries and cafes. When Joe, thinking about how Elvira would love the place, saw the sign and awning of the hotel Lebanon, he said, "Hey, let's check out the main accommodations."

"The Navy is expecting us," Mark said.

"There's lodging on the base," Phil said, "for anyone here for the duration of the installation and field tests."

"Those Navy barracks will never be adequate," Joe gave Phil an assured look: *you know there will be a need for temporary, private lodging, comfortable accommodations.*

There was no further argument for the moment.

The Lebanon, though a standard Soviet four story red brick hotel building, seemed to Joe to be a charming inn. It was not far from the town center. Beside it stood an ancient cathedral. Across the street a an inviting café was busy with eager patrons. Inside, they were greeted by a surprisingly young man, for he seemed to be in charge of the hotel. "Good afternoon, allow me to offer you the services of Hotel Lebanon?" Khalid Islamov's Russian was clear, his tone unusually courteous.

Phil and Mark, who did not really want to waste time there, said nothing. Joe, also taken aback, said, "Well, we'd like to know what's available."

"We have single rooms, double rooms, rooms with double beds. Would you like to see our overnight accommodations?" Again Joe was struck by the lack of indifference he had grown used to in Leningrad from people in service positions.

"That's not—" Phil was interrupted.

"—Sure, let's have a look," Joe said.

"Fine," said young Islamov. He called softly out and a

young woman took his place at the front desk, nodding in a friendly fashion and greeting them in Latvian with a smile.

The Hotel Lebanon was modern and though physically much alike the hotels built in many Soviet cities, it was impeccably clean; the floors were polished and there was an unobtrusive scent of turpentine. The rooms as well as the corridors were decorated with ceramic flowers and birds. The attendants and maids they encountered were also courteous and friendly. They were shown small single rooms, double rooms with two or three single beds. Joe asked, "You said you have rooms with larger beds where a couple could sleep together?"

"Absolutely," Khalid said, "as long as both have proper city ID, that's fine, but of course the single bed rooms are much less costly." Islamov showed them a room with a double bed and then a rather luxurious suite which brought a smile to Joe's face.

Phil observed Joe nodding approvingly, "Sure, of course, of course," Joe was saying, "but on special occasions it could be worth a little extra expense."

The Lebanon seemed quite wonderful and even had its own cozy restaurant just off the lobby, smelling of fresh bread and spicy dishes.

Outside, Phil said to Joe, "Don't get any ideas about bringing Elvira into Liepāja. There's no way I'm going to vouch for her as a part of our work here."

"Of course not," Joe said genially.

"There's no other way she'd get official identity papers."

"Well, I wasn't thinking so much about that," Joe said, only slightly abashed.

"What then, sneak her in, in the trunk of your Volga?"

"Don't be ridiculous," Joe chuckled. "The thought barely crossed my mind."

"Seriously," Phil said. "We're doing all right with this one; let's not fuck it up with some scandalous nonsense that for certain the Leningrad Obkom will cook up if they are given half a chance."

"Of course, of course," Joe said, "I was only asking about the beds to get an idea of what kind of place it is. Who else might be staying here."

"It's a nice quiet hotel," Phil insisted, "mostly used by officials moving around from place to place."

"Well," Mark said, "let's get to the base and see what we're getting for laboratory space."

On the way to the bridge which crossed into Karosta and the naval base, they passed a wide variety of stores and small cafes, crowded masterpieces of the national cuisine. Joe stopped at the market where they found products long lost to memory in Leningrad and Moscow. He insisted on buying two boxes of salted herring, available only in the Baltic. *One for Elvira and one for Vera.* Phil and Mark each bought a box. But before Joe could buy anything else, Phil insisted they get to the Navy base.

At the bridge, they reached a check point and were waved on quickly after displaying their identity documents. Clearly the two armed guards had been made aware of their impending visit. Just on the other side of the bridge, the road forked and they took the left hand road as per directions volunteered by the bridge guards.

They drove through an industrial zone where Joe, appreciative, noted evidence of a metallurgical plant, and ship repair plants, places with the right tooling to manufacture improvised engineering solutions to almost anything.

At the more heavily guarded base gate, the three men were met by a captain, second rank, who greeted them cordially and took them to a rear admiral's office in one of red brick two story buildings built along the high embankment between the artificial submarine harbor and the Baltic Sea.

The Soviet Navy had set up its Baltic headquarters here. One-third of the city was taken up with the naval base. The 14th Submarine Squadron of the Baltic Fleet's 16 submarines included Project 613 which was designated, Whiskey Class by NATO, Project 629a designated Golf Class by NATO and Project 651, Juliett Class by NATO. Also at the Liepāja base was the 6th group of Rear Supply of the Baltic Fleet, and the 81st Design Bureau and Baltic Reserve Command Center. Most were housed close by in the buildings surrounding the manmade berth harbor, which was nicknamed, 'the Bucket'.

Rear Admiral Suvorov was as plain and ordinary a man as

could be. After introductions to the LKB men, Suvorov, looking out upon the submarine berths in the narrow harbor, explained that though some 16 submarines were based there, many were currently at sea. "Would you like to tour one of the submarines presently in port? There is a Project 641 here at present..." He waited politely.

"Sure," said Joe and Mark together.

Then Phil said, "I think we better look first at possible laboratory space."

"Certainly," Suvorov said.

Their laboratory was to be in one of the more well appointed red brick buildings of a dozen Fleet Division structures along the embankment facing the shallows of the Baltic Sea on one side and the bucket on the other.

Staros did not mention to Suvorov that he at least had already been shown the inside of a 641 sub, one with the tactical ID of B-103, by its captain, Commander Eric Golonov himself, in Kronstadt.

After satisfying themselves that there was ample space and electricity in the large empty first floor, so convenient to the submarine berths, Phil released Mark and Joe to visit the submarine while he went back to Suvorov's offices to make phone calls.

Once alongside the immense black hull, Joe eyed the rough surface with its welded plates and rough coats of finish with a sort of awe. Up close, there was a primitive, almost brutal simplicity to an object so obviously manmade, a giant weapon to be launched into the ocean. To Joe's warmest lights, it represented the success and power of Socialism and a Communist state.

Once having descended the narrow stairway of open grid steel steps, seeing through them down three flights, Joe was soon moving along the narrow passages of the operations deck. Each chamber of the sub's six chambers was sealed from its neighbors by a heavy air-and water tight hatch. Joe was struck by the incredible number and constant presence of dials, gauges and valve handles, round shapes at every turn, along every surface, hundreds of dials and gauges to watch over with nearby valves to turn in response to the analog data. *No wonder it takes a crew of 78 to operate this ship,* Joel thought, *all of it should be digital, computer controlled. ...But at least we have a start. Keeping track of ten active torpedoes, navigation of the boat, integrating all sonar and radar data, will be hard enough, calculating distance and changing position of five enemy vessels and firing torpedoes at three of them simultaneously? At least we're not expected to integrate the data from the endless analog meters or control all these valves. Not yet...*

Upon seeing the long, red labeled torpedoes and the open torpedo tubes, Joel felt a sense of relief that Mark was in charge of the project. *It involves heavy objects with heavy consequences.*

Even their short tour of the boat, gave both Mark and Joe a new perspective on the challenges they faced. They would need to install the Uzel and several display screens that they were building with as large a screen and as small an electronic component package as they could manage in the very limited space. It would mean running cables to the sonar and torpedo systems and elsewhere, a formidable task because nearly every square centimeter of each partition wall was in use.

Joe was already thinking about using several UM-2 processors: one for direct torpedo control, a central master unit and another for navigation. It would eliminate a lot of trouble-prone cabling and connections. *I bet Mark is already thinking about that, but hasn't said anything yet.*

BY MARCH 1, THE COOPERATION BETWEEN the Soviet Navy's submarine command and the large team of engineers at LKB in Leningrad and at the Kronstadt Plant, had for the most part become a comfortable symbiotic working relationship, in large part due to the skills and knowledge of Rear Admiral Oscar Solomonovich Zhukovsky. Zhukovsky, despite the fact that officially he was retired and had never been more than a rear admiral, wielded power and influence at the highest levels of the Soviet Navy. Both naval officers and LKB leaders understood that they would soon be working together at the large Liepāja naval installation in Latvia. Phil Staros, Joe Berg and Mark Galperin had spent enough time there to see that the place was a splendid seaside spot, with beautiful long beaches, all in a country with far better food and more comfortable cultural traditions than could be found even in Leningrad or Moscow. So they let it be known that postings in Liepāja might not be a constant hardship.

Everywhere in the world, in 1968, there were stirrings of unrest and protest. Even in the Soviet Bloc, on March 8, student protests sparked a political crisis in Poland. On March 12, in the New Hampshire Democratic primary, Lyndon Johnson barely edged out antiwar candidate Eugene McCarthy. Two days later, Senator Robert F. Kennedy entered the race for the Democratic Party's presidential nomination. The day after that, a violent demonstration against the Vietnam war broke out in London with hundreds of arrests. On March 22, the "Red Brigade" initiated a period of revolution in France with an attack on the University of Nanterre. On March 31, Lyndon Johnson announced he would not seek re-election.

On April 4, J. Edgar Hoover's assassins murdered Martin Luther King, Jr. in Memphis. It was Hoover's response to King's fulminations against the Vietnam war and his long struggle against Jim Crow. Riots erupted in major American cities, lasting for several days. Edgar spent the morning after King's murder having his portrait taken for publicity purposes. His afternoon was spent as usual at the racetrack. Even after murdering the revered civil rights leader, Edgar continued to smear him, hoping to prevent a national holiday in his name.

As if to distract from the terrible murder, the last Saturn V test of unmanned Apollo 6 was launched successfully. Despite serious problems, the heat shield, the command module and the Moon orbiting navigator were cleared for a manned attempt.

"Apollo 6…" Phil said to Joe.

"They've scheduled twenty of them," Joe said. "the relentless redundancy is stupendous."

Joe and Phil didn't talk about it further, but they both knew they were both thinking about the UM-2S probably gathering dust in Mishin's offices. To have been that close to installation on the Soyuz craft bound for a manned Moon landing made the Uzel seem like a consolation prize, however vital it might be to their survival. They both knew the Apollo missions would keep coming and that the Soyuz efforts would probably also be ongoing, but without them and their innovative thinking.

On April 6 1968, two days after King's murder, a shootout between Black Panthers and Oakland police resulted in several arrests and deaths, including 16-year-old Panther Bobby Hutton. Five days later, President Johnson signed the Civil Rights Act of 1968. Less than two weeks later, for eight days, Columbia College students took over administration buildings and shut down the university. Two weeks after that, on May 13, Paris students rioted and one million protesters marched through Paris streets. On May 17, nine anti-war activists entered the Selective Service offices in Catonsville, Maryland, removed and burned the draft records with napalm. Five days later, the US nuclear-powered submarine Scorpion sank with ninety-nine men aboard.

There were lots of quips and comments among the team of LKB engineers and Soviet Navy officers about the Scorpion disaster:

"Maybe it was a computer glitch."

"They should have had a better control system."

But beneath any such dark humor was the knowledge of the recent disappearance of the Soviet K-129, a Soviet ballistic missile submarine lost on March 8. The anger, the fear and sadness of the Kronstadt naval officers affected LKB as the two sides worked together and grew closer.

ON JUNE 5, ROBERT F. KENNEDY WAS SHOT,

and died the next day. Multiple shooters were covered up by a lone gunman patsy. On June 8, James Earl Ray was arrested for murdering Martin Luther King, Jr. Under torture, he confessed, but later declared that he'd been framed to cover up the FBI assassination.

By late June, Joe Berg's children, Vivian, Robert, Alena and Anton were out of school. Vera and the children returned to Prague and to her family's nearby home in the country, their customary practice for the summer. It was Vera's escape from Russia, to be free of the summer ills of Leningrad and from Joe's relative indifference. This year, their departure occurred at much the same time as Joe began to work in Kronstadt on developing the Uzel system, occasionally in the closed Baltic port of Liepāja in setting up the LKB laboratory near the submarine berths there. It was an inviting prospect. Not only was there the Baltic Sea, its beaches and dunes, but there was Latvia's food, music, and people. In short, for LKB and for Joe, a paradise to enjoy and to look forward to next summer.

With his family's departure, Joe and Elvira could be together, with time away from her alienated husband and the two girl children by Joe that Joe had never seen. As summer waxed, and the routines at the naval base in Kronstadt became established, Joe was busy with interesting technical problems to solve on fitting the Uzel system to the submarine. Even so, he worked on the UM-1NKh, constantly improving the design with every new installation in factories and power plants throughout the Union.

On July 1, the CIA began a program of kidnapping, torturing and murdering Viet Cong leaders in Vietnam. US desperation in the face of a losing war became ever more reckless and cruel, to American's lasting shame. Soviet aid to Vietnam was calculated to prolong the fight, to stretch and broaden US loss of life and prestige across the world.

The space and missile race was closely coupled with the microelectronics race. The cumbersome response of the uneducated, aging and heavily medicated Soviet leadership slowed Soviet development of microelectronics. The US had its share of ignorance and blindness, but it also had huge financial superiority and barely-regulated free-enterprise under a central organizing agency, NASA.

On July 18, Intel Corporation was founded in Santa Clara, California for the sole purpose of designing and manufacturing semiconductor microelectronics. Intel would become a signpost for Joe during the rest of his life. He'd always ask, *"What is Intel going to do next? How did Intel solve that problem?"*

THIRTY-NINE

"There's always something suspect about an intellectual on the winning side."
—*Vaclav Havel*

LATE ON AUGUST 20 WHEN JOE RETURNED TO Kronstadt from a few days of camping with Elvira, clearly relaxed, he was unprepared for the shock he received from Mark, who took one look at Joe's deep tan and said:

"So where have you been; you haven't heard have you?" Seeing Joe's puzzled look, Mark went on, "the Prague Spring is over. Czechoslovakia has been invaded by half a million Soviet troops, thousands of tanks and a thousand airplanes. The whole country is being occupied; Dubček is out. People are fleeing the country for the West. The entire Warsaw Pact is involved in a military crackdown."

Joe's suddenly paler expression was tinged with guilt and fear. "Damn, Vera and the kids are there. I have to get in touch; I've got to get them out. It could be Hungary all over again. And with Brezhnev in charge there is no telling what may happen…"

"Do what you need to do, Josef Veniaminovich. I can assure you there are no crises on the Uzel that I can't deal with. And, as I understand, Philip Georgievich will arrive tomorrow."

"Well, that may change. I'm going to try to call Vera." Joe was not sure whether Mark was aware that he had been languishing with Elvira all weekend. If Mark knew or disapproved, he showed no sign. After a few hours of trying to reach Vera in Prague, Joe found Elvira who had already heard the news of the Soviet invasion. "I haven't been able to reach Vera and the kids," he told her. "I must go to Moscow, and see what I can do to get them out of there."

"I'll take the bus and train back to Leningrad," Elvira said.

"No, I'll drive you then go on to Moscow, if need be. Perhaps I can do whatever can be done from Leningrad." *But Viktor Taroikin and Alexsandr Shokin are probably both in Moscow...*

They set out almost immediately in the Volga for Leningrad. With Joe most concerned for his wife and children, the precarious nature of their own relationship was evident to Elvira, but it troubled her little. Such was her love for Joe that she thought mostly of what she might do to help him protect his family. "Joe," she said, her blonde hair, bleached by the sun, framed her lovely tanned face, "you need to rest. Let me drive. You stretch out in the back and sleep."

"I suppose I could try." He pulled the Volga off the road and was sound asleep within minutes. Elvira smiled at his snoring as she drove and would have frowned had it stopped. Their life together was on a precipice, but it lacked nothing of respect and love. In Leningrad, they said good-bye. She did not need to say that she hoped he would soon find his family safe. There were no such doubts between them.

From the apartment on Budapeshtskaya Street, Joe tried once more to reach Vera. The busy signals were not ordinary, but were sounds he had not heard before. Either that, or his calls simply ended in dead air. After an hour, he called an LKB operator at home and asked her to use her connections to international phone operators to get through to Prague. She called back an hour later. "I can do nothing. They will only tell me that there is no phone service at the moment and they have not been informed as to when it will be working."

Incoming phone traffic to Czechoslovakia has been restricted. I must go there, but no doubt air travel is also a problem...Can I drive there? ...There must be some trains running.

Next, Joe tried to reach Viktor Taroikin, who was not in Leningrad but in Moscow, as he often was of late. When Joe reached Major Taroikin in Moscow, Viktor told him, "I'll see what I can do. Things are complicated there now. Is there any chance you'll be in Moscow any time soon?"

"I can be, of course."

"Stay there. I'll call you tomorrow."

"If I could only talk to Vera and the kids, to know they're alright..."

"I'll call you when I know how to do that."

Joe called Aeroflot. Flights to Moscow were apparently undisturbed. *I should go there. Maybe Shokin will help.* After changing his mind back and forth several times, Joe decided to wait until morning. The following day, as he prepared to go to the airport, Taroikin called. "I'll be in Moscow this afternoon," Joe exclaimed, "I'm on my way to the plane right now."

"But I'm in Leningrad. Come to my office, we'll call Vera from here."

"You think you can reach them?"

"I now know how to do it." Again, Joe sensed Viktor's own obvious certainty of his connection to power and control. Joe could not recall any time Viktor had ever lied to him. Nor had Viktor been wrong about a promise or advice for that matter. But Viktor's certainty was not quite his own as Joe drove north into central Leningrad, a twenty minute drive. He parked on Shpalernaya street around the corner from Liteyny Avenue, not far from he Neva River at the Liteyny Bridge. Soon he was at the entrance to the Bolshoi Dom, Leningrad home of 'the Soviet secret police' since the early 1930s. After showing his ID to the guard at the entrance desk, Joe was escorted by a young officer to a lower floor where he waited only minutes before being ushered into Major Taroikin's office. Viktor greeted him with a sympathetic smile. "Let's see how quickly we can find them," he said.

"What's going on there? They could be killed or-or-or arrested. They know nothing of politics—or anything like this. They're musicians, all of them. When I think about what happened in Budapest in '56, I—"

"Relax, Joe. This is nothing like Budapest. The rebels are all peaceful, non-violent deviationists. No one is throwing rocks or gas bombs. Soldiers are not being killed."

"...What's it all about then?"

"Dubcek went too far, too fast, nearly declaring a withdrawal from the Soviet sphere of influence." Viktor waved Joe to a seat and sat behind his desk, drawing one of the several telephones closer, a red one.

Taroikin was graying at the temples Joe noticed as Viktor dialed three digits then repeated first one and then a second code number. A moment later, he repeated the telephone number for Vera's father's house. Joe sat gripping the edge of his chair, his knuckles white. Then: "Good morning, Gospasha Bergova, I have your husband here, eager to speak with you."

Joe took the phone. "Vera? Are you alright?" he said in Czech then in Russian, "The kids?"

"We are all okay," Vera said in Czech, "but I'm very frightened. Everywhere there are soldiers; there have been rapes and beatings. People have been killed. Where have you been? I expected you to call days ago. Have they arrested you? You're in Taroikin's custody?"

"No. No, no. I'm fine. I was in Kronstadt. But phone service to Czechoslovakia has been…" Joe met Viktor's eyes in a quick glance, "have been difficult…I'm here with Viktor to make sure I'd get through to you, that's all."

"Well, there seems to be no travel from here, and it's soon time for the children to return to the conservatory. But I don't dare go into Prague and look for a way—"

"—No, no. I will come and get you."

Viktor raised his eyebrows, non-committal.

"Yes, I want *you*," Vera said. "Not some guard detail of Viktor's. I don't know who to trust. How soon will you come?"

"I'm going to come to you, as soon as I can." Again, Joe looked to Viktor who gave him a sort of concerned and conditional nod. Of hope more than agreement. "Well it may take a few days." Again, Viktor's eyes told him he could not yet promise, "but so you feel safe there?" Joe switched to Czech, "Stay there, be careful. I'll come get you as soon as I can."

"I don't suppose you miss me?"

"Of course I do, all of you. Do you miss me, and our nice big apartment?"

"I miss you a little. But not Leningrad."

"Well…"

"Okay, come as soon as you can."

"Let me say hello to the kids…"

"They're outside with my uncle and the dogs."

"Vivian, too?"

"…Yes."

Strange, Joe thought, *I feel suddenly uneasy.* "Well, will you give them a big hug for me?"

"Come soon and hug them yourself. But I will. They miss you."

Off the phone, Joe looked to Viktor who said, "Things are in some turmoil there. It may take some time to arrange. And perhaps it would be better for you not to go yourself…"

"She's quite frightened. She says there have been rapes and killings. How can I rest until I know they're safe?"

"There is little violence between the civilian population and the soldiers. According to our people there."

"Oh? But certainly there must be friction; the soldiers were sent there for a reason."

"There is civilian resistance. They've had it easier than the rest of us and they don't want to follow the rules anymore. The women are luring the soldiers and fooling them; the men are removing and changing the street signs. They managed to re-route an entire division back out of the country."

"Really?" Joe doubted Viktor would make that up.

"Days after marching to Prague from Poland," Viktor said, "they found themselves back in Poland."

They both laughed. After all, it was funny.

"But she says there have been killings."

"I doubt it is policy. Khrushchev's reaction in Hungary did us little good. But of course when there is defiance of curfews and disruption of civil order, there will be some bruises…"

"How soon can I get there, I wonder."

"I recommend that you contact Aleksandr Shokin. He's a minister. He reaches the highest levels."

"You think it will take help from the highest levels to—"

"Some of my higher-ups think it will all be over and settled in less than a week and they will therefore be reluctant to arrange anything special unless your family was in immediate danger. Personally, I'm more afraid these resisters will insure that the curfews and strict civil order will continue for some time."

"So, we can do nothing without Shokin?"

"You are important to him; you and Phil made him a minister. If he's going to see you risk your life in any way, he'll want to have a hand in it."

"So there's nothing you can do?"

"I've tried, and been told to wait, that it will soon be over. Of course, I will keep trying to find a way."

Joe's eyes met those of the tall lean and handsome KGB officer. Though anxious, he appreciated Viktor's frankness and his obvious concern. "Well," Joe said, "I'll put in a call to Shokin."

"No need. We've arranged for you to meet with him tomorrow, here in Leningrad. He is meeting Staros, and will meet with you separately. Keep in mind this is not the only crisis in the world; the police are beating journalists and elected politicians in Chicago, making the Democratic party convention a bloody riot. The French are exploding hydrogen bombs now. My colleagues are busy on all fronts you might say."

The following day, Joe did see Shokin briefly, after his meeting with Phil. "Let's wait a few days till things settle down," Shokin said. "Your family is safe where they are. I've arranged for a guard detail to keep an eye on them."

"They need to get back to the conservatory. The term is starting soon."

"Understood. Joe, go back to your normal life as much as you can. Within a day or two you can call them again, from your home, here in Leningrad. Tomorrow someone will call you with a code for the operator."

Shokin was in a hurry to leave and Joe followed him to his car at Shokin's suggestion. "The best thing you can do, my friend, is relax and reassure your wife that the wait for a return to normal will not be a long one. Best for everyone if you keep working."

FORTY

"Isn't it the moment of most profound doubt that gives birth to new certainties? Perhaps hopelessness is the very soil that nourishes human hope; perhaps one could never find sense in life without first experiencing absurdity." —Václav Havel

FOR A MOMENT, AFTER SHOKIN STEPPED INTO his car and was gone, as Joe turned to go, he felt elated. *I'll spend time with Elvira on Budapeshtkaya street, listen to music, surrounded by all the comforts of home.* Instant guilt quelled his elation with a reminder of how he'd feel for the rest of his life if anything happened to his family. *Not until they're back, safe and sound...but that doesn't mean I can't spend an afternoon or evening with her...*

The following day, Taroikin called Joe with a five digit code he was to use in reaching Vera. It worked.

"I've been told we must wait a few days until things settle down," he said.

"Joe, I'm frightened here," Vera said sharply.

"They've sent a guard detail to watch out for you."

"I've seen them. I wouldn't trust them with anything."

"They're there just in case."

"Things here were fine, good again, until this ugly, brutal invasion."

"Now, now, best to be patient." *And not curse the government on the KGB telephone.*

"The kids need to be in classes; there are four of them, if you remember."

"We need to be patient, Vera. Let me talk to the kids."

"Here's Vivian. Robert is here. Anton and Alena are out somewhere with uncle Cyrus."

"Vivie? Everything all right?" Joe's voice was warm, comfortable, as he always felt with his oldest, his favorite.

"Mom is hard to live with, constantly complaining about what is happening here."

"Be patient with her. If you are not worried, it will help her not to worry. Keep practicing your music so you'll be ready when you get back."

"I'm not worried. You will take care of us. I practice every day. We can't go anywhere so there's not much else to do. I love you Papa, see you soon I hope. Here's Robert."

"Hi Papa." Robert's voice held a certain reserve which had characterized his response to Joe of late, as if he'd realized his father was merely human. They spoke briefly, assuring each other of love and connection.

Days went by. Both Taroikin and Shokin reassured Joe, but insisted that he wait. There were still no commercial flights to Prague. Elvira came to stay a night with him twice, the first times she'd ever been in his home. Then one morning when Elvira was there, Taroikin called:

"I've arranged for a special detail to collect Vera and the kids and bring them safely to Leningrad, but when the officer in charge of their guard detail asked Vera to pack and be ready, she refused to move unless you come for her."

"I'll go immediately. But how?"

"That will not be useful. It will take far too long and complicate things. You'd better call and convince her to move. It's all arranged and waiting; she'll be on a special plane."

"She's not going to be happy."

After minutes on the phone with an exasperated and unhappy Vera, she at last agreed to accompany the detail that was now waiting outside the old family homestead. "You'll all be home safe and sound this evening. We'll dine out, all of us."

"Tell me again why you are too busy to come for us."

"The powers that be find it inconvenient to include me. Probably with good reason."

"And you don't mind?"

"Without their help, you'd be there for some time."

Off the phone, Joe saw that Elvira, though not

understanding Czech, had understood most of what had been said. A bit glum, she finished dressing and brushing out her hair. Joe, embarrassed that she'd been there in Vera's bed while he was on the phone, felt a resurge of warmth for her as she stood and took a quick look at herself in the mirror. She turned to him with a smile, "I have to go anyway. You will have time to rest."

"First, I'll drive you home."

Nearing her apartment bloc, Elvira spotted her husband and ducked down, telling Joe to drive farther, another reminder of how precarious their lives were. A block away she kissed him quickly and stepped from the car, to right herself and prepare to meet her husband.

THAT EVENING, AT A SPECIAL GATE AT PULKOVO, Joe met his family. He'd scoured the Volga and the bedroom upholstery, sheets and floors, carefully plucking up every blonde hair he could find. He'd convinced himself there was no aura of Elvira or her perfume.

They were all happy to see each other, but as he drove home, answering and asking questions, he could not break the ice with Vera. Robert was distant. Vivian was affectionate and constant as ever, happy to be home. Anton and Alena talked about school and friends they would see again.

Once Vera was alone with her husband she curtailed polite exchanges by remarking, "Your Stalinists have demoralized us. They have destroyed what was becoming again a happy country."

"Nonsense, Vera. The Czechs can't just decide to introduce a different form of government."

"That's just what we need to do. We are sick and tired of this Soviet bludgeon hanging over us."

"I think Dubcek went too far; it's only logical that he not be allowed to deal independently with the West."

"I'm talking about freedom of speech, the conduct of a civil society."

"There have to be certain standards…"

"Oh, and do you follow these certain standards?"

"What are you talking about?" *Did she see or smell something?*

"You and your secret police buddies do what you want."

"They brought you home safe. Out of the mess your Dubcek got you into."

"What's the use of talking to you! You still worship Stalin and all his lackeys."

For days they both understood the wisdom of not discussing what for Vera was a heartbreaking moral destruction of her native land. For Joe it was an attack on his closely held beliefs, his devoted hope for Communism. They both knew their children would not countenance any loss of either of them or any continuing hostility between them. After a week, Joe met Elvira in his garage. They did the business at 3 in the morning in the backseat of the Volga as they comforted themselves with having had a good summer.

ON SEPTEMBER 21 1968, THE SOVIET'S SOYUZ program for a manned Moon landing seemed to advance by a significant step: the *Zond 5* unmanned lunar flyby mission returned to Earth orbit. The following day, the re-entry capsule, landed with a diverse biological payload alive. The tortoises had lost a little weight but remained active and hungry. Zond 5 also brought excellent photos of earth from the Moon. Joe and Phil could not help feeling some hope. But, due to some technical glitches, Zond 5 splashed down in the Indian Ocean instead of landing in the Khazak desert. Soviet recovery ships quickly rescued it, but not before a US spy ship had taken photographs of the descent module bobbing in the ocean, an object to all appearances designed for humans. NASA had been tracking Zond 5 for its entire flight and these photographs seemed proof enough that the Soviets were planning—at least—a manned flight around the Moon. Thus spurred, NASA decided to launch Apollo 8 to the Moon in December instead of its originally planned mission of testing the lunar module in high Earth orbit.

On October 11, NASA launched Apollo 7, the first manned Apollo mission, the first three-person American space mission, and the first live TV broadcast from an American spacecraft. It was an 11-day Earth-orbital test flight to check out the lunar module docking maneuvers with a crew on board. On

October 16, as the Apollo 7 astronauts orbited Earth, at the Olympic games in Mexico City, African-American athletes Tommie Smith and John Carlos raised their arms in a black power salute after winning gold and bronze medals.

The Apollo 7 mission, as it splashed down on October 22, was a complete technical success despite a near mutiny of the crew. It reassured NASA for an Apollo 8 trip around the Moon two months later, but certainly without Schirra, Eisele or Cunningham. They never flew again and eventually made public their near total dissatisfaction with ground control and the annoying, impractical orders they received from mission control.

As the space race seemed to be drawing close to a tie, Joe and Phil saw there was no longer a microelectronics race between the USSR and the USA; the West was winning. They were still fighting off competitors designing computers using vacuum tubes. In mid-December they read of what would later be called 'The Mother of All Demos' in San Francisco where Douglas Engelbart introduced NLS, the revolutionary hypertext system, along with the computer mouse. Engelbart had opened the door to a new age of human-computer interface, including via the internet. Joe and Phil were stunned at the news and among the few Soviet scientists who saw the near and far term implications.

On December 24, US spacecraft Apollo 8 entered orbit around the Moon. Astronauts Frank Borman, Jim Lovell and William A. Anders became the first humans to see the far side of the Moon and to see the entire Earth from space. NASA might be pulling ahead of the Soyuz program.

Staros now seemed tireless, using every allotted ruble and kopek, and doing everything possible to maximize and stimulate the premiums and other forms of co-payment. He organized day and night shifts on the system, including Saturdays, Sundays and public holidays, doing anything and everything to move them toward completion. Hundreds of design changes were being made as a result of Navy Commission bench tests in Kronstadt. Joe knew there were glitches the Commission didn't find, possibly harmless ones that perhaps never need be dealt with? Much of the changing design had been harried and would have to be redone, first in Kronstadt, and then in Liepāja. Components of the Uzel system were going to be placed in four of the six compartments of submarine B-103, including at both ends. There would be over one hundred sockets, thousands of pin-connectors on miles of cable. The documentation was prepared in a hurry and must be corrected to represent the working system. Again, Firdman's early CADCAM work was the sweet peppermint lifesaver.

ON THE EVE OF 1969, IT HAD BEEN DECIDED, submarine B-103 would be moved from Kronstadt toward Liepāja to be moored at berth number 16. It was a short distance across the Gulf of Finland and down into the Baltic Sea, but in a virtually new boat whose accumulated problems may or may not have been corrected at the Kronstadt plant. The severe winter conditions were not a problem; B-103 was built to feel at home anywhere in the world's oceans. But after a year's break in combat training, after the replacement of a large part of the crew and with new officers, experienced specialists not fully ready on certain needed tasks in running a submarine, especially under emergency conditions, there were some strong doubts about making the move while depending on the Uzel. On the other hand, Commander of B-103, Captain Eric V. Golovanov was long experienced and one of the best divers in the Soviet Navy. Executive Officer, commander Vladimir T. Bulgakov was a seasoned and demanding master of the ship, fully prepared to act as Captain if need be.

But sober voices said it would be better to be safe than sorry, better to move with the Uzel system shut down. One admiral cautioned, "The so called Node is still not ready, admit it. And you do not have enough trained personnel either, do you?"

The installed Uzel system, in comparison with the state of the boat, seemed satisfactory. Installed less than three months from the date of delivery, it was connected to the power supply and started working, though everyone agreed, including the Navy Commission that there had not been enough time to test everything. It was only the second example of a full system, after the Chief Designer's Stand, with a possible third unit in production at LKB in Leningrad.

"If that attitude of waiting until all details are ironed out prevails," Joe told B-103's Commander Golovanov, "our detractors in Moscow will say that Staros turned a perfectly good submarine into a pile of scrap metal." Joe thought of Vasily Mishin, *He didn't have the balls to go ahead with us. He let some crony talk him into some half-assed computer for the Soyuz.* "I'm all too familiar with that attitude," he added.

Golovanov then went so far as to voice his confidence in the operations of the Uzel, certainly at least as far as handling air circulation and wastewater disposal.

"But do you feel confident about the rest of it? Dead reckoning? Torpedo firing?"

"I've seen how your system works. It doesn't stall or crash or get hung up on anything."

"So we both hope they go with the Uzel operating the boat on the way to Liepāja, starting with navigation?"

"Certainly," Eric Golovanov said. "It's better than what we had before, I can tell you that."

As would often happen in these hesitant or ambiguous situations, Rear Admiral Oscar Solomonovich Zhukovsky was capable of expressing a sharp, rigid opinion. He gathered the leading developers, both Navy and LKB, and he said, "Listen you puppies, you would-be war criminals, I promise to pay for your military tribunal; but we must move forward." He was prepared, he said, to enlist former subordinates, officers, heads of the Institute. He contacted the commander in chief, Sergei G. Gorshkov on a closed naval communications link then immediately flew to Moscow to further enlist his support. That put an end to all doubts about moving on January 31.

Zhukovsky, until his dying day, retained a full admiral's rights, habits and contacts. But due to lingering doubts about an untested system, it was decided that two capable LKB engineers, Bindichenko and Troshkov must be aboard B-103 going to Liepāja. It would be the second or third New Years' celebration they would miss for the LKB team, but they understood the need to win this one. They were given very little time to finish bench testing the Commission's changes before bringing the equipment to life. They performed an intensive last debugging of the now living system as a part of the shipboard electronic system, the vital data entry into a massive weapon. The new specialists were told to prepare for the unexpected and to accept risks greater than under normal conditions of military service.

FORTY-ONE

One sits the whole day at the desk and appetite is standing next to me. 'Away with you', I say. But Comrade Appetite does not budge from the spot. --*Leonid I. Brezhnev*

SOVIET NAVY SUBMARINE B-103 ARRIVED IN LIEPĀJA at daybreak on January 3 1969. Commander Eric Golovanov watched every move as the nearly 100 meter long submarine made its way inside the narrow channels, aligning itself with the first of a series of buoys and then taking the direction of a second and third buoy to crawl at an almost imperceptible rate through the narrow, shallow channel to enter the long, artificial bay only 200 meters wide called the Bucket This Bucket contained 16 submarine berths, and was separated from the sea by a high bank along which were built the two story buildings of the submarine division headquarters. Parallel to the division headquarters, officer's barracks, workshops and laboratories, there was a long row of stately old trees that formed a shady lane.

B-103 moved at a crawl down the length of the bucket to the very end. The submarine berths were at an angle to the shore as in the roadside angled parking of cars on a city street. At berth 16, the farthest spot from prying eyes, there was a large sheet of iron with the words printed in large letters: 'Beat savage imperialism!' There was a small memorial site including a plaque with the names of famous divers, Heroes of the Soviet Union.

In one division headquarters building, on the first floor, was LKB's laboratory. This building, built in the nineteenth century of dark cherry-red bricks, was the most attractive of the entire row, none of which were considered architectural monuments. LKB engineers, used to the Leningrad standard of architectural beauty—the great theaters, churches, monuments and museums—did not appreciate the beauty of this simple factory building. But because its brick was darker and redder than any of the others, it found its way to memory and affection.

Not only was the entire city of Liepāja carefully guarded, and closed to all ground and sea traffic, but security was omnipresent anywhere near the naval base and was even more intense close to submarine B-103. The Navy-LKB team was working on a top secret weapons program. Admiral Sergei Gorshkov led Soviet military thinking with a certainty that submarines were the one weapon that could out-maneuver US forces and maintain a balance of power. It had the ability to move unseen and to strike from anywhere. For Gorshkov, under the sea was the Soviet battleground, not the surface of the oceans, nor on land or in the air, but with stealth, in the dark, ready to launch nuclear ballistic missiles from anywhere in the world, including Chesapeake Bay and the St. Lawrence River. What could be better than building a mighty submarine fleet of overwhelming superiority?

FLYING FROM LENINGRAD TO LIEPĀJA TOOK a little more than two hours in good weather. There was a stopover in Riga, at a small airfield, which could land planes no larger than the twin turboprop Antonov AN-24. The young LKB engineers enjoyed a sense of holiday and Baltic freedom when the plane landed in Riga, with half-an-hour to run to the bar and drink a cup of delicious coffee and eat an exotic pastry. And even have a small glass of brandy. This Riga buffet was dramatically different from all the food serving establishments LKB engineers had known in Leningrad. They were pleased by the Latvian pastries, the welcoming smiles and a wonderful word 'Ludzy' to which the answer was 'Paldies'.

Another twenty minutes of flight, and they were in Liepāja's airport which handled only three or four flights a day. Its only structure was a small shed, which provided an escape from sun, wind, rain and sleet, before flying. There was a small canopy over the crossing point on the field. But because Liepāja was a major naval base, the airport supplied buses to fetch ranking officers and a bus that brought passengers to the Hotel Lebanon itself. Those with heavy baggage had to arrange to be met by someone in a separate vehicle. In order for LKB to meet major military officers and even their own bosses, there was Staros's Volga, model GAZ-21, known in Leningrad and Moscow as '*the tank in evening dress*'.

Three minutes away, they were at the Hotel Lebanon where a special concierge, Khalid Islamov, welcomed them and explained that he would always be worried for their sake. He became host and protector to this whole carefree horde of seeming idlers who were really great and essential workers. They suffered one great fault only be cured by time: youth. Once Islamov had identified and registered them, he had an envelope for each holding multi-stamped ID cards and travel documents for movement in and around the closed city. There was one ID to pass the gates of the naval base, another for the submarine division and another for '*on, or in the vicinity of*', submarine B-103.

The LKB team had barely arrived in Liepāja when Oscar Zhukovsky introduced a hard order. He argued that the project could not lose at least a week by team members going home for the New Year Holidays. "If we fall behind schedule we'll have no one to forgive us," he said. "We will have only ourselves to blame." Without much serious complaint, everyone agreed. To compensate, Oscar Solomonovich offered the option of inviting family members to join them, to feast and celebrate in Liepāja. Mark Galperin, in an effort to lead such a cooperative plan, invited his family for part of the holidays. But few others did; most were not averse to celebrating independently from family, with comrades.

Galperin's daughter, Anya, was still a young teenager so the team, including Mark's wife, Raisa, decided that he should stay at the hotel with Anya while Raisa, due a break, would accompany several handsome gentlemen to a luxurious restaurant. They all knew each other well and had spent a pleasant afternoon and early evening together, but when it came time for Mark to stay and the company to depart, Mark was very sorry to miss out and was not happy to hear only jokes at his expense. The entire city of Liepāja was gong to be out celebrating without him.

Anya, who had enjoyed the afternoon's dashing adult

company, was soon asleep and Mark lay down on the living room couch of his Hotel Lebanon suite with a book to read, thus to pass his lonely time. It wasn't long before he felt himself drifting off to sleep for a nap, as good a way as any to pass the time until Raisa and his companions returned.

Galperin awoke much later to a dashing song of multiple voices. He rushed to the window to see Raisa, *the life of the party,* conducting the choir. She was wearing the cap and badge of Captain Gregory S. Kubatyan. The captain's bald head reflected the light of a street lamp and he stared up at Galperin with a mischievous smile. Mark responded to the exuberance of their song by throwing his hands in the air whereupon the crowd happily rushed to the hotel entrance. Quickly ducking under his blanket, Mark picked up his book and was ready to insist on not being further disturbed. But, hearing them coming down the corridor, he spotted his work shoes beside the couch and grabbed one. As soon as the door opened, he threw the heavy shoe without looking. It landed on Captain Kubatyan's bald head. Mark did not get to fire the next shot because the whole gang fell upon him in a rousing boisterous drunken reunion. Mark was grateful that Anya, in the next room, slept soundly through the epic evening's end. But the same officers and rowdy companions told Anya all about it at breakfast.

Part of the story of Liepāja in the year 1969 was the story of five top engineers, fun loving young men and deputy chief designers, each in charge of specific areas of the Uzel project with their own teams of five to ten second deputies. Zhukov, Kuznetsov, Pankin, Maslenikov and Nikitin shared exhausting work seven days a week, with only occasional visits to the family. They shared their time of recreation and release.

There was a famous restaurant, Jura, of a modern design, featuring a high cuisine of traditional Latvian dishes. It was staffed by courteous and efficient young people. Along with dinner there was a culturally rich variety show, something unheard of in Moscow or Leningrad. Three times a week these shows went on until near midnight. The programs and groups changed at least once a month. After midnight, dancing and partying at the Jura often continued until 3 AM. When fights or loud arguments broke out, there was a professional bouncer, Matveyich. He was ever present and, in spite of his small stature and mature age, he instantly wrung the most zealous fighters down the stairs with their caps flying after them. At the bottom of the stairs, these rowdies were taken hold of by the patrol officers. In the mornings, commanders hurried to the garrison guardhouse to rescue their young brawlers from further trouble.

One day, the weather was bad enough to prevent flights from Leningrad so that certain supplies were lacking. This led to improvisation which had embarrassing results. Certain would-be musicians, knowing Joe's weakness for music, created a song about it, and practiced it so often that everyone on the upper floors of the Lebanon was nearly forced to hum the melody. If not actually internalized, the song became familiar enough. Very late one night, on a weekend when the restaurant Jura was open until 3 AM, suddenly through the frosty air and the surrounding silence came this concert of *Vanished Pain at Leningrad Design Bureau!* It was an evening when the company consisted mainly of senior officers, directors and members of the State Commission, who were forced to stay in Liepāja.

JOE SOON HAD A CHANCE TO TALK AGAIN with Commander Eric Golovanov, captain of Project 641 submarine B-103 to ask how the Uzel had performed during his recent voyage. Golovanov was the man now most familiar with its use, their ultimate customer. It was unusual for ether man to be at a meeting of the joint Navy-LKB team on a Sunday morning in mid January and it was remarkable that they were both there.

Joe thought Captain Golovanov's written report on his voyage to Liepāja from Kronstadt seemed cautious, perhaps intentionally restrained. As they left the meeting room and the dark cherry red brick building, they began walking around the end of the manmade submarine harbor. Golovanov apparently heading toward B-103, no doubt to check up before doing anything else for the day. Joe walked with him, saying, "I've read your excellent report, Commander, but I'd love to hear whether or not your confidence in the Uzel was fully sustained."

Over the years Joe had improved his skills at human relations, starting when he sought younger brother Arthur's allegiance in fending off the overbearing psychology of older brother Bernie. Joe's way of getting at what people thought wasn't just the questions he asked or any hint of psychological reward for opening up, it was more Joe's tone of voice, the confidence he had in being open with you, in sharing salient matter-of-fact observations. His generous inclusion was in his voice and presence, right there in plain sight, without pissing anyone off.

To Commander Eric Golovanov, Dr. Joseph Berg was an odd duck, but clearly operating on a high level of intelligence. Eric thought of Joe as he had first seen him: Berg's humble even sloppy dress, with mismatched socks, his badly tied necktie hanging askew, the way he moved, flexible, nimble, but erratically, with his too large jacket flapping as he moved.

"There were a few surprises," Golovanov said, "I'm sure the Leningrad Design Bureau still has work to do."

"Of course, that's why we are here. No, you outlined your observed anomalies in sufficient detail. I suppose I'm asking how it felt."

It was a cold morning 18 degrees below zero, Celius with moisture in the air. Their breathing made clouds as they walked several paces without speaking. Both were wearing heavy sheepskin parkas; Joe's was older and less well maintained. Rounding the corner of the submarine basin, they were soon at the ramps up to B-103's high deck and conning tower. Golovanov slowed perceptively, saying, "I'm not sure what you mean, but I can say that it felt alright. My hopes for your computer's possibly important future were not disappointed. Does that answer your question?"

"Walk with me a ways?" Joe waved his hand out, his arm suddenly fully extended then dropping instantly to his side.

Golovanov smiled at the innocence of any politics or social structure in Berg's question, yet a question both personal and sincere. "Why not," Eric said, "I've got a pair of land legs that shouldn't be wasted."

As they moved on past the access ramp, Joe met

Golovanov's gaze with a look of delight that could not be mistaken. He told Joe:

"The navigation was precise and much faster than the old ways, rendering positions in real time. It wasn't in my report, but we checked and rechecked the Uzel's reckoning data, using the old ways. When there was any difference between the two, I came to believe the Uzel."

"Really?" Joe said. "Yes that's the kind of thing."

Golovanov smiled, happy to see the look of wonder on Berg's face. "Of course, how well it does on firing torpedoes at three different moving target while tracking five targets simultaneously will be another matter entirely."

"Of course, but there will be field trials to prove or disprove that."

"Do you consider that a truly a realistic goal?"

"Well, that's what we calculated as possible."

"If so," Eric turned and met Joe's eyes, "I don't know anything that could beat us. The Americans can't do such a thing."

"Well that is possible and I believe we will see it certified, eventually." Joe knew they weren't there yet on tracking five enemy subs and shooting torpedoes at three of them, simultaneously, but he felt confident they were only a few inventions and solutions away. A larger memory cube was one thing..

"Your system operates the boat smoothly," Golovanov said. "Once a course command is initiated the reaction is immediate. It's like I'm talking to the boat and it answers me."

"Some day there will be voice commands, so that a captain can talk directly to the computer."

"Are you saying that during final development here in Liepāja I will be able to tell my boat what to do? In plain Russian?" Golovanov's respect for this odd, strangely engaging scientist, was soaring toward awe as his gaze reached again for Berg's eyes.

"Oh, Gosh no," Joe said, blushing and smiling sheepishly, "I'm merely saying that once you start converting information into ones and zeros, there's no limit to what can be accomplished. And will be accomplished. Some day."

"To be perfectly honest Joseph Veniaminovich, you had me going there. Next, you'd have had me practicing my voice for speaking to the computer. Not the way I'd speak to my father or my wife."

Joe laughed good naturedly, "Well sorry if I got your hopes up."

They walked past several submarine berths, some with submarines being resupplied or undergoing minor repairs. Other berths were empty, some already frozen over.

Joe remained quiet as they walked. Then Golovanov, exclaimed, "If the Uzel gives me the power to engage five enemy submarines or surface vessels on an instant to instant basis, I will have the most formidable weapon of the seas."

"Joe nodded agreeably without saying anything, apparently quite content with himself and his companion, but there was a ferocity in Golovanov despite his boyish appearance, that gave Joe pause.

"But I'll tell you what," Golovanov said. "Now don't quote me on this, at least not while I'm still alive, but your Uzel? …Its going to be a challenge. With control so precise, it will be hard to fault the equipment if I miss my target in torpedo shooting exercises."

Joe shivered, not from the cold, but from a sweep of awe for the depth of this indirect endorsement by an often decorated battle ready diver, with supreme hope for the combat power of his weapon.

"Thank you Commander for confiding in me," Joe said.

"Well," Golovanov stopped walking, for emphasis, "please let's arrange for you to come out with us to the proving grounds. So you can see the Uzel in action?" Golovanov turned to go back up the long pier. To Joe it seemed as if he meant to lead the way to B-103 and an adventure into the depths.

"From what I understand, Commander Golovanov," Joe said as he turned back as well, "those trips are long; you're out there for weeks at a time. I can barely afford to escape for a few hours." *Except with Elvira.*

"I'm sure I can come up with a good reason for a short

foray, or find a sudden need to cut short a longer mission. Perhaps you can set aside a day or two?"

"I'll think about it," Joe said and tried to imagine finding that much time. *Might be tedious and boring most of the time, too,* he thought and more or less dismissed the idea.

MANY SOVIET MILITARY ENGINEERS HAVE been forced to test their endeavors in the Arctic or in deserted Central Asian steppes or in Siberian forests, somewhere in the middle of nowhere hundreds of kilometers from the nearest settlement. As a result, they have stories of hardship with which to proudly regale friends and family. Born in such hardships they may have friendships that last a lifetime. But it is hard for them to say of such exercises that they were entirely enjoyable.

It is true: Liepāja was a military base, a place for ship trials, professionally well-equipped with metallurgical and ship repair plants and a strategic submarine base relatively close to deep water. It was a closed city, with 26,000 Soviet Navy personnel from admirals to sailors to civilian staff, with numerous KGB agents there to keep it tight. But the stories from Liepāja, 1969, were different than the spare stories of struggles and hardships from elsewhere in the land of Socialism.

For these scientists and engineers, Liepāja was a charming ancient town full of pleasant Baltic life and European customs. There was the Sea, the beaches, restaurants, small cozy cafes and shops full of Latvian national souvenirs made of ceramics, amber and wood. There were ceramic bottles and bottles with "Riga Balsam" a small shot of which not only gave a special charm to a cup of coffee, but when added to vodka, it made the 'drink of the gods'.

FORTY-TWO

While you're saving your face, you're losing your ass
--Lyndon B. Johnson

JANUARY 14 1969, THE SOVIET UNION LAUNCHED Soyuz 4 followed the next day by Soyuz 5, which docked with Soyuz 4 in orbit. It was the first docking of two crewed spacecraft of any nation, and the first transfer of crew from one space vehicle to another. It was the only time a transfer was accomplished with a space walk. This was two months before the United States Apollo 9 mission performed the first internal crew transfer. But Soyuz 5's service module did not separate. It entered the atmosphere nose-first, leaving cosmonaut Boris Volynov hanging by his restraining straps. The atmosphere burned through the module, but the craft righted itself before the escape hatch was burned through. Then, the parachute lines tangled and the landing rockets failed, resulting in a hard landing which broke kosmonaut Volynov's teeth.

On January 16, Student Jan Palach set himself on fire in Prague's Wenceslas Square to protest the Soviet invasion of Czechoslovakia. Three painful days later, he died. His sacrifice spurred other similar sacrifices and demonstrations against Soviet rule. Vera Bergova, Joe's wife, had all she could do to contain her fury. *That anyone would do that over these despicable brutes!*

On January 20, Richard Milhouse Nixon succeeded Lyndon Baines Johnson as the 37th President of the United States. He would be kicked around for years to come.

IN LATE JANUARY, AFTER MORTON SOBELL, THE coconspirator convicted with the Rosenbergs, was released from his 30 year sentence for espionage, having served 18 years, Phil Staros read about it in the *International Herald Tribune* at breakfast in Moscow's hotel Metropole. As usual he was enjoying the company of close friends. He was heard by Eric Firdman to say almost under his breath, "I'd be free now. I'd never have done more time than Morty."

Joe wasn't with Phil that morning, perhaps inventing another technical solution, or off with Elvira. But he read the same news about Sobell and reacted differently.

Unlike Al Sarant, Joel Barr did not consider that being forced to flee the USA to the USSR had deprived him of something he might have had, or should have had. Joel was living his dream, of finding the true Socialist state and becoming part of it. Of course the reaction of capitalism toward losing its secrets was wrathful and punitive. It was to be expected. But his friends from the Soviet intelligence service had made sure the US intelligence service didn't get to punish him. Joel was equally glad Al had also escaped. And, he'd never yet regretted his promise to Al that day in Moscow when Al demanded to be the decision maker in their new partnership. Joel truly loved Al who had offered whole-hearted friendship from the start, a welcoming hand up and out from ethno-centric Judaism, Joel's first *goy* friend, who accepted him as he felt himself: a man, an atheist, a scientist, a communist and a friend. Joe understood Al, admired his incredible skills of concentration, communication and influence, but of course he thought Phil's approach to Soviet politics was overwrought. *Maybe we should have taken the shot at Zelenograd, accepted what was offered, played the game. Who the fuck did we think we were? Two Yanks about to take over the whole Soviet electronics business?* Joel smiled, it was almost really funny, the absurdity of it: *But if it comes out that we are not even Czechs but Americans, we'll be torn to pieces.*

So yes, Joel/Joe was both glad Morty had made it through alive, but he was saddened by the terrible penalty his old friend had paid. Unlike Al/Phil, Joe was not focusing on Morty now being 'free' in the United States, but about the terrible waste of Morty's life and his brilliant, creative mind. From those sad thoughts of Morty, Joel again felt that almost numbing sense of gratitude, a breathless awe of his own good fortune: *to be here, doing advanced work, at the top of my skills, to have a family, Elvira, my best friend as a partner… If I were religious I'd tell everyone it was a miracle. …And ask for donations.* Joel laughed but he knew in his heart that Phil, despite all his humanitarian enlightenment, believed in *just deserts. He believes he deserves to be rewarded for his genius and hard work…As though there is an entity of higher judgement that decides fairly the deserves and the deserve-nots.* But as far as Joel was concerned, a good communist thought instead about the opportunity to contribute to the human community. *Deserves? I certainly have received in life far more than I ever deserved. I'm glad Phil gave me the UM-1NKh to manage. The trips with Elvira to the factories… Do you hold it against us, Morty…against Julie? For getting you mixed up in it? Poor Morty. You'd never admit or show it if you did, would you?*

LIEPĀJA, WORKING, CHEERFUL AND WELCOMING,

it was a time when the young Leningrad Design Bureau engineers woke up every morning with the thought: *today there will be something important in my life. Victory is still only a few days and nights of hard work away.* They were perfectly happy and they slept soundly. They were having fun, enjoying life as if on a permanent vacation, when victory is celebrated with a reckless feast, and the next day there is a new challenge or surprising adventure. And they all knew how to work without rest for many days in a row.

The plentiful items of culinary delight in Liepāja's shops and market, products never seen in Russian cities, were prizes bought by LKB team members to enjoy in their hotel rooms or were taken home to friends and family on rare leaves to Leningrad. Another great gift, besides boxes of Baltic herring, was Latvian pig fat, especially smoked to preserve and flavor it, as found at the small butcher shop in town. Many Russians believed the best cure for a hangover was a large chunk of this fat washed down with another shot of vodka.

Hotel Lebanon was home away from home. At times, the LKB team in Liepāja would number up to 120 people, and the hotel roster included not only LKB employees, but also numerous officers who helped to carry out the inevitable changes in algorithms for solving problems. There were many contractors, boat designers who carried out tests. The officers of the central apparatus of the Naval Fleet stayed there. The Lebanon took them all. Sometimes, when there was no room, Khalid Islamov provided cots for one or two nights. Such times were never considered a hardship by hard working young men and women who could have slept standing up after their long shifts. But, regardless of reckless recreation, their most common habit was hard work, and not immoderate drinking. Controlling alcohol consumption was particularly difficult in a technological enterprise that required ethanol. Legitimate use was hard to pin down. Blame for shortages necessarily had to be widely shared.

But of course the LKB team and the closely associated Naval personnel and even the entire submarine division itself, were only part of life in Liepāja. All the people who worked in the "Baltic Navy were in town. Also based there were a number of smaller surface warships, minesweepers, patrol ships and support vessels, meant to protect local waters. Liepāja had no capacity for large deep draft vessels. Those went to the deep water ports of Riga and Ventspils.

Liepāja's main attraction for many of the Russian speaking people there was, an ancient cathedral next to the hotel, nearly identical to the Kronstadt Naval Cathedral, familiar to all Soviet Navy sailors. On Sundays, this old Russian church attracted a number of LKB members who afterward discussed their impressions of the musical accompaniment to the services.

On Sundays, as well as every other day, at 7:45 AM, the LKB team was on the bus, joshing each other and remarking on the high and low points of the past evening's activities. Then, as they crossed the bridge into Karosta, the northern section of Liepāja, all trivial talk evaporated and was quickly replaced by serious concerns in solving the problems they would face at their laboratory and inside submarine B-103.

After the bridge, the road forked and the bus made its way through the industrial zone of the city, past the metallurgical plant and ship repair plant, both part of Soviet Navy's work, and thus familiar to LKB engineering. Sometimes, there were large orders associated with the imminent introduction of changes in the testing process. Sometimes a simple but vital component could be produced within a few minutes after a quick negotiation over the phone with individuals who knew a glass or a bottle would be forthcoming.

Even the most hungover and sleep deprived on the morning bus could be restored to life by a particularly interesting discussion. Sometimes there were several topics, sometimes there was unanimous interest in a single question that occupied them to the end of the journey, like how to seal tight the Uzel's cable passages between compartments of the submarine.

At the base, a sailor ran to lift the gate of the Naval Division headquarters and the LKB team was proud that no one checked their documents. Their vehicles had a permanent pass with the inscription 'Do not check'. Every time they passed through and walked from the bus to the berth of B-103 or a little farther to their nearby lab, they felt proud that they were so thoroughly trusted.

FEBRUARY 21 1969, THE SOVIET SPACE PROGRAM

made its first attempt to launch the huge and complex 30 engine rocket, the N-1, designed under Sergei Korolev to carry Soviet cosmonauts to the Moon. This first attempt was to be an unmanned Moon orbital mission. But, a few seconds into the launch, a transient voltage caused KORD, the Rocket Engine Control system, to shut down engine number 12 and, in order to maintain symmetrical thrust, KORD shut down the opposite engine, number 24. Seconds later, oscillation in the number 2 engine tore components loose and started a propellant leak. Further vibrations ruptured a fuel line which spilled fuel into the hot booster, starting a fire which burned through wiring in the power supply, causing electrical arcing that caused KORD to shut down the entire first stage at 68 seconds into launch. This signal also locked the second and third stages preventing ground command from starting their engines. The N-1 hit the ground 52 kilometers from the launch pad, 183 seconds after launch. Vasily Mishin blamed the generators for the failure, because he could not think of any other reason for all 30 engines to shut down at once. But Mishin was quickly proven wrong when the generators were recovered from the crash site, were refurbished and worked without any problems during further bench tests. The KORD was found to have a number of serious design flaws and poorly programmed logic; its operating frequency perfectly coincided with vibrations generated by the propulsion system.

Though Joe and Phil could only speculate as to what happened to the N-1 launch and Major Taroikin was not forthcoming with any details, they assumed that Vasily Mishin's drunken leadership was at fault. They did not blame Sergei Korolev's design, but the N-1's failure further discouraged, but did nor entirely extinguish, any hope they had of a Soviet manned Moon landing.

FORTY-THREE

Once you get into this great stream of history, you can't get out. --*Richard M. Nixon*

ON MARCH 3 1969 NASA LAUNCHED APOLLO 9 with a three astronaut crew. Four days later, Apollo 9 returned safely to Earth after successfully testing the Lunar Module. Joe and Phil, after the N-1 launch failure, felt the inevitable pace of the American race to the Moon. They vowed to themselves not to let it distract them from successfully completing the Uzel mission.

Hotel Lebanon, by late March 1969, had become a great place for music. Several LKB team members had guitars and played for friends in their hotel rooms. Yuri M. Rozanov always had his guitar and could sing folk songs all night long, even after a hard day. He was fond of sitting on the windowsill of his room with his legs dangling out into the night, even on very cool nights, singing and playing for whoever might be listening.

Phil Staros would come for a few days with a small suitcase, an even smaller essential tool kit that he never parted with, and his guitar. He trusted no one to touch or move his guitar. But very few had heard him play and some said carrying a guitar and playing the guitar were two very different things.

Joe said to Phil one day when they were alone in the Volga, after Phil had carefully cradled the guitar case in the back seat, "Maybe make the guitar less of a mystery. These bright engineers are into singing and playing guitars or the piano every chance they get, so naturally they wonder what you do with your guitar."

"So let them wonder or let them ask," Phil said.

"I know how good you are," Joe said. "I came to appreciated folk songs from you many years ago."

"You still don't really like folk songs much," Phil said.

"But why have our present colleagues never heard you? How many times did you play your favorite songs for our crowd at 65 Morton Street in apartment 6-I? Do you want our best engineers to think you play only for yourself?"

"It's not anybody's concern why I want my guitar close at hand. It connects me to a time when I was happy and had no serious worries. That is not something that is easy to explain given our present situation. Playing American folk songs could be a dead giveaway."

"So don't explain it," Joe said, "but play some of those favorite tunes for this crowd. After all, our old friends who could understand precisely what your songs mean for you are gone, some of them forever."

"It's not the same. The old crowd helped write my songs, or inspired them."

But one night Staros invited Galperin, Zhukov. Kuznetsov, Nikitin and a few trusted others to join him in his room on the fourth floor of the Lebanon. Though always neatly dressed, Phil now wore a dazzling clean and ironed shirt with slightly cuffed sleeves, sharply creased trousers and freshly shined sparkling black boots. The guitar case was open on the bed and the guitar's richly hued wooden surface shone as it lay ready to be seen and heard.

In an unusually shy tone, Phil said, looking from one to another of his guests as he reached for his guitar, "I want to play and sing for you a few favorite songs. It seems I have not shared my interest in music as I might have."

When all had settled down and exchanged minor phrases, Phil placed his left booted foot on the clean white bed and rested the guitar on his raised leg. He ran his fingers lightly over the guitar strings. "I will choose personally memorable songs that I think you will like." He moved his mustache from side to side in a slow preparatory way.

As Staros played, he began to sing as if to himself, in what was almost a whisper at first, so that it was not so much the words as the mood of the song the others felt. Then he sang songs softly in full voice in English, in German, but most were

Greek or Latin-American songs. All the songs seemed melancholy and were performed from the heart. It was apparent to those close to him that for all his extraordinary charisma, he was a very lonely man.

In the small cafes, crowded masterpieces of the Latvian national cuisine, there were a dozen different salads, rolls, cold beef, boiled and jellied in two or three combinations. Latvia was particularly rich in a variety of apples. In unusually rich Latvian markets in small villages and just at the side of the roads, there would be vegetables, fresh summer savory, winter forest and garden berries and mushrooms. Best of all were the little roadside cafés in the countryside right next to a dairy farm offering a great variety of dairy products, as important a part of Latvian culture as the songs, costumes, ceramic arts and even the Latvian language itself. There was everything that can be made from milk: sour cream, cottage cheese, Baltic soft and hard cheeses, and whipped cream! This whipped cream was not the whipped mass which was sold in cans and looked more like shaving cream, but cream that has just been whipped in modest but tall, narrow glasses with chocolate, strawberry, lemon, or caramel sauces. At the window of a small cafe, hearts stopped in anticipation and it was necessary to try something new and better, each time.

Beyond all of Liepāja's charms, for the LKB team and their Naval cohorts, the most important source of joy and spiritual vigor was the sea. The beaches, famous for lime trees growing not far from the water, were attractive even in cold weather, even when shrouded in heavy mist. A walk along the beach, breathing the fresh sea air was a tonic they all appreciated.

IT DID NOT TAKE LONG TO DISCOVER JUST how difficult a problem the cabling from the central control room was going to be. The first cable run from central command amidships through the compartment walls revealed that there would be no air- or water-tight seal unless new methods were discovered or invented. The cable bundles themselves would leak water under the slightest pressure. They tried different methods to prevent the leakage of air or water and began testing their efforts by putting one end of the cable into a beaker of water and blowing on the other end. If there were bubbles, or even the slightest stirring of the water, their efforts were considered a failure.

Someone, no one was later sure who, suggested that rubber condoms could be used to seal the cable passages at junction points. So a team went out and bought every condom for sale in the pharmacies of Liepāja and even emptied the pharmaceutical supply depots. They kidded about how there would be a baby boom in the closed city nine or ten months away. Some cynical voices said that using Soviet condoms was futile as they were notorious for frequent leakage. Some truly unpatriotic souls even went so far as to suggest they needed American or French condoms.

But sealing the conduits with rubbers was only a good try; it almost worked. Next it was bicycle inner tubes which were emptied from sports stores. The bike innertubes worked better than the rubbers, but did not entirely solve the problem either. Joe suggested to Phil they needed to have the cabling specially manufactured.

"We'll get the Kronstadt factory to do it," Phil agreed. "Everyone knows I can contact Admiral Gorshkov if need be. We'll get it done."

"It needs to have a complete seal around all the separate filaments, bonded to the outside jacket every meter, or two meters at the most."

"I'll give them those specifications," Phil said. "Probably Mark can take care of it." Joe shot Phil a look: *maybe you better make sure; you're the big dog.* Phil caught Joe's expression and nodded with the slightest leftward move of his mustache.

Questions about the sealed integrity of the boat due to the Uzel cabling would remain unanswered for some time to come. While they waited for the cabling to be manufactured, other problems arose.

TOWARD THE END OF APRIL, IN LENINGRAD, Joe had finally prevailed on Phil to submit the UM 1NKh for the State (Stalin) prize. They included the names of several other LKB engineers who had worked hard to improve the computer.

It did not take long for the powerful Leningrad Party Committee to denounce their application and refuse any support for it. Joe had worked hard as had two other LKB engineers in preparing extensive circuit diagrams, detailed drawings, explanatory texts and other documentation of their current factory installations. Rejection was a bitter pill to swallow though not entirely surprising. Certainly not surprising to Phil who had called it a fool's errand throughout their discussions. But Phil had made the UM-1Nkh Joe's baby so he had eventually gone along with the application. He refrained from offering any response similar to: *too bad, but nice try.* He showed only a silent unsurprised patience.

THERE CAME A DAY IN EARLY MAY, ONE OF those rare northern days that combine more than 16 hours of daylight with a deep blue cloudless sky and shirtsleeve warmth, a day when you can almost see the trees growing from tiny green bud tips to sharp young leaves. A day when you want to be outside seeing birds fly and watching trees grow. Joe knew this day and he knew people. He'd understood all this from his early days as a tentative atheist following his *bar mitzvah* party. And even before, when he broke into his Brooklyn neighborhood's sandlot baseball league. He had long recognized the power of the human spirit, how unstoppable men and women could be when they were inspired and fueled with hope. It was such a day.

This wonderful day in Liepāja happened to be the day before Staros was due to arrive with top Navy brass, to inspect, to question, to comment, to suggest and perhaps to encourage or at least to urge them to earlier completion. A formidable prospect to be sure, but whenever Phil wasn't present, Joe Berg was the boss, even over Uzel's Chief Designer Mark Galperin. But intelligent followers do not follow their recognized leader blindly. So, when Joe announced that the entire LKB team was to take a bus to the beach at Bernati for the day, there was not only astonishment, but doubt, and with doubt came hesitation and resistance.

Typical of those who didn't feel comfortable with a day of leisure at the beach, a day that looked too good to be true, was programmer Boris Baranov. He was particularly puzzled, if not bewildered, by Joe's clearly insistent announcement. Baranov's irritation grew strong enough that he dared challenge Joe with an albeit polite question:

"With Philip Georgievich arriving tomorrow, does a day at the beach seem entirely prudent?"

"Did you see their faces this morning?" Joe said. "Did you see how worried everybody was? How anxious? Of course they are worried about tomorrow, about the problems from weeks ago that still exist, how Staros and the Navy chiefs will react. But they are so busy worrying, they have forgotten what they have already achieved. Let today be to celebrate that. We are going to cut the development time for a fully operating Combat Information and Control System from eight years to five or less." Even as Joe spoke he moved and urged others toward the bus waiting just outside their dark cherry red brick laboratory.

"I suppose you could look at it that way," Barnanov said, moving reluctantly along with Joe, feeling unsatisfied with Dr. Berg's explanation. Berg seemed too lax and unregimented. *Or* Boris wondered, *is he trying to become more popular with the troops than his partner, Staros, a strict and efficient boss?*

"Then too," Joe said, smiling and confident that he could win over this recalcitrant fellow, "for us to have a successful meeting tomorrow, everyone must arrive knowing that behind us, we owe nothing." We must not look drawn and sick at heart, but confident and assured. That is what is really important, that everybody feels good."

"That's an unusual view," Baranov said mulishly.

"Okay. Can you think of anything more likely to make everyone feel proud of accomplishments and confident of coming success than a day at Bernati?"

Boris didn't answer. Only many years later would he realize that the missing piece of the puzzle that Dr. Berg exhibited that morning, the seeming illogical and arbitrary behavior, was American behavior: a never quite comprehended whimsical, generous scheming toward mutual good fortune.

Joe found Baranov stiff and cranky, but he decided not to hold it against him. *Let's see how he likes a day at the beach... Let's see who has no guilt and therefore no qualms about a carefree day...*

In less than an hour, the bus carrying sixty surprised but happy LKB and Navy members arrived at Bernati, an abandoned resort located half an hour south of the center of Liepāja.

A wide, luxurious beach stretched along a narrow strip of dunes covered with a dry pine forest. Behind the dunes was a road in the direction of Ventspils to the north and to the Lithuanian border to the south. The road was almost empty and the beach, too, was so deserted that they felt little need for bathing suits, even though the water was still cold and a short dip in the sea was enough. There were some border guards who passed occasionally but steered clear of any confrontations. The road led a kilometer away to the small village, one of the most beautiful of all the places on the Baltic coast, Bernati.

By the time they were on their way back from Bernati, Joe felt sure it had been a good idea. Certainly he had gained a much better idea about the characters of the team. Baranov seemed still somewhat put off, but had had moments of relaxation anyway. *Kuznetsov and Zhukov are certainly a mischievous pair, and their musical aspirations seem more frivolous than serious.*

On May 18 1969, Apollo 10 was launched with a three man crew, the full dress-rehearsal for the Moon landing. Four days later, Apollo 10's lunar module flew to within 16 kilometers of the Moon's surface. Four days after that, on May 26, Apollo 10 returned to Earth, after a successful 8-day test of all the components needed for a successful manned Moon landing.

THERE WAS ANOTHER GROUP THAT PLAYED music in Lebanon hotel rooms. They adopted the name *Koratron*, not to be confused with electronic terms such as, Pozitron or magnetron. No, Koratron was the name of a Hungarian firm that imported dress pants to be sold at the hotel's department store, *Kurzeme*. Imported clothing was itself a pleasant surprise, so such items were quickly bought up by this group of deputy Chief Designers, Kuznetsov, Zhukov and Nikitin, friends who were used to having dinner together in their rooms and talking about music. They soon realized that they had acquired more than just trousers. Fastened to each pair was a label of fifty square centimeters, black with large gold letters, KORATRON. They understood that a musical ensemble could gain both a strong name and an attractive uniform. It was enough of an incentive to prompt further steps toward the formation of a musical group; they needed only musical instruments.

In a toy store, Kuznetsov found the only instrument capable of a melody. It was a children's pipe, equipped with a small accordion keyboard. Zhukov came up with a child's balalaika, the Russian three stringed instrument with a triangular wooden, hollow body and a fretted wooden neck.

Schoolboy pals, Valodya Kuznetsov and Gesha Zhukov convinced Ed Nikitin to take up a small children's drum. These three Uzel Deputy Chief Designers, the core of the LKB team along with Pankin and Maleninkov, deep in their work, burdened with responsibilities, never lost their sense of humor, nor their great respect and devotion to their teacher and leader Phillip G. Staros.

The three young musicians soon added a fourth member, Vladimir Mikhailich, Chief Observer of the 24th Naval Research Institute. A seemingly dry, neat and conservative man, Vlad was transformed in joining the band. He brought some lightness, delicacy and a very subtle and kind wit to the group. He devised his own instrument, a resonant tin dust bin. But, instead of banging on it with a stick or serving spoon, Mikhailich purchased a toilet bowl brush. He kept it in a secluded place so no one would use it for its intended purpose. Blows to the dust bin were loud, dramatic and were clearly used to highlight a particular musical phrase or a significant, telltale lyric.

The Koratron quartet enjoyed great success among the LKB and Navy team. But very late one night Staros came unannounced from Leningrad. His late flight had been further delayed by the weather. By midnight Koratron and their fans were sure Staros would not arrive so late. But Phil had managed to reach Mark Galperin just before finally boarding the plane in Riga, once the rain and hail had stopped and the fog had lifted. Only Mark knew Staros was still coming and he barely managed a glass of strong hot tea before heading to the airport shed. Hoping to chat privately with Staros, Mark found his boss too exhausted to engage. At the hotel, Staros thanked him, said good night and set out immediately to his fourth floor room, "for a late but good night's sleep," he added.

According to the daily schedule, the morning shift woke up at 7 AM and after breakfast were on the bus to the submarine base at 7:45. Staros, disciplined man that he was, left earlier in his car. As was customary, the first shift began with a short meeting with all the deputy chief designers. Staros, though neatly dressed and clean shaven, seemed very tired and sleepy. It seemed his obvious fatigue might be due to the late and tiring flight. But, when Galperin commented, "It is unfortunate that your flight was so delayed," Staros explained:

"That was only one thing. The fact is I didn't sleep a single wink all night long." He now had the meeting's full attention and sympathy. "As I settled in my comfortable hotel bed to sleep, an African band began rehearsing just below my room. They went on all night, playing almost directly into my eardrums."

There were sheepish droops to some of the sympathetic faces due to knowledge that it was Koratron that had been holding forth to great merriment. With the words of this unfortunate circumstance barely out of Phil's mouth, the same happy musicians arrived, clearly tired and hung over. They were startled alert to see the big boss. Even as Staros said in conclusion, "Besides the horrible high pitched sounds like a cat being strangled, there was this loud crashing boom coming irregularly up through the floor."

The core of deputy chief designers took their seats in the meeting with shamefaced expressions. It was an awkward moment which teetered precariously over an abyss of tragedy and laughter. It would take time, but eventually everyone concerned would get at least a chuckle out of a somewhat secretly shared memory.

It was a long drive from Leningrad to Liepāja, and the Lebanon hotel, was often crowded. As per Phil's admonition, Joe did not contemplate bringing Elvira to the closed city. When she could arrange for her children to be with her mother, when her husband was away, as he was more often than not, Joe would drive her to the countryside near Liepāja where they would camp, making love by an open fire, in the cool night air from the Baltic Sea. Vera and the children were going back to Prague for the coming summer, despite last summer's chaotic crackdown on the Prague Spring of -Alexander Dubček. For Joe, there was much to look forward to in the summer of 1969.

FORTY-FOUR

Finishing second in the Olympics gets you a silver medal, finishing second in politics gets you oblivion.
                                                    --Richard M. Nixon

BY EARLY JUNE, INTERMITTENT SHORTS IN A number of RAM memory blocs were wreaking havoc with the operation of major circuits in the prototype Uzel on B-103. The system would work fine from start up for an hour then became what might as well be a patch of tangled hay baling wire. Haywire. Unpredictable circuit failure or corrupted data. The most vulnerable part of the system was the permanent memory block which held the computer operating program. These blocks included modules consisting of small ferrite rings with an inner diameter of 2 mm, made manually by winding the finest copper wire with enamel insulation around a sewing needle. For many years, these RAM blocks had provided superior reliability. But now there was a problem in the one single place that was supposed to be permanent, unchanged and thoroughly debugged.

Eventually it was decided that the problem might be due to microcracks in the enamel insulation of the coils resulting in intermittent short circuits between the windings so that the program read 0 instead of 1, or vice versa. Most often, the evidence did not show as failures, but as random errors, no doubt increased by the high temperature in the boat of 95 degrees Fahrenheit and nearly 100 percent humidity!

Therefore, after a number of attempts to find a compromise between constantly swapping out modules and trying to control temperature and humidity, Staros decided, with tacit agreement from Berg, to close off the area, use dry ice and baked desiccants. After much placing and re-baking of desiccants at high temperature, a constant hassle, it did dramatically increase the intervals of stable operation. But Mark commented, "We are only replacing a catastrophe with an extremely bad situation."

Next, the decision from Staros and Galperin was to set up a schedule for rewinding and replacing coils on a continual basis. This also helped, but was still not a solution. These experiments and half measures were taking up valuable time. Joe was becoming increasingly anxious and irritable because he could not see the solution.

After two days of not calling Vera in Leningrad to say good night to his family, which followed a period of familial and conjugal neglect in preceding weeks, when Joe did call, Vera was adamant that he return to Leningrad. "If we are married," she said, "I should see you. The kids miss you; they are growing up. You don't miss me at all?"

"Oh please, Vera, of course I miss you, but I've got big problems here in Latvia."

"All the more reason to take a break. Your family has to matter. We will be going to Prague soon, probably without you, yes?"

"Let me talk to the kids."

They say they will talk to you when you come home."

"What? Now you are turning them against me?"

"They say they want a papa who is not just a voice on the telephone. Here's Vivian."

"Hi Papa."

"Vivie," Joe was warmed by the sound of her voice, "I'm so busy and have some serious problems. But I miss you all the time."

"Papa, come home; we are not the same without you. Here's Mama."

"Vera, please, let me talk to Robert."

"They all say come home."

"I simply can't leave here now...Let me see."

THAT EVENING, AT BUDAPESHTSKAYA STREET, when Joe arrived, after driving to Riga and flying from Riga to Leningrad, he was met with four happily surprised children and a blushing wife. He couldn't help being warmed and touched by their reactions even as he suffered guilty feelings toward Vera for his recent infidelity.

Vera smiled at him, happy that she had won his allegiance in this way, feeling that she must still matter to him.

When tears were dry, kisses and hugs were satisfied and happy laughter had subsided, Joe told them, "Well of course I'm glad to see you, but I'm afraid I'm very tired and I'll have to go back to work tomorrow. We'd better all get ready for a good night's sleep."

"It's not bed time yet," Robert said, already well aware that adult rules could be stretched and ignored.

"Papa play your Viola for us," Vivian said. "It has been gathering dust here without you."

The sheer emotional weight and intense cognitive input had driven the Uzel's troublesome memory cubes and their tricky coils from Joe's mind. And he could not refuse such a sweet request from his favorite, Vivian."

As he was fetching his viola and they gathered in the big music room, Vivian coaxed Robert, "Where's your clarinet, let's play some of those Bach pieces that Papa loves."

Anton asked, as he stood with Alena, "Can we play, too?"

"Of course, of course," Joe said as he came back in with his viola and its bow.

"Get your instruments," Vera said to Anton and Alena. "I'll help you if you like."

JOE BERG ARRIVED BACK IN LIEPĀJA TWO DAYS after he'd disappeared. He seemed quieter but in a good frame of mind as he sat behind a microscope in the LKB lab. He was studying the modules that had been removed due to the most extreme instability. Without attracting attention, Joe called in turn the most experienced developers and technicians of these memory blocks and held whispered discussions with them. They did some measurements. Then they cooled and heated the modules and took more measurements.

Joseph Veniaminovich surprised everyone at breakfast the next day with a galley table set with fresh warm pancakes and real coffee. He called all the military men off the boat including B-103's captain, Commander Eric Golovanov. In his strange but characteristic Brooklyn accent he announced, "As you know these intermittent circuit problems have become a serious stumbling block, a roadblock even. I have an idea that I think may be a solution, but it will take the entire day to try it and I'll have to shut down the entire system to do it. Not only that, it also involves heating these coils to a high temperature for an extended period of time. The inside of this boat is going to be very warm. There were glum and apprehensive looks around the room. Joe met their gazes with a warm, slightly embarrassed smile, "So what that means," he said, "is that there is nothing much you can do here today. I am going to make it more than a strong suggestion; you will take the bus to the beach. Back to Bernati."

As it was one of the first warm, clear days in June, such a directive was not a hard order to like, or even follow. They still enjoyed memories of the last time Joe had given everyone a day off. The man made a joke of it, but again he wasn't kidding.

"Take along plenty to eat and drink, Joe said, "and try to enjoy yourselves." As if he felt the need to plead with them simply to have fun. Perhaps he was feeling a good Communist's conscientious pang that he should not be the only one to enjoy the great opportunities of a summer in the dunes by the sea.

"You give us no choice, Gesha Zhukov said as if being coerced, "we're forced to blow the day off."

"I recommend a barbecue, with plenty to drink," Joe said.

"Really?" Ed Nikitin asked seriously.

"Leave me only one good tech volunteer and the water gang."

The 'water gang' was what the specialists in B-103's cooling system were called.

"But I should—"

"If I stay I could get at—"

Berg waved off all objections He made it even clearer vacating to the resort beach was not merely a suggestion. To Mark Galperin, it seemed like a truly barbaric action and Berg refused to discuss it with him. "This is my final decision as Chief

Engineer," Joe said, "I take full responsibility."

Mark thought to himself, *He says suddenly relax in the middle of a crisis. It reminds me of the story of a family putting the fat Christmas goose in good, hot oven and sat themselves down to drink vodka. They only remembered the goose when there was smoke and a smell. Their oven contained only charred bones. Joe's experiment will end in disaster…which means the tests will be postponed for a few months…which will lead to a terrible scandal…and to closing down our operation. Maybe he wants us out so no one will see a huge failure…*

"I am certainly not going to take part in some picnic," Mark said, "it is like having a feast during the plague."

"You need some time off to relax," Joe said, "get some sun on your face. For a young man you look too pale. It's no good just beating yourselves up here, day after day."

Mark was not pleased or hopeful, but when Phil was not there, Joe was the big boss. And then too, it seemed somehow unlikely to Mark that Joe would fail. "So you seriously want all of us, engineers, techs, software nerds, everybody, out?"

"Off the boat and off to Bernati. Here, take along this bottle of konyak. Take some pressure off."

Mark would not go, but most everyone else boarded the bus, already noisy, cheerful and energetic with growing anticipation. By 9 AM the submarine and the LKB lab were nearly abandoned; only the duty officers, those in the control room and the KGB staff were still there, maybe one or two others.

Mark clearly meant to sulk away the time until the climax of the experiment. But he said no more and kept himself busy taking inventory of electronic components. He found that there were no back-ups for the memory blocks being tested. Not here in Liepāja. They would have to be re-supplied from Kronstadt or Leninggrad. He couldn't get the image of the charred smoldering blocks out of his mind. *What are we going to do then?*

Once most of the team were on the bus and gone to the beach, those few left behind were instructed to place inside a sealed enclosure temperature gauges and to shut off the water system heat dissipation. "Check the safety of the insulation on the inside of the enclosure," Joe told them, "Leave enabled internal fans to stir the air and level the temperature field. Most important, turn up the heat. I'm going to use a temperature inside at a level that I'm not going to mention in order to spare your nervous systems. By midnight, we'll disable the automatic warm-up and begin a slow direct cooling and wait to achieve a stable temperature inside. We'll need to document the temperatures along the way."

Late that evening, Mark, in a mood of doom-facing chagrin heard the sound of the bus driving up outside the laboratory windows at around 11 PM. His cheerful team members were, loose and relaxed and still talking about the spectacular sunset they had watched over the peaceful sea that lay golden before them.

The next morning, without having slept in his Lebanon hotel room, Mark skipped breakfast, didn't wait for a bus and took a taxi to the boat.

Inside, he met a tanned, happy and proud in victory Joe Berg who had not slept unless it was a nap on the boat. When Mark questioned him with his eyes, Joe said, "The circuits have been running without missing a beat for…" he looked at his watch, "six hours and twenty-two minutes."

Mark took a seat, waiting for the telltale signs of trouble. An hour went by and there weren't any. The system was up and running and continued to do so for several hours more. "What happened?" Mark finally asked.

"You're going to realize you knew all along when I tell you," Joe said.

"I hope so."

"The coils baked for four hours at one hundred fifty degrees," Joe said. "I expected some damage, but I only had to replace one chip; it might have gone anyway."

"But the high heat fixed the problem?"

"The problem was, those coils were never properly cured. The enamel coating was not fully hardened; under moderate heat and some physical pressure they shorted."

"Don't you think the fix will be temporary?" Mark asked. "Won't they revert to whatever condition you baked out of them?"

"No, I don't think so," Joe said. "I feel pretty sure the coating on the coil wire was never hardened as it should be It was not the fault of the enamel or the idea but of timing in the final process."

"I suppose you could be right," Mark said.

"So here, in this hot submarine," Joe said, "in a lot of humidity, we had shorts which changed the output values."

"I guess we'll se," Mark said.

"I think they are set now," Joe said evenly "and will last as long as any components can last in this heat and damp."

Joe was proven right in the week that followed and the team admired him as well as adored him for the wonderful day they'd had at the beach in Bernati.

Mark recovered from his funk, delighted that now work could go forward, glad to learn from someone so intuitive and yet modest. *We are saved because we are a team,* he thought. *We believe in our system and and can now be confident of victory.*

Whenever Mark tried to explain how terrible he'd felt and how dangerous it was, his friends laughed and said, "That's nonsense! Everything turned out just great!"

For Mark, the result of this crisis, this scare he'd had, was that preparation for the tests went even faster, and it brought out the difference in the way Phil and Joe solved problems.

AS AN INTERNATIONAL COMMUNIST MEETING began in Moscow, in Liepāja, in the mornings, the LKB team might have a crowd swim at June's early dawn, hours before the day shift would start again. Sometimes there were individual days off and in Liepāja there were very decent tennis courts. Opposite the courts, in the same recreation area, there was a summer theater. Every day a troop from Tbilisi either rehearsed or performed there. It was great fun to see and hear these strong performances, not that there were any of the famous Georgian stars there. But the most special time at the beach was, of course, in July, especially if the summer was hot, as it was in 1969. After a hard shift in such heat, especially inside the submarine docked at its berth, people parched and barely alive raced to the hotel then to the sea, and some went to the beach without stopping at the hotel, their fatigue crying out for instant relief. Forever young and full of energy, it took only minutes for the slow moving shadows from inside the submarine to become energetic athletes, playing football and volleyball, now tireless. Or, taking turns on the tennis court, also good in forgetting a hard day.

THE SECOND SOVIET N-1 ROCKET VEHICLE was launched on July 3 1969 and carried a modified L1 Zond spacecraft and an escape tower. There would be claims that a lunar module was also carried; however, only the L1S-2 and booster stages were on the official record. Launch took place at 11:18 PM Moscow time.

For a few moments, the rocket lifted into the night sky, seemingly bound for a Moon orbit and to obtain photographs of possible crew landing sites. But, clear of the tower, there was a flash of light, and debris fell from the bottom of the first stage. KORD, the Rocket Engine Control System, instantly shut down all engines except number 18. This caused the N-1 to lean over at a 45-degree angle and drop back onto the launch pad. The 2300 tons of propellant on board triggered a massive blast. The shock wave shattered windows across the launch complex and sent debris flying as far as 10 kilometers away from ground zero.

FORTY-FIVE

"This is one small step for a man, one giant leap for mankind."   *--Neil Armstrong*

IT BECAME UNUSUALLY HOT, EVEN FOR JULY IN LIEPĀJA, and it was nearly impossible to breathe inside the submarine. While B-103 was moored in its berth with its engines silent, there was not enough power to drive the boat's ventilation system. It had become clear to Joe in June, even as July approached, that productive work on the <u>Uzel</u> inside the submarine was going to be nearly impossible. The heat and humidity inside the submarine grew daily as July's days arrived, causing new equipment problems and an ever greater toll on the boat's crew and the team of scientists working on the top secret Combat Information and Control System. Everyone agreed and understood that most of these minor and rare major equipment failures would not occur when the submarine was underway. Then, there would be no such intense, stagnant conditions inside. But here and now, sweat dripped from every centimeter of their bodies, stung their eyes and fell into the delicate equipment. Tempers became short and frayed, thinking was seriously blurred.

One morning, weeks after the memory blocs were fixed, during the first few days of July, Joe drove off in the wreck of a Moskvitch sedan he'd bought to use in Liepāja. His Volga was with Elvira, for her comfort and safety while she stayed in a nearby north coastal town at a decent inn.

There were rumors that Joe was working on a new invention with the management of the metallurgical plant. Evil tongues said it was to replace all the fenders on the wretched Moskvich sedan. Berg was not above improving a car, even one just off the assembly line. Those who saw Joe leave in the miserable Mosckvitch, so unsuited for a major scientist and design bureau boss, those who watched him go might have had some inkling about Elvira or at least a notion that there was a woman not far away in Joe's life. Or maybe, it was also thought, the heat and humidity were too much even for Communist Number One, his nickname still echoing from Prague. Maybe he was just taking off to the beach for one of his thoughtful long walks near the surf? And who was to say he didn't deserve such a break?

Joe smiled as he drove. Once again, he hadn't talked about his ideas or plans. He wanted to arrive at a solution before there was any second-guessing.

Late in the hot, sweltering day, two trucks arrived at the dock, one with a crane. They were followed by a van full of workers and tools. At the same time, Joe arrived at berth 16 in the disreputable Moskvich. The workers, using the crane, unloaded from beneath a tarpaulin on the other truck what was undoubtedly the largest motor driven enclosed fan ever made in the USSR. Joe, planning since mid June, with the help of a supervisor at the ship-repair plant, had designed and built this huge self-contained fan. Next, the workers unloaded a large cylindrical coil which, over the course of half-an-hour became fifty meters of collapsible tubing more than a meter in diameter. One end was fastened securely to the fan which was being anchored to the dock, just to one side of the access ramps. The tube was lashed to the ramps and then to the hatch in the B-103's conning tower. This too, had been engineered not to interfere with coming and going access to the boat.

All of this, unloading, securing the tube, fastening the giant fan to the dock, bringing and attaching power to the fan motor's switch box, took nearly two hours. But it took only minutes, once the tube began making its way to the open submarine port, for the able wordsmiths of the Soviet Navy and their companion scientific team from the Leningrad Design Bureau to name Joe's invention, 'Berg's Elephant'.

The Elephant didn't just help; it was transformative. The enclosed fan, the Elephant's head, pumped fresh sea air down into the boat through its trunk so vigorously that stagnant air was blown from open vents and completely replaced continuously within a matter of minutes. The advantage to the Uzel project was immeasurable: the time saved not chasing down problems that would never exist in normal operations of the boat was only one great saving. The restored health of employees meant they could work productively. The Elephant provided not only welcome relief for both engineering crew and sailors as well as the hard pressed memory blocks and other components of the Uzel CICS, the Elephant fueled the spirit of appreciation for Joe and the ingenuity of his concern for others.

Again Joe was happy like a child. After all, he was not just an unusual engineer, he was a furious inventor! In all the memories of participants in these events Berg would remain as a bright, unusual and sometimes eccentric person and the creator of the famous Elephant in the hot seaside summer of 1969.

JOE HAD HEARD ABOUT THE LATEST FAILURE of the N-1 rocket launch through Phil from Shokin. For years, they'd kept their ears open to any news of the Soviet manned Moon mission. But weeks after the latest disaster, Joe was with Viktor Taroikin who was unusually outspoken, generous and emphatic in sharing what he knew about the second failed N-1 launch:

"Joe, it's a miracle it wasn't much, much worse. Launch crews were only allowed outside thirty minutes after the accident. But when they did go out, droplets of unburned fuel was still raining down from the sky. As much as 85% of the propellant did not go up in that massive explosion." Viktor's eyes narrowed, "Can you imagine if all of it had exploded? It was already one of mankind's two or three largest non-nuclear explosions, visible 35 kilometers away in Leninsk. Fortunately, the launch escape system activated at engine shutdown and pulled the capsule to safety two kilometers away. The launch pad was thoroughly leveled, the concrete pad caved in and one of the towers twisted around itself. Despite the devastation, most of the telemetry tapes were found intact."

"Fantastic," Joe said, "and what...?"

"Engine 18, which had caused the booster to lean over 45 degrees, continued operating until impact, something engineers aren't able to explain. Nor do they know why the number 8 turbopump exploded. Vasily Mishin believed that a pump rotor had disintegrated, but engine designer Kuznetsov, a sober man, answered Mishin that the N-1 engines were entirely blameless. You see, Mishin defended Kuznetsov's engines two years ago and can't publicly condemn them. Kuznetsov got the investigative committee to rule that engine failure was due to 'ingestion of foreign debris'. So future flights will have fuel filters they probably don't need."

"Of course," Joe said, *Mishin! What corruption...* "It's terrible..." *But so pathetic....*

"The director of Baikonur launch facilities wants the rocket control system to be locked for the first 20 seconds of flight to prevent a KORD shutdown command before the booster clears the launch pad." Viktor shook his head.

"They'll try again?" Joe asked, sympathetic.

"Of course, and no doubt American spy satellites have shown the Union is building a Moon rocket."

The next day, after meeting with the KGB Major, on July 16 1969, Joe heard the news on the BBC: Apollo 11 with Neil Armstrong, Buzz Aldrin and Michael Collings had been launched with the aim of making it the mission of the first manned Moon landing. *Of course, it's finally over,* Joe thought, *but no, it has been over for quite some time. Since January 1966. We just haven't wanted to admit it.*

All through July the late night carousing at Liepāja's Jura restaurant continued; the various musical efforts within the LKB team lasted late into the nights and escapes to the beaches at dawn ran at full pace. One night, long after midnight, in the middle of July, Yuri Rozanov was sitting on his hotel room windowsill, dangling his legs from the third floor of the Lebanon. Those with him in the room were used to Rozanov playing for the surrounding area below. They paid little attention to his songs, barely bothering to applaud in an off hand sort of way. But someone out there in the streets and walkways called the police. The cops came and the room was cordoned off and several engineers were taken out and questioned, documents scrutinized, notes taken. Several hours of this punishment made it even later when it was finally all over. The still drunken engineers and Liepāja's disturbed peace were moved to the beach.

JULY 20 1969 THE US LUNAR MODULE EAGLE

landed on the lunar surface at what its pilots, Neil Armstrong and Buzz Aldrin named Tranquility Base. An estimated 500 million people worldwide watched in awe as Neil Armstrong took humankind's historic first steps on the Moon at 10:56 pm ET.

Joe and Phil didn't see it until much later, but they read about it and believed it. It was as though a shadow crossed their paths and left them with mournful thoughts of Sergei Pavlovich Korolev. And they thought of Vasily Mishin, whose rocket expertise was purloined from the Third Reich and nothing more. The two American engineers felt sure it hadn't had to be that way. *We could have beat the West to the Moon.* If it was possible for them to commit more deeply to the Uzel, they did so.

One night in late July there was a violent storm that swept along Latvia's Baltic coast. The next morning broke warm, clear and sunny. The sea had subsided somewhat, but hard waves hit the shore, jumping over the shallows, knocking bathers down and tossing up all sorts of personal items people had tried to dispose of in shameful hope. There were fishing net fragments, pieces of wood from the skeletons of old fishing boats whose owners' bones had also washed up from where they had perished in the depths of the sea. But among all sorts of debris, it was a good day to scour the beach for an occasional treasure.

There were beaches much closer than Bernati, one just south of the channel inlet into the bucket. After an early morning LKB staff meeting, Joe Berg decided to take advantage of the beautiful clear morning and the fresh air to have a walk along this local beach. After leaving the LKB lab and walking to the mouth of the bucket, he was surprised to meet Commander Eric Golovanov and two Navy midshipmen, who were also there to catch the motor launch across the inlet to the beach. Joe and Eric greeted each other warmly, both pleased at the encounter. Upon stepping free onto the opposite wharf, Joe assumed Golovanov and the two young officers were headed somewhere together, but the two young men in uniform set off for business elsewhere.

With friendly nods, Joe and Eric set off together along the beach.

"Are you up for a stroll, Dr. Berg," Golovanov asked.

"Of course," Joe said as they took steps toward the surf.

"Everyone's garbage has come back to haunt us," Golovnov commented after a few meters, heading south. "Keep your eye peeled for bits of amber and a rare piece of hardwood carved by the sea."

After they'd walked another fifty meters and stopped once or twice, Golovanov asked, "Have you thought any more about coming along with us next time we go out?"

Joe shot Golovanov a quick glance, wanting to gauge the mood and depth of his casual question. Joe nodded and kept walking for few paces. "Of course I've thought about it, but I have certain time constraints, which I have to avoid breaking. It doesn't really seem likely."

"My submarine is a relatively slow moving boat," Golovanov said affably. "It takes time, maneuvering into deep water and crawling back to berth 16, so I understand it might be inconvenient."

Joe stopped and bent down to retrieve a tightly stoppered bottle which had washed ashore in a tangle of sea weed and rotted fishing net. He held the completely empty bottle up to the light and wondered why it was so carefully sealed. Golovanov was watching him.

"I guess I'm looking to see if there was a note from some poor soul," Joe said, "someone who has lost all hope of salvation, a desperate sailor perhaps, calling out to his sweetheart, hoping he can die thinking at least she may someday know that he never stopped loving her."

Golovanov was again puzzled and amused by Berg, *such an odd duck*, "So you could find her, Dr. Berg, and deliver the message, just a few decades late?"

"But, who knows," Joe said, delighted that Eric appreciated his conceit, "perhaps not too late?"

Golovanov laughed. "But you know," his tone conciliatory, "of course that empty bottle asked you what reason there was for sealing it?" Golovanov stopped. "—Wait, the storm coughed up not only trash from the deep, but something good;

look here…" The slight, graceful sailor leaned over and brushed aside sandy seaweed to reveal what looked like a bright stone, resting in the algae like a diamond on velvet. He retrieved it, brushing it with the cuff of his jacket before handing it to Joe. "You know what this is?"

Taking it, Joe said, "It's amber isn't it…" He wet his finger with spit and rubbed it on the lump of fossilized tree sap, revealing the deep, nearly transparent, yellow brown interior of the stone. Taking a few steps, Joe rinsed the nearly teardrop shaped lump in the froth of a wave rolling in nearby. Admiring it, he moved back to Golovanov, offering with a jovial smile to hand it back to the submarine commander."

"No," Eric smiled, "it is for you, a small token of my appreciation."

Joe, surprised, somewhat reluctant, pocketed the stone as they strode on, "Appreciation for what exactly…?" he muttered.

"For your consideration of my crew, with your elephant, for one thing, for the Uzel. It will provide every submarine commander who has it, a better chance of victory and survival in combat. Please call me Eric by the way?"

"As you know, Eric, nearly everybody calls me Joe. That's stupendous! Thank you. Well," don't thank me for the Uzel, it is a joint effort, not only Staros and Galperin, but all of LKB and especially the Soviet Navy itself, ministers and other leaders have made it happen."

Golovanov was nodding amiably as Joe spoke, "Of course, but you are the Uzel's mascot."

Joe shot Golovanov an affable look of puzzlement.

"You are the mood of practical success for its creation."

"…?…Very high praise. Thank you. I'll do what I can do."

Eric paused and stood looking out to sea. The horizon was clear. There were two smaller Navy boats a few kilometers from shore. He turned to Joe, "I must head back to base," he took a step back and Joe joined him saying:

"I too have things to do." He thought of the lump of amber in his pocket, *I'll have it made into a pendant for Elvira.*

COMING FROM THE BEACH AT BERNATI,
LKB members passed one of the more popular places in Liepāja,
the restaurant and drinking establishment, *Banga*. (Wave) They
often stopped there, but they did not go to eat, and certainly not
to have a drink. When they stopped at Banga, they stopped to
look around and then leave. *Banga* was a large wooden shed built
around strong wooden columns Each column was covered with
nails and on each nail hung someone's sea cap, left there by men
and women of the sea who felt at home in *Banga*.

Jura was from a European restaurant culture, *Banga* was
simpler and more Russian. At Jura, brilliant naval lieutenants and
senior officers were expected on any holiday, but *Banga* buzzed
with fishermen's talk and fleet warrant officers talking out loud.
At *Braga* the heavy drinking and carousing began even before
dark in the winter time. If someone started a drunken brawl at
Banga, only the fighters and the police paid attention. One needed
to be on one's own at the *Banga*. The specialized young scientists
and engineers from the Leningrad Design Bureau just wanted to
be reminded that normal life continued and that the Earth was
still spinning in the right direction.

The beach decorated their difficult lives. Some LKB team
members needed to be with submarine B-103 beneath the sea, to
sleep on the boat during distress sometimes, during tests in the
underwater naval proving grounds. So of course they had to have
recreation, first, and then maybe later sleep and rest, or maybe
not. The young were capable of staying up till dawn singing and
playing guitars or suddenly deciding in the middle of the night,
the whole gang, to go to the beach and to swim naked in the dark
Baltic Sea

While they were in Liepāja, and not some cold or dark and
lonely outpost, they went to the beach, restaurants, sang songs in
their favorite rooms of the hotel Lebanon. In due time they
would forget the hardships, setbacks and mistakes to remember
only all that was cheerful, young and joyful.

DAYS AFTER THE STORM, AFTER AMBER HUNTERS
had disappeared—having been extremely lucky or more likely
disappointed in their search for an elusive piece of happiness—

Joe and Eric Golovanov were once again walking, at 8:30 in the morning, along the beach south of the inlet channel. Joe enjoyed the sea air as well as Golovanov's often instructive company. Eric was ever more convinced that if Berg were to see the submarine in action, under combat conditions, he would discover practical improvements or see future problems. *Staros is with the admirals and ministers; Dr. Berg is right here, his spindly frame moving easily along, more and more like a friend.*

As they walked farther south, saying little, both knew in their weighted silence the question: Would Joe accompany Golovanov and B-103 on a field test and training mission? Neither broke that silence.

There were a number of fishermen on the beach with huge two wheeled carts, wheels over a meter in diameter. The fishermen waded into the shallows and came out carrying armfuls of seaweed. *Sea vegetables?* Seeing Joe's obvious curiosity, Golovanov said:

"It is the season to begin collecting these plants. They take them and dry them and sell them for a good price at various collection points."

Joe flashed a smile of friendly encouragement: *Then what?*

"I don't know," Golovanov continued," "from there they send it to some plant somewhere to extract certain substances critical to the national interest perhaps. I don't know what, even something strategically important?"

"Well, you are quite right about it being in the national interest," Joe said with generously sparkling brown eyes. "I didn't know until just now that this is how it was harvested, but of course, they extract agar, and what would we Soviet citizens do without our Russian pink and white marshmallows? Made from this seaweed? ...Indirectly, of course." Joe thought of 'Elvira's delight at roasting marsh mellows over an open fire and his own pleasure in sharing it with her.

"Of course," Golovanov agreed. "By the way, Dr. Berg, there will be a field test of torpedo firing in late August or early September. It will test dead reckoning in real situations."

"Yes, I'm aware that there are such tests coming up," Joe said.

"They will be in simulated combat conditions," Golovanov said. "I can tell you this because I know you have the highest First Form clearance. There will be at least eight other vessels involved including other submarines."

"It will be a real test of what we have promised," Joe said.

"Will you join us?"

"I doubt I'd be cleared for it, either by my partner, Philip Georgievich, or by the electronics ministry."

"I've convinced Zhukovsky and he has talked to Gorshkov, and I believe Sergey Georgyevich Gorshkov has spoken to everyone else. It seems we all agree; the probable benefit outweighs the relatively small risk."

"Well," Joe said stretching the word out to encompass a host of hesitations, "my wife and four kids are going to be coming back from Prague about that time; I'll need to be around to greet them... And I have other responsibilities...How long a...mission will it be?"

"At least four days."

"That's a good chunk of time..."

"You'll let me know?"

"Of course, of course," Joe said munificently.

IN MID-JULY, ONE EVENING, JOE CALLED VERA in Prague. He had not called every evening to catch up on the day's doings and say good night, not by a long measure: once a week was more like it.

"Where have you been?" Vera asked right off. "I've tried calling you, even at that hotel in Latvia. Didn't the ever so polite man, Islalmov give you my message?"

"No, what was the message?"

Vera sighed, "To call me of course."

"Okay, well now at least I've called you. Is everything all right?"

"Here, Joe, Vivian has something to say to you."

"Hi Papa."

"Vivie, how are you?"

"I'm fine, but I want to have a dog."

"No, now that's just not practical."

"We can name him Lenin, Leo, for short."

"That's not a convincing argument Vivian."

"Oh, Papa, we get so lonely when you are not with us; you always do fun things."

"We'll get together again soon, back home in Leningrad and do fun things."

"Papa, we really want a dog. We all do; even Mom says she could get used to having a dog."

"Well, we'll have to see."

"Please Papa. Please?"

"Oh all right, I suppose so."

"Yeeeeahh, Oh, thank you Papa."

"Okay, Okay."

"His name is really Saba. Uncle Cyrus found him. You'll love him."

"You already have him."

"Yes, but we can call him Lenin, okay? Here's Mom."

"Well, I hope you know it's a done deal now."

"As though I had much to do with it,' Joe said.

"Are you angry?"

"Of course not."

FORTY-SIX

"Nobody cares about the bronze or silver medals."
--Buzz Aldrin

ON JULY 24 1969, THE APOLLO 11 ASTRONAUTS returned to Earth, the first successful men on the Moon, but they were placed in biological isolation for days. Mission Control believed in Moon microbes. Later, they realized; *no air, no life.* The Space Race to the Moon was over and the Soviet Union had lost. The Soviet Politburo turned toward the problem on Earth: the Soviet military had no way to compete with US military, either. They had no aircraft carriers, no way to strike from a mobile location, except submarines. As if to distract from the sensational Apollo story, the Politburo released Gerald Brooke from his sentence as a British spy, in exchange for Soviet Spies Morris and Lona Cohen, UK prisoners, code named Peter and Helen Kroger, who had been messengers delivering atomic secrets to the KGB from Klaus Fuchs in Los Alamos and Harwell.

On August 9, in Los Angeles, followers of Charles Manson murdered Sharon Tate, Abigail Folger, Wojciech Frykowski, and Hollywood hairstylist Jay Sebring at the home of Tate and her husband, movie director Roman Polanski. The news was the beginning of a series of revelations that would eventually cast a dark shadow over the hopeful peace and love flowering of hippiedom.

From August 15 through August 18, The Woodstock Music Festival was held in New York state, featuring the top rock musicians. It was a shock to American society due to the sudden vast popularity of the new revolutionary youth culture. One of the most peaceful mass gatherings in world history, one million agitated rock fans conducted themselves without a squabble for days and without the presence of the police.

AS SHORTENING DAYS OF AUGUST PASSED,

the sense that their good summer would soon be over spurred Joe and Elvira to seek greater happiness. Elvira had rented a room in the quaint seaside town of Pavilosta, little more than thirty minutes away by car from Liepāja. She had the use of Joe's Volga while he continued to use his battered, multi-owned Moskvitch, the awe of young Navy officers and LKB staff, that a top scientist should be seen in such disgrace. Those who knew Joe, merely smiled.

Joe and Elvira had decided to spend most of the week of August 17-22 camping along the Latvian coast at various spots close to the beach. Their plan had some of the feel of a honeymoon, as a dedication to their carnal union, but it was also a goodbye. Soon no such sojourn would be possible. Who knew for how long? To satisfy the elan of his physical devotion and his romantic feelings of a coming separation, Joe now had the amber pendant, the stone Eric Golovanov had given him, *found for me,* polished and held in a silver setting handcrafted to the shape of the stone. At their first campsite, Joe pulled it from his pack and gave it to Elvira.

She was delighted. He watched her take pleasure in it. As she examined and admired the amber stone, he told her the story of it, giving her time.

"It's perfect," she said, "and always funny, the captain of the submarine gives you nature's most eternal, jewel of the sea."

"It's true," Joe said, "amber is far from common along these shores, even after a heavy storm."

"It is very significant and also funny, as you like the life, yes? It reminds me of the children's story about the lost sailor and his fabulous gifts from the king and queen of the sea. Probably nobody remembers this old fairy tale now, but me." She pulled up the silver clasped stone by its chain and held it between their eyes. "It is so beautiful Joe, like a piece of the sun for me to keep near my heart."

They were both deeply tanned. They camped at night well off the beach in the little valleys of the dunes. They talked and joked and spoke about engineering puzzles before and after they made love. They were moving slowly north by day along the beach, swimming in the sea, sometimes using bathing suits, or going without if there was no one around. They saw almost no one, partly because there were very few people around and partly because they avoided those that were. Sometimes, they'd camp away from the sun in a grove of lime trees during the day and swim at night.

It was Thursday, August 21, when Joe and Elvira were camped again at the most deserted spot they'd found during their days of moving up and down the coast. In the sand dunes only five or six kilometers from the Liepāja naval base in Karosta, their tent was tucked behind a high dune which fell away steeply to the sea. After love making, they lay naked in the warm sun. The splashing of waves closely below them at high tide awakened them. They rolled down the dune—their eyes closed to avoid the swirling sand—and splashed into the water. Marching naked across the shallow water of high tide, they plunged into the deeper water and swam, laughing and talking. As the tide ebbed they came ashore and trudged up the dune toward their camp. At the top of the rise, Elvira took Joe's hand and pulled him down playfully on the sand, to begin rolling down again. As they rolled, laughing, their wet bodies gathered sand.

As they opened their eyes and began to get up, holding hands, they realized they were not alone. A uniformed KGB officer, assigned to the military, was approaching them along the beach. His attention to them was clear in his emphatic strides toward them. They stood motionless by the water, covered in light sand. Even Elvira stood unabashed.

"Good day," Joe said as the officer arrived before them, "what beautiful weather, eh?"

"You are trespassing in a restricted military area. All civilian traffic is forbidden here."

"I was just saying to my girlfriend," Joe declared confidently, "how remarkable it was that we had such a fine place all to ourselves. I couldn't help wondering. That explains it."

Hearing Joe's foreign accent the man asked, "What on earth are you doing here? Besides the obvious? Clearly you have no documents. I could arrest you as a spy."

Joe enjoyed the irony, though he did feel at a loss, never

before having been so completely without his fine collection of multiple sealed, stamped and very convincing documents "You're quite right comrade," Joe offered, "we're just a couple of civilians, but actually I'm working with the Navy, supervising a small gang of civilian workers on a project at the base. We're on a break for a day or so."

"Of course you cannot prove any of this, but what sort of work do you claim in the strictly closed city of Liepāja?"

"Unfortunately, even my humble efforts are strictly classified. We are strongly discouraged from discussing anything work-related even among ourselves when away from the base."

"Where are your clothes, if you have any?"

"We left them up in the dunes," Elvira waved her hand as Joe confirmed her statement with a nod, glad she had not mentioned their camp.

The officer glanced down at his polished black shoes which already bore stains of sand, salt and water then upwards to the sandy dune above. "Well, get your clothes and put them on. Then leave this restricted area immediately. I'm giving you an undeserved break."

"Thank you," Joe and Elvira said in unison.

The young officer shook his head, suppressing a smile, "If I arrest you as you are I will hear about it for the remainder of my career." When Joe and Elvira moved toward the receding waters, he told them, "Do I need to remind you that you must leave immediately?"

"We need to rinse off," Elvira said in a confidential inclusive way that reached the officer's better nature. He nodded with a shrug and once again they plunged into deep water and splashed each other. He was still there when they came out.

"Let me ask you," Joe said, approaching the man as he prepared to continue his patrol along the beach, "since it is our last time together this summer and for quite a while to come, would it be alright for us to stay here tonight and leave first thing in the morning?"

The man scowled, resting a hand on his sidearm for a moment. *It's late in the day,* he thought. Then he shook his head in demonstrative incredulity. "If I lay eyes on either one of you again, with or without your clothes, I will take you in."

"You won't. Big thanks." They stood happily side-by-side as the officer walked away. When he was gone, they plunged back into the sea. "By tomorrow morning," Elvira said, "it will be time for us to go anyhow."

At sunrise, they made their way back to Joe's Moskvitch. "Get some rest," he told her when he dropped her off at her room in the village. "I'll come by around eight. We'll plan from there."

When Joe reached the LKB lab at the submarine base, he heard the news: There had been protests in Prague and Brno, Czechoslovakia's second largest city. The demonstrations had been met with violent repression by military force. After a long effort to reach Major Taroikin, Viktor told him:

"The Prague spring is finally over."

"But my family is there."

"Did you try calling them?"

"You think there's a chance I'll get through?"

"I don't think there's much chance you won't."

Joe didn't say anything.

"Order has been fully restored," Viktor said. "You should have no problem."

"So the protest has been dealt with harshly?" *What if Vera and the kids got caught in a crowd near the demonstrations… She hates the Soviet presence there so much, she might've…* "Yes," Joe said, "sorry to bother you, Major."

"I doubt you'll have any problem."

Am I going to go through this all over again? Joe sat for a while in the little cubicle he shared with Phil, and Mark, who used it when neither boss was there. Joe retrieved the phone and dialed the base operator to ask assistance in reaching Vera at her father's house near Prague.

"Well," the operator said, "Long distance is a little busy right now. Why not let me call you back when I've reached your wife? Are you going to be at this number for awhile?"

"Well, not for very long," Joe said. *It's the same all over again. Last year, it took us months to get back on cordial speaking terms.* Joe knew their strong opposition to each other over Soviet rule in

Czechoslovakia was fueled by Vera's angry discontent. She smoldered in unhappy deficit without his full affection. Joe stepped away from the phone and the cubicle and walked across the open space with a few desks and drafting tables to a window looking out on the Baltic Sea. He had only started to fully contemplate having to deal with getting through to Vera and the kids, *how to get them out of Prague,* when the phone rang in the corner cubicle.

"I have your wife on the line, Dr. Berg," the young base operator said.

"Hello, Vera?" Joe said in his best Czech.

"Did you finally think of us? I've been calling you and calling you!"

"Where?"

"Kronstadt, at your offices and at our home."

"I'm in Latvia." He wanted Vera to remember he shouldn't talk about where he was or about his work, over the phone.

"We're on our way home," Vera said. "This is now a strictly occupied city. I hoped you might come and join us for the last few days we're here and take us back."

"I'll get down there right away." *As long as the planes are flying.*

"Don't bother, we are about to leave for the airport. Uncle Cyrus is taking us. "We're all packed. Really. I have our tickets."

"Are you sure? There's no problem with…"

"Prague has been crushed, you don't think that is a problem? Probably not."

"What time does the plane land? Maybe if I leave here now I could meet you."

"Who knows? Don't bother. We'll take a taxi when we get to the airport. But you'll be back tomorrow won't you?"

"Of course, of course."

Joe left the dark cherry red brick lab building with some misgiving. Vera seemed to assume that he was no longer useful to her. He needed to pick up Elvira and head back to Leningrad.

WHEN JOE ARRIVED HOME IN LENINGRAD

at the apartment on Budapeshtskaya Street, he was already thinking about returning to Liepāja and to seeing Elvira again, perhaps his last chance to contemplate a spate of happiness for a day or so. But all such thoughts were swept from his mind when the door opened to four children smiling and calling out greetings, a dog jumping at him, and his wife, Vera, standing behind this young crowd eyeing him speculatively: *How are you going to take this?*

The dog, a mongrel puppy of untraceable origins with mottled, mixed features, but somewhat brown in color, was licking Joe, up on hind legs and down, obviously caught up in the spirit of the occasion. Joe made his way through them, ignoring the dog, patting heads and sharing kisses, hugging his children and Vera, whose embrace they both eagerly shared as reassurance to their children.

"They let you bring that dog on the airplane?" Joe asked, realizing he'd hoped they would leave the dog in Prague.

"Papa," Robert said, "he's only a little dog. I put him in my carry on bag before we went to the airport. Can't we keep him?"

"That small size is a temporary condition. Look at those paws."

"It's a female by the way," Vera said to Robert, glancing at Joe.

"A girl dog? Robert said.

"Yes," Vivian said, "so I guess we can't name her Lenin, or Leo."

"Or Leonid," Joe joked, thinking of Brezhnev.

"Papa, let's take Saba for a walk," Anton shrilled.

"Let's fix Papa something to eat first," Vera said then to Joe, "I have everything ready, let's all sit down."

"Sure, let me get out of these clothes," he said sniffing involuntarily for Elvira's traces.

Once he was in khakis and a T-shirt, they all took seats at the table, the lawless growing animal reigning chaos with the kids until Vera, sensing Joe's irritation and the pandemonium said to Robert, "Put Saba in the kitchen and close the door."

Robert, trading glances with his mother, understood compromise was better than a quite possible loss. He did as he was told.

The frantic door scratching and howls of misery, the half-breath whines of desperation soon won out. "I guess we have a new member of the family," Joe said, "whether all of us like it all of the time or not."

"Good Papa," Vivian said.

"You have to be practical in life," Joe said. "And that means no feeding the dog at the table while we're eating."

"Why?" Anton asked.

"She has a name," Vivian said, "and it's Saba. *Saba Sabaka.*"

"You can feed her scraps if we're finished with them, later on," Vera said.

"That doesn't mean save your meal for the dog," Joe said.

"Saba," Anton said.

They ate, looking to Joe often, glad he was home.

"Anton, finish up your dinner," Vera said so we can take Saba for a walk in the park."

"I'm not that hungry," Anton said.

"He's saving it for Saba," Alena said.

"I am not," Anton lied.

"Put it aside until we come back from out walk," Joe instructed. "You might be hungry then. We have other good things for Saba to eat."

IN LATE AUGUST, SHARP CORPORATION SURPRISED ITS competitors, and engineers everywhere, by announcing the launch of the Sharp QT-8D Microcompet, a micro-calculator based on four Rockwell Metal Oxide Semiconductors (MOS) large scale integrated (LSI) chips that had been developed for the Apollo program. This was at a time when most of Soviet industry and commerce used the abacus for numerical calculation. Therefore, Microcompet burst on the scene like a bomb going off, replacing typewriter sized devices around the world. It would soon strongly influence Joe's and Phil's chances of survival

FORTY-SEVEN

"You only have power over people so long as you don't take everything away from them. But when you've robbed a man of everything, he's no longer in your power - he's free again."

--Aleksandr Solzhenitsyn

SEPTEMBER 4 1969, B-103 DEPARTED THE BUCKET, shortly after dawn. It was followed by two other submarines, K-78, a Project 651 outfitted with the Cloud CICS, and D-128, a project 629 recently upgraded with two Scud missile tubes. Captain Eric Golovanov stood in the central control room as B-103 crawled down the artificial inlet and followed the narrow channel toward deeper open water. Joe Berg was with Golovanov. Joe had at last overcome his reluctance other obstacles real and imagined. He was flattered by Golovanov's idea of his value, his certainty that it would be a valuable experience for both of them. They were on their way to the Soviet Naval Proving ground in deep water of the Baltic Sea.

"We are going to take a devious route," Eric said in rapid Russian, "to approach from the north, undetected...until..."

"...You gain a tactical advantage?" Joe offered. Golovanov's tone was unlike the sound of his conversation while walking along the beach or even in the meetings of their professional joint efforts. His tone was a harmony of certainties that every soul onboard was under his command. *Command is in his blood,* Joe thought. *The fate of the Uzel is in his hands now as well. But I'm not here to babysit the Uzel, that's Toshkov's job. Eric persuaded me to come to 'the first crucial battle conditions field trials'. The navigational trials were successful, so there is every reason to hope this will go well, but this time it is live or die for the Uzel and it's in the hands of an impulsive...*

warrior. But he is the Uzel's ultimate customer.

"Joe," Golovanov said, "you had better go have a look at the bright wide world while you can. We'll dive in a few minutes. We may be under water for days."

By this time Joe and Eric used first names when talking privately. Eric's inbred and embedded prejudice against Jews had been eroded as his sharp curiosity about odd duck Dr. Berg had revealed Joe's lack of any religious connection to Judaism. At Berg's core, Golovanov could see no insistent adherence to, or carefully maintained celebration of belief. Joe had liked Golovanov from the start and enjoyed getting to know him. With Staros, the commander shared the magnetic charisma of a man of slight stature but tall in pluck and deft of life force.

"As you reminded me," Joe said, "I told no one where I was going or how long I'd be gone, not even Mark or Phil." This mission is highly classified. So I'd just as soon no one see me on deck now. Do you think it will really be four days?".

"It could be a week if nothing decisive happens," Golovanov warned. "Or longer. Keep the tower between you and the port when you're on deck. We'll soon be well away." Eric appreciated Joe's assent to the secret mission and was glad Joe had the highest first form clearance.

Joe nodded somewhat numbly, thinking what might happen in his life during that stretch of time when he was completely out of touch.

"Then ,too," Eric added, "I'll do my best to make short work of the opposition and get you back before anybody misses you."

"You made it plain from the start," Joe said "that it could take a while. I'll be alright."

"Get some fresh air. You are my doctor of fresh air, go! Or don't tell me later how you miss fresh air and sunlight."

Joe of course knew the inside of B-103 very well; he had worked there off and on for months, had even slept there briefly once or twice during long troubleshooting investigations. With easy familiarity he climbed to the tower hatch, already uncomfortable with the idea of being trapped inside for days.

With one hand on a post that held the deck rail cable,

Joe's dark slacks, black T-shirt and deep blue lightweight windbreaker jacket whipped in the breeze. He looked back at Liepāja, the polluted harbor,, the brick buildings and other moving Navy vessels. In the distance, church towers stood up. *To reach for the sky and an imaginary god? Or to escape, at least in thought, the squalor and pain of human life? To have something semi-solid to look up to? The tower of a building.* Joe had mused over the phenomena of religious belief since reading *Of Human Bondage* when he was 13 and had first understood that he did not believe in God, or in the Bible, either.

There were two other men on the submarine's deck, sailors, one at the deck's bow, the other by the tower hatch. Both were still in uniform. All three men were aware that the boat was soon to dive. They waited together for the signal. Joe believed he shared this with the seamen. It was enough. *Our time in the sun and sky is short.*

There was a surge in power from the screws and the boat picked up speed from 1 or 2 knots to 10. The diesel engines ran strong. They were free of the approach channels and headed for the open sea, for 15 minutes, changing course twice, then continued for another 10 minutes. Abruptly, the screws reversed and the boat stopped, floating awash in its own wake for a moment. There was no horn sounding to alert them to a dive. To Joe, it felt like a problem, not a calculated decision. The two sailors seemed to be equally alerted, but they did not move from their posts as Joe made for the hatch. *There's no way now the Uzel is not involved in every aspect of the boats operation, including this sudden shutdown!* Joe hurried down to the central control deck where Golovanov stood at the Uzel console.

"What's happened?" Joe asked.

Executive Officer, Commander Vladimir T. Bulgakov looked sharply at Joe but looked away as Golovnov answered:

"Your Uzel is telling me we have no clearance below the hull."

"Are you sure—I mean what data is being used in the calculation?"

"A direct sonar reading under the hull gives me 16 meters," Bulgakov said.

"Yes, I see, of course there may be a problem." Joe moved to the control console, "Are we okay for a moment? Let me just see…" As he suspected, the perceived depth was a composite of several sonar inputs including directly below, ahead and to port and starboard. He shifted the data as XO Commander Bulgakov showed a concerned frown, not quite a scowl. When forward sonar was read alone, Joe saw where the shallow depth reading had come from. When he turned up the frequency and intensity of the sonar pinging, he saw there was an obstruction dead ahead. Joe punched a few more keys and the image of a sunken coastal freighter was discernible on the monitor. Closer examination showed that apparently the shipwreck had been shifted by a recent storm so that the stern was buried deep and the prow was up at an angle close to 45 degrees. The sharp end of its broken bowsprit would have met them head on in ten seconds at the rate they had been moving.

"An almost suspicious arrangement," Bulgakov said. "It would have done serious damage to the outer hull."

"Maybe there was cargo that shifted astern in the storm," Joe offered, "helping to sustain that crazy angle?"

Bulgakov didn't shift a whisker to agree or disagree with Joe's speculation.

"It's good we paid attention to the Uzel's alarm," Golovanov said, "and the XO," he nodded at the stocky Bulgakov, "reversed engines when he did."

Of course,' Joe said. "Absolutely."

"That is one smart as hell computer," Golovanov said, to look ahead and warn us about bad clearance ahead."

"Well," Joe said, "it wasn't actually programmed that way."

"How not?"

"Well, it should not have been a mystery," Joe said, glad Golovanov appreciated the Uzel. "It read and gave the most critical reading. We can fix that; the message should be *danger ahead*, not *you've hit bottom*." It prioritized the worst case reading, but it should be closer to plain Russian."

"It may have saved our ass," Golovanov said.

"Why didn't an alert come specifically for an object

ahead?" Bulgakov asked sharply .

"Exactly," Joe said. "We'll fix that."

"A sober sailor watching a sonar scope would have caught that," Bulgakov added.

"I have no argument," Joe said. *But the Uzel is thinking ahead, before we do. In a way.*

They were soon underway, pursuing Golovanov's roundabout route to the battlegrounds. In another few minutes a horn sounded to announce their dive. Joe felt the boat tilt downward and heard the sounds of water enclosing them. A shiver rattled his bowels: *trapped, not for hours but for days…?*

Submerged 100 meters, they moved along at 25kph for thirty minutes, changing direction several times as Golovanov put the Uzel navigation software through its paces. Joe faced not only edgy claustrophobia, but extended inactivity with not enough to think about to keep him from wondering what might be happening to his life back there on dry land. *Not a good combination*, he thought, *the deadly focused boredom of one's fears.*

Golovanov saw Berg's frustration and suggested he rest and occupy himself in a lieutenant's cubicle, providing him with paper and pencils.

"Call me if anything more comes up," Joe said, feeling slightly queasy and tired. He stretched out on the bunk, apparently his for the duration of the trial. He soon fell asleep.

Golovanov knew he would be facing at least two other submarines and at least two armed surface vessels, torpedo boats. He counted on being able to outmaneuver a destroyer or frigate, both of which he was sure would be part of these exercises.

Though Eric Golovanov didn't know it yet, there would be four submarines, two more besides the two that had followed him from the bucket at Liepāja: K-78 and D-128. He would be surprised to see S-177, a Project 613, and K-208, a Project 651 equipped and operating with the Uzel's competing Accord CICS, the vacuum tube based computer system distinct from the Cloud CICS and all predecessors for its single centralized controller.

Whatever the 24th Naval Research Institute and Oscar Zhukovsky threw at him, Golovanov was confident, eager for battle. *If Joe's Uzel works like it did on the bench in Kronstadt and during the trials so far, saving us a collision, I can handle whatever they've got.* He knew that psychologically his adversaries would expect him to come from the south. Coming down from the north, might not give him any advantage at all, but it might delude those hunting him into mistaking B-103 for an ally. Even a hesitant minute or two could give him an advantage.

Hours later when Joe woke up, he realized he had needed sleep for days and this confinement had given him the chance to shut down. He found Bulgakov at the Uzel console. The LKB tech, Toshkov, was standing by and nodded to Joe, as much to say, *no problems you need to worry about.*

"The captain is also having a nap," Bulgakov told Joe as if answering a question. "He will be fully prepared for battle."

Joe returned to his temporary berth to do some thinking. Later, he returned to the control deck just as Golovanov reappeared, not looking as if he had slept, but did seem energetic and in good-humor. Bulgakov read aloud their position, from the navigation monitor and made a silent offer to relinquish control of B-103 to her commander.

Golovanov waved off Bulgakov's gesture, "Take her up to periscope depth."

Soon they were looking out across the open water. The day was somewhat overcast. It was late afternoon. The sea was relatively calm and clear in all directions, land masses in the far distance, a couple of fishing boats, a trawler, a small freighter. No warships, no Soviet Navy. Not yet.

Joe had no idea where they were and asked.

"We're north of the proving grounds," Eric answered.

"Are we going to surface? Joe wondered.

"No, we are going to move slowly at 100 meters." Golovanov said, nodding to the XO.

"Taking her to 100 meters," Bulgakov said.

"It will be night soon," Joe remarked as he steadied the idea in his mind of moving slowly through the dark black deep water. *No one knows we're here. Room for mistakes to be made…* For a moment he was terrified, just being there.

Golovanov, sensing Joe trepidation said, "Soon it will be time to shoot at real targets with real torpedoes, Dr. Berg." *If you are worried already, what about that?*

"And be shot at by real torpedoes," Bulgakov added.

"Let's dodge them all!" Golovanov studied Joe, his mood unchanged. "Is the Uzel ready?"

"I'm not going to speculate," Joe said; "we'll know soon enough, won't we?"

Bulgakov smiled, but as if reluctant to admit Joe's point.

Comrade Golovanov is so calm, Joe thought. *Is it possible he doesn't care whether Uzel comes out smelling bad? He cares most about his own performance? Of course.*

Class 53 torpedoes were used by all Soviet combat submarines. (53cm/21in) Among the 22 onboard B-103 were electrically propelled and peroxide propelled, some were wake-honing (so effective against surface ships) some were sound-honing, some heat seeking. There were two experimental sonar-guided electrically driven prototypes. In these sea trials everything was tested, recorded and would be examined. The Uzel kept track of the technical specifications of each torpedo, the exact time and coordinates where it was fired. Oscar Zhukovsky, top 24th Naval Research officials, the State Commission and torpedo designers would have access to all the data.

B-103 moved yet further north then east before moving slowly southward. Some hours later, around 2200, Golovanov told Joe, "We are now on the northern edge of the Soviet Navy's Baltic proving grounds."

The boat slowed and proceeded submerged at 80 meters. An hour later they lost all forward motion as B-103 rose amidst the changing sounds of water. The periscope and radar antennae broke the surface with scarcely a bubble.

What Joe saw through the scope was a surprisingly populated horizon in nearly full moonlight. In the near darkness of the Moon beams as the scope scanned 360, there were dots of light which Joe realized were smaller boats. The larger ships, a destroyer and a frigate, also displayed electric light. Joe said to Golovanov but included Bulgakov, "There are quite a number of vessels out there. How close are the closest ones?"

"I doubt they've picked us up. We're a good ways off. We're using the magnified scope." As in most military submarines, B-103 was equipped with two periscopes.

This is chaos about to happen, Joe thought. *The chance of confusion and disaster is obvious!* "Is it your job to outmaneuver all of them? There are no friendlies out there?"

"Well, there's the destroyer; what would any exercise be without at least one destroyer? And you saw the other one, the frigate? At least one, yes...?"

"But there are another dozen or two..."

"Supply vessels, patrol boats, torpedo boats, officer excursion launches. And torpedo chasers. It's a grand occasion all around."

"Torpedo chasers?" Joe asked.

"The Soviet People's Navy is not in the habit of losing or discarding valuable resources," Golovanov's eyes seemed to stop just short of an amused twinkle.

So light hearted... "So how do they--I mean how can they...:"

"They keep track. After it's all over, they'll retrieve them remotely."

"What a chore. It's too bad they're not on a leash of some kind." Joe always started with an ideal solution and worked backward.

"It's much easier if we don't miss," Golovanov said. "Otherwise they can travel for kilometers, down a canyon somewhere."

Joe supposed Golovanov might be exaggerating, that certainly the torpedoes were under better control. *Limit their fuel so they can't go far...* He knew the B-103 carried 22 torpedoes with 6 ready to fire from the bow tubes and 4 ready in the stern tubes.

There was a beep from the Uzel and Bulgakov said, *"Vot, ostorozhno tam. Look watchout there.*

At the very edge of the sonar scan there was a new bright spot on the green. Golovanov took over control and, with a nod, ordered Bulgakov to stand by to fire torpedoes. Then he said as he hit the keys, "Down scope,drop to 100 meters."

"Another sub?" Joe asked as he noticed the eager aggression in Golovanov's face and movements. *He is relishing an attack.*

"Yes," Golovanov said, "here to hunt us. Unless we are fortunate and they mistake us for one of the hunters. Maybe until it is too late."

"So you are going to fire real torpedoes?" Joe asked in a forced jovial almost rhetorical way. "I hope none of them are armed, are they?"

"Not with explosives."

So how do you know when there's a hit?"

"They are armed with a signal sender."

"Which is also used by these torpedo chasers?"

"Correct." Golovanov nodded, then twisted his head away from Joe's conversation to monitor incoming data. Using the Uzel to calculate, he received a vertical and horizontal distance readings; their first adversary was 200 meters down at 8 kilometers. Eric knew what the other blips on the screen were; he'd had them on radar and had seem them through the scope. He wondered, *Where are the rest of my diver pals and how many of you are there?*

Minutes passed as they sat floating, motors silent, drifting slowly in a subsurface current. Then another sonar blip appeared. Far to the west of the first sub, which had moved very little. This new one was moving east.

Golovanov waited, unsure which of the smaller surface vessels might be in play, torpedo boats ready to pounce . *I'll know when they shoot at me.* The Uzel was now tracking both submarines and three of the four most proximate surface vessels. Theoretically, B-103 was ready to fire at any three of those five. But Golovanov suspected there might be another submarine and he waited.

When a third sub showed up to the west of the other two, Golovanov moved, but slowly at first and at an angle, Joe realized, that would bring all three within nearly optimum shooting range of less than a kilometer, assuming no radical changes in speeds or directions of all four boats. *From the point of view of any one of the other subs,* Joe thought, *B-103 is not directly approaching any of them. Do we appear as a possible ally?* Imagining for a moment that Golovnov might be preparing to attack all three subs, Joe shivered with nervous dread. *A make or break test of all our work for the past four years. Our life's work, for that matter…*

Suddenly another blip appeared on the screen or rather separated itself rom their first sighting, the submarine on their port side toward the eastern edge of the battleground. Instantly, Golovanov reset Uzel to separately track both submarines. They were S-177 and K-208. He was now tracking four submarines and the nearest surface vessel.

Golovanov wondered, *Are they both facing south toward Liepāja, waiting for me?* He fired three torpedoes nearly simultaneously then, seconds later, a fourth. Joe felt the repercussion in the deck. Two torpedoes bracketed each of the two closest submarines. "Goose the torpedo gang," Golovanov told Bulgakov, who wasted no time urging the seamen in the forward torpedo room to reload.

B-103 increased speed, shortening the distance to both submarines. But now two more blips appeared, smaller blips, torpedoes moving much faster toward them at the center of the green scanning circle. Golovanov went for a steep dive moving toward the incoming torpedoes, aiming to duck under quickly. He set Uzel to track the torpedo boat that had fired instead of the more proximate surface vessel. The attacking torpedoes passed well above while the bow shot Golovanov had taken was on target. Then there was a loud beep and an overhead loudspeaker crackled. "Torpedo A-622 destroyed.S-177 disabled." *One down!* Then another abrupt announcement, "K-208 hit, still underway, no serious damage."

"Ohhahh," Golovanov groaned, "A hit is a hit. Cheaters must die…" There was invigorated fury in his eyes. *Happy animosity,* Joe thought as Golovanov fired the remaining bow torpedoes at the closest of the other two subs, D-128.

Leveling the dive at 210 meters, Golovanov turned B-103 north, away from the fleet of surface and submarine vessels. D-128 was firing back, two torpedoes. B-103 zagged hard to starboard and headed for the surface, firing two stern torpedoes at D-128, before suddenly turning back at another odd angle.

Joe would always have trouble remembering exactly what happened next. D-128 was disabled. They were fired at. Then there was a lot of dodging and maneuvering, constant sudden speed, direction and depth changes.

Golovanov dodged and held his fire. At last it seemed B-103 drew the remaining two subs and three surface vessel in pursuit. But Joe would always remember that, with two submarines attacking and torpedoes being fired from everywhere, Golovanov fired all six of the bow torpedoes at the two submarines and the closest surface attacker. B-103 was constantly moving, surging, ballast tanks blowing or gurgling, the deck like a live animal under Joe's feet.

There were beeps of sound and the loudspeaker was going off to announce hits. Then they were hit, a heavy thud on the outer hull. Golovanov kept moving. Bulgakov made sure the last of the torpdeoes were loaded and armed. But soon came the announcement that all but one surface attacker had been disabled. Or "sunk. The timeline would later show that B-103 had taken out its adversaries before being hit itself. Golovanov had dodged twelve torpedoes to be hit by one.

Joe looked wide-eyed, full of trepidation and wonder, and Golovanov laughed, "We'll be headed home now Joe; back in time to celebrate on the beach and watch the sunset."

"That's it?" Joe said, disbelieving.

"They've got plenty to think about, not only Gorshkov, but Kuznetsov as well, Krushchev's heirs for a world force navy. We're going home proud and free."

"We got hit, probably done for, but you don't seem unhappy."

"I did what any good diver would do, and took out six to my one."

"Sure. Of course," Joe said, "if you look at it that way."

"Your little box of scrambled wires and plastic is the hero. You and your partner, Philip Geogieovich, can be very proud."

"He is going to be annoyed with me; I didn't say I was going to accompany this field test."

"He'll feel better when he sees how we celebrate tonight. The brass? The big bosses, they're not going to pin any medals on you yet. But we know what happened and we'll tell anyone who is cleared for it."

"Tonight?" Joe asked.

"If it's nice, we'll get everybody down to the beach. Even if it's not so nice."

"Phil is due in Liepāja on Saturday or Sunday to go over the results of the field test. To look at the data and talk to people."

"Surprise," Golovanov laughed, "they thought it would take till Monday to see what was what."

They both laughed, Joe a bit surprised at himself, "Well," he said, "they have to write it up, cross check all the data…"

"Of course," Eric said, "they need to do it, not us. We already know."

As it would turn out, the top Soviet Naval engineers were especially happy with Golovanov; he had put their torpedoes to the test as well as the Uzel."

Whenever Joe thought about the last 30 hours as a field test for the Uzel, he glowed with its success, but he didn't think of it that way most of the time. The feral lethality of the attacks and counter attacks, the vast numbers of men occupied with it, the vast energy spent training them, equipping them. *Torpedo Chasers! How is Phil going to take all this?* "So, are we headed back submerged?" Joe asked.

"We need to recharge the batteries before reaching Leipaja. We're going to pop up on the surface, no need to hide now. So hold on to your ass." Golovanov watched Bulgakov handling the boat and asked his XO, "*Gatov Prizhok-Kita?*" Ready for a whale jump?"

Their surface maneuver wasn't the emergency surfacing that is so abrupt the boat is partially free of the water, the whole forward hull exposed, like a whale jumping up for air and sunshine. It was not quite a whale jump, but there was a furious popping up, water rushing from the boat as it came up. The bow came down and sent waves rippling outward. Joe was beside the seaman ready to open the tower hatch. He was suddenly acutely aware of how much he wanted fresh air and sunshine.

Suddenly there was the sky and morning sunshine from a sun low in the east. The boat was still rocking in its own turbulence, the screws motionless, the diesel engines still not restarted. There was only the sound of water slapping against the sleek, black outer hull. Joe stood on the narrow deck, his hand firm on one of the wet rail posts. He took several full deep breaths, surprised to feel so relieved and thankful as he looked around.

A pair of ducks were calmly floating on the chop beside the dripping glistening 100 meter long submarine. The ducks, ten meters away, barely glanced up at B-103, as if at an entirely harmless and familiar fellow creature of the sea. For Joe, there was no mistaking the attitude of the ducks toward the submarine and the tall thin man in dark T-shirt and slacks: *This is our sea, but we are willing to share it.*

They arrived in Liepāja in the late afternoon. Joe, Eric and Bulgakov napped on the way. It was the same day that US Army Lieutenant William Calley was charged with 6 counts of premeditated murder, for the 1968 deaths of 109 Vietnamese civilians in My Lai, Vietnam. The event had been covered up by the army until a GI wrote letters to all the top hypocrites who then pretended it was a rare, isolated incident. Calley, who could have received the death sentence when found guilty, was found guilty, but would serve only three years of house arrest instead.

FORTY-EIGHT

"We were young, we were foolish, we were arrogant, but we were right."   *--Daniel Ellsberg*

A CONVIVIAL GROUP BEGAN ARRIVING AT BERNATI around five in the evening. Golovanov, Bulgakov, the top crew of B-103, anyone who had been near the control deck of the submarine during the combat trial, were among the first, soon followed by the leaders of the pack at LKB, who brought friends. They had all been there before, at their favorite spot on the wide white sands. As word spread among LKB that Joe had been along for the crucial combat trials, he was included in all the toasts with jovial accounts of the Elephant story and fond reminders of other days at the same beach decreed by Joe during the glorious struggle that was their summer. Among the sailors, the Navy men, there was a clear confidence in their victory, any doubts left in the rest of the crowd were swept away in the power of righteous celebration.

Even without a strong hot summer, the Baltic Sea remained warm in September and the summer of 1969 was unusually warm. The water temperature that late afternoon and evening was around 65 degrees Fahrenheit, (18 C). Not exactly a warm bathtub, but good for a comfortable plunge and short swim.

The need for oblivion and release from their tense, abstinent mission was evident in chain smoking and the heavy consumption of vodka by the victorious sailors. Of course, there was plenty of wine and beer. The guitars were playing accompanied by songs. Koratron was there spinning out their intricately absurd musical comedies and blatant joy. It was a warm evening of soft air.

Later in the evening, Phil arrived, earlier than planned

apparently upon hearing about the impressive performance of B-103 and the Uzel CICS.

Staros came from Pskov, an ancient city almost on the flight path from Leningrad to Liepāja. He'd spent two days there speaking with a factory management about manufacturing an updated UM-2 designed for process automation control. Apparently the meetings with the factory council had been frustrating and Phil was stiff and a bit cranky, at first. But he stopped short of scolding Joe for going off on the sea trial and listened to Joe's account of the Uzel providing only one data source, the vital point, though it had not been programmed to deal with an odd situation like that sunken freighter. "It's thinking ahead," Joe joked, chuckling to himself.

"Yes, Staros said agreeably, "we need to make that clear to operators, program in the emergency selection." But Phil kept dampening Joe's enthusiasm by reminding him, "The Soviet Navy hasn't signed off even on the navigation field trial yet, let alone the combat field trial. Firing off a dozen torpedoes successfully is no where near having the Uzel fully accepted."

Golovanov is quite confident. He says Zhukovsky loves it and the old devil will be all in."

When is your friend Golovanov ever not confident? Just think how far we still are from being set up in mass production for installation in regiments of advanced Soviet submarines." That was what Phil clung to, a possible outcome that might return them to a position of respect and leadership.

"Shag za shagum," Joe said. Step by step.

Golovanov, drunk, wearing only dark blue bathing trunks, seeing Joe and Phil apparently arguing and as if he'd heard his name, though he had not, was padding across a wide stretch of sand toward them. He knew Joe was worried about Phil's reaction and he fondly embraced Philip Staros, proclaiming, "You did it. You are a genius!" And he added in a quiet, gruff voice, "Your little box of wires and plastic is a miracle." He glanced at Joe with a raised eyebrow. "Joe was there; he saw it all." Eric nodded affectionately at Dr. Berg. "Your friend here was very reluctant to go. He was afraid to be cooped up for days. But with the help of Uzel, I made short work of it."

Phil smiled at the captain and Joe could see he was relaxing slightly, as if forced to join the fun.

"Hey," Golovanov said, "If we'd have taken another day, even half-a-day, I could have got all of them. Without a scratch, but we proved our point well enough, I'd say." Golovanov stared at each of them in turn with no apparent expectation then stared off into the sea with the same blank expression.

"Yes, I understand you had a successful trial," Phil said, still somewhat formal, "but we have a long way to go. There are a number of changes, additions, that need to be made as a result of the trial, don't you agree?"

Golovanov waved his arm aloft as if clearing hanging cobwebs from his path, "All that will come Philip Georgievich, but *we* know *now*. Trust me..." and he lay a friendly, sandy hand on Phil's shoulder, "You don't need to worry dear Philip Georgievich, your dreams will come true." This was said as if generously to a child at bedtime. "*We* know. *Now* we know." He walked off and returned two minutes later with a half-full liter bottle of Stolichnaya. He handed it to Phil without a word. Phil won Eric's approval by taking several gulps from the bottle before handing it to Joe.

The two men, one in bathing trunks, the other in ironed clothes and polished shoes, were the same height and build Joe observed. *They are alike in other ways, why I like them both, driven, relentless. Pure elements...in a way.*

SUNDAY MORNING, SEPTEMBER 7, JOE AND PHIL were nearly alone in LKB's lab at the submarine basin. They were going over the data from the field trials. It was clear the Uzel had performed well. But already the theory was being introduced that much of Uzel's apparent success was due to the skill of its highly decorated captain. Joe, knowing Phil was at least mildly annoyed with him for going alone unannounced, was expecting some conversation from Phil toward acknowledgement of this *faux pas* on Joe's part. After Phil had reviewed the data file for an hour, he said, "Golovanov was not only putting the Uzel and the sub through their paces, he was testing the torpedoes. He never fired similar types at the same target. As much as possible, he mixed their honing characteristics and propulsion methods."

"Yes," Joe said, "he mentioned how much the navy scientists would appreciate his selections."

When Phil finally spoke personally to Joe, aside from the significance of the data and the modifications they needed to implement, he spoke not in Russian, but in Czech:

"Goddamn, I can't even think straight. My mind is so befuddled."

Joe was alarmed. He responded in Czech, "What are you talking about?" He doubted anyone else around spoke Czech, and hoped they didn't.

"I'm still so hung over from Friday's beach party," Phil explained pleasantly, "my brain is in limbo shock."

"Oh," Joe said in relief, *is that all?* "Of course. Right now I couldn't invent the solution to a square meal. But give it a day or two..."

"Sure, *eventually*, we'll be alright."

"The human physiology is surprisingly resilient." Joe felt generously cheerful. They could fully agree on this at least.

"Sure," Phil said, "but the time wasted; the pain of it all. Why do they have to drink so goddamn much? It sends everything backwards."

"I know; I know," Joe said.

"There has to be a way to avoid the damage. At least some of it."

"Well, it's very hard," Joe wore an amused smile, "to turn down a drink from a friendly Russian comrade."

That's it, if you are going to work together, become friends, you can't turn down a drink." It's part of trust itself.

"Some consider it one of the best qualities of socialism," Joe joked.

"Well, we don't have to take part in all of them," Phil said. "I, at least, shouldn't have gone to the beach and started drinking on Friday."

"But you got to know Golovanov better," Joe offered.

"Yes he made a point of getting me drunk, like ordering his crew."

"He means well, unless you are an enemy warship."

"Was it him or was it the Uzel? What made it happen so well?"

"I watched a warrior in peak performance with his weapon. The power of destruction was breathtaking as he fully trusted that weapon."

"Still, I'm not sorry I missed it," Phil said evenly.

FRIDAY'S BEACH PARTY WAS NOT THE LAST that autumn for the collective of Soviet Navy and the Leningrad Design Bureau. The water grew steadily cooler and the swimming shorter.

On October 2, a US 1.2 megaton thermonuclear bomb was detonated at Amchitka Island, Alaska, less than 400 miles from Russian islands in the Bering Sea. Less than two weeks later, hundreds of thousands of people flooded the United States in a Moratorium to End the War in Vietnam. Nixon showed no signs of yielding to the now inevitable loss of the war.

On another late October day, perhaps the last time any local native would leave a beach in Latvia to venture even an ankle into the water, Gesha Zhukov ran into the surf at Bernati with a thermometer dangling from his neck. With water at his waist, he leaned over to submerge the thermometer then shouted, "Nine degrees!" (48 Fahrenheit) "Come on in!"

Some 15 or 20 people, both young and mature, scientists, engineers and technicians, whooped, whistled and rushed into the water, vowing that they would continue to swim while the sharp edges of coastal ice were not a danger to the skin of their feet. On such cold cloudy days, if there was no rain, a minute or two was enough.

JOE WAS ASTONISHED ON THE MORNING OF November 9 1969 when a woman who worked with Andrei Tupolev, Olga Konstantinova, who Joe had flirted with at Tupolev's design bureau, called him at home in Leningrad. She said: "I haven't seen you in months and months and I had nearly forgotten about you... Then I saw your name in *Pravda*, this morning."

"Oh, you did, did you?" *What have we been accused of this*

time? Joe wondered.

"Congratulations. You must be very proud. And congratulate your partner Philip Georgievich as well, though he is not so friendly as you are."

"...Excuse me, but I'm not aware..."

"It's Olga from Tupolev."

"No, of course but what are you saying..."

...You mean you don't know...? The State Prize!" Olga's tone held a strong sense of disbelief. You mean you really didn't know? I'm the first one to tell you?" She seemed pleased at that idea.

"Yes, please enlighten me."

"You and your team have won the State Prize for your computer, the UM-Nikita. How could you not know? If you submitted it, you have been waiting to hear the results, no?"

"Well, yes, but I didn't know and that's a long story."

"Perhaps you will tell me about it during your next visit to Andrei Nikolayevich?"

"Of course, Olga, certainly, of course. Thanks for calling me."

Joe, Staros and several team members had been awarded the premier State Prize for the UM-1NKh, the Soviet Union's most prestigious prize, formally known as the Stalin Prize. Somehow their application had found its way past the Leningrad Party Committee into the hands of the nominating Commission in Moscow. The State prize had been approved and was signed by Mtyslav Keldysh, President of the Soviet Academy of Science who would soon officially congratulate them.

At first, Staros and Berg were thrilled, as is normal for anyone winning a prestigious prize. Joe thought how proud Vivian and Robert would be. Phil thought such recognition would buoy them toward a restored position. But they soon realized that it had plunged them into greater danger. The Leningrad Obkom officials had also been surprised to read the same article in *Pravda*, and they were horrified that the international community would learn that two foreigners were responsible for the advanced level of microelectronics in the Soviet Union. Grigory Romanov was further enraged because it seemed *'that nest of Zionist vipers'* had snuck their application for the State Prize past them. It was completely unacceptable.

Joe and Phil were escorted into Obkom headquarters by adjutants of Grigory Romanov. Romanov demanded their resignations.

"I am certainly not going to do that," Phil said.

"Nor will I resign," Joe said. "It would only encourage you."

"What? You dare to poke the bear? I will make sure you are finished forever. We will dig through all you have done, all you have tainted."

Once back on the street, Phil said, "Their next move will be to kick us out of the ministry. They just need time to make up the lies to explain it."

"They could skip all that, Joe half-joked, "just have us arrested and locked up."

"Look," Phil said, "we have the ideas that can beat the West; we know how to do it. If we can make even a few on the Central Committee and the Politburo understand that, they are not going to lock us up."

"What Romanov wants is a prison think tank for us, a *sharashka*. If we're lucky."

But when they tried to interest Shokin and Dementyev in their plans to beat US and Japan, their arguments fell on deafened ears. America had beaten USSR's early lead in space with the Apollo 11 mission in July, and Brezhnev and the Soviet military were rapidly adopting the view that it was impossible to catch up with the West. It would be better to copy their successful technology than to waste resources trying to innovate their own. Brezhnev was far less willing than Khrushchev to spend precious resources on projects which did little but boost Soviet prestige. If the Americans hadn't done it, it wasn't worth doing.

Staros and Berg were infuriated as they encountered a wall of skepticism, vilification and refusal. They were informed that Soviet priorities had changed after losing the Moon race, the Politburo was freshly concerned with military vulnerabilities on Earth. Joe and Phil were left without any new prospects or hopes, with only the possible eventual success of the Uzel to sustain any hope of returning to the leadership in microelectronic development in the land of Socialism.

Two days after the announcement of their State Prize in Pravda, Sharp released the eagerly awaited QT-8D Micro Compet, the first mass-produced calculator to have its logic circuitry entirely implemented with large-scale semi-conductor integrated circuits (LSIs). Sharp would sell over 1 million QT-8D units, setting .off competition around the world.

On November 12, Independent investigative journalist Seymour Hersh broke the story of the March 1968 My Lai Massacre. The story further undermined public support for the Vietnam war. Two days later, NASA launched Apollo 12 with Pete Conrad, Richard Gordon and Alan Bean for a second manned mission to the Moon. The next day, the accident prone, disaster prone Soviet submarine known as 'the widow maker' because of all the crew members killed in it, K-19 collided with the USS Gato in the Barents Sea. The Gato, barely damaged, continued its underwater patrols while K-19 barely made it back to port for repairs. On that same day, November 15, in Washington, D.C., over 400,00 protesters demonstrated against the war, some calling it the 'March Against Death'. On November 17, negotiations between the USSR and the USA began in Helsinki to develop the SALT I treaty aimed at limiting the number of nuclear weapons on both sides. On November 19, Apollo 12 astronauts Charles Conrad and Alan Bean landed at Oceanus Procellarum (Ocean of Storms), becoming the third and fourth humans to walk on the Moon. They splashed down safely in the Pacific five days later. This second manned Moon mission and the fact that the US planned a half dozen more such missions decisively defeating the USSR's plans for doing so. It would be self-defeating now to try.

As 1969 drew to a close, with work on the Uzel still continuing, but now without much need for close supervision by Phil Staros or Joe Berg and with strongly renewed hostility by the Leningrad Party Obkom, especially from Grigory Romanov, their future seemed bleak and at loose ends. The LKB continued to further refine and developed the UM-2 for automation control systems. They used it in Computer Aided Design and built computerized and automated testing equipment based on the UM-1NKh. But they had no major project to sustain them.

FORTY-NINE

"The development of events in the world arena demands from us the highest vigilance, restraint, firmness and unremitting attention to the strengthening of the country's defense capability... Perhaps never before in the postwar decades has the situation in the world arena been as tense as it is now... Comrades! The international situation at present is white hot, thoroughly white hot"

--Grigory Romanov

THE NEW YEAR 1970 DID NOT OFFER NEW PROMISE or hope for LKB. The fate of the Uzel was in the hands of the Navy Commission and Mark Galperin's small team. There would be further tests and demonstrations. The contract for the first submarine installation was nearly fulfilled. But it had not been certified and the remaining parts of the contract could still be overturned. In February they tried to contact Marshal Dmitry Ustinov several times. He had become even more powerful and had issued a directive which ordered the Chelomei design bureau to combine its Almaz space station with OKB-1's Salyut space station, now headed by Vasily Mishin. According to Ustinov, the two Chief Designers were to create a perfect Salyut space station. It was widely known that Uncle Mitya had been Chelomei's stolid personal adversary for decades. Joe and Phil didn't hear back from Ustinov's office.

Not exactly a ray of hope, but a factory in Pskov had agreed to manufacture the Elektronika K-200, a further refined and miniaturized version of the UM-2. It was a prospect more like probation than a return to station, more pension than sinecure.

March 5 The Nuclear Non-Proliferation Treaty went into effect, after ratification by 56 nations.

In the first quarter of 1970, Soviet submarine B-103 ventured out of Liepāja several times for further tests and demonstrations, some at maximum test depths in deep water. The Uzel routinely handled complex maneuvers and simultaneous torpedo firing at multiple targets. Also during this first few months of 1970, they obtained and incorporated ever more reliable data on acoustics. As far as Phil, Joe, Mark and the LKB deputy chief designers were concerned, the boat was operating reliably and the system requirements had been fully met, or as Joe pointed out, "Some specifications are slightly shy of the mark, but on the whole we've done better than the requirements. We far exceeded expectations, Above all, we delivered on time, besting the competition by at least two years."

They all knew what keeping to the relentless schedule had cost them, and what sort of pride and comradeship had inspired them.

"Too bad Grigory Romanov doesn't see that as a good thing," Zhukov said.

Kuznetsov half-grunted a chuckle of approval.

"No one can argue with the divers themselves," Joe said, "They are happy."

Zhukov, Nikitin and Kuznetsov nodded agreement.

"So we wait and hope the Navy agrees with you?" Mark said.

"They will accept it, I believe," Phil said, doing his best to be reassuring.

Staros was not mistaken. And Golovanov was right; they knew after the combat trials in September. The State Committee on March 30, 1970 signed an act to make official their successful completion of the prototype. To commemorate the event a medal was produced, an emblem of Liepāja with the text of Liepāja's 16th submarine berth poster: 'Beat savage imperialism!'

In recognition of their success, the official act decreed that:

"1. The Navy now has another team capable of designing a Combat Information and Control System at a very high technical level to provide adequate tactical and algorithmic formulation of the needed software.

2. The Navy has received an example of a prototype CICS developed 'from scratch" in 5 years instead of 7-8 while making the original instrument equipment instead of using stock items.

3. By using a dynamic vertically integrated electronic enterprise, incorporating latest developments, a complex technical system has implemented solutions for the Navy, 5-10 years ahead of similar systems from other enterprises."

It was a great victory and a great relief. And there was of course great celebration. Joe and Phil celebrated whole-heartedly; though once again they reminded each other of the damage to clear thinking.

"Maybe we should drink cognac, it's less lethal," Joe suggested.

"Maybe," Phil said, "cognac is almost as socially acceptable as vodka."

"One for one, we'd be better off."

"We could try it," Phil said.

"We'd still need to accept several toasts of vodka."

Their hangovers were no less painful despite their vows to do better. But even more devastating than the metabolic poisoning of ethyl alcohol, was the telegram they received on the first of April: LKB ceased to exist as an independent organization and was now a member of the Scientific and Production Association Pozitron. Phil and Joe would report to the director of Pozitron. It was Grigory Romanov's next move.

"Pozitron," Phil gasped. "They make ceramic capacitors and have nothing to do with the direction of our work!" Phil was pale feverish and sick to his stomach. Everyone at LKB was in shock, but soon the team rallied and prevailed upon Staros to remember that they now had behind them a very big victory, which could not be forgotten because of the value of what they had done. Their achievement was now officially recognized and that meant more than one Chief Designer, one team, one boat and one system. Joe said to his partner and their close colleagues, "Never mind submarines and spaceships, we opened the development of domestic microelectronics."

"Yes," was Phil's half-hearted answer, "and we are going to have to defend it, and work even harder."

The slow transition to Pozitron began. Phil remained crushed and bitter. They knew Grigory Romanov wasn't going to let up. But no one at LKB understood yet, not even Mark Galperin, that Pozitron had the weight and power to play a crucial role in a final success for the Uzel: general acceptance and the high demand made possible through mass production or, to begin with serial production, one unit system a time but one right after another. Uzel now needed a factory behind it. For the coming months they worked toward developing the K-200 as a potentially mass produced item and they further developed computer aided design as a tool of multiple manufacturing. They also began using the UM-1NKh as the basis for new precision test instruments. It seemed to be the best they could do.

ON APRIL 11, APOLLO 13 WAS LAUNCHED FOR the Moon with Jim Lovell, Fred Haise and Jack Swigert. On April 13, an oxygen tank exploded, voiding two tanks of oxygen into space. Mission Control aborted and put the three men in the Lunar Module, designed for 2 men for 2 days not 3 men for 4 days. Four man/days as opposed to 12. They went once around the Moon then back they came on rationed food, reduced oxygen, not enough water and in a crowded, painful, damp, cold potential coffin. The drama of life near death renewed public interest in the Apollo program. Countless millions watched the Pacific Ocean splashdown.

On May 1 1970, President Richard Nixon ordered US forces into neutral Cambodia, widening the Vietnam War and sparking nationwide riots. On May 4, a great early spring day to be outside on the rolling grassy campus grounds of Kent State University in Ohio, National Guardsman fired a fusillade of over sixty rifle rounds at several hundred peaceful student demonstrators and non-demonstrating idle students. They killed 4 young students, permanently paralyzed another and seriously injured 8 more. The murder of these students, and subsequent killings of student protestors at other US campuses, triggered the largest student strike in US history. But in a national poll, taken immediately after the murders, nearly 60 per cent said they thought the students deserved it.

On September 20 1970, the USSR's Luna 16 landed on the Moon and lifted off the next day with Moon samples. Back on Earth four days later, the world hardly noticed.

On October 8, Soviet author Aleksandr Solzhenitsyn was awarded the Nobel Prize for Literature. Many in the Russian *intelligentsia* suspected the CIA had manipulated the Nobel prize committee to grant the award for its anti-Soviet value. "He should be ashamed of himself for being part of such a charade," they said.

On October 20, the USSR launched the Zond 8 lunar probe. It circumnavigated the Moon, less than 700 miles from the surface, sending back detailed photographs of both Moon and Earth from different distances along the way.

IN LATE OCTOBER, GRIGORY ROMANOV TOOK over Leningrad party control from Vasily Tolstikov who was put in charge of promoting USSR technology to Mongolia. One of Romanov's first acts was to use Pozitron to further censure and restrict Staros and Berg.

Phil and Joe had been largely at loose ends with the future of the Uzel still not secured, even as Mark's team worked on the next two Uzel systems for the new Project 641-B submarines. Phil was horrified and despairing, Joe depressed, but they didn't wait for Romanov's next move. They contacted Shokin and Peter Dementyev, the man who had brought them from Prague to Leningrad, one of their earliest supporters. They received only off-hand, vague and thus discouraging answers from both Shokin and Dementyev or their ministry aides. Joe arranged to meet with Major Viktor Taroikin.

"Our future in the Soviet Union is finished and done for," Phil said as soon as they were seated in Taroikin's Moscow office. "These latest threats and restrictions are just the beginning. Romanov plans to have us locked up somewhere."

"That is not going to happen," Viktor said. "I can assure you of that much."

"Even so, without new work, a chance to prove ourselves,

we might as well be placed under house arrest," Joe said.

"You must be patient, give Romanov a chance to make his moves against you, so that I can arrange for a counter move. He is on an upward path under Brezhnev, and will not be easy to stop. I hope you are maintaining a good relationship with GKET Minister Aleksandr Shokin?"

"We are in touch, but he, too, seems wary of offending Romanov."

"Be patient and you can be sure I will do what I can, as opportunities develop."

Not much reassured, Joe and Phil returned to Leningrad, Joe at least, glad they still had their salaries, their lab and offices.

On November 9 1970, the Soviet Union launched Luna 17 from Earth orbit for the Moon. On November 17, Luna 17 landed and released the Lunokhod 1, the first roving remote-controlled robot to land on another world. It would operate on the Moon for 11 months, traveling 7 kilometers, testing soil, recording cosmic ray activity and sending back hundreds of high definition photographs including panoramic views of the Lunar landscape. But there seemed to be no glory in it, anymore.

The next blow came in late November when the earlier decree merging the Leningrad Design Bureau, LKB, with the Pozitron Scientific Production Association was followed by an order for Joe and Phil to report to the director of Pozitron on a daily basis. The first act of this new boss was to order them to immediately dismantle two clean rooms and stop work on another clean room, all necessary for the production of high density large scale integrated circuits. Clear to the two Americans was the rapidly approaching end of their scientific careers in the Soviet Union. It would not be long before Romanov was included in the state secret that they were not only foreigners, but Americans. On top of this dread, they chafed under the increased restrictions and humiliations inflicted by Romanov and Pozitron.

JOE, VERA TOO, WERE PROUD THAT ALL FOUR children were students at the Leningrad Conservatory of Music, the famous institution whose alumni included Pyotr Tchaikovsky, Sergei Prokofiev and Dmitri Shostakovich. Shostakovich taught there during the 1960s and Nikolai Rimsky-Korsakov taught there for almost forty years following its inception in the mid-nineteenth century. His bronze monument still stood in Theatre Square.

It was Joe's ambition coming true, that Vivian, Robert, Alena and Anton would become professional musicians. After promising to spend the weekend at home, he looked forward to playing music with them as a quintet. On Saturday afternoon, while Vera was out shopping, Joe was alone, a quiet moment in Leningrad. He dialed Elvira, letting it ring twice before hanging up. Hoping she would call him right back, he waited. thinking it would be wonderful to see her even for a few hours, sometime before the busy next week. As five minutes passed, Joe grew less hopeful. Feeling the need to move around, he began to get, up then sat back down and dialed Aleksandr Shokin's office. Shokin's assistant, Marina Leotovskaya, recognized Joe's voice instantly:

"Oh, Zhosef Veniaminovich, how are you today? You just missed him, but I think he will be back soon."

"Well, I'm fine," Joe said, "how are you, Marina? Still as smart and glorious as ever?"

"Thank you, Dr. Berg... Shall I ask him to call you?"

"Within the hour? Sure, please."

"You are at your office?"

"No, at home. the number is—"

"—No of course I have that number."

Joe waited but neither Elvira nor Shokin called. Vera returned and sensing Joe's melancholy mood, she left him alone. In the kitchen, she began to prepare for a large family meal. After an hour or two, the children arrived back fromm their short day at the Conservatory. Vivian and Robert greeted him somewhat formally as they removed their wraps, but Alena and Anton, who just wanted Joe's usual treats, whether it be an instant poem of lavish compliments, or candy, pastry or a fresh pack of playing cards, as it was today, two packs, offered with optimistic admonishments to share.

"What do you say we listen to that Bach cantata recording," Joe offered. "We'll see if we can play it just as well."

"Oh, Papa," Vivian laughed.

"Why not?" Joe asked. "If not now, why not before much longer?"

"Don't get started on that just yet," Vera said. "Dinner will be ready in twenty minutes."

"Fine," Joe said, "we'll listen to Bach while we eat."

Vera gave him a smile which he returned. Then the phone rang and Joe answered, prepared to say it was a wrong number if it was Elvira. But it was Shokin.

"Something up that I should know about on a Saturday? Shokin asked.

The Bach selection began playing on the high fidelity system in the large open room, providing clear high notes and rolling base sounds.

"Well," Joe said to Shokin, "I'm worried that our talents are going to waste, we've got lots of good ideas the Americans haven't thought of yet."

Just then Alena screamed at Anton, "Give me one of the packs you selfish brat. You can't hold all the cards."

"Not before your dinner, Robert," Vera exclaimed as Robert slid one of Joe's candy bars off the table.

Joe put his hand over the mouth piece and made a silent plea to Vera to quiet the kids. "Be quiet you two," she said to Alena and Anton. "Papa is talking to someone important." Joe cringed thinking of what Shokin was hearing.

God, what bedlam, Shokin thought. Then, "But Joe, you've made a habit of angering some important people. So that opening up new or experimental projects to you is full of risk."

"It's such a waste to just put us out to pasture while Party people work to discredit us entirely."

Shokin heard a crash of dishes, another loud squawk from Alena, then Robert, saying to his mother, "Yes, Mom, I'm hungry. I thought we were supposed to have dinner? When is it?"

"Be patient, Robert," Vera cried nodding her head toward her husband and placing a finger across her lips.

The man is wrangling monkeys on all sides, Shokin thought. For a moment or two, he saw Joe as the confused and lonely foreigner he was. In that light, Joe and Phil seemed more manageable, more easily guided and kept out of trouble. "Tell you what," Shokin said, "maybe I can come up with an idea or two. Why don't you and Phil come and see me in Moscow on Monday, around 1300 (1PM) would be good."

Shokin's offer to meet had not fully reassured Joe but it was enough that he joined his family for dinner quite cheerfully. He started playing the Bach recording again, occasionally emphasizing certain passages to his children with movement of hands and arms or humming the melodies.

PHIL AND JOE ARRIVED AT SHOKIN'S OFFICE

late Monday afternoon. Shokin kept them waiting less than 30 minutes before they were ushered in to the GKET Minister's office. He looked at each of them carefully in turn and said, "So you hope I can rescue you once again, is that it?"

"We are here to offer our services in advancing Soviet microelectronics," Phil said.

Joe looked directly into Shokin's eyes as he nodded, a gesture perhaps more effective than words: *Staros and Berg United.*

"You've heard of the new micro calculator, I'm sure," Shokin said, "the Sharp company's Micro Compet?"

"We are familiar with it, yes?"

"Sure, of course," Joe said.

"Have you studied it? Or even actually had one to study?"

"No," both Americans said.

"Well, in that case, let me introduce you," Shokin produced a new Sharp MicroCompet from his desk drawer and handed it to Phil. "Believe me," he added, "it can do everything and more of what the big desk models do."

Joe glanced at the handheld calculator as it passed into Phil's hands, then he looked to Shokin: *So what? What's that to do with us?*

Phil merely looked at the plastic device then went to return it, but Shokin, waved him away, saying magnanimously, "No keep it, it's yours; consider it a gift and a possible lesson."

Both Joe and Phil looked at him, puzzled.

I am able to offer you," Shokin said, "the same opportunity I have offered to two other design groups in my ministry. To reverse-engineer this amazing little machine and produce a fully functioning prototype by March 30th next year, in time for the 24th Party Congress."

"In less than four months?" Joe said.

"Correct."

"I'm pretty sure we can do that," Joe said quickly.

Phil was barely able to suppress his rage enough to appear calm and thoughtful.

"If you can do that," Shokin said, "I can more or less promise you it will help restore your reputations. After all, to produce the Union's very own state-of-the-art micro calculator...would go a long way."

Joe cringed knowing Phil was about to scream at Shokin's awe of this calculator, let alone that they could slavishly imitate Japanese technology and call it 'state-of-the-art'.

Shokin, too, was thinking. If he succeeded, he would prevent other Soviet ministries from being awarded contracts for microelectronic devices. He would also be credited with making good use of these disgraced foreigners. Shokin was pretty sure he could sell the deal to Brezhnev on the promise that it would be ready for the Soviet supreme leader to present at the 24th Party Congress in April 1971. He continued to study Joe and Phil, waiting for Phil's answer or reaction. Then he said, "But keep in mind before you agree to take on this challenge, that it has to be on my desk by March 30th and it has to work just as well as that one."

"We agree," Phil said reluctantly, moving the calculator to is briefcase, "but we'd better get started." He made a motion to leave, barely able to keep himself from pounding in rage on Shokin's desk.

"This new device, if you make it in time, will be called the Elektronika 24-71, for the 24th Party congress in 1971."

"In getting started on this," Phil said, "it would help if we didn't get so much interference from our adversaries."

"I'll see what I can do," Shokin said.

Accepting the challenge did provide relief from immediate persecutions. Pozitron's boss was told to back off and leave them to work independently. It did not take them long to discover that the two other design bureaus Shokin had selected were aiming to make an exact copy of the Sharp Micro Compet. Phil had been utterly humiliated by the demotion into Pozitron—he, much more so than Joe, who constantly reminded himself that there was plenty of room for things to get much worse. Phil was now further disturbed and angered by the *meet-the-deadline-or-else* nature of this humiliating 24-71 deal and the pointless uselessness of it.

When they were alone, far from Russian ears, Al Sarant said in plain New York English to Joel Barr, dedicated Soviet patriot from Brooklyn, "We're being made fools! Copying Japan and the US is pure bullshit. We can do so much better; we proved it with the UM-1NKh and the Uzel."

Joel, worried about Al's blood pressure, offered, "But of course we have the UM-2, further developed now."

"They want a copy of Sharp's Micro Compet. Four months from now, there will be newer and better devices from the US and Japan."

Undertaking such a desperate crash program meant making chips with close to 2,000 elements when, in late 1969-70, the most complex Soviet chips contained at most 40 elements.

"We'll use the UM-2 circuit and software but shrink it even further than on the Elektonika K-200' we'll have it down into LSIs."

"Memory storage that small is not going to be easy, either," Al said, "or cheap."

No one else has the UM-2. We merely need to miniaturize it. So you can put it in your briefcase or coat pocket."

"Merely!" Al said. "In three months! "It's so utterly stupid to abandon creative, innovative programs."

"I certainly won't argue that," Joel said. "but let's see what good old American ingenuity can do?"

It took them only a day to realize that without a higher precision photo repeater, they would never be able to make the dense LSI chips required to produce a small powerful calculator like the Sharp Micro Compet. To make LSI's with up to 2000 elements they would need photo engraving techniques to etch and layer silicon wafers far superior to anything available in the Soviet Union.

On December 15 1970, the USSR's Venera 7 became the first spacecraft to land successfully on Venus and transmit data back to Earth. The data from the surface of Venus revealed that its dense atmosphere was 96% carbon dioxide, its surface temperature was close to 900 degrees Fahrenheit and atmospheric pressure at its surface was nearly 100 times the pressure at Earth's surface. Venera 7 put to death any hope of Venus being a place humans might visit.

FIFTY

"When I won the world championship, the United States had an image of, you know, a football country, a baseball country, but nobody thought of it as an intellectual country."   *--Bobby Fischer*

IN AN AMERICAN TECHNICAL MAGAZINE, ERIC Firdman discovered an advertisement for a David Mann 3600 photo repeater capable of defining lines down to one micron wide. Bringing this to Phil's and Joe's attention, they found further documentation on how the pioneering US chip companies used this same machine to make the photo masks for their dense LSI chips.

When Staros informed Shokin that the Elektronika 24-71 project could not possibly succeed without a high precision photo repeater,' Shokin promised to look into it. He quoted them the standard line about how sale of this advanced equipment was forbidden to any entity behind the so called iron curtain. They listened to his boring account of the process used to disguise its final destination by first selling it to a fictious company then smuggling it into Russia. "Which costs a great deal of hard currency, and takes a long time."

"You and I both know," Staros said, "that if we do this, it will be the one. The best. So let's get us this machine or one we can use." Phil pressed Shokin unrelentingly until Shokin admitted that he had already purchased the machine for a another design bureau within his ministry. It was being delivered elsewhere in Leningrad as they spoke.

Phil and Eric conspired and performed a number on Shokin's vanity and ego and soon made him agree to let them have access to this machine immediately. Even then, it was no simple matter to pressure the recalcitrant director of the other design bureau to produce the photo patterns from their CADCAM files into three sets of photo masks. Weeks later, they had viable LSI chips, produced at a very low yield, but they had proved that precise photo masks were the key to making large scale integrated circuits and small computers.

They worked on their odious task day and night in various unhappy states of mind; Phil was far more depressed than Joe and they went often to Moscow to get away from Romanov and even Shokin.

On January 31 1971 Apollo 14 was launched with three men hoping for a third successful lunar landing. Right after the launch, a bomb exploded in a men's room at the US Capitol. The militant anti-war Weather Underground took credit for the bomb and promised many more until the Vietnam war ended. It put a lot people up tight. Then the three astronauts came back from the Moon. Going there began to seem routine again.

On March 8 1971, the Citizens' Commission to Investigate the FBI broke into FBI offices in Pennsylvania and took all the files.

On March 15, a non-military version of the UM 2, an improved design, the Elektronika K-200, was manufactured in Pskov. A US magazine review of the Elecktronika K-200 declared it the top thing in process control automation and expressed admiration and surprise at the sophisticated English brochure, concluding the review, "The Elektronika K-200 may presage a whole new direction in Soviet cybernetics."

In late March, they managed to assemble a working prototype of the Elektronika 24-71 for the March, 30 1971 deadline. It was placed on Brezhnez's desk by Shokin as he had promised. Aleksandr Shokin then arranged for a celebration which included a number of interested industry individuals. Certainly they were all very proud at LKB that they had pulled off the 24-71 challenge successfully. Again Joe and Phil and Eric took part in some excessive drinking and though they drank cognac much of the time, they suffered regrets. The more successful they were, it seemed, the more they had to drink.

Later, Staros gathered nine or ten colleagues, including

Joe, Eric and Mark for a private celebration. "Though the Elektronika 24-71 is clearly superior to the Sharp MicroCompet," he said, "as predicted, it is nowhere near current state-of-the-art. Japanese and American companies have moved ahead. We cannot be proud of the device itself, but only in beating the deadline." As they commented on what a Soviet calculator meant to Soviet citizens and scientists who might use it, Staros offered a toast and then a prediction:

"You all know, all this micro calculator stuff is nothing. Today we are opening a new era for mankind, the era of personal computers."

Everyone was surprised. "What do you mean?" Kuznetov asked.

"I mean what I have just said. In five to ten years individuals like you and I will be able to afford their own computer at home and it will be as powerful as today's latest military computers."

It was a remarkable prophecy at the time. In the West, it took Ed Roberts over three years to coin the phrase, 'personal computer'. Those who heard Phil say it, would watch in awe the next few years as his prediction proved conservative.

After being dumped unceremoniously into Pozitron, Philip Staros was crushed as he watched the disbanding and dispersal of the LKB team. Certainly Joe was not happy about it although Joe was not angered or particularly surprised. He licked his wounds and moved on. Mark Galperin continued to be the Chief Designer of the Uzel, shepherding it through the contract with the Soviet Navy, including the installation of two additional submarines after B-103, also classified as experimental combat vessels. Ultimately, Mark, unlike Phil and Joe, was not disappointed in being joined with Pozitron. The next step in their Navy contract provided that a factory would take over producing an additional three units for three more submarines, for the final and thorough trial. The problem now facing Mark was that there was no factory ready and willing to manufacture the Uzel. The Navy's position was that Staros and what was left of LKB would need to produce the next three Uzel installations, as they had so successfully done the second and third boats. Mark decided to go to the director of Pozitron and ask for his help, without informing Staros or Berg. He surmised that getting Staros involved might create confrontations. Joe, on the other hand might be sympathetic, but might not.

Mark was told, wait a few days, "I think there will be a solution," the director said.

In April 1971, an order was signed for the Pskov factory radio parts shop number 20 to take up the manufacture of computer technology. The USSR was over productive of ceramic capacitors. During the week before the new order, the Pskov factory had hired LKB's chief of the design department, Anatoly S. Sobolev, to head up the new computer production unit, the man who was most familiar with the design documentation for CICS Uzel, a man Mark knew very well. Another LKB Deputy Chief who had supervised the work on the Uzel and Elektronika K-200, working closely with Staros for 10 years, was also hired by the new Pskov factory unit.

APRIL 19 1971 THE SOVIET UNION LAUNCHED

Salyut 1 into low Earth orbit, Earth's first space station. The Salyut program followed this with five more successful launches of seven station modules. The final module, *Zvezda*, (Star) became the core of the Russian contribution to the International Space Station and remained in use in the 21st century. Salyut 1 was visited by Soyuz 10 and Soyuz 11. The hard-docking of Soyuz 10 failed and the crew had to abort the mission and return safely to Earth. The Soyuz 11 crew achieved a successful hard docking and performed experiments in Salyut 1 for 23 days, but were killed by asphyxiation caused by valve failure just prior to Earth re-entry.

ON MAY 9 US MARINER 8 CRASHED INTO

the Atlantic Ocean minutes after launch. Ten days later, MARS 2 was launched by the Soviet Union as a part of a series of crewless Mars probes and landers. The Mars 2 and Mars 3 missions consisted of identical spacecraft, each with an orbiter and an attached lander. The Mars 2 lander became the first human-made object to reach the surface of Mars although the landing system failed and the lander was lost. These two orbiters were meant to image the Martian topography and clouds, take Mars temperature, study the composition and physical properties of the surface, measure the atmosphere, monitor the solar wind, measure the interplanetary and Martian magnetic fields and be the communications relay to send signals from the landers to Earth. A large dust storm on Mars nearly ruined the missions. Unable to re-program the mission computers, both Mars 2 and Mars 3 had dispatched their landers immediately, and the orbiters used limited data resources in snapping images of the featureless dust clouds rather than mapping the surface.

ON MAY 30 US MARINER 9 WAS LAUNCHED toward Mars, a robotic space probe which reached the planet on November 14 1971, becoming the first spacecraft to orbit another planet, narrowly beating Mars 2 and Mars 3 which arrived weeks later. After encountering dust storms on the planet for several months following its arrival, Mariner 9 managed to send back clear pictures of the surface and successfully returned 7,329 images over the course of its mission.

On June 12 1971, J. Edgar Hoover announced at Tricia Nixon's wedding ceremony, all smiles for the press, that he had no plans for retiring and intended to stay on as director of the FBI indefinitely. The next day, the New York Times began to publish the Pentagon Papers revealing the devastating facts of the losing war.

On June 26 1971 the Soviet space authority made another attempt to launch the N-1 rocket, which had been designed to carry Soviet cosmonauts to the Moon. Soon after lift-off, due to unexpected eddies and counter-currents at the base of the first stage, the N-1 experienced an uncontrolled roll beyond the capability of the control system to compensate. The KORD sensed an abnormal situation and sent a shutdown command to the first stage, but the guidance program had been modified to prevent this from happening until 50 seconds into launch. The roll, which had initially been 6° per second, began rapidly accelerating. At T+39 seconds, the booster was rolling at nearly 40° per second, causing the inertial guidance system to lock at T+48 seconds and the interstage truss between the second and third stages twisted apart and the third stage separated from the stack and at T+50 seconds, the cutoff command to the first stage was unblocked and the engines immediately shut down. The upper stages impacted about 7 kilometers from the launch complex. Despite the engine shutoff, the first and second stages still had enough momentum to travel about 15 kilometers from the launch complex to blast a 15-meter-deep crater in the Kazakh steppe.

On June 30, in the New York Times Co. v. United States, the US Supreme Court rejected the government injunctions against publishing the Pentagon Papers as unconstitutional prior restraint.

On July 26 Apollo 15, carrying three more guys, was launched. Five days later, two of the crew members became the first to ride in a lunar rover, a day after landing on the Moon. On August 7, Apollo 15 and its three man crew returned to Earth.

On September 21, Britain expelled 90 KGB and GRU officials; 15 were not allowed to return.

On November 15, Intel Corporation released the world's first microprocessor, the Intel 4004.

In December, Hoover and the FBI, still chasing Barr, theorized that because there was no news of him elsewhere, he must still be underground in Europe or the United States.

When Joe and Phil asked Shokin for further relief from Romanov and his minions, there was talk of a new project, to be called the Elektronika K-300, but there was no specific offer or arrangement made. They did not feel much restored to respect or confidence.

FIFTY-ONE

"I regret to say that we of the FBI are powerless to act in cases of oral-genital intimacy, unless it has in some way obstructed interstate commerce."

–J. Edgar Hoover

ON JANUARY 4 1972, THE FIRST SCIENTIFIC HAND held calculator was introduced by Hewlett-Packard at $395). The next day, President Nixon ordered the development of a space shuttle program. On February 5, US airlines began mandatory inspection of passengers and their baggage. On February 21, the Soviet unmanned spaceship Luna 20 landed on the Moon.

Also on February 21, President Richard M. Nixon made an unprecedented 8-day visit to the People's Republic of China and met with Mao Zedong, to be credited with 'opening the door to China'. He was the same man who had done so much in the early 1950s to close the doors on China after the Communist victory over Chiang Kai-Shek in 1949. Nixon reaped political capital at both ends.

On February 26, Luna 20 returned to Earth with less than two ounces of lunar soil. On March 2, the US Pioneer 10 spacecraft was launched from Cape Kennedy to be the first man-made satellite to leave the solar system.

On March 6 the Elektronika 24-71 began manufacture in Leningrad. Staros again predicted that it was nothing compared to what was coming. Their struggle to escape Romanov and Shokin had come to nothing. Romanov and Shokin were too strong. Joe was bruised a bit by Firdman taking over mass production of the UM-1Nkh. Joe's methods were brilliant, intuitive, but haphazard.

On April 16 1972, Apollo 16 was launched with three

more crew members. During the mission, the astronauts achieved a lunar rover speed record of 18 kph.

Days after Neil Gallagher confronted J. Edgar Hoover on his 'homosexual lifestyle', Hoover died on May 2 1972. His position as the US chief of police had covered up, protected and financially provided for an extravagant lifestyle. He also used his position to protect his criminal acquisition of material evidence to use, throughout his career, in blackmailing top politicians and judges, including eight US presidents. He had also abused his power to promote right-wing political schemes and to provide himself and Clyde Tolson with frequent lavish vacations and to feather their nest financially. In 1963 and 1964 he ignored and destroyed evidence in the Kennedy murder investigation. In addition to a corrupt, criminal career, Hoover could fuck-up a free lunch like the keystone cops: He blabbed the news of Red Spy Queen Elizabeth Bentley's confession, so that the KGB knew within days that their top American agent was naming 100 secret KGB sources. Hoover gave the Soviet intelligence service plenty of time to cover their tracks. Ever arrogant, Hoover was photographed giving oral sex to Tolson, second in command of the FBI. As a result, he himself was blackmailed into denying for 13 years that organized crime existed.

On May 26 Richard Nixon just missed a planned visit to Zelenograd, when negotiations ran late as he and Leonid Brezhnev prepared to sign the SALT I treaty in Moscow as well as the Anti-Ballistic Missile Treaty. Several members of Nixon's delegation did visit Zelenograd, but did not pick up any hint about its American creators. By this time though, those who worked closely with Joe and Phil, such as Eric Firdman and Mark Galperin, were sure the two Czech scientist engineers were not only not Czechs, but were Americans. Still, very few outside the Politburo suspected they were ever spies.

On June 17, five White House operatives were arrested for burglarizing the offices of the Democratic National Committee. The scandal and investigation that followed would lead to Nixon's resignation two years later.

On July 8, the US sold grain to the Soviet Union for $750 million. The transaction was marred by sabotage when the bulk loading of grain was mixed with broken glass.

On August 15 1972, LKB was moved into an enormous electronics conglomerate, NPO Svetlana. For Staros and Berg, it was an even greater demotion and humiliation. Founded in 1889 Svetlana was a large well established enterprise with 30,000 employees which, under Brezhnev's new organizational structure, had been given control over a dozen design bureaus and basic research institutes. The transfer from Pozitron to Svetlana was justified because Svetlana's profile was closer to LKB than Pozitron's in as much as Svetlana was involved in manufacturing transistors, though so far it had produced no integrated circuits. The theory was that the combination of LKB's design powers with Svetlana's immense production capacities would be a winner. In reality, it was Romanov's and Shokin's joint idea that Pozitron's handling of LKB and Staros was too soft.

Svetlana's general director, Oleg Filatov. was known as Romanov's protege and a tough boss. Filatov looked like a storm trooper: a tall redhead with pale blue expressionless eyes who liked to show off his power by inflicting pain and suffering. Shokin had squeezed everything he could from Staros who, considering Romanov's hatred, had become a liability and no longer worth protecting or supporting. For Shokin, it was time to throw Staros to the wolves and Oleg Filatov was the right wolf. Shokin was also aware of Staros and Berg's attempts to get away from his ministry. The environment at this high level of government controlled industry made secret meetings impossible. The day after Staros met with the chief of another defense ministry, Shokin asked him what they had discussed. He knew the answer but wanted to test Staros's loyalty. In fact, there was no loyalty left on either side and Shokin was thinking, *The little shit has not learned his lesson so I'll make him pay for his disloyalty by dumping them into Svetlana where he will be under the guns of my man Oleg Filatov.*

Filatov called Staros, Berg, Firdman and Galperin into his office and verbally abused them then announced that LKB had three high priorities: 1) completing the Uzel project's serial production for boats 4, 5 and 6, 2) organizing the mass production of the Electronika 24-71 and 3) developing LSIs, high yield, large scale, integrated circuit production. Filatov told

Firdman he did not give a shit about Eric's scientific artificial intelligence interests:

"You will be given production quotas for the 24-71," he said. "I will fire you and make sure you don't work elsewhere if you do not meet the quotas."

Again their titles were demoted or erased. Firdman knew he would be fired even if he met the quotas. Is so, he wouldn't be needed. He reported to a new chief engineer sent to LKB from Svetlana. Filatov was undoubtedly told that Firdman held the keys to LSI technology and Electronika 24-71 production, but because he was not a manufacturing expert, he knew someone with manufacturing experience would take over Electronika 24-71 production as soon as it was up and running. Firdman wanted only to go back to artificial intelligence research.

Staros and Berg could not imagine how to operate effectively inside a behemoth like Svetlana. Ambitious for higher office, Grigory Romanov had vowed to install the defense industry in Leningrad, particularly the electronics sector. He meant to make Leningrad a showplace for Brezhnev's organizational reforms. Having foreigners running a highly visible military microelectronics R&D operation didn't fit that plan. Romanov instructed Filatov to cancel LKB operations and denounce its leaders within one year. "Out on the streets. You've got one year to get it done," was the way he put it.

But at first, things as Svetlana went well enough for the LKB, having successfully produced prototype LSI chips. On this basis, Staros and Berg appealed to Shokin for a David Mann 3600 photo repeater like the one they'd used earlier, an essential piece of equipment for making the photo masks needed to make integrated circuits. Without it, their yields were too low to mass produce LSI chips. Despite the Western restrictions against selling high-tech equipment to the Soviet Bloc, the ban proved only a minor inconvenience. It took three months from the time they convinced Shokin to order the state-of-the-art photo repeater for it to arrive. The machine had been purchased by a cooperative West German company that quickly resold it at a profit to a Yugoslavia company which marked it up again and sent it to Leningrad. With this vital piece of equipment in hand, the LKB dramatically increased LSI yield, and began to meet Svetlana's LSI production targets, a tricky proposition for Staros and Berg who hadn't been involved in mass manufacturing for the two decades since they had left Western Electric and Bell Labs. Meanwhile, after seven years, the Uzel, originally envisioned as a quick project, was finally nearing completion.

ON NOVEMBER 23 1972 THERE WAS YET ANOTHER Soviet N-1 launch for a Moon flyby. The lift-off went well. At T+90 seconds, a programmed shutdown of the core propulsion system, consisting of the six center engines, was performed to reduce structural stress on the booster. Because of excessive dynamic loads caused by a hydraulic shock wave when the six engines were shut down abruptly, lines for feeding fuel and oxidizer to the core propulsion system burst and a fire started in the boat tail of the booster. In addition, the #4 engine exploded. The first stage broke up at T+107 seconds. The launch escape system activated and pulled the Soyuz craft to safety. The upper stages were ejected from the stack and crashed into the steppe, yet another failure.

On December 7 1972, Apollo 17, with yet another three man crew, the last Apollo manned Moon mission, was launched. Four days later, Apollo 17 landed on the Moon. On December 14, Eugene Cernan was the last person to walk on the Moon after he and Harrison Schmitt completed the third and final extra-vehicular activity. On December 19, Apollo 17 returned to Earth, concluding the program of lunar exploration for a nation now bored with trips from the Earth to the Moon.

FIFTY-TWO

"In the 1970s in New York, everyone slept till noon. It was a grungy, dangerous, bankrupt city without normal services most of the time. The garbage piled up and stank during long strikes by the sanitation workers. A major blackout led to days and days of looting. The city seemed either frightening or laughable to the rest of the nation."

---Edmund White

JANUARY 14 1973, ELVIS PRESLEY'S HAWAIIAN Concert broke the Apollo Moon landing records for the size of the worldwide TV audience. On January 20, Richard Nixon was sworn in for the second time as US President, the only person to be sworn in twice as both Vice President and President.

It was in the evening, one of the last days of January, just after the Paris peace talks had brought an end to the Vietnam war. Joe was glad he didn't need to venture outside in order to visit his partner. On the streets of Leningrad, the temperature was low enough to freeze mucus in the nose with each intake of breath and the sidewalks were covered with black ice. Joe was pretty sure Phil was at home, that the whole family would be there. He wanted to see Anna and of course he considered himself the doting uncle, so it was time to visit the children. He'd brought a Beatles recording, chocolate eggs, other sweets, and something special for Anna.

Joe and Phil seemed bound to each other for life and there were times when given a choice Phil was not happy with that. What he had admired so much in Joel Barr continued to be what maintained his boomeranging admiration, not only Joe's highly intelligent mind, but the casual confidence Joe always had about his own intellect. *Never proud and boasting as he could,* Phil thought. *He lays down the golden ideas without counting points, always as if you already knew...very generous. But done so you'll agree to it...* No, Phil was glad Joe had called saying he wanted to drop in, hoping it wasn't too late.

Anna greeted Joe at their threshold. He was taken aback by how drawn and weary she looked. *Such a stunningly beautiful woman so diminished.* "Hi, Joe," she said with a smile that brightened her. Her eyes offered familiar warmth and trust. As they embraced, she whispered in English, "He has something he wants to tell you about, but he's worried about telling you."

Joe knew how Carol loved to use her native language. It was Carol not Anna who had whispered to him, using the only language she really knew. "Here," he whispered back in English, "this is for you, a token of my admiration," and he handed her a box of special chocolates.

She kissed his cheek in thanks. "He's in his den," Anna said in her simple Czech, "Go. The kids will come see you."

After shaking hands and embracing, Phil insisted Joe take a seat on the sofa beside him. He spoke Russian. The rule was they didn't speak English around the children.

"Anna says you have news of some kind," Joe said, wanting Phil to feel more comfortable knowing he was ready to listen.

"She did, did she," Phil said. "Well, it may not be good news or even the sign of good news to come. But I suppose it is meant as an honor. I've been invited to go on a demonstration cruise in the first Project 641B submarine. It was launched in September but has not been commissioned yet."

"But as far as I know," Joe said, "from talking to Mark, the Uzel is functioning properly on that new boat."

"Yes, fortunately the Uzel is not delaying its commission, and apparently they are now close to certification as there will be all the top admirals and ministers along for the ride."

"So, what's worrying you? There will be more vodka?"

"No. The fact that they didn't specifically invite you."

"No, I was not invited."

"But shouldn't you come along?"

"No," Joe said, "it's a special honor for the Chief Designer, the head of the firm, part of your role." Joe noted Phil's immediate look of relief and he added, "I had my Jules Verne cruise in B-103, that was enough for me. You will be with a gang of hard-drinking Russian submariners..."

"As you know, I'm naturally claustrophobic and of course none of what the boat is capable of can be demonstrated while it operates on the surface."

"Of course," Joe said, "but you'll be alright. Look, Phil, this *is* good news. It means at least the Soviet Navy supports and trusts us."

"Yes," Phil said, further at ease, "I can agree with that. Gorshkov doesn't care about the politics. My job is to accept their compliments gracefully and assure them that it is all taken in stride...That we never had a doubt about the ultimate success."

Joe was nodding approval as Phil spoke then he asked, "When is this occasion to be?"

"A couple of weeks, I think."

Just then, Kolya and Kristina came in, calling out favorite greetings for their uncle Joe. Kolya, the oldest, was in his late teens.

Joe handed out the treats, but the two teenagers seemed barely interested, though polite in accepting them, allowing that the younger children, Mila and Tonya would be interested, but were already in bed.

Kolya and Kristina spoke Russian like their father, unlike Joe's children who spoke Czech at home. "Uncle Joe, did Dad tell you, he's going for a ride in a submarine?" Kolya asked.

"Are you going too, uncle Joe?" Kristina asked.

"No, no," Joe said, "that's just a special outing for the big boss."

"He had his ride," Phil said, "going off on one of the first combat trials without me."

The two children paused, glancing at the two adults, to make sure there were no hard feelings. Seeing none, Kolya asked, "So you saw them shoot torpedoes from the submarine?"

"Indeed I did," Joe said. "It was rather frightening, all the power of it, and the idea of sinking other ships in the deep ocean."

"Will it be safe for Dad?" Kristina asked.

"Don't worry,," Joe said with a big smile, "the 'Soviet Navy will take very good care of your father."

At nearly 100 meters long, the 641B, the largest diesel-electric submarine ever built, now controlled by the Soviet Navy's first digital computer, was soon to be commission as B-443. Project 641B was already worrying Western military thinkers. Coated with a rubber-like sonar-absorbing material, armed with electronically guided torpedoes, the 641B's were a formidable threat, well designed to hunt American submarines and guard the USSR's undersea bastions where Soviet submarines equipped with nuclear missiles waited.

Inside the submerged submarine, with somewhat restored pride, Phil Staros watched as his brainchild correlated sonar, radar, hull sensor and engine data to plot its own location and track 5 targets so that highly accurate torpedoes could be fired at any instant. It was all there to see on the display monitors LKB had designed and built. Even preferring cognac, Phil drank more than he intended, but socially the voyage was a success. The senior officers loved showing off what the Uzel could do, almost as if Phil couldn't possibly imagine it without their clear demonstration.

His comment to Joe was, "What's a day of throbbing headaches, if we are the toast of the Soviet Navy? Anyway our stock is up. If the Navy needs another miracle they'll ask us first."

MARCH 3 1973, STAROS WAS AWARDED THE ORDER of the Submariner, a unique medal and honor. Phil and Joe, along with their wives, were invited to celebrate the Uzel's success at a banquet in Moscow on March 21 1973.

"It means," Phil said, "we are not back on top, exactly..."

"But," Joel finished, "we have successfully bounced up from the bottom."

"Yes, we're on the way up, I think." Phil feared optimism's painful disappointments.

"We'll have to perform well at this banquet," Joe reminded Phil, "everyone will be there."

"With Vera and Anna?" Phil said. "They will find it to be…"

"…a tedious affair," Joe said.

"Which will be a gripe for days."

"Not to mention that it will take days afterward to sober up," Joe added.

"So don't drink so much; take sips," Phil said.

"Even so, you have to join in on dozens of toasts. It is really…"

"…you're right," Phil said, "each one of these celebrations wipes out a week of work and concentration. Drinking only cognac helps, but even so, turning down a shot of vodka is not polite."

"Not to mention," Joe said, "you lose track of what you are agreeing to, what is being understood during all those drinks. There must be a way to avoid all that, to politely not drink. Maybe a doctor's order that one drink will kill you."

"We could always bring our own?" Phil made it Joe's question.

"Why would we do that?" Joe said. "Like their cognac isn't good enough?"

"We could say we preferred our own cognac," Phil said, maybe water it down a bit, and bring several bottles of the best…"

"What if we substituted amber tea in a cognac bottle," Joe said, "we could carry on in a sober fashion with our wits about us, for a change."

"No, absolutely not," Phil said.

"Because it would be terrible to get caught."

"Of course, that, too," Phil said.

Much like in America, liquor is used by Russians to break the ice. But in Russia the ice is much thicker. To drink with someone meaningfully in Russia, just the two of you, let's say, in Moscow or Leningrad for example, it's not going to be one drink. Your host opens a liter bottle and throws away the cap. You are both opening yourselves to each other, allowing and offering vulnerability, letting the alcohol overwhelm all pretense and façade. You do this on purpose, to plumb the depths of friend and foe, to bravely seek the heart of the matter.

If you cannot be imagined crawling on all fours across the threshold of your domicile, how can you really be trusted? So Phil was well aware of what utter folly it would be to bring a cognac bottle full of non-alcoholic tea to a drinking orgy, especially one celebrating the Uzel and honoring him with the Order of the Submariner.

JOE DID NOT INFORM VERA RIGHT AWAY OF

the banquet in Moscow. As he often did, he put off telling his wife things she would not want to hear. So when he did tell her and he began to emphasize what an honor it all was, what hope it offered that he and Phil would soon be on top again, Vera said:

"That's in five days. In Moscow of all places. Just how am I supposed to prepare in five days?"

"Well," Joe said, "you should get yourself a new dress, new shoes, whatever you want. Money is no object."

"How can I do any of that in five days? In Leningrad of all places? In Prague something might be possible. Have you thought about who will look after your children while I go off to Moscow with you for this great honor?"

"Well, I thought—"

"Let Phil and Anna go; we'll look after their kids. The banquet is to honor Phil, isn't it, not you?"

Joe wondered how easy it might be to convince Phil that he and Phil should go alone. But Joe did not want to deprive Anna of a chance to get away from captivity, to shine a few hours at large in the world. He said, "I'm sure it won't be a problem to find someone to stay here with the kids. I'll pay whatever it takes. We'll fly down in the early afternoon, check in to the Metropole, but if you like, we take the late train back in the sleeping car, in our own room, if you'd rather not stay in Moscow overnight."

"I can not go; I have nothing to wear," Vera said evenly.

Joe wished for a moment he could bring Elvira, how she would dazzle everyone and so enjoy all the Navy men in their crisp clean uniforms. Then he said, "Vera, please, as a special favor to me, and to Phil, and Anna, please find something nice to wear, pay a seamstress to make you something elegant. Maybe you have a dress that fits you just the way you like to use as a model for something new? A pattern, you understand, we can make it worth her while."

"But you won't quibble if she wants an arm and a leg? You know who I'm thinking of?"

"Yes, but she does good work. I won't quibble unless she's not happy with the arm and the leg."

THE EVENING OF MARCH 21 1973, JOE, VERA, Phil and Anna arrived together in a ZIL limousine at the 21 story Rossiya hotel in Moscow, the largest hotel in the world when it was completed in 1967, to remain so for more than another 20 years. Next to Red Square, the Rossiya was a giant that overshadowed the high red brick walls of the Kremlin. The hotel could accommodate 4000 persons, offered shops, salons and even its own police station and jail. The State Central Concert Hall which seated 2500 people, was directly beyond the high ceilinged lobby. The Rossiya was designed for important Soviet parties and celebrations.

Vera was wearing a full skirted burgundy dress, new, fitting her perfectly. She was not a bad looking woman, not like a woman who'd given birth to four children. Anna was wearing her elegant dark green dress. Through the weariness shone the beautiful woman that she was.

The two couples were greeted at the lavish entrance hall by liveried ushers and guided to a grand banquet chamber adjacent to the State Concert Hall. They were the honored guests of the Soviet Navy. The banquet table was set for sixty places, a bottle of 100 proof Stolichnaya at each place, along with nearby bottles of red and white wine. Admiral of the Fleet of the Soviet Union and Deputy Minister of Defense, Sergei Gorshkov, was seated at the head of the table. Philip Staros was seated on his right followed Anna Staros then Joe and Vera. On Gorshkov's left were GKET Minister Aleksandr Shokin and "Admiral Oscar Zhukovsky with their wives. Amidst other top Soviet Navy brass and scientists involved in the success of the Uzel CICS, Joe was happy to see Commander Eric Golovanov, captain of B-103. *He is now part of the northern fleet,* Joe thought, *Eric made a special arrangement to be here!* They exchanged a friendly greeting across the table.

When Phil had taken his seat, he removed a one liter bottle of Soviet Red Star Cognac containing a dark rich brown liquid. He said to Gorshkov in his perfect Russian, "Sergei Georgievich, I brought my own cognac; My doctor advises that vodka is damaging for my heart."

"If it's better for you, Dr. Staros, I'm all for it," Gorshkov said.

Anna leaned toward Gorshkov to say in her minimal Russian, "Vodka is too strong for him. The cognac is only half."

Anna, looking after four kids in Leningrad for a faithless husband, had not learned Russian well. She meant the cognac was only half the proof of the vodka. She had not been informed by Joel or Al that the liquid in the premium cognac bottle was boiled tea, meticulously strained. Joe had suggested and Phil had brought along a bottle of the real unopened Red Star Konyak still in his briefcase along with more disguised bottles of tea.

After a champagne toast to the success and strength of the Soviet Navy, another to the Philip Staros and the Uzel, as dishes of salads and smoked fish were served and eagerly sampled, the dinner then progressed through nearly endless courses of rich, delicious Russian food. Nearly everyone made a speech, it seemed, some little more than quickly introducing themselves, barely mentioning any personal contribution to the glory of the occasion.

In addition to intimate toasts offered between those sitting close to each other, there were toasts which often widened to include the whole gathering. through the Russian tradition of adding words of emphasis or further dedication to the toasts proposed by others. This extended the interval between actual drinks. Diners held on to their glasses, waiting for the latest generous, supplemental phrases to conclude. Sometimes, this interval was shortened by a glance from Gorshkov to the speaker so that they all could at last raise glass to lips and swallow their medicine, enjoying *Druzhba*, friendship, sharing sincere good wishes and fond memories with generous empathy for their struggles together. It was a good time. Both Anna and Vera noticed that Phil and Joe were not loud or slurring conversations.

Neither knew why. Joe pretended relative indifference to the cognac, taking vodka from time to time, mostly keeping some in his glass, as though he were continually drinking it.

As the momentum of the dinner was winding down, after most had had their say or had decided not to say much, Admiral Gorshkov turned to Phil and said:

"Phil, I drink to you in memory of that first meeting eleven years ago in the attic on Volkovskaya Street. You see, I knew then that one day we would work together. I was just beginning to be successful in convincing my military colleagues that submarines, armed with long range missiles and accurate torpedoes were the ultimate defense of the Union. But you, you had no such idea, back then, am I right?"

"I was very grateful for such important attention," Phil said in his perfect Russian. "And of course I had no idea about any such partnerships."

"How did I know it?" Gorshkov asked rhetorically. "Well, I saw who you were, your belief in everything you said, in all that you were doing. And Dr. Berg, so clearly a brilliant scientist and so devoted to you. It struck me that you made an unbeatable team." Gorshkov was obviously relaxed and comfortable, a little tipsy, but comfortable enough to share his inebriation as part of the good feelings he had in Phil's company.

Phil had had several drinks, several glasses of champagne and shots of vodka; his mood was not entirely guarded. He poured himself a generous shot from the cognac bottle, then passed it to Joe who was thinking, *Let Phil do his thing; he's so very good at it.* Anna encouraged a waiter to pour her a glass of red wine. Joe set the cognac bottle down as he continued to talk with Zhukovsky and Golovanov. They had all enjoyed working together; the two Navy men were kidding Joe about the Elephant. Oscar asked:

"What did that son-of-a-bitch who runs the metallurgical plant in Liepāja have to say to you about building such a giant enclosed fan?"

"How did you do it?" Eric added. "I know you didn't bribe him. Or did you?" He laughed.

Phil touched glasses with Gorshkov, they raised their

drinks and downed them. Gorshkov made no secret of the fact that he was celebrating his brilliance in finding and believing in Philip Staros.

After several choices of rich desert, as Phil and Admiral Gorshkov continued their discussion of computers and cybernetic weapon control, and as the waiters were clearing dessert dishes, the bottle of premium vodka at Gorshkov's place came up empty and he turned to order another but when no waiter was immediately attentive, and perhaps because it was time for a postprandial brandy, Gorshkove gave a yelp of comradeship and reached across to take hold of the Red Star Cognac from Phil's place.

"Oh here," Phil cried, reaching for the real bottle of proudly produced Red Star Konyak. "We'll open a fresh bottle!"

"Nonsense, Dr. Staros," Gorshkov said in kind, fraternal gruffness, "We drink from the same bottle. Though cognac is not my customary beverage, I'm happy to drink cognac with you." With that, he uncapped the boiled tea and poured himself a generous glass.

Phil and Joe sat completely paralyzed in tipsy horror, more and more white faced.

Not to drink with a Russian colleague is bad enough, a startling example of uncouth rudeness, but to fool him into thinking that you are opening your heart and soul in the bonds of friendship and trust? That is among the worst social felonies.

Helpless, Phil took hold of his glass of tea with white knuckled fingers; his hand was shaking as he raised his glass. They drank.

Gorshkov's face revealed utter disbelief and consternation as he spat the tea all over the table cloth. He uttered several astonished oaths not usually expressed except in the company of other seasoned Russian sailors.

Amidst mumbled and fruitless apologies and further curses from their hosts as news of the crime spread, Joe realized they should skip all the formal good-byes and beat a hasty retreat. He could not help looking to Eric Golovanov, allowing himself an exchange of expressions. Eric's was not angry or even terribly surprised, but sad, puzzled. But it seemed a final goodbye without spite: *You poor odd duck, even when you walk you seem to be moving in all directions at once.*

Joe grabbed Vera's hand and headed for the exit, followed by Phil and Anna.

Vera and Anna both had a fine time of it, both a little tipsy, and had no idea why they were being suddenly dragged out. Already reluctant to race along with Joe, not wanting to ruin her new shoes, Vera cried out as Joe raced her into the lobby and headed for the front entrance, "Our coats! Where are you going?"

Joe had forgotten about checking their wraps. For an entire second, Joe thought seriously of leaving their coats behind. But then Vera said, "I want my fur coat, whether you care or not."

They waited at the cloakroom counter, Joe nervous, Phil stone faced with bitter chagrin. Joe held a five ruble note loosely in his right hand, hoping it would help achieve rapid retrieval of their outer garments before anyone showed up from the banquet. He imagined a general discussion of their crimes taking place around the dinner table as the party began to disperse.

A WEEK OR SO LATER, GRIGORY ROMANOV was made a candidate member of the Soviet Politburo, the supreme ruling body of the Soviet Union. In particular, Romanov was made supreme sentinel of the electronic industry. Only Brezhnev could countermand him there. Shokin was a mere underling. For Joe and Phil, it was a nightmare come true. Romanov would now certainly know they were renegade Americans and would hate them even more.

They didn't have to wait long for the next blow. Days later, Svetlana's boss, Oleg Filatov further demoted Berg and Staros so that they were bosses over nobody, without titles or statff. LKB was renamed the Leningrad Design and Technological Bureau, LKTB.

Beside themselves with fear and worry, they appealed to Marshall Dmitry Ustinov but he wouldn't see them. They were utterly disgraced and they knew they would never win another Soviet military contract. The two Americans were now in a no man's land of a down-bound purgatory. They wondered if even

Major Viktor Taroikin would speak to them. Would he offer any hope, any suggestion for a way out of their trapped lives?

Communist Number One, Volume III, to be published next year, in 2022, will be subtitled: *The Life and Times of Joel Barr, St. Petersburg Music Man, Back in the U.S.S.A.*

In Volume III, Joe and Phil react differently to their disgrace at the Soviet Navy's honorarium banquet for Saros. The information of who they really are, American ex-spies, begins to leak out and spread. Their children become independent and begin going their separate ways. This final volume will also contain an extensive bibliography of the author's source material.

Made in the USA
Monee, IL
31 August 2021

76959547R00233